P9-DTP-879

CROSSING THE LINE

CROSSING THE LINE

Meghan Rogers

PHILOMEL BOOKS

Philomel Books
an imprint of Penguin Random House LLC
375 Hudson Street, New York, NY 10014

Copyright © 2016 by Meghan Rogers.

Penguin supports copyright. Copyright fuels creativity, encourages diverse voices, promotes free speech, and creates a vibrant culture. Thank you for buying an authorized edition of this book and for complying with copyright laws by not reproducing, scanning, or distributing any part of it in any form without permission. You are supporting writers and allowing Penguin to continue to publish books for every reader.

Philomel Books is a registered trademark of Penguin Random House LLC.

Library of Congress Cataloging-in-Publication Data
Rogers, Meghan.
Crossing the line / Meghan Rogers.
pages cm.—(The Raven files ; 1)
Summary: Jocelyn Steely was kidnapped as a child and trained as a North Korean spy, but the tables turn when she becomes a double agent for the very American spy organization she has been sent to destroy.
[1. Spies—Fiction. 2. Kidnapping—Fiction. 3. Brainwashing—Fiction.] I. Title.
PZ7.1.R66Cr 2016   [Fic]—dc23   2015007510

Printed in the United States of America.
ISBN 978-0-399-17617-3
10 9 8 7 6 5 4 3 2 1

Edited by Jill Santopolo.   Design by Semadar Megged.   Text set in 11.5/17.5-point Adobe Devanagari.
This is a work of fiction. Names, characters, places, and incidents either are the product of the author's imagination or are used fictitiously, and any resemblance to actual persons, living or dead, businesses, companies, events, or locales is entirely coincidental.

To my parents, Marianne and Frank,
who never gave me any idea that this wouldn't happen.

To my sister, Katie, who entertains
every crazy thought that floats through my head.

And to my cousin Hunter, who is very much my brother—
this one absolutely would not have happened without you.

Chapter One

SHOTS FIRED

I scanned the room I was about to break into from the inside of the ventilation shaft. The duct was large and opened through the side of a wall, giving me a clear view of a big concrete area—the perfect space for testing and developing cutting-edge military technology.

I drew a slow breath through my nose, giving myself one last moment to think about the alternative. This Japanese research facility was mere miles from a U.S. military base, which meant this was the closest I'd come to American soil since I was kidnapped by the North Koreans when I was eight. From the moment my KATO handler assigned me this mission, I had thoughts of using it to escape. But I knew I could never pull it off. After nine years of teaching and training, KATO thought they had me brainwashed to be their ideal spy. And while I had more independent thoughts than they could ever comprehend, they *did* control me in other ways. No matter how desperately I wanted to break free, I knew I could never get away with defying them.

I pushed the dangerous thoughts away and forced myself to focus. If I didn't come back with the files for Project Pegasus, KATO would go out of their way to remind me just how much they owned me.

The duct I was in opened up onto a ramp, which led to a platform with a row of computers that overlooked the open testing area. Those computers had what I needed. I leaned back and put my feet up against the grate, preparing to kick it in. Before I could, a rope fell from the ceiling, dangling in front of me. A few seconds later, a tall, broad figure rappelled down.

I slid away from the grate, doing my best to hide in the shadows. I caught a glimpse of his face and knew exactly who it was.

His code name was Scorpion. He worked out of the U.S.-based International Defense Agency—the IDA. They were KATO's number one enemy, and Scorpion was mine. We had squared off several times in the past, trading punches and wounds and barely escaping. In almost every instance, I'd gotten what I'd come for and left him empty-handed. Still, he was a complication.

I quickly thought of ways to modify my plan. It didn't matter how many problems came up, KATO was still expecting a successful mission. It had been a while since I'd dealt with the consequences of disappointing them, and I wanted to keep it that way.

Scorpion did a quick sweep of the room, seeming to look for anything that might be out of place.

"Everything looks clear so far," he said, using the communication system in his ear to report back to his headquarters. KATO didn't give their agents that kind of support.

Scorpion slowly stepped away from me and headed up the ramp. He plugged a drive into the computer and started typing.

"I'm not seeing any Project Pegasus," he said into his comm. I swallowed. He was here for the same thing I was. "Oh no, now I've got it." He kept typing, his fingers sliding effortlessly over the keyboard.

I glanced around the room. The only way Scorpion could get off that platform was if he came back down the ramp. And if he did that, he'd have to pass by my air duct.

"I've got the files copied and the computer wiped." He unplugged the drive from the computer. "I'm moving to the extraction point."

I sat back, realigning my feet against the vent and leaning to pull my gun out of my holster. I waited until he had stepped just in front of me, then put all of my effort into kicking out the grate. It flew out of the wall, completely nailing Scorpion's upper body. He was so stunned that the force of the hit sent him flying, knocking the round metal rail loose from the top joint as he fell into the open testing area.

I popped effortlessly out of the vent, slid under the railing, and landed a few feet away from him. Scorpion had just gotten to his feet. He recovered quickly. He had his gun out of his holster and trained on me, just as mine was on him, before I could get any more of a jump on him. I glanced at the floor between us and saw the drive lying on the ground.

He caught my eye and smirked. "Go ahead, Viper." He was taunting me. "Take it."

I eyed him carefully as I edged closer to the drive, waiting for him to make a move.

I was two steps from the device—and four steps from him—when he finally struck. In one quick motion he reached for the loosened railing and swung it in my direction. It hit my arm and sent my gun flying across the room.

I launched myself at him, not giving Scorpion the chance to get a clean shot. I landed a punch to his jaw with one hand and used the other to knock his gun to the floor. It dropped close to the drive. He got in a hit to my stomach while I threw one to his throat, but neither of us slowed down. I ducked a blow to the head and spun to ram my elbow into his chest. We fell into a fierce rhythm, taking turns between blocking and landing our hits. I did my best to back up as we fought, putting myself next to the drive and Scorpion's gun. I could see the drive at my feet, and I knew exactly how I was going to get it. I picked my moment, then faked a move to Scorpion's right. He took the bait, leaning in that direction and giving me the perfect shot at his left arm. I grabbed his wrist and twisted it behind his back as quickly as I could, not stopping until I heard it crack. He stumbled in pain and I used his momentum to push him forward. I had the drive in my pocket and his gun in my hand before he could even turn around.

We were both panting. Scorpion and I had always been evenly matched—it was the only reason we had both walked away from our previous battles. And in each of those instances, this was the moment I was afraid might happen. That one time, I would truly gain the upper hand. And now I had.

My gun was on him, and KATO's directive demanded that enemy agents be put down at every opportunity. He wouldn't be the first enemy agent I'd killed, and the fact that he had started backing away told me he knew that.

I didn't want to kill him, but I pulled the trigger anyway—I had to.

Although, when I did, I pivoted the gun to the right just enough to put the two bullets through his shoulder instead of his chest. It was a quick and subtle move. One that would no doubt be written off by the IDA as luck. But I knew the truth, and I was terrified KATO would too.

Scorpion cried out in pain as I jumped into the ventilation shaft.

I didn't look back. I had to move as if I thought I had killed him. My heart pounded with a furious fear as I worked my way to my extraction point. I had never disregarded a directive before, but other agents had, and KATO *always* found out.

Yet, in the back of my mind I couldn't shake the thought that maybe—just maybe—if I could get away with this, then I might have a shot at finding a way out.

Chapter Two

One year later

I walked as slowly as I could to the security house on the edge of the IDA's Wilmington, Delaware, headquarters, trying not to think about the number of ways this plan could end me.

A security officer stopped me before I could get within five feet of the house. He looked to be only a little older than I was, and his expression was all business. "Do you need help with something?" he asked.

I looped my thumbs through the straps of my backpack to hide the fact that my hands were shaking and took a steady step forward. "Yes," I said. "You can tell the director that Jocelyn Steely is here to see him."

His stance stiffened as his hand moved slowly to his hip, where I was sure he had a gun. "I'm not sure what you think—"

"I know exactly what happens here, and I'm asking you to tell Director Simmonds that I need to see him." I was too anxious to be patient with this guy.

His eyes narrowed and his gun made its way to his hand. It wasn't trained on me yet, but I had no doubt it would be if I pushed him any further. He studied me, clearly weighing his options. It was a long moment before he took a step backward. "Come with me," he said.

I gripped the straps of the backpack tighter and pulled myself forward. He led me into the guardhouse, past a couple of his coworkers, and came to a stop at a door that required an access code. He typed quickly, then held the door open for me, told me to wait, and shut me inside. The room was set up like a standard interrogation room. Small and square with a table in the center and chairs on either side. I raked my nails across my scalp and started pacing. After about fifteen minutes, the door opened again. I pivoted to a stop and found myself face-to-face with the director of the International Defense Agency.

Director Simmonds's eyes had a tired harshness to them, but his tall build and confident demeanor made it easy to see why he was the person in charge. He stared at me evenly and I was afraid to move. "I heard you were asking for me." His voice had a quiet power that made speaking to him even more intimidating than the idea of it had been in my mind.

"Yes." I took a deep breath, knowing I had one chance to tell him everything. "KATO sent me here to act as a double agent for them." His eyebrows arched in surprise. "I'm supposed to tell you that I'm the kidnapping victim you've been searching for, which I guess in a sense I am." I waited for his reaction. There was none, so I continued. "They gave me a story about how I escaped from them that you're supposed to believe. Ideally, over time I'd be accepted enough to be integrated into the IDA. Then I'm supposed to pass any information I can back to them."

Simmonds's gaze was unblinking and intense. It made me feel like he could see inside my mind. I shifted uneasily, feeling better that the table was in between us.

"Is this the tactic?" He sounded very unimpressed. "You show up and confess everything so I believe you're on our side?"

"I'm telling the truth." I couldn't keep the desperate edge out of my voice. "I don't want to work for them. I *never* did. And I know my family has roots here." I was targeted by KATO ten years ago because my parents were IDA spies. That fact was the one thing that helped me keep my brain intact.

"Then why did it take you this long to reach out?" Simmonds took a step closer. "You've had plenty of opportunities over the years."

I took off the backpack and put it on the table. "Because of this." I swallowed hard and pushed it closer to him, hesitating briefly before letting go.

He gave me a curious look, but opened the bag. He pulled out one of the four transparent plastic water bottles and studied the clear liquid inside.

"It looks like water, but it's not," I said, crossing my arms. "It's a drug called Gerex. KATO engineered it." I pulled my arms in even closer. "And I need it in a way you can't possibly understand."

Simmonds looked up at me sharply. "You're addicted?"

I held his gaze. "Yes." I hated the term, but it was true. If he dug deeper into the bag, he'd find a needle. "I can only get it from KATO. It's how they knew I would always come back. And how they think they can send me in here and trust I won't betray them. If you can help get me off it, I'll tell you everything I know about their operations. I can be *your* double agent." A chill shot through me at the thought, but this had to happen. I would never be able to get away from KATO if I couldn't survive without the thing they used to control me.

"Let's not get ahead of ourselves," Simmonds said. "But for

argument's sake, if I were to believe you, what else would you want out of all of this?"

I bit my lip for a moment, thinking. I didn't want to look like I came in with an agenda, but lying right now wouldn't help my case. I answered him honestly. "I want a chance to damage KATO's recruitment program." I wanted to keep them from doing to other kids what they had done to me. "I know a lot about their headquarters and operations, but they've got recruitment safe houses all over the world. I want to find them."

"Well," Simmonds said. "I think we both would have an interest in that." He shifted the bottle in his hand, examining it for a few more seconds before looking back up at me. "There's some missing from here."

I nodded. "KATO thinks the IDA's headquarters is in New Jersey, so that's where they dropped me. It took me a couple days to get here."

He was quiet for a moment, considering me. "And why would they think we're in New Jersey?" he asked.

I relaxed slightly, relieved to move on from the Gerex. "Because that's what I told them."

He stared at me again. "I'm going to have our medical team run some tests on this." He picked the backpack up off the table. "If it has the effect you're saying it does, we might be able to work something out."

I forced myself not to react or show any sign of excitement. He could be lying to me or, at the very least, buying himself time to work on a strategy. He moved toward the door, Gerex in hand. My heart rate spiked.

"Sir," I said, panicking at the idea of being separated from the drug. He looked back to me. "No matter what you may think about all of this, I *do* need that." I gestured to the water bottle. "Once every twenty-four hours. If you're not going to help me—" I paused to make myself to calm down. I didn't want to beg. "Please don't make me go without it."

Again he took his time to answer, his eyes scanning my face, looking for some kind of sign. Then he took another step toward the door. "I'll make the necessary arrangements," he said. "You'll stay here for now. I'll be back when we've investigated all of this further."

He closed the door behind him and I exhaled a tense breath that did nothing to take away my stress. I lowered myself down onto the floor in the corner of the room, pulling my knees to my chest and pressing my back against the wall, trying to convince myself I'd made the right call.

True to his word, Simmonds sent the IDA's resident physician, Dr. March, to give me a daily Gerex injection while they finished running tests on the drug. Dr. March was tall and sticklike, but warm and maternal even to me. I wasn't in good shape when she came to me the first day. It had been over twenty-four hours since I had injected, and there's a component to the Gerex that makes going without it physically painful. It felt like a fire was spreading through my veins, suffocating me from the inside out.

Dr. March had found me curled up in a ball in the corner of the room shaking with my crazy curly hair plastered to my sweaty forehead and tears running down my face. All from the pain of missing my injection. I was barely aware of it when she pulled me to her, holding me tight as she held out my arm and pushed the drug into me.

"It's okay," she said as I continued to shake, waiting for it to kick in. "You're going to be okay." She kept a hold on me until she was sure I was stable, and even then she seemed hesitant to let go. She didn't say much else, and she didn't stay too much longer than she needed to to do her job, yet somehow I felt safe with her. She had taken care of me in a way no one else had in a very long time. And even though I knew logically I shouldn't trust anyone at the IDA at this point, I couldn't help but feel better when she entered the room.

Which was why I was relieved when she came in with Director Simmonds three days after I had arrived. Dr. March took a seat on one side of the table and indicated I should do the same. Simmonds stood behind her. His expression seemed softer toward me, but still had an underlying suspicion.

"I've done all the tests I can think of on the Gerex you gave us," Dr. March said. "Between that and what I've seen from you I can honestly say it's like nothing I've ever come across before."

I sat up straighter. "Are you saying you can't get me off it?"

"No, I'm pretty sure I can, but I think it's going to be extremely difficult and painful for you." She met my eyes briefly before continuing. "Usually, in a situation like this there are medications that help with detox and lessen withdrawal symptoms, but in this case—with a drug this strong and complex—I'm afraid to put anything new into your system."

"You think I can be easily addicted to something else?" I asked.

"I honestly don't know," she said. "But it's not a risk I'm willing to take. You'll probably have cravings for some time after your detox, but I'm looking into some alternative techniques to relieve those. In the meantime, if you want this, we're going to have to do it cold."

"I can take it," I said, even though I wasn't sure I could. I was so close to being free I would have agreed to almost anything. "I need this out of me."

No one spoke for a moment. Dr. March glanced up at Simmonds, who nodded. "We'll have you moved to the medical wing and get you started today."

That was when the realization slapped me in the face. I had already had my last dose of Gerex. I balled my fists to keep myself under control, and reminded myself that this was what I wanted.

Simmonds led me to the medical wing through a series of underground tunnels. It made sense that he would want to keep my presence a secret until he knew more, one way or the other.

Dr. March showed me to a sterile white room, complete with a bed. She knew I had a few hours until I would feel any symptoms and left me to get settled.

But I couldn't settle. I paced the room anxiously, trying to push down the fear and prepare myself for what was coming. It had been years since KATO had truly denied me Gerex. I tried to convince myself that I could handle it, but it didn't work.

I felt the shaking start just before the pain did. Dr. March appeared shortly after the symptoms set in. She held me while I screamed until I eventually passed out from the pain and exhaustion of the struggle. I felt like my eyes had barely closed before the same excruciating burning sensation that had knocked me out jolted me back awake.

I lost all track of time, screaming and crying and fighting to breathe. I wanted the Gerex *desperately*, and it took everything I had not to give in—not to tear the building apart looking for the bottles I had brought in with me.

After a while, the suffocating fire died inside me, and left me sore and aching. That was when the sweating and vomiting started. Nothing I ate stayed in my stomach. Even the water Dr. March forced into me was too much to keep down. The number of times I had fallen asleep sobbing was more than I could count. And even though I was sweating, I couldn't seem to stop shivering. Dr. March had brought in extra blankets to try and make me as comfortable as possible, but nothing she did helped.

Toward the end of all of it, I finally started to level out. I still craved the Gerex fiercely, but I didn't depend on it to exist like I used to. It probably helped that my body was beyond exhausted, and I found myself floating out of consciousness without meaning to.

Despite this, there were several occasions where I would wake up from a dead sleep in a cold shaking sweat, panting and *needing* the Gerex in my blood. Dr. March helped me fight through it a few times before trying an acupuncture technique she had researched. Each time she did it, my symptoms faded within minutes.

"I think," Dr. March said to me one day about a month after I'd first arrived at the IDA, "you are officially clean."

I bit my lip, afraid to believe what she was saying. "Are you sure?" I asked.

She put her hand on my shoulder and smiled. "I'm sure." She sounded calm and confident and after everything I couldn't help but trust her completely. "Remember, these symptoms will probably stick with you for a while, but your appetite has improved, you're keeping food down, and for the most part, you're sleeping through the night. At this point, I'm comfortable releasing you to Director Simmonds."

Before Dr. March let me go, she scheduled a series of regular check-ups with me. She also made me promise I'd come to her for acupuncture whenever I needed it.

I agreed to everything easily. It had taken a month, but for the first time in seven years I could finally be considered sober.

Chapter Three

INTEGRATION

A security member took me down a floor, and deposited me in a room. I breathed deeply the whole way, feeling like the air was the freshest I had ever taken in.

"The director will be with you momentarily," the security officer said, shutting the door soundly behind him.

Director Simmonds's office was the size of a small conference room. There was a desk to the left of the door and the wall behind it was lined with several monitors. Only one of the monitors was on. It displayed a map of the world with twelve blinking dots at various points. Most of the dots where either green or yellow, while some were open white circles. I didn't know what the colors meant, but I could guess that the dots themselves indicated the locations of active missions.

The reality of the situation started to sink in. I was a KATO agent standing in the director of the IDA's office. It was enough to make me feel suffocated, caged, and anxious. I had survived my detox, but I had another fight ahead of me. I needed to convince Simmonds I was on his side and do everything I could to keep myself out of KATO's reach for as long as possible. I wasn't deluded enough to believe I'd ever completely escape them, but that was a confrontation I couldn't think about.

I found myself craving the Gerex and shook away the thought, refusing to give it power.

The door opened behind me and I spun around, briefly meeting Director Simmonds's eyes. He seemed considerably more relaxed than he had been the last time I'd seen him.

"Jocelyn." His voice was gentler than I was expecting. "Why don't you take a seat?"

He sat behind his desk and I eased into the chair across from him, resting my elbows on the arms and casually lacing my fingers together. I tried to act like this was just another job.

"How are you doing?" he asked. I was a little thrown by the genuine concern in his voice.

"I'm—better," I said, not looking to go into any more detail.

He scanned me briefly, then nodded and pulled a file—my file—closer. He studied it for a moment, then leaned comfortably back in his chair. "I'd like you to tell me everything you know about KATO."

I blinked a few times, replaying the question in my head. If he was really asking me for information, then it could only mean one thing. "You believe me?"

He nodded solemnly and I saw pity on his face for half a second before he hid it. "I've seen detoxes before," he said. "But yours was the most difficult and painful I've ever had to watch."

I sat up a little straighter. "You were there?" I didn't remember seeing him.

"I was." He met my eyes. "And I can't imagine a KATO agent who was truly brainwashed would put themselves through that. You had to want it."

I gripped the arms of the chair, trying not to think of how good it felt to have the Gerex in my blood.

"So," he said, bringing me back. "What can you tell me about KATO?"

I moved to the edge of my seat, preparing myself. I didn't waste time asking what he already knew. Instead I told him everything I could, starting with KATO's original intentions. The organization was designed to be a division of North Korea's intelligence agency with a special focus on utilizing the skills of younger agents. The program was so successful, it quickly became a priority to recruit potential agents as young as possible. The younger KATO could get their claws into someone, the more power and control they would have, which was why kids became their target.

Some parents gave over their kids willingly, thinking they were giving a great service to their country, while others were blackmailed into the situation. They got the rest of their agents by taking advantage of easily manipulated orphans. As far as I knew, I was the only kid taken to send some kind of message.

I also told Simmonds where their headquarters was, and how they operated. I told him about some of the things I had stolen and the people I'd killed, but I kept it limited to the bigger assignments. I'd done far too much damage on KATO's behalf to list everything. The whole exchange took hours, and it was as equally freeing as it was terrifying.

Simmonds listened attentively, and waited until I had finished to speak. "I can imagine they told you some tales about the IDA?"

I nodded. "They spent the first four years drilling into me how meddlesome, intrusive, and evil all of you were," I said. "They did everything they could to make me hate you, but it never felt right." I rubbed my palms anxiously on my knees. "When they thought they had me, they told me my parents were IDA spies. I didn't believe them at first, but they had video and other evidence. It was supposed to motivate me against them and against the IDA even more. They wanted me to feel betrayed that my parents not only lied to me, but were working for the people I was supposed to hate. But ultimately, it made me feel like I had a way out."

Simmonds studied me momentarily, then shifted a little closer. "You should know that I've been trying to get you back since they took you. It was six years before they put you in the field, correct?"

I nodded, my face tight and focused, unable to hide how much he had just surprised me.

"Once they did, you were so well trained that I couldn't get to you," he said. "And based on what we know now, it seems it would have been hard to persuade you to leave." He shook his head. "I had hoped when you were finally retrieved you wouldn't still be tied to them."

A small humorless laugh snuck out of me. "I'll always be tied to them." His expression didn't change. "Did you work here when I was kidnapped?"

"I did," he said.

"Then you knew my parents?"

His eyes darkened a fraction. "I was very close with them."

I swallowed hard and ignored the weight that dropped in my stomach. "They're dead, aren't they?"

He held my eyes, preparing me. But I was prepared. I'd been

prepared for years—since KATO first told me the truth. "Your mother is."

I sat up a little straighter. "And my—my father?"

"He's alive," Simmonds said with a small smile. "At least, as far as we know. He left the agency after he lost you and your mother, and he made sure no one could find him. We don't have any idea where he is or how to get in touch with him, but we'll get someone on it."

My gut turned in an unexpected way and I shook my head. "It's okay. Given the situation it's probably better if he's left alone."

Simmonds's face twisted in confusion. "He would want to know." He sounded so sure, but I didn't respond. I didn't know how he could understand. "And he will be very unhappy with me if he finds out you've been recovered and we didn't try to track him down."

I gave him a small insincere smile, fighting the impulse to push the issue. "Can you tell me anything about them?"

Simmonds smiled lightly. "Your parents and I were some of the first spies this organization had. They were on their way back from a vacation in Paris with you when my predecessor asked them to make a stop in South Korea. It was supposed to be a safe, quick job. That's the only reason they agreed to it, especially with you along for the ride. Your mom was going to stay in a hotel room with you while your dad went to pick up a package. You wouldn't have been on the ground for more than an hour."

"KATO found out," I said hoarsely. It didn't matter that I was eight at the time, or that ten years had passed. I still remembered being dragged away from my mom by a man in a mask.

"They did." He leaned forward. "They took you and killed your mother. It took us a while to find her body, but once we did, your father left the agency and made sure he couldn't be tracked. He didn't want to be around when you were found."

"You mean when my *body* was found," I said.

Simmonds didn't say anything after that. He didn't need to.

I leaned back into my chair, doing my best to turn off my emotions. "So, what happens now?" I asked, desperately needing to change the subject. "I get to work on stopping KATO's recruitment?"

Simmonds continued paging through my file. "Yes," he said. "And I will help you where I can, but we need to be clear on how the IDA operates. Our goal is drastically different from KATO's. We don't run on a direct political agenda. We were formed to combat agencies like KATO, which means that while we do have ties to the U.S., Canada, and the core counties of the European Union, we aren't officially affiliated with any one government. This gives us a larger reach since we're not bound by a single diplomatic or foreign policy, but it also means we have no military backing. Everything that goes on here is solely on us, unless we can persuade another agency or government to get involved."

"What are you getting at?" I asked.

"I'm saying, I don't have a problem moving on what you're planning, but I am not in the business of sending agents into the field until we have a full and well-developed plan based on credible intel. You can't rush this." He held my eyes evenly, like he was trying to stress the importance of this.

"Trust me," I said, meeting his gaze. "I know I don't have nearly enough resources to pull this off yet. It may take a while, but I'll make this happen."

"Okay, then." Simmonds nodded. "Now, as for your in-house

cover story. None of the agents, outside of myself, Dr. March, and a handful of others, will know you've been sent here as a KATO spy. We'll tell everyone exactly what KATO expects us to: That you were kidnapped from this agency as a child, and now we've gotten you back."

I shook my head, doubtfully. "That's not going to go over well. I've spent the last four years fighting against this agency. I almost killed some of your agents—"

"But you never did."

I tilted my head to the side. "A few times I came pretty close."

Simmonds leaned forward. "If KATO ever gets a hold of an agent and that person says something—" He didn't need to say what KATO would do to get the truth out of someone. "It would jeopardize you, your mission, and this agency's ultimate goals."

"I know," I said. "I just think it's going to be a hard sell."

"It will be," Simmonds said. "But we both know it's necessary."

I rubbed my forehead, irritated that this was the best option. But I knew what I was getting into when I showed up on campus. "Okay, you're right. What else?"

"Your KATO contact." He turned to another page in the file. "You'll communicate with them as they requested, and we'll talk before and after you do. I'll be telling you what to say to them and how we're going to handle this whole situation," he said. "Did KATO ask anything specific for your first contact?"

"Yes." I sat straighter, and began to feel more comfortable. We were discussing an assignment, and there was nothing I was more familiar with. "They want me to find out everything the IDA has on them."

Simmonds pursed his lips in thought. "Very well. I'll come up with something you can tell them. We'll go over everything before you get in touch."

"Okay," I said. My palms started to sweat at the thought of making that contact. I wiped them on my pants and did my best to focus on Simmonds, who had moved on.

"You'll have unlimited access to Dr. March," he said. "She's told me you'll need it."

"And what's the cover story there?" I asked.

"That you've spent ten years in a North Korean facility and you're drastically behind on the necessary medical care."

I nodded. He seemed to have thought of everything. "Anything else I need to know?"

Simmonds closed my file and gave me his full attention. "You know you're going to take a lot of abuse from the agents here until they get used to you."

I gave him a small smile. "I've been through a lot worse." I survived the detox and I managed to get Simmonds to trust me. I could handle this.

He grimaced. "You may need more help than you think. I'm putting Travis Elton in charge of you."

I shrugged, not understanding.

"You know him as Scorpion."

My eyes widened. "There has to be someone else."

Simmonds shook his head. "No one that I trust enough to handle something this important."

I ran my hand through my curls. "If I had to pick a 'biggest enemy' it would be him."

Simmonds nodded. "I know. But you need someone to look out

for you." I opened my mouth to argue, but he didn't let me. "If we really had just gotten you back, I would put someone in charge of your transition. If I didn't, it would raise suspicion."

I sighed and remembered pointing that gun at Scorpion all too clearly. "But isn't there *anyone* else?" I tried not to sound desperate, but I failed. Simmonds was right, this was going to be a lot harder than I had originally planned.

"He's the best we've got, and I'm not trusting someone less with this."

I arched an eyebrow. "And how does he feel about that?"

Now Simmonds wavered. "He—hasn't been told yet." A light flashed on the desk and he pushed a button, which seemed to buzz the door open. "But he's about to be."

I took a deep, helpless breath and put my game face on. The office door swung open and Scorpion walked in, his tall, broad frame filling the room. He froze when he saw me. It took all of two seconds for him to have his gun out of his holster and aimed at my chest.

I sat back in my chair and leaned on the arm casually. "Well. That didn't take very long, did it?"

His shoulders were tight and squared, and his eyes locked on me. When he spoke, his voice was stiff and controlled. "How the fuck did you get in here?"

"Agent Elton, put the gun away." Simmonds's voice boomed with a power that reminded me of the first time I'd met him.

Scorpion's eyes snapped to him, but his gun didn't move an inch. "Sir, do you have any idea who this is?"

"I know exactly who she is, and I'm telling you to put the gun down."

Scorpion faltered, but lowered the weapon. His attention was back on me. "I think you need to tell me what's going on here, sir."

Simmonds stood and leaned on the front of the desk, facing the two of us. He gave Scorpion my cover story and I worked to keep my face neutral.

"She's been on campus for a month," Simmonds said when he was finished. "Now it's time to take her out of isolation and officially integrate her into the IDA."

Scorpion's face contorted as if Simmonds had suggested he set himself on fire. "You have got to be kidding me." Scorpion was still staring down at me. I wiggled my eyebrows and smiled just to irritate him. His nostrils flared.

"You know I've never been one for jokes," Simmonds said in the calmest voice he could have used.

"You really think KATO's Viper isn't playing you?"

I inhaled sharply to keep myself from flinching at my former code name.

But Scorpion didn't notice. "I have a bullet scar on my shoulder from her!" He pounded the front of his left shoulder to make a point.

"Yes," Simmonds said. "And you're one of our best agents, which means it would take someone pretty talented to put you in that position."

Now it was Scorpion's turn to glare. "That's not the point."

"It's exactly the point." Simmonds went back behind the desk and opened the top drawer. "We have an unbelievably skilled agent with information on our enemy. We would be foolish not to use it."

Scorpion opened his mouth, but Simmonds kept talking. "She will live on the base and attend some of the academy's classes."

A vein bulged in Scorpion's neck. "You want to put her in a school? With kids?"

I sat up straighter, losing my casual façade. "You know," I said, "school was never something we discussed."

Simmonds dropped an envelope on the top of the desk and slammed the desk drawer shut, which effectively kept Scorpion from speaking. He put his attention on me. "Jocelyn, you are an exceptionally trained spy with a minimal and exceedingly skewed education. We have a school on campus, which trains and educates future agents so they are field ready when they turn eighteen. I don't think practical combat or basic espionage classes are needed, but I would feel better if you weren't limited to KATO's tactical philosophies and worldview. Some time at the academy will do you good." He held out the envelope to me. "This is everything you need to know about your schedule and classes."

I bit my lip. I hadn't been in a true school setting since I was in third grade and I wanted to keep it that way. But I didn't have any other choice. I took the envelope from him and slid back in my seat.

"We also have a few other guidelines I want to go over," Simmonds said. "Travis, you will assist with Jocelyn's integration until she completes her first assignment. Your job is to make sure she gets where she needs to go and to minimize conflict as much as possible. You're to act as a guide, not a security guard."

Scorpion's face compressed with livid irritation, but he didn't say a word.

I nodded, getting more uneasy with each word, but I would never show it. I hated the idea that I would have to rely on him of all people. But this was the mission. That's what I had to keep reminding myself.

This whole thing was one big mission, and I had to earn these agents' trust. The only people I didn't have to pretend around were Simmonds and Dr. March.

Simmonds turned to Scorpion. "As for her being with academy students, you can't possibly believe that I would endanger the students of this school."

Scorpion ran his hand over his hair. "Right now, sir, I don't really know what to believe."

Simmonds's face went stony. "Jocelyn," he said, "will you wait outside for a minute?"

I hesitated, shooting him a questioning look.

"I need to talk to Agent Elton alone."

I paused for another moment, and Simmonds raised his eyebrows at me. "Yeah," I said finally. "Sure."

I pushed out of my chair and maneuvered around Scorpion, who made no effort to get out of my way. I went into the small hall outside of the director's office. I couldn't hear anything that was being said, but I had a hard time staying still. I rocked back and forth on my feet, continually pushing myself higher. They couldn't have talked for more than five minutes before the door was yanked open and Scorpion came angrily storming out.

"Let's go." I knew he was talking to me, even if he wouldn't look in my direction or stop to see if I was following.

I glanced at Simmonds, who gave me a small nod. "Just remember what your goal is and you'll be fine."

"Right," I said, though I didn't completely believe him.

"He'll look out for you better than anyone else," he said. "He may not be nice to you, and he may not trust you, but I made you his responsibility. He'll take that seriously."

I nodded once and relaxed a fraction. "Thank you."

He gave me a sad smile, and I sprinted to catch up to my tour guide.

Chapter Four

COMFORTABLY UNCOMFORTABLE

I barely slept my first night in my new room. It didn't matter that it was way nicer than I was used to. I couldn't care less that it had its own bathroom, or that the yellow paint on the wall was just bright enough to be cozy without being a distraction. It didn't make a difference that the bed was the most comfortable I'd ever tried. The whole room was warm and comforting and peaceful and so unfamiliar that I could hardly stand it. Plus, I was more anxious about my first day than I cared to acknowledge. I needed to be calm, together, and tough, which I could handle. These were all things I was used to being.

I dragged my blanket and pillow onto the floor, hoping the familiarity of a hard surface would help me sleep, but it didn't. Instead, I stayed up replaying my conversation with Simmonds. My dad was alive. That wasn't part of my plan. The only memories I had of my parents were at least ten years old, and I'd since come to learn that there was a lot I didn't know about them. Now I was sitting on the base that had been their second home for years. Once I got more comfortable here, I'd make it a point to dig up whatever I could.

But in the meantime, I was determined to stay focused on my

goal. I had to stop KATO. As long as I concentrated on that, I'd be able to keep it together.

I stopped pretending to sleep at six, assuming Scorpion would be by for me early. He hadn't been too forthcoming with information the night before. I considered myself lucky that he got me to my room without cutting my head off, no matter what Simmonds said. I wore the workout clothes I found stacked on top of the dresser, which I assumed were for me. I was never more grateful for my dark, thick, curly hair than I was that morning. I had it tightly secured in a ponytail over my left shoulder, designed to hide the ugly circular burn scar below my ear.

I was still in my room at seven and I was starting to get impatient. By seven thirty I was pacing in circles, and fighting the urge to snap something in half. When Scorpion finally knocked on my door at eight, I was ready to pounce. I pulled the door open so fast that his eyebrows shot up. His surprise lasted only a few seconds before he covered it with an aggravated scowl. He glared at me, then took in the room—my bed pulled apart and reassembled on the floor—before refocusing on me.

"You ready?" His gruff, agitated demeanor hadn't changed.

I slipped into the casual, confident persona I needed for this mission and tossed my head to the side. "What, no gun today?"

He turned and walked down the hall, completely unamused. I jogged to catch up and fell into step next to him. "You know, I kind of thought you'd be dragging me out of bed as early as you possibly could," I said.

His jaw tightened, and I knew I was on to something.

"Oh, I get it," I said when it hit me. "The morning schedule starts at eight, right?" He stared straight ahead, ignoring me. I couldn't help but find the whole thing mildly amusing. "So if everyone else is already training or in class, no one will be in the cafeteria to see you with me."

He rounded on me, bringing us both to a stop. "I don't know what you're doing here, Viper." I forced a cocky smile to keep myself from flinching. "And I don't know how you managed to snowball Simmonds, but there is no way you're not KATO controlled. Simmonds may have asked me to be your guide, but as far as you and I are concerned, I'm in charge of you. You don't go anywhere without me."

I arched an eyebrow, completely unfazed. "Your name's Travis, right?"

His eyes narrowed and filled with an anger and fierceness I'd only seen when I had fought him. "You don't get to call me that." His voice was quiet, but just barely in control. "And you're going to listen to me. I won't let you compromise this agency. The people here have worked too hard and done too much good for you to turn everything over to KATO. If you don't listen to me, I'm going consider you a double agent, and no one will *ever* give you a chance here."

"It's not like they will anyway," I said, then dropped my smile. "But that's not why I'm here."

Scorpion let out a sardonic laugh. "Yeah, right. I don't believe for a second you could be on our side. Not after everything you've done. Someone as cold and ruthless as you doesn't just switch sides like that. You may have belonged to us at one point, but they raised you."

Anger ignited in my chest as every drug injection and broken bone flashed in my mind. I steeled myself and let my overconfident act slip. "You don't know the first thing about being raised by them." I stared him down. If we were going to be stuck together, I wasn't going to let him get to me. "Actually, when I think about it, you don't know much of anything." I stepped closer, purposely invading his personal space, making the narrow hall feel smaller. "All you know are your orders."

Every inch of him was visibly contracted. "You have no idea what I know."

"No." I shook my head and stepped back. "You have no idea what you *don't*."

His jaw clenched, but he stayed quiet. I started walking again, even though I didn't know where I was going. I was sure he would take the lead again quickly, which he did.

I never had a lot of information about the agents I'd faced in the past. In fact, I made it a point to know only what I needed to beat them. But Scorpion was different. He was easily my biggest challenge, so I'd learned a little more about him. He was twenty-one years old. He'd been with the IDA since he was fourteen and spent four years training in their academy before going on his first mission when he was eighteen. I was eighteen and I'd been a field agent for four years. The other thing I knew about Scorpion was that he was most comfortable when he had control of a situation. And if I had to guess, the reason he was so quiet on the walk down to the cafeteria was because he knew when it came to me he'd never have the control he wanted.

The cafeteria was in the basement of the student housing building, which was where my room was now. When we got there, a tall, light-haired, wiry guy, who seemed a little older than Scorpion, stood by the door. He looked up at us and gave Scorpion a nod. His eyes were a fierce, honest emerald green. And they weren't happy to see me.

"Cody, what are you doing here?" Scorpion asked.

"Dude, what do you think?" Cody tilted his head to the side as if he had just been asked a very stupid question. "I'd leave you to deal with *this* alone?" He scrutinized me with a look of disgust on his face. I narrowed my eyes at him, but stayed quiet.

Scorpion shook his head. "This isn't your responsibility."

Cody rolled his eyes. "Well, it shouldn't be yours either."

"And who are you?" I asked, looking from one to the other.

Scorpion ground his teeth together. "We need to eat before it's gone."

I tried to ask more questions, but Scorpion pushed the swinging door open before I could. It snapped shut in my face. I put my palm on the door, channeling my patience, then opened it. Cody glanced at me out of the corner of his eye, like he was daring me to say something. But since that was what he wanted, I went out of my way to do the opposite. Instead I just followed them to the breakfast buffet without a word. I walked a few paces behind them, studying their dynamic. I could tell they were close, and seemed to relax slightly once I got quiet. They kept glancing back at me, but they had fallen into a comfortable banter.

I froze when I got to the table, forgetting about Cody and Scorpion completely. I hadn't eaten a real breakfast since I was eight. Even during the past month, the withdrawal made it hard to keep food down, and when I could, I just ate what was put in front of me. Now the scent of meat and grease assaulted my nose and I found myself staring at an entire spread of food, not knowing where to start.

"Let's go, make up your mind," Scorpion said, sliding a plate in my direction. "I've got a lot to do today, and I'm not wasting an hour while you make a breakfast decision."

"Right," I said, still distracted by the food.

I watched him out of the corner of my eye, piling scrambled eggs onto his plate. I hadn't had eggs quite like this since before I was taken. I took some after him and added a piece of toast. I knew I couldn't eat too much. I was used to KATO's portion sizes, which were basically just enough to keep me strong and alive.

Scorpion and Cody sat themselves down at a table. I chose the seat across from them, and took a bite. It reminded me of the breakfasts I ate as a kid—warm and full of flavor. Scorpion kept his focus on his food. Cody, on the other hand, didn't take his eyes off me. "So you're KATO's amateur attempt at a double agent," he said. "You have to know we would never trust you enough to tell you anything useful."

I squinted my eyes into a tight glare. I didn't have to defend myself to anyone here, let alone this nobody.

"It's funny that you're so quiet now," Scorpion said, glancing up. "You couldn't shut up on the way down."

"Well, *Travis*, you weren't nearly as confident on your own as you are now that you have a friend."

His hand balled into a fist when I said his name, and I smiled.

"Let's review how things are going to work here," Scorpion said. He launched into the same set of rules he'd gone over on the way down, but ended his lecture with orders he seemed to think I should follow. "If I tell you to do something, you do it. No questions. If I tell you to stand in the hall, you stand in the hall. If I tell you to jump off a roof, you jump off the goddamn roof. Got it?"

I arched my eyebrow. "This sounds a little more like a guard than a guide," I said. "And I didn't make it this far just to jump off a roof because you told me to."

Cody rolled his eyes. "Yeah, I'm sure you've been through a lot. It must have been so hard when KATO dropped you in the U.S. and sent you to infiltrate our base."

I gripped my fork tightly, but barely felt the metal edge digging deeply into my skin. My lips thinned and I turned away from Cody, giving Scorpion my full attention. "There are two things you're going to have to accept." His eyes tightened and he opened his mouth, ready to snap at me, but I plowed on before he could. "First, as we've been over, you don't know as much as you think you do. Your job is to do what Simmonds asks you without putting your own spin on it. Stop giving me empty orders and do your job."

Based on the death glare I was getting, I had no doubt Scorpion was picturing himself jumping across the table and strangling me.

"You motherf—" Cody started to stand, but Scorpion grabbed his arm and pulled him back into his seat.

Scorpion gritted his teeth. "What's the second thing?"

I bit back a smile. "The second thing is that I can drop you so fast you won't know what happened. I've done it before, and I'll do it again if I have to. You have less power over me than you think, so you might as well keep the threats to yourself."

His nostrils flared. "You can't take me. Not like you think you can."

I stared him down. "That bullet scar on your shoulder tells a different story."

Cody's temper boiled and his voice turned to an angry growl. "You really want to stop talking *now*."

I didn't like using the shooting against him, but I leaned back and enjoyed their reactions anyway. I was pushing, and it was getting to both of them. Scorpion was a good enough agent to hide it from most people, but I could pick up on the small things. The way his pupils dilated just a fraction. And the way his breathing hitched before forcibly leveling out. He was working hard to keep himself in check. "I guess you're forgetting about the stomach gash I gave you in Thailand," he said. "You really so sure you can take me as easily as you think?"

I shrugged and slid back in my seat. "You may have drawn blood, but you didn't win. I got out of there with exactly what I came for."

"And what was that?" He leaned closer, squinting like he was trying to crack an encrypted code. "Plutonium for a North Korean nuclear weapon? A tool to help KATO kill millions of people they don't agree with?" My insides shuddered, but I didn't let him see that he'd hit a nerve. "I may be ordered not to hurt you—for now—but you better believe that'll change if you do *anything* to threaten this agency."

I didn't blink or say a word. I didn't give him any hint that he had fazed me. "You have no idea how motivated I can be in life-or-death situations."

Cody leaned forward slightly, pointedly twirling a sharp knife in his hand. "Want to give us a demonstration?"

My jaw locked at the threat and I shoved the table to their chests. Cody took the brunt of it and dropped the knife in surprise. It was in my hand in under second. I flung it across the table hitting my target as the tip burrowed into the back of Cody's wooden chair, right next to his shoulder. Both of them stared at me wide-eyed.

I shoveled a forkful of eggs into my mouth. They were cold, but I didn't care. I swallowed and stood up. "There's your demonstration."

I left the student housing building determined to find the training and tech facility on my own. The IDA's campus was comprised of four buildings surrounding a modest courtyard. It easily passed for a small college. I made it about halfway across the courtyard before Scorpion caught up to me. He'd left Cody behind.

"Don't you ever think about threatening the life of an agent again," he said, practically barking at me.

I rolled my eyes. "Please. If I were 'threatening his life,' he'd be dead right now."

"He got lucky," Scorpion growled. "You missed."

I glanced up at him and smiled. "It's cute that you think that."

He jumped in front of me as we got to the training facility's doors. He leaned in menacingly close. "You pull shit like this again and I'll report it to Simmonds."

I inhaled sharply. I knew the limb Simmonds was on for believing me. I didn't want to make things harder for him. Scorpion held my gaze for another moment before turning his back on me and heading inside.

Just inside the training facility's door was a long hallway, with a set of double doors right in front of us. Up until yesterday I had never left the Operations Building, so all of this was new to me. I was processing every detail. I wanted to know all I could about this place—the swifter I could move around, the better off I would be.

The first floor was a wide-open gym with punching bags hanging from the ceiling, and mats that spread from one wall to the other like a rug—probably for sparring. The walls were lined with different combat weapons. Most were dulled or made for practice, but a few looked sharp enough to do some damage. On the right was a glass wall and behind it was the cardio equipment. There was a faint smell of sweat in the air, but it was heavily masked. This was a huge upgrade from the cold cement floors I was used to. And at KATO we used one another as punching bags.

I barely had a chance to take all this in before someone attacked me. One of her hands squeezed my shoulder while her other forearm pressed just below my neck. She pushed me backward, slamming me against the wall. For a moment, all I could see was her hard ice-blue eyes.

"How dare you come here?" Her voice was low and full of anger.

I stayed frozen, studying her face, trying to figure her out. She seemed even angrier than the others. "How can you be here after what you did?"

This was something personal. "What did I do to you?"

It was her turn to look shocked. "You don't even remember." She pressed her arm harder into my collarbone. "You drove a knife into my ribs and you don't even remember it was me?"

Scorpion came up behind her, but he didn't react right away. He wore a satisfied, condescending expression, giving the girl some time. After another minute, he exhaled reluctantly and pulled her away. "Come on, Rachel."

"*No.*" She struggled against him, trying to get back to me. "Even if I believed that she isn't working for KATO—which I *don't*—she doesn't get to just come in and train like she's one of us."

"Simmonds says she does," Scorpion said with a harsh, angry edge.

"And you're on board with this?" Her voice was reaching a panicked shriek.

He gave her a long, even look that made it clear he wasn't, but he also was set on honoring Simmonds's request.

Rachel's eyes widened, angrier than before. "This is bullshit!" She stormed off through another set of doors on the other side of the room, her straight, perfect light-brown hair swinging behind her. When she was gone, the only sound was the hum of the radiator.

I suddenly realized just how many people were in the room. There had to be about sixty to seventy agents, all positioned in various places around the facility. Some were training with one another while others worked agility courses and punching bags. Or at least that's what they had been doing. Now everyone was staring at me. Scorpion turned back to me with a triumphant look, then he walked off to the corner, toward Cody and a dark-haired girl I didn't know. I rolled my shoulders back and refused to worry about anyone else. It was the only survival tactic I had, and it had kept me alive so far. According to my schedule, this was agents-only gym time. The facility was shared between active agents and academy students. This was the one time of the day that only active agents were allowed in.

I moved past the faces, heading toward the punching bags in the back of the room. I had to pass my trusted guide and his friends to get there. Cody had been talking to Scorpion, but the closer I got, the more he focused on me, his stance got more and more defensive. His head was clearly still back in the cafeteria. "You're one crazy bitch, you know that?" he said. "I don't care what agency you're from. You don't get to pull that kind of shit here."

He stood half a step in front of Scorpion with his arms crossed. Just as protective as he had been earlier. He was either his brother or a really good friend. I shrugged a shoulder casually. "You asked for a demonstration."

He laughed harshly, with an edge of disbelief. "Right. Like it would have mattered. You would have found another reason." I crossed my arms and squared myself, waiting as he stepped closer. "You think we all don't know *everything* about you? You're one of KATO's best cold killers. The damage you've done is jaw-dropping."

I'd heard the term "cold killer" before and it made my blood turn to ice. It was for spies who killed innocents to prove a point. KATO was famous for it and I was their best. I did it to survive. And to get high, which seemed like the same thing most of the time. I fought all of this off and smiled. "That's funny. I still don't have the faintest idea who you are—I guess you're not too impressive around here."

He tensed. "You *fucking*—" He took a step toward me, but Scorpion pulled him back.

"Cody, don't. Simmonds will have you out of the field for a year." He glared at me. "Besides, I think Rachel got the point across."

I crossed my arms and held my ground, determined. No one here had the power they thought they did.

"We may have to put up with you," Cody said through gritted teeth, "but the less time you spend around us, the better off we all are."

"Then stop talking to me, and leave me alone."

Cody still wanted to fight, but Scorpion, who hadn't let go of his arm, tugged him back.

He refocused his group into their normal routine, trying to save them all from getting in trouble because of me. There was still one girl from their group who hadn't come after me yet, but I figured that was just a matter of time. I found a corner with a punching bag off to the side, and spent the gym time working to get myself back in shape. But the one thing that wasn't lost on me was the attention I was getting from Scorpion. Even though he was yards away and wrapped up in his own training, he never stopped scrutinizing. He was just waiting for me to start something. I shut the rest of the gym out. I had too much on the line. It would be a while before I was anywhere near ready to go after KATO, but I was determined to be prepared when the time came.

Chapter Five

FIRST DAY OF SCHOOL

S corpion dropped me off for my first class fifteen minutes early, then stood outside waiting for the teacher to arrive. I had four classes in the afternoon and was trusted enough to get to each of them on my own. But Scorpion wasn't about to leave me unsupervised for more than the five minutes in between classes.

I took a seat in the back corner of the room, hoping to stay as far out of the way as humanly possible. I didn't know what to expect from a situational assessment class, but the room itself was a little surprising. I was used to sitting on the floor in a small room while some older operative drilled information into my head. This couldn't have been more different.

The room was big enough for two columns of two-person tables, with each column five rows deep. In the front there was a wider table with a computer in the corner, and behind that table, slightly to the left, was a white slab mounted on the wall. I had no idea what the purpose of *that* was. As a whole, the setup vaguely reminded me of my classroom experience before I was taken. Except the rooms seemed smaller back then and somehow less intimidating. Nothing about this IDA situation was comfortable. I could handle the name-calling and aggressive agents, but a classroom with students was another story. I had never felt more out of place.

"You must be Jocelyn." A kind voice startled me back to reality.

I fixed a sardonic smile on my lips and ran my finger across the table as if I couldn't care less. "That would be me."

The woman was average height and in shape, even though from what I'd overheard, teachers weren't active in the field. She put her bag down on the desk, pulled out a pen and notebook, then came and took the seat next to me. "It's good that you're early. It gives us a chance to talk," she said. "I'm Agent Lee." Up close I could see she had kind brown eyes—which put me on guard.

She put the notebook and pen on the table and slid them over to me as kids started to fill in the room around us. Agent Lee ignored them, even the few that called out her name. "I figured no one would take the time to get you any kind of supplies. You can use this notebook for your notes, and you'll find textbooks have been sent to your room. It's school policy to save the reading for outside of class, so you don't need to worry about bringing them back and forth."

I arched my eyebrows. "Reading?"

Concern flashed across her face. "You *do* know how to read, don't you?"

I rolled my eyes. "I'm fluent in six languages and functional in four others. *Of course* I know how to read. I just haven't had to do it for school in a while."

Agent Lee smiled and relaxed. "I would imagine it'll take some time to get adjusted to a new lifestyle, but you'll get the hang of it. You've only missed a couple weeks of class, so you're not too far behind, but for now, why don't you just focus on learning the new material and we'll catch you up on the old stuff when you're acclimated."

I nodded uncertainly. She was nice. And I couldn't figure out how much of it was an act.

"Excellent."

"How old is everyone else?" I asked, glancing around at the few kids in the room. I was expecting them to be my age, but they looked younger.

"In this class, most are sixteen." The bell rang and she stood up, leaning a little closer as she did. "You're going to be fine." She tapped the table reassuringly, then moved back to the front of the room to get started.

Without Agent Lee to distract me, I noticed the buzz, whispers, and glances that were flying around the room. I had no doubt they were all about me.

There were two girls sitting at the table in front of me in deep conversation. The smaller one probably didn't even hit five feet tall but she had her blond hair piled high on her head to give an illusion of height. Her friend was just shorter than me. Granted, I was a little on the taller side. Suddenly, the blond girl turned around. "So, are you really a double agent? We're *dying* to know."

I blinked. Surprised by the open directness of the question. "No. I'm really not."

The girl shrugged casually. "That's what I figured. Simmonds is pretty protective of this place."

Her friend glanced at her. "You never know."

But the first girl just rolled her eyes and turned back to me. "But you *are* a field agent, right? You've been on actual *missions*?"

"I guess." I shifted, uncomfortable with the attention. "Yeah."

Her eyes widened. "That's *so* cool."

"What grade are you in?" the friend asked, squinting to study me. "You look too old to be a sophomore like the rest of us."

I could just barely get around their easy acceptance to process the question. "I don't think I'm in a grade."

"Oh," the blond said. This seemed to throw them off. "Well, what track are you in?" She tilted her head to the side. "Are you even in a track?"

Now I was the one confused. "I don't know what you're talking about," I said.

"Really?" She leaned closer, all too eager to explain. "Well, after this year we get to pick an area to specialize in, then we take classes designed to make us experts in our areas." She searched my face for some kind of recognition, but I was still in the dark. "For example, I'm planning on specializing in grifting, so after this year most of my classes will focus on acting, psychology, and stuff like that."

"So you'll only go on missions that require grifting?" I asked.

"Not *only* grifting," she said. "All agents can handle any assignment, but we all have our skill sets, and the IDA wants us using them as much as possible." KATO played to my strengths in a similar way, but instead of training me to be the best, I had to prove that I was. "I'm Gwen, by the way." Then she gestured to her friend. "And this is Olivia. She's looking to specialize in observational intelligence, but she also has an amazing brain for strategic planning."

"*Gwen.*" Olivia glared at her friend.

"Sorry," Gwen said with a shrug. "But it's true." Then she turned back to me. "What about you? We know your code name, but I'm assuming you have a real one." She gave me a smile so true it caught me off guard.

"I'm—Jocelyn," I said. I hadn't said my name once at KATO, and I'd barely used it since I'd been back. I was surprised by how thick and unfamiliar it felt on my tongue. "And I guess retrieval would be my specialty." That and assassination had been my strengths at KATO, but I didn't think I needed to tell them about the second one.

"Retrieval?" Olivia asked. "I wonder if you'll end up on the in-house team."

I arched an eyebrow at the term, and Gwen read my confusion. "The IDA gets a piece of its budget by retrieving stolen items—especially art—in exchange for reward money. It's the in-house team's job to track and retrieve the missing items."

I tipped my head doubtfully. "I don't think anyone would be too comfortable with me being that deep into the internal operations of this place." I had never known the IDA was partially self-funded, but it made sense. It would make it a lot harder for one country to have complete control if the agency had a say their budget.

"You never know," Gwen said before moving on. "Everyone's been talking about you since word got out last night. Is Agent Elton really your handler?"

"All right, everyone," Agent Lee said from the front of the room, sparing me an answer. "Today we're going to continue our immediate assessment unit. We've already discussed the elements to consider and potential approaches. Now it's time to put that into practice."

Before she could continue, a short, dark-haired boy sauntered into the room, just a little too relaxed for someone who was almost five minutes late.

"Sam. I'm so sorry I didn't wait for you to start class," Agent Lee said, her voice laced with sarcasm. "But the bell rang and it just—*meant* something to me."

I bit my lip to hide a smile. In my experience, teachers didn't have a sense of humor, just a deadly temper.

Sam beamed. "It's okay, Agent Lee, I understand." He started across the room, but stopped when he spotted me. He turned back to Lee. "You let the new girl sit in my seat?"

Lee shrugged. "She was on time."

Sam smiled and shook his head before heading back toward me and dropping in the empty seat to my left. Sam pulled out his phone and started playing some kind of game, unconcerned by the fact that Agent Lee was trying to teach. I couldn't help but notice he was also the only person who was completely unaffected by me. So far, people either antagonized me or were curious about me. But Sam didn't seem to care whether I was in the room or not.

I turned my attention back to Lee, who had picked up a stack of index cards from her desk, fanned them out in front of her, and continued her instructions. "Each of these cards has on it a situation that would require immediate action. On a separate piece of paper, you're going to write down the number that's on the top corner of the card, followed by how you would handle the situation. You have fifteen seconds to make your assessment and pass the card to the person next to you."

"Is this a test?" a boy on the other side of the room asked.

"I think you can answer that for yourself, Adam," Agent Lee said as she started handing out the cards, making sure to put them facedown.

Adam sighed. "Everything's a test because everything counts in the field." He sounded bored, as if this was something that had been repeated in the past.

Agent Lee nodded and continued moving around the room. When she got to me, she paused. "Just give this a shot, and try not to overthink it, okay?"

I nodded and pulled the card closer, waiting for a sign to start. Everyone flipped their card over when Agent Lee gave the signal and I did the same. I scanned the card. It was a short description involving a retrieval assignment and approaching enemy agents. I picked up my pen to answer, but then I paused. I knew how KATO had trained me to answer, but I was sure it wasn't what the IDA was looking for. Lee told us to switch before I had even written a word down. No one else seemed to have a problem.

By the end, I didn't have a single complete answer. I wasn't even questioning my strategy for most of them. I trusted myself to react in any of the situations I'd read, but I struggled to explain how.

After Agent Lee collected our papers, she spent the rest of the time talking in the front of the room while the class scribbled in their notebooks. I had no idea what they were writing. The only person who didn't seem to bother was Sam, next to me. He pulled his phone out like he had when he first sat down and started tapping the screen. When the bell rang he put his phone in his pocket and headed out the door with the others right behind him. No one waited for any kind of formal dismissal from Agent Lee.

I let out a tight breath, picked up my notebook and pen, and moved toward the exit.

"Have a good day, Jocelyn," Agent Lee said, erasing the white slab, which I had learned was called a whiteboard.

I paused and studied her for a moment, searching her body language for any sign that she was insincere. But I couldn't find one. I nodded slowly. "Thanks."

I stepped into the hallway, hating that all of this had me so overwhelmed.

The rest of my day wasn't any better. In addition to the classes themselves, none of the other teachers were as welcoming as Agent Lee. My second class was Weapons and Arms with Mark Reynolds. He was older, with glasses and salt-and-pepper hair, and he couldn't go more than five minutes without throwing out a phrase with a double meaning that was unquestionably meant for me. My third class was Oppositional Protocol with Wayne Scott, who didn't seem to like me any more than Reynolds did. His method was simply to ignore me, which I was fine with.

I couldn't keep up with these classes any better than I could Agent Lee's, and I still didn't understand why everyone else kept *writing*. I held on to my pen just to have something to do. I was also having a hard time with the other kids. It felt like in some ways they looked up to me, which ate at me in a way I hadn't expected. Sure, I was a field agent, but with all the things I'd done I definitely wasn't the kind of person designed to be a role model. The attention made my skin crawl. I felt the craving creep into my system and I had to grip my pen tighter to steady myself.

But I was keeping it together. My greatest challenge came with my last class, Global Dynamics with Agent Sidney Harper. He was younger than the other teachers, all of whom seemed to be in their thirties or forties. Agent Harper looked like he could have been around twenty-five, which put him a few years older than Scorpion, but right in the age range of the agents he had trained with earlier in the day.

And he had the same attitude toward me that they had. "Viper." He said my name with an evil twist to his lips. I sat up straight and defensive. "Can you name the country most commonly associated with a dictatorship?"

I clenched my teeth and focused on the blank page in front of me. I thought I was prepared to have my past talked about, but Harper was proving me wrong. The next thing I knew he was standing over me and his hand slammed against the table with enough force to startle Sam, who was again sitting next to me. But I didn't jump. I didn't even flinch. If I moved more than I had to I was going to give my weakness away. He was doing this to get at the part of me that was a brainwashed kidnapped victim, but that version of me didn't fit this mission.

I slowly and evenly looked up at Agent Harper. I could feel everyone's eyes on me.

"Do you need me to repeat the question?" he asked. "Or should I say it in Korean so you can understand?"

"North Korea." I held his glare. I wasn't about to let him win, but he *was* getting to me. The craving was getting harder to fight off. I balled my fists on my lap to keep myself in check.

He smirked. "You would know, wouldn't you?"

My nails dug into my palms. I hated that after a month I could still be pushed into feeling like this. No matter what Dr. March had said, it shouldn't take this little to put me on the edge. I should be better than this.

"I bet you think you're doing right by the Great Leader, coming in here to spy on us."

Most of my day had been spent with agents implying I was a traitor, but Agent Harper was direct enough to draw the anger and emotion out of me. "I'm *not* working for KATO." My words were startlingly forceful.

Harper's lips stretched into a condescending smile. "That's just what you want us to believe." He stared me down for a moment before turning and strolling back to the front of the room. "Why don't we look at how much you don't know?"

I bit my tongue.

"What's the first amendment to the Constitution?" he asked. I stayed quiet, refusing to admit that I didn't know. Agent Harper laughed. "Do you even know what the Constitution is?"

Again, I kept my mouth shut, focusing on anything but the attention I was getting from the rest of the class. I had heard about the Constitution, but I didn't know the details. KATO was good at keeping us away from things they didn't want us to know. He spent the rest of the class making a spectacle, pointing out how little I knew. I kept trying to tell myself I'd been through worse, but it didn't matter. Every question spurred a dark emotion in me, which made me crave the drug in a way I wasn't expecting.

Every time he said something to me the whole class would glance back like I was going to explode at any moment. Which by the end was actually not far from the truth. I found it harder to remember my mission. But I had to. My plans were too big to let someone like Agent Harper get to me.

The only way I made it through the class was by pulling my mind back and tuning everything out. When the last bell rang I got my stuff together and left as quickly as I could. At that point, seeing Scorpion waiting impatiently for me in the hallway was a welcome sight.

Scorpion took off down the hall when I came out of Harper's room. I urged myself to keep up, angry that I was feeling more unstable with every step. I took a moment to get myself together, which Scorpion didn't appreciate. "Let's go," he said when we got outside. "I'm missing the afternoon training for this."

I had an appointment with Dr. March, and Scorpion had to take me. I forced an eye roll. "I don't see why that's my problem."

He spun around and glared at me. "It's your problem because you're the person holding me back." His eyes narrowed. "For someone who claims to be on our side, you spend an awful lot of time getting in my way."

"You haven't even been with me a full day," I said. "And no one said you have to wait for me. All you have to do is guide me from one place to another. You decided to make it more."

He looked ready to attack, but instead he turned on his heel and stalked off ahead of me, staying silent until we were on the top floor of the Operations Building outside the medical wing. "Don't take too long."

"I'll be out when I'm *done*."

He glared at me, and I ignored him. I stepped past him and pushed the door open. Dr. March was waiting for me in the lobby.

She smiled when I first came in but once she got a good look at me, her smile faded and her eyebrows knitted together. "Jocelyn."

"I'm fine," I said. "I just—" I closed my eyes, hiding how much I was struggling.

"You're not fine," Dr. March said. "You're fighting it."

I shook my head, but hearing it out loud broke my resolve. Suddenly I couldn't stop shaking. She put her arm around me and quickly led me to one of the back rooms. She sat me on the bed and guided me back onto the pillows. I hated that I still needed to be taken care of.

I rolled onto my back and curbed the urge to curl up in a ball, still fighting for control and craving the high. Dr. March stepped away for a moment, then came back with a tray. She sat on the edge of the bed and brushed my hair away from my left ear. "You'll be okay in a minute," she said. I closed my eyes as she reached back for the tray. A few seconds later I felt the acupuncture needles settle in and around my ear. She did the same to the other ear. The effects were almost immediate.

Dr. March ran a hand through my hair. "I'll let you rest for a while."

I let myself relax once the door closed. It was the first time I had been truly alone since Scorpion picked me up for breakfast. I let the alternative medicine work its magic. Dr. March came back after—I don't know how long. She took the needles out of my ears, and when I was ready, I sat up. She looked at me with the sad but nurturing expression I had gotten accustomed to. "Do I even have to ask how your first day went?"

"It wasn't that bad," I said. She gave me a doubtful look and I rubbed my eyelids. "I should be able handle this. None of this has been easy, but KATO was so much worse."

"At KATO you were high all the time. That numbed you in ways I'm not even sure you realized," she said, writing in my file.

I exhaled heavily and shook my head. "I should be stronger."

She stopped writing and looked up. "You are the strongest person I've ever had in this office."

I bit back a disbelieving laugh. "It doesn't feel that way."

"This isn't something you ever really get over. Not completely. And with this drug"—she shook her head—"it's going to take you longer than most. Every addict has triggers that make them want to get high again, and the closer you are to the drug, the stronger and more frequent that want will be."

I ran a hand along my forehead. "Tell me about it."

"What you're going to find is that some triggers are stronger than others," she said. "Today was stressful, even for someone who's survived what you have. Certain things are going to set you off more. It may take you by surprise at first, but once you can anticipate it you'll have an easier time counteracting it. In the meantime we'll keep up with the acupuncture treatments."

I nodded.

"You should also be aware that the drug has a steroid component to it," she continued. "So don't be too surprised if your senses or reflexes are a little slower than you're used to." I looked at her sharply. Those were two of my most important defense systems. Dr. March sensed my panic. "You'll adjust." She put a reassuring hand on my knee. "It just may take time." She stood up and dipped her head slightly so she could look me in the eye. "We're going to figure all of this out, okay? But for now, you're good to go. Come back if you feel your symptoms building up. It doesn't matter what time it is."

I smiled at her weakly. "Thank you."

She gave my shoulder a squeeze and left the room, giving me a minute to myself before I headed out.

Scorpion was leaning against the wall, arms crossed with one foot propped up. His face tightened in annoyance when he saw me. "What could you have possibly been doing that took so long?"

I had been in with Dr. March for forty-five minutes, but from the way he was acting, it was like I'd been gone for hours. I moved in front of him and headed toward the training facility. "None of your business."

He grabbed my shoulder and turned me around to face him. "Were you casing the place?"

"What?" I tried to pull away but his grip was too strong. "No."

"What did you steal?" He scanned me, searching for any sign of a lie. "Medical files? Research?"

I struggled against him, matching his gaze. "I didn't take anything!" He didn't believe me.

His jaw flexed and he spun me around against the wall.

I pushed back. "What are you doing?" I was livid.

"If you've got nothing to hide, then prove it," he said. He was pissed he had to wait and he was looking for a fight I couldn't afford to give him. The mission was too important. He muscled me back around and frisked me expertly. I bit down hard on my lip, fighting the urge to punch him.

I whipped around when he was finished, furious.

But Scorpion didn't care. "I *will* find out what you're up to." His voice was full of determination.

"There's nothing to find out!" I growled. I breathed heavily and made myself calm down a fraction. Then I smiled bitterly. "But even if there was, you'd never find it. We both know how good I am. Isn't that right, *Travis.*"

His lips thinned and he let out a frustrated grunt. "Don't. Call me that!"

I pushed myself off the wall, away from him and toward the exit.

Chapter Six

QUESTIONS NORMAL PEOPLE ASK

It took me a few days to settle into the routine, but even then I never let down my guard. Scorpion's angry condescension hadn't lessened, and Cody and Rachel had taken a run at me every chance they got. But I could handle them. My classes were still overwhelming, but so far the first day had been the worst. Gwen had even worked out that I didn't know how to take notes and walked me through it. Still, the best part of my day became the afternoon workout sessions. They gave me the chance to go off by myself in a corner and pound the punching bag. Agent Harper still rubbed me the wrong way, so punching something helped keep the cravings at bay.

The downside was that the afternoon training sessions were open to both agents and academy students. The kids missed the morning sessions because they had their more practical combat and espionage classes. The afternoon sessions were also open to their teachers. Most of the instructors were older and out of the field, so they didn't have too much of a presence in the training facility. But Agent Harper was younger and still actively training—he lived to torture me. He tried to bait me into a fight, but after the Cody incident I did my best to avoid all of them.

Scorpion kept an eye on me, but he also stayed as far away as he possibly could. And the other agents did the same, aside from a few glares and glances, which was why it was so surprising when I realized one of Scorpion's friends was standing next to my bag—she was the only one from his group I hadn't talked to yet. She waited patiently with her arms crossed. I tried to ignore her, but the longer she stood the more determined she seemed. Eventually, my resolve cracked and I stopped punching. "What are you doing here?"

She flipped her long dark ponytail over her shoulder and smiled. "I want to talk to you."

I blinked. The addition of the students had made the afternoon training sessions louder than the morning ones, and I was convinced that over the grunts and hits and laughter, I couldn't possibly have heard her right. "You what?"

She smiled. "The only agents you've talked to are Travis, Cody, Rachel, and Sidney Harper, and none of them are all that interested in hearing your side."

My eyes widened in disbelief. "And *you* are?"

She shrugged. "I like to give people the benefit of the doubt. I figure if you're telling the truth and you aren't brainwashed, then things must have been pretty awful for you. And I thought you could use someone to train with."

I stood stiff, unsure of how to react. I may have been here only a few days, but so far not one agent had even considered that I might be telling the truth. I wasn't prepared for the flood of KATO memories that came with that acknowledgment.

I didn't know what to say, but it didn't matter. She kept talking. "I'm Nikki, by the way."

"You already know who I am." I kept my stance guarded. "You're friends with Rachel, right?"

"Yes," she said with a skeptical tone.

"I can't imagine she would be too excited about you talking to me." I glanced behind her and past several sparring agents to Rachel, who was glaring back at me.

"She's not," Nikki said. "But she'll get over it. I have a habit of talking to people no one else likes. Though you should know that just because we're talking, doesn't mean I trust you. Because I don't."

"Then what are you doing here?" I asked, irritated that she'd brought any of this up to begin with.

She shrugged. "Every other agent wants to keep away. *I* want to get to know you. Because if you're telling the truth, you're going to need a friend. And if you're not, I want to be the first to know."

I considered her for a moment. It wouldn't be the worst thing in the world to have someone else on my side. "Fine," I said. "But I'm not looking for a sparring partner today."

She nodded. "I'll give you some time, but you'll have to learn to adjust because I'm going to be around."

She walked away without another word. When she got back to the group, everyone seemed to have a question, but Nikki just shook her head and pulled Rachel aside to train.

Scorpion stalked over to me at the end of the training session, a determined scowl etched in his face. "What did Nikki want with you?"

I kept punching. "Why don't you ask her about it?"

He pulled the bag back, so I'd miss my next punch. I glared at him. "I did," he said. "She wouldn't tell me."

"Then I guess it's none of your business." I tried to continue my workout, but he stepped in front of the bag, blocking me.

"You don't get to decide that." His expression was strained and angry. "Now tell me. What did she want?"

I sighed, too tired to fight him anymore. "She said she'll be keeping an eye on me. Just like everybody else. You happy?"

He didn't say anything, but when I pushed him aside to get to the bag, he went without a struggle.

I'd been at the IDA a week before I met with Simmonds again. Scorpion had been just as brusque and irritating as he had been on day one. And Agent Harper and Cody hadn't gotten tired of giving me a hard time. From what I could tell, their disdain for me was the only thing the two of them ever agreed on. Nikki had kept her promise to be "around." She started training closer to me and even threw a few friendly comments my way. I also started finding my way on campus. I had more or less managed to get the layouts of all the buildings. I had made it a point to know everything I could about KATO so I could find a way out. I hadn't planned on needing the same thing for the IDA, but I wasn't leaving anything to chance.

It had been five weeks since I'd left KATO, which meant it was about time I made my first contact. They were expecting it to be a while before I was trusted with anything, but the sooner I got in touch with them, the better. Simmonds was waiting for me when I showed up at his office before my classes.

"How have you been?" he asked as I sat across from him. The mission map on the monitor above his head caught my eye. There were nine dots now, and in different locations from the last time I had been in the office.

"Good," I said, forcing my focus back on him. He gave me a doubtful look and I conceded. "I'm okay."

"You came in with four bottles of Gerex," he said. "How long is that supposed to last?"

"Until mid-December," I said, shifting uncomfortably. "Each bottle has a month's supply."

"Is there a way they planned to get more to you if you need it?" he asked.

I shrugged. "They said that there is, and that they'd let me know when the time comes."

"Very well." Simmonds tapped the file folder on his desk with his thumbs. "Are you ready for this?"

"Yeah," I said. I had to be. "If we wait too much longer they might get suspicious."

"How are you supposed to contact them?" he asked.

"They gave me a series of websites and message boards to memorize. First I have to check the temperature in Berlin on a KATO-controlled weather site. The temperature dictates what message board I'm supposed to go to. Then each site has a coded protocol that's designed to fit the language of the website." I rattled off everything as KATO had trained me to.

Simmonds furrowed his brow. "KATO had to know we'd catch on. We monitor computer activity, and you'd have no reason to be on a message board of any kind. We would have known you were a double agent."

"They gave me a spoof server to go to first," I said. "I put in the right

URL and it takes me to a site that masks my history. It was designed specifically for the IDA's computer system."

Simmonds's eyes darkened. "How does KATO know our computer system?"

I shook my head. "I don't know. I don't think they have anyone else in here. They would have told me if I had an ally and they wouldn't have been as desperate to get me in."

Simmonds nodded, considering this. "Okay, I'll handle it." He pushed the folder across the desk. "Here's what you'll tell them. You said they're looking for what we have on them, correct?" I nodded and flipped through the folder that contained all the details I'd need. "We obviously aren't going to turn all of that over, but we did come up with a mixture of information that's true, though slightly outdated, and information that's close to true, but more immediate. You need to type this information *exactly* as it's written. It's a code designed to give us a small window into their computer."

"They'll be able to find that," I said.

"They won't. It's too small to be detected. It only gives us a peek at the files they have open. We'll have people monitoring the window, and compiling the data that comes across." He was direct and straightforward.

"They won't know it came from me, right?" I couldn't hide my sharp tone.

Simmonds's face softened. "They'll never know you did anything intentionally."

"And the intel that's close to the truth—it's close enough that they won't think twice about it?"

He gave me a single headshake. "They'll think we're close enough to be tracking them, but that they're still good enough to keep us guessing. And the truth is, aside from what you've told us, we really *don't* have too much recent intel that would interest them."

"Okay," I said, letting out a breath I hadn't meant to hold.

"I expect to meet with you after you get a response from them," Simmonds said.

I nodded uneasily. If I slipped up once, KATO would know I'd turned. I would only be able to hide from them for so long and when they got a hold of me—

I shook the thoughts away. I could do this. I was *trained* to do this. And if I couldn't do this much I would never be able to stop their recruitment regime. "Yes, sir," I said, feeling my confidence building.

"Good." He shifted a little closer. "Now, we need to discuss your bigger mission. How are you planning on getting to KATO's recruitment operations?"

"I don't have enough to go on yet," I said. "They either convince most recruits to join as kids or blackmail them by threatening their families. They've also gotten families to turn their kids over under the guise of serving their country. I haven't found anyone else who was kidnapped. They have recruitment centers at various points all over the world. I know rough locations of most, but I need to figure out the rest of the plan—mainly, what to do with the brainwashed agents who had their lives stolen and are now stealing other people's lives."

Simmonds's expression was even, but I noticed a small spark in his eye. "If you can figure out those locations, I'll supply you with people to help with the infiltrations and provide a place for those agents to go."

I eyed him uncertainly. I could tell this was about more than just damaging KATO. And taking on that many enemy agents was asking a lot. "What's in it for you?"

He gave me a small smile. "Don't worry about it." He read my uneasiness and tipped his head. "Jocelyn, you're trusting me with your life. If you plan on making this happen, you're going to have to trust me with this too."

I bit my lip and conceded a nod.

"All right, then," he said after a moment. "You have a way you can get to a computer to make your contact?"

"I'll come up with something," I said, smiling. "Got to pretend I'm a double agent, right?"

Simmonds nodded gravely. "Be careful. If any of our agents catch you—"

"They'll think I have a mystery game hobby," I said, though even I didn't believe myself. I dropped my smile. "I'll be fine. I've been doing this a long time."

I was more anxious than I was expecting to be the night before my first KATO contact and I couldn't relax enough to fall asleep. My mind came floating back to my parents, which it did a lot when I didn't have something else to distract me. I had so many questions. Some of which I didn't think that much about until I'd gotten to the IDA. Were they good agents? What were their strengths? Did my dad ever try to find me? Was I like them at all?

The later it got, the more questions I had and the more restless I felt. By one in the morning, I found myself pacing the room. I had to do something—anything. I couldn't stay suffocated in this room all night. I was going to get answers.

I had located the IDA's archives room in the lower level of the Operations Building a few days earlier. It housed a copy of every mission and personnel file in the IDA's system. I hadn't considered investigating further until that moment.

I crept across the courtyard. It was a new moon, which made it practically pitch-black out. I tugged on the door, and wasn't surprised to find it was unlocked. With missions occurring all over the world, I had no doubt that the IDA had someone in this building at all times. I stood by the door, listening for anyone who might be coming down the hall. Simmonds didn't tell me any place was off-limits, but I knew most people wouldn't agree. When I was sure I was alone, I moved stealthily down the hallway pausing outside the archives door, which I was stunned to find open.

Once I saw the setup of the room, I understood why it was so easy to get inside. The room itself didn't have too much in it, with the exception of four computers that lined the back wall. Each computer required an agent security code for access. I was clearance level two, which got me access to the most basic files—past missions, basic personal details, employment records, and other trivial information. Most agents were level four, higher agents levels five or six, with seven and eight being reserved for the highest-ranking IDA members. I punched my security code into the closest computer and logged on.

Once I was in I started combing through the files. I didn't see any kind of easy search bar. These files were sorted as if this were a physical filing cabinet. I had to tab through the virtual drawers and folders to find what I was looking for. I slid closer to the screen, causing the chair to squeak slightly. I hadn't gotten far when the light flicked on. I whirled around to find Nikki standing at the door, her eyes wide as she took in the scene. "What are you doing?" Her voice was far too calm for the look of livid disbelief she was wearing. "You sneak into our archives and we're supposed to believe you're not a spy?"

"I didn't sneak," I said. "I used my code. Simmonds'll know all about this by morning." And he'd given me every indication that he was trusting me as much as I was trusting him.

She relaxed slightly, her face turning curious. "What are you up to?"

I glanced up at her reluctantly. This wasn't something I ever planned on discussing with anyone. It was too personal. "It's none of your business." I turned back to the screen and continued flipping through the folders.

"Simmonds may be okay with this, but what makes you think the rest of us will be?"

I spun on my chair to face her, a panic rising in my chest. "I'm not doing anything wrong," I said, speaking through my teeth.

"Maybe not, but your history is just a little too sketchy for me to take you at your word." She crossed her arms. "I said I'd give you a chance. Now you're going to give me one. If you tell me what you're up to and it's as innocent as you say it is, I'll keep your secret."

I let out a deep breath. I didn't have a choice. "I was looking for my parents' files."

Her eyes widened slightly. I'd surprised her. "Your parents? That's what this is about?" I looked away, feeling far more exposed than I was comfortable with. "No, it's good," she said. "I just wasn't expecting that." She came and sat at the computer next to me.

My defenses went up. "What are you doing?"

"Helping." She smiled a small fraction as she logged into the computer. "What clearance level are you? I need to set the computer so I don't give you anything above your clearance." I answered her question, but I was stunned. It must have showed because her smile got a little wider. "Your parents had the same last name as you, right?"

I nodded, still trying to comprehend what was happening. Nikki got to work quickly, and a few seconds later she came up with two files side by side on her screen. She slid over so I could see and my breath caught when I read their names; Alexa and Christopher Steely.

She opened my father's file without another word and passed the mouse to me. I glanced at his picture, but couldn't bring myself to study his face too closely. I scanned the file, taking in the information quickly. "Most of this is blacked out," I said, not looking at Nikki. She came a little closer and I didn't try to stop her. There wasn't anything too personal for her to see, just basic information—when he started, how long he worked there, and a handful of his more minor missions.

"It's probably above your classification level, which isn't too surprising." She flipped back to the front of the file. "Yeah, look here." She pointed at a small number next to one of the blacked-out sections. Seven. My mom's was the same. Nikki squinted at the number, seeming perplexed. "That's interesting."

"There's something off about that?" I asked.

Nikki shrugged. "I don't know if there's something *off*, but it looks like your parents were involved in some pretty big things. Most files this old aren't above level four."

I opened my mom's file. Her picture, I couldn't look away from it. We didn't look too much alike—her features were much more delicate than mine—but we had the same hair. It was crazy and curly and nearly impossible to manage. Her file was even more blacked out than my dad's. The only details I could make out were what I already knew—her employment time, and that her body was found in South Korea. I closed the file quickly, angry that she was dead and that I couldn't get any more information about her.

"We can look into a few things," Nikki said. "The IDA has other resources. We may be able to piece some things together."

I snapped out of my trance and focused on Nikki. "What?"

Her forehead tightened in confusion. "There are a few other places we can check. Files may be level seven, but some reports and other articles aren't as high up. We may be able to find something more."

"Okay." I spoke slowly, trying to process this. I wanted to ask her why, but when I opened my mouth different questions came out. "How did you know I was in here? What are you even doing here this late?"

"I just got back from a mission and Simmonds asked me to drop the file off in the filing and processing room next door. I was on my way out when heard the chair squeak. Which probably wouldn't have seemed that weird if the light weren't off." She tilted her head to the side. "If you want to look less suspicious, you should probably stop sneaking around in the dark."

"Yeah." I rubbed the back of my neck. "Right."

She let out a big yawn. "Anyway, I should get home before I fall over." She logged off her computer. "I've got the day off tomorrow, but train with me when I get back. We'll work out a plan."

I nodded and she headed for the door. "Nikki." She turned back around, giving me a patient, expectant look. "Thank you."

She smiled. "Don't stay here too late."

Chapter Seven

FIRST CONTACT

I stayed in the archives room poring over my parents' blacked-out files much later than I should have. I eventually managed my way back to my room to get some sleep. By the time I woke up I was able to tuck everything I learned to the back of my mind. I had something more important to do and I couldn't afford to be distracted.

I knew there had to be computers in the Academy Building even if I hadn't found them yet. I had the layout for each of the buildings down, save for a floor here and there. We had five minutes between each class, which was just long enough for me to get my message out to KATO. I spent the time in between my first and second classes finding the room, which turned out to be in the basement. I waited until in between my third and fourth class to actually make contact, and did my best to avoid drawing any more attention to myself than I did on a regular basis.

By the time I got downstairs, I had four minutes to pull this off and get back to Harper's class. It was the closest I'd come to a true field assignment in months. I sat at the computer trying to type while adrenaline rushed through me. I wasn't used to working after so much time off, or this sober. It was a simple assignment, but I found it so much more exhilarating than I normally would have.

It took me a beat longer than I would have liked to key in the firewall spoof correctly. Once I did, I entered the designated KATO weather website. Thirteen degrees Celsius. An odd number in the teens. I jumped over to the Dell computer technical support message board and followed KATO's directions. I found the fifth post that mentioned a keyboard problem and clicked.

I scanned the post and quickly decoded the message KATO had left. It was short, and didn't give me too much information, saying only that they were awaiting the details of the request they had previously assigned me. It also said I should check back as soon as possible to see the status of my report, which probably meant that I'd get more instruction the next time I logged on.

When I started typing, my heart picked up for a different reason. This post was my first true attempt to mislead KATO and the reality of that slammed into me. I felt the craving start to eat at my insides, and it threw me for a moment. But I pushed on, ignoring it.

I typed in the details of the intel that the IDA had on KATO to the letter, like Simmonds had said. My heart pounded furiously when I finally pushed the post button, as if I had just run for miles. But I had only thirty seconds to log out and get back upstairs to Agent Harper's room, and I refused to let something as stupid as a message board post put me back in Dr. March's office.

Sam gave me a questioning look when I slid into my seat. It was one of the few times I got to class after him.

"What were you up to?" he asked.

"Nothing." I was breathless and I used that to hide the uneasy note in my voice. "I just got held up in the bathroom."

He studied me for a moment, then nodded. I couldn't tell whether he believed me or not, but either way he didn't feel the need to ask any more questions.

I couldn't stop fidgeting in my seat. I had no idea what Agent Harper was teaching, and I made no effort to figure it out. I was sure there were more than a few jabs at me, but right then I couldn't be bothered to care.

It took me a while to fall asleep that night, and then I found my-self awake at five in the morning, sweating, shaking, and fighting the urge to throw up. I thought I had gotten it together. I thought I would be fine until my appointment with Dr. March later that day. But right then, I couldn't ignore how much I *needed* the drug.

I had to get to Dr. March.

I shook the whole time as I got dressed and crossed the court-yard to the Operations Building. I had never been more grateful for the elevator. I knocked on Dr. March's door, which was right next to the medical wing. She lived on campus and had told me that she was always on call.

"Jocelyn," Dr. March said when she opened her door. She looked disheveled, but surprisingly alert. I didn't have to say anything. She grabbed my elbow and led me across the hall into the medical ward. She put me in a room and immediately began the acupuncture. I ex-haled audibly when she left me to relax.

When she came back, she sat down on the bed. "You shouldn't have let it get that bad," she said.

"I didn't know it was," I said, glancing up at her.

She gave me a doubtful look. "There's no way you didn't feel this building." I broke eye contact and she sighed. "Look, I get what you're trying to do. But you're not going to beat this that way. Not with the kind of drugs you were on."

"I thought I could do better," I said, still unable to meet her eyes.

"You will." She brushed a hand through my hair. "It's just going to take some time. You'll get stronger." I bit my lip and stared at the ceiling. "Get some sleep. I'll wake you before the morning schedule starts."

She left me before I could argue.

I woke up two hours later when the door banged open. "Why the hell can't you follow directions?" Scorpion yelled.

I sat up so fast I felt dizzy and blinked a few times to clear my head.

Dr. March was right behind him. "You can't just barge in here! This is a medical ward!"

Scorpion didn't even acknowledge her. "You have absolutely *no* business going anywhere on this campus at night!" He glared at me, his eyes livid. "Let's go. We're leaving!"

"No we're not," I said, fighting to keep my voice controlled.

"I'm not asking." He glared down at me, like he owned me. The same way my overbearing KATO handler used to.

I was too groggy to think fast enough to fight. I used to wake up sharp and alert. Another side effect of the Gerex. Now without it I needed time to get my brain moving. "Give me a minute."

"You haven't *earned*—"

"I said I need a minute!" I could feel a headache building. I stared him down like he was a dog, determined not to be the one to blink first. "Get. Out."

His fists were balled and his arms shook slightly like he was trying to get himself in check, yet he seemed more pissed off with each breath. When he finally got it together enough to try and argue, Dr. March took the opportunity to drag him out of the room. She shut the door behind her, and I let the quiet hang in the air, giving myself a moment to think. Then I pulled my hair into a side ponytail, splashed some water on my face, and met Scorpion in the hallway.

I was impressed to see that Dr. March had managed to get him all the way out of the medical wing. He was pacing in front of the door when I found him.

"You need to understand something, right now." He was so far beyond angry that he had to work to keep his voice at a reasonable volume. "When I tell you to go *nowhere* without me, that means absolutely nowhere. Not to class, not the training room, and not the medical wing. It doesn't matter if you cut your arm off. You can bleed to death for all I care, but you *do not* leave your room without me." He scanned me from head to toe. "I don't even see any bandages, so it couldn't have been that much of an emergency."

I took three steps forward so that I was in his personal space. "I get that you *think* you're in charge of me, but you keep forgetting that *you* were the person who gave yourself that responsibility. So it means *nothing* to me. You don't know everything about the situation and you have no idea why I was here."

He ground his teeth together, getting angrier. "Then fill me in. Put my mind at ease."

"I can't tell you anything you don't already know. You need to do your job, which is what Simmonds tells you to do. He trusts me enough to move around here without a constant guard." I was in his face, glaring up at him, my eyes level with his pursed lips. I could practically see his mind searching for a comeback. "Now, are we going to train, or what?"

He glowered, then strutted down the hall without another word.

Scorpion didn't speak to me until we got into the gym. "You don't leave this room until I tell you to, okay?"

"When are you going to understand that you don't get a say in where I go?" I asked.

He attempted to reply, but Cody was next to him before he could get a word out. "Is this about the stunt she pulled this morning?" he asked Scorpion.

"I didn't pull a stunt." My frustration level was growing. My tolerance for Cody was nearly shot, and after the last two days, I wasn't feeling particularly patient. "And no one asked you to get involved."

Nikki and Rachel, who weren't standing too far away, came closer. "Don't you *dare* talk to him like that," Rachel snapped.

I moved forward to meet Rachel head on, but Nikki stepped in my path.

"Let's go," she said to me. "You promised me a workout today."

"I'm not done here." I glared at the others over her shoulder.

"*Everyone* is done here," Nikki said, pushing me away. Scorpion, Cody, and Rachel were shooting me aggressive, agitated looks. She didn't so much as glance at them. "Come on." She backed me into the corner, away from everyone.

"Why are you doing this?" I asked. "You keep involving yourself in my problems. And your friends hate you for talking to me."

"I'm friends with Sidney," she said. "They're used to this type of thing."

I gaped at her. "You're *friends* with Agent *Harper*?" I couldn't picture how someone as good-natured as Nikki could be friends with *that*.

"Really?" she asked. "You're judging *me*? The only person on your side?"

I faltered, but recovered quickly. "He's an asshole," I said. "And not just to me."

"And you've done some pretty serious damage to my friends," she pointed out. "Things involving guns. And knives."

I swallowed, then nodded. "Okay, fine. That's fair."

"I knew you'd see it my way." She smirked and put her arms up in front of her. "We've got a lot to discuss. We might as well spar and get a workout in."

I eyed her fists wearily. "I don't know if that's such a good idea."

She tilted her head to the side, like I was being ridiculous. "Come on. If you keep it clean, I'll keep it clean. I'm on your side, remember?"

"What do you mean by 'clean'?"

"No hits to the head, and nothing that's going to do any actual damage," she explained. "We try to take each other down, but not hurt each other."

Everything at KATO was a fight that counted. If you won, you got Gerex. If you lost, they kept it from you. I didn't know how to fight for "practice." But I found myself nodding. Nikki had my back twice this week. She *was* on my side—and in a way no one ever had been before. I didn't want to lose that.

I put my hands up in front of me and bounced en garde, waiting for her to make the first move. She swung at my side, which I blocked easily. My steps were hesitant at first, but I got the hang of it. After a few minutes, I hooked the back of her leg and brought her to the ground. I stood above her, waiting for her to pop up and launch herself at me.

But instead, she laughed. I furrowed my eyebrow, confused as she reached forward holding her hand out. It took me a moment to figure out she wanted me to help her up.

"You're good, I'll give you that," she said as I pulled her to her feet. "Want to go again?"

"Sure," I said, and I meant it.

She smiled and got ready to fight. "I haven't forgotten about your parents," she said. "If you're okay with going late to the afternoon training, I can meet you after your classes and we can start our search."

"That would be great." I was a little stunned that she remembered.

She took a shot to my bicep. "We can go back to the archives room and see what mission files and medical reports we can get access to. Then we can figure out where to go from there."

I was surprised at how excited the prospect made me. We may not have access to everything, but Nikki knew her way around the IDA's system better than I did. I had to believe I could use that to my advantage.

We kept sparring, and Nikki took the opportunity to start asking questions. "So, do you want to tell me what happened this morning?" I narrowed my eyes, making it pretty clear I didn't. Nikki just sighed. "Come on, what did we say about trust?"

I dodged her punch, feeling the desperate urge to keep my mouth shut. But this was my chance to win her over. I couldn't blow it. "I had a medical emergency," I said.

She considered me. "That's what Travis said. But he also said you didn't look that hurt."

I swallowed. "It was a different kind of emergency." She stopped fighting for a moment, giving me a searching look. "KATO didn't exactly give the best medical care. I'm behind on a lot of things."

She nodded and raised her hands again. We dropped back into our dance. "Travis is pretty pissed about it."

"I know." It came out harsher than I meant, but I was irritated. "It's none of his business."

"It takes a lot to get him worked up," she said. "He's one of the most lighthearted people I know."

This surprised me enough that I dropped my guard. Nikki's fist landed in my side. I grunted, but hid most of the pain as I was trained to.

Her eyes went wide and her face was tight and apologetic. "I'm sorry," she said. I shook my head like it was nothing, but she didn't buy it. She grabbed my elbow and guided me over to the other side of the gym to a giant blue box. She lifted the top and I realized it was a water chest. She opened a bottle and handed it to me, then waited until I had a few sips before she said anything else.

"I surprised you," she said.

I shook my head. "You didn't—"

"I did." She wasn't buying my bullshit. "I just didn't expect to. You were that surprised to find out Travis is easygoing?"

I let out a laugh. "He's never been anything but a serious, guarded asshole."

She shrugged. "He takes his job seriously, and he takes you more seriously than almost anything I've ever seen. But that's not who he is; it's just how he works."

I fell quiet, not entirely sure what to say. So instead I changed the subject. "I should go," I said. "I have classes soon."

"Okay," she said. "I'll meet you after your classes and we'll see what we can find out about your parents."

"Sure." I gave her a small smile. "Thanks." I headed for the door, not at all surprised to find Scorpion hovering right behind me before I could even get close to it.

Chapter Eight

TRAINING PARTNER

Nikki was waiting for me when I got out of Agent Harper's class. We crossed the courtyard to the Operations Building and went down to the archives room. The first thing I noticed when Nikki opened the door was that we weren't alone. I'd recognize Scorpion's broad build anywhere—even hunched over a keyboard with his back to me. He froze when the door opened, then quickly closed the program he had open, and locked the computer.

"Of course," I said. "It's like he's put a tracking device on me."

Scorpion spun around on his chair. "What are you doing here?" he asked. "I thought Nikki was getting you."

Nikki waved from the door. "Nikki *did*."

"And this isn't *your* archives room," I said. "I can be here."

Scorpion stood up, annoyed. He pushed past me and turned to Nikki. "She's your charity case. She's your problem."

Nikki rolled her eyes. "Don't be a noodle."

Scorpion glared at her. "Shut up." He stepped around her, into the hallway.

"You first, *noodle!*" she yelled after him. She refused to give him the last word. It was pathetic and childish, and it irritated Scorpion just enough to make me happy. She shook her head after him.

"What's a noodle?" I asked.

Nikki laughed and rolled her eyes. "It's something that Cody started when he was at the academy. You're probably better off not knowing the details."

I laughed lightly. "Yeah, I think you're right."

She sat down at the computer and pushed out the chair next to her. "Come on, let's get to work."

I slid into the seat and logged onto a computer as Nikki did the same. "What are we looking for?"

"I'm going to go through medical reports, and I'll show you where to find the mission history files," she said. "You still probably won't have access to most of the details, but if you sift through what you can, we might be able to piece some things together." Nikki helped me navigate the files and before long I was flipping through my parents' mission history. Six years of partially redacted trips and assignments. At least, that's what my dad's had, but there was something different about my mom's.

"Is it weird that my mom didn't go on any missions for the first four years she was at the IDA?" I asked Nikki.

Nikki glanced at the file. "Not necessarily. She could have been working in another department. Like operations or tech or something. But whatever she was doing during that time could explain why her file has a higher clearance level." She turned back to her computer and left me to wonder, only to break through my thoughts a few minutes later.

"I think I found something else," she said.

"What is it?" I leaned closer.

Nikki skimmed the report. "It's your mom's autopsy." Needles ran down my spine. "When did you say she was found?"

"Simmonds said after I was taken."

Nikki grimaced. "Well, he wasn't lying. She was found three *years* after you were taken. In South Korea near the DMZ."

My eyes jumped down the report. "It took them three years to find her?" Nikki bit her lip, and I could tell she was holding something back. "What is it?"

She watched me closely for a moment. "She hadn't been dead for that long when they found her. She'd been, uh"—she hesitated—"killed within days of being recovered."

My heart dropped to my stomach. Simmonds had lied to me.

I went straight to Simmonds's office from the archives room. Nikki tried to come with me, but I wouldn't let her. I needed to talk to Simmonds alone. I paced the space in front of his door while I waited for him to finish up a meeting with someone else.

"Jocelyn," Simmonds said as I brushed past the exiting agent. "Can I help you with something?"

"You lied to me about my mom," I said. My voice was calm enough, but it was an act. He'd asked me to trust him, and I had. Now it was taking everything I had not to completely lose my temper on the person giving me a way out of KATO. I stood in front of him, tapping on the edge of the desk.

He looked confused, then the realization dawned on him. "You found your parents' files the other night. You've done some more research since then, haven't you?"

I nodded, a little surprised he wasn't trying to hide his lie. "I wanted to know about them."

He nodded, resigned. "What did you find?"

I wanted to be more upset with him, but he had information I wanted. I swallowed. "My mom was alive for three years after I was taken. I thought they killed her to get to me, but they kept her alive. They *used* her for something."

"We don't know that for sure," Simmonds said. "All we have is speculation, but we never found any proof. We can't even say for sure that KATO had her, it just makes the most sense."

"I don't need proof," I said. "They took her. I know how they work. They keep people as long as they're useful, and then they kill them. They put her in South Korea so you would find her." I massaged my forehead, processing everything. "Today I learned that she was here for four years before she went into the field. What was she doing then?"

Simmonds kept his face neutral, but his pupils dilated a fraction. "That's classified." My eyes narrowed in irritation and he sighed. "Jocelyn, I knew both of your parents very well. The three of us were among the IDA's first agents. We helped get this place off the ground. And before that we worked together at the CIA. There's a lot about them I can share with you, but I cannot discuss the work they did here."

"There has to be some information you can give me." I pulled my fists tight against my sides. "I thought I knew what happened to her, and I don't. I need something to go on."

Simmonds considered me carefully. "I can tell you that the work she did during those four years was in the development division," he said. "But that's it."

I met his gaze. I was still annoyed he'd kept this from me, but I believed right now he was telling me all he could. I ran a hand over my hair. "If it was development, then that has to be what KATO used her for." It was all adding up.

He tipped his head to the side. "I know you found your way around that facility. Do you really think she was in there and you had no idea?"

"At that point, yes, I do," I said. "I was eleven when she died and still afraid of them. They could have had her in the room next door and I never would have known."

He was quiet for a moment, then said, "If you have any questions about your father, I could try to answer those."

I shook my head harder than I meant to. He was out there, they were looking for him, and I wasn't so sure I wanted to find him. I didn't know how to be a daughter. And I'd worked for the enemy. I'd already let him down in more ways than I could count. So no. I didn't want to know any more about him. I didn't want to know all the other ways I'd disappointed him.

Simmonds studied me for a moment. "I'm not going to stop you from researching, but I can't give you anything more," he said. "And if you keep digging, I'm fairly certain you're not going to like what you find."

I swallowed hard. I believed he was being honest, but I had no intentions of giving this up. "I understand," I said. "Thank you."

I stood up, ready to leave, but Simmonds stopped me. "Before you go, I have a few things I've been wanting to talk to you about."

I sat back down.

"I've been checking in on you," he said. "Agent Elton and Dr. March have been keeping me well informed."

A small laugh got away from me. "I'm betting their reports have a lot of differences in them."

Simmonds smiled. "That's putting it mildly. But at the moment, I have two concerns. The first being about what happened this morning."

I shook my head, annoyed. "Scorpion can't tell me what to do."

"That's not my issue," Simmonds said. "We're getting to the point where we're going to be looking to put you in the field." I sat up straighter. I hadn't expected the conversation to go in this direction. "But I can't do that if you can't be honest about how you're feeling. You become too much of a liability if the agency has to worry about you struggling with cravings on an assignment."

"You won't. I'll make sure it's taken care of ahead of time." I didn't care how eager I sounded.

"I need to know you can admit it when you're craving the drug," Simmonds said. "Until you can, we can't believe you when you say you're under control."

I pursed my lips, seeing a handful of other issues. "How are you even going to convince anyone to let me out in the field?"

"That's my problem," Simmonds said. "Your job is to be ready when the time comes."

I took a deep breath and nodded. "I can work on that."

"Good." He kept the conversation moving, barely acknowledging how hesitant I was. "Now for my second concern. Agent Elton's reports spend a lot of time focusing on training room confrontations."

"His friends, aside from Nikki, like to push me," I said before he could finish.

"That's not the part of the situation that concerns me. I knew putting you with other agents would lead to a certain level of conflict. My problem is that when talking to Agent Elton, I was left with the impression that you train either by yourself or with Agent Nikki Edwards, is that correct?"

"Well, yeah," I said with a small shrug. "She's pretty much the only person who can stand to be around me."

A ghost of a smile crossed his lips. "She tends to do that for a lot of people." He thought for a moment. "Agent Edwards is good, but she's not the kind of challenge you need if you're going to be in top form for fieldwork. You'll train with Elton from now on."

My defenses went up. "I'd rather be by myself."

"That may be, but you can't challenge yourself the way an opponent can," he said. I tried to argue, but he cut me off. "I need you to do this. I'm taking a risk keeping you here and pushing to have you in the field. I need you at your best."

I sat back in my seat and crossed my arms. He was right. I owed him. "You think he's going to go for this?"

"I don't care what he wants. He's the only person in this place who can give you a real workout and who won't try to kill you if put in that kind of situation."

I gave him a doubtful look. "I wouldn't be so sure about that."

"He has the strongest sense of duty," Simmonds said. "If I give him the assignment, he'll carry it through."

I arched an eyebrow. "Do you want to tell him or should I?"

Simmonds stood and walked around his desk. "I'll handle it. I called him down shortly before you showed up. He should be waiting outside."

"Can I stay and watch?" I asked, smiling at the thought.

Simmonds tried to keep a straight face, but I caught him holding back a laugh. "I think it'd be better if I spoke with him alone. Send him in when you leave."

I leaned against the wall across from Simmonds's office, waiting for Scorpion to finish his meeting. I knew he'd be pissed, but if we had to work together, there was no point putting it off. A couple of girls had showed up after a few minutes. They seemed around my age and took it upon themselves to wait as far away from me as they could.

It was about fifteen minutes before the door was flung open.

Scorpion's nostrils flared in frustration, which quickly turned to aggravation when he saw me. "What did you say to him?" The two girls at the end of the hallway glanced, wide-eyed, at each other, before skirting around Scorpion and disappearing into Simmonds's office.

"I didn't say anything." I shrugged innocently as the door shut behind him. "According to Simmonds, *you* were the one telling him about my training habits."

His shoulders tensed as his annoyance grew. He sauntered ahead of me and I kept pace with him. "We have to do this." He was practically spitting. "He'll be checking up on me."

"I'm not exactly thrilled about this either," I said.

He snorted. "Right. What do you have to complain about?"

"Do you really think I want to spend time with you?" He looked at me out of the corner of his eye and I could see I'd surprised him. "We spent the last three years fighting each other. I don't like you any more than you like me. And despite what Simmonds says, I don't trust you not to kill me."

He kicked his jaw out and laughed. "If I wanted to kill you, Simmonds wouldn't be able to stop me. And you wouldn't stand a chance."

I arched an eyebrow. "Oh, really, *Travis*? So all those times we squared off you just *let* me go?" He glared at me out of the corner of his eye, but didn't speak. "China. Russia. *Thailand*. You weren't actually *trying* to kill me there, is that what you're saying?" Again, he stayed quiet. "Yeah. That's what I thought."

I yanked on the door to the training room, but Scorpion came up behind me and shoved it closed. "If we're going to do this, we're going to do it my way."

I let my hand drop to my side. "Of course. *Everything* gets done your way."

He shook his head, his irritation increasing. "What is that supposed to mean?"

I rolled my eyes. "You've wanted complete control from day one." He gritted his teeth, but didn't interrupt. "Now we're doing what *I* say. If you don't like it, you can fight me over it."

He ignored me. "There are private training rooms in the back. We're going where no one can watch."

I cocked my head to the side. "You're that embarrassed to be seen with me?"

His lips were pressed together so firmly, they practically disappeared. I was on the very last of his extremely frayed nerves. "It's bad enough we have to do this; I don't want to spend the rest of today explaining myself to everyone else. Everything doesn't have to go my way, but this does."

He stalked off down the hall, not bothering to wait for me. I followed him, more because not following would be seen as not cooperating, which he could use against me.

The private workout room was like a smaller, slightly less equipped version of the gym. The walls and floor were covered with padded gym mats, and an assortment of weapons hung in a case on the upper half of the wall. There was also a punching bag in the corner, as well some other training equipment scattered around the edges of the room. Scorpion had taken off his sweatshirt and thrown it in the corner by the time I had caught up to him.

He didn't say anything else, he just rounded on me and rocked up on the balls of his feet, his arms bent in front of him waiting for a fight.

I followed suit. I wasn't much for playing defense but, in this case, I wanted to see what he was going to throw at me before I committed to anything. And I knew he was too impatient to wait me out. He lasted all of ten seconds before he threw the first punch, which I dodged easily. I swung a punch of my own, knowing he would sidestep, then I swiped my leg at his knees. He recovered in enough time to jump, but just barely. He hit me hard in the stomach. Harder than Nikki had earlier, and he didn't feel even a little bit bad.

I breathed tightly through my nose, pushing away the pain. I couldn't slow down. I couldn't show any weakness. He picked up the pace and I struggled to keep up. We traded punches and kicks, dancing across the mat. I lost track of everything—time, space, and even the addiction. Nothing else mattered. He was taking out years of pent-up frustration on me, and I had to fight to find the motivation or endurance to match his pace. I have no idea how long we were going at it before I finally got the upper hand. I grabbed Scorpion's wrist, turned so my back was to him, then flipped him over my shoulder.

But he was quick enough to grab my forearm. He slammed into the mat and used his momentum to pull me down with him, twisting me until we were both lying on our backs panting. Simmonds was right. It was the best workout I'd had since I got out of KATO.

Scorpion didn't rest for more than a moment. He popped up before I could get to my feet, and grabbed two wooden staffs that were stored on the wall with the other practice weapons. He tossed one at me as I stood, and I caught it just in time to keep it from hitting me in the face. "Let's make this a little more interesting," he said.

I curled my fingers around the staff, shifting uneasily. I was breathing hard, feeling more winded than usual, but I refused to quit. Scorpion seemed faster than I was used to him being, but I could tell I was starting to wear him out. Still, he had caught his breath much more quickly than I had, and he didn't wait for me to recover. He spun the staff at my head and when I moved to block it, he flicked his wrist and swung at my side. I pulled my staff down, just stopping his from colliding with my ribs. I jabbed it back into Scorpion's stomach but it didn't slow him down. He retaliated quickly, striking my side, and this time I couldn't avoid it. My rib cage throbbed. He hit me so hard I wouldn't have been surprised if a rib was broken.

He cut up and chopped at my collarbone, but I dodged it just enough to lessen the impact. My breathing was more labored than ever, and the pain in my ribs was making it worse. He pulled the staff back and pushed it toward me, aimed at my throat. I caught it just in time. The two staffs pressed on each other, and the pain in my side spread through my torso.

I bit my lip hard enough to taste blood. It was the only thing keeping me from crying out. I struggled to push back as I realized my vision had started to blur.

Then something flickered in Scorpion's face and he lifted the staff. I was about to relax when he swung down, swiping at my legs and taking them out from under me. I slammed down onto my back, every muscle throbbing.

Scorpion pressed the base of the staff into the ground and leaned over me. I could barely make out his arrogant face in between the stars. "Don't you ever think for a second that I can't take you."

He started to walk away from me, and I swung my staff, hitting his knees and bringing him down next to me. "And don't *you* ever think that means you've won."

He pushed himself off the ground, still pissed, and strutted out of the room. I stayed down, trying to catch my breath and find the strength to move.

I was way more out of shape than I realized.

Chapter Nine

HOW THE DAY ENDS

My ribs hurt for the rest of the night. I knew I should go to Dr. March—especially after my talk with Simmonds, but it was that same conversation that held me back. I needed to get into the field to get closer to my mission. To do that, I needed to be training with Scorpion, and I needed to develop some level of trust among the other agents. That was never going to happen if I went to March with something like this. There wasn't anything she could have done for me anyway. I knew enough about rib injuries to know they were only bruised.

My room came with a small fridge, which had a freezer full of ice, so I strapped several bags around my torso to ease the swelling. The afternoon wasn't a total loss. I had more power over Scorpion than he liked to think. I could push him, and I knew I could get to him enough to make him snap. I was close today. Scorpion didn't want this on Simmonds's radar any more than I did, otherwise I was sure my ribs would be broken. Getting my ass kicked wasn't exactly how I wanted to use this power, but given time, I'd find a way to make it work to my advantage.

I still had trouble sleeping in the bed, but that night it felt good to stretch out on something soft. I fell asleep propped up against the wall at an awkward angle and, when I did, I dreamed I was back at KATO.

"For some of you, this will be your last fight," one of the other handlers said. I was thirteen and there were ten of us who had been training together. We were paired off. He circled us, barking orders, while the other handlers watched from the side. My handler, Chin Ho, stood staring at me, evenly. This was a fight designed to weed out the weaker trainees. The winners got to become field agents. The losers ended up dead.

Chin Ho held out a vial for me to see, and I understood. It was more than just my life I was fighting for. It was Gerex.

A whistle blew and the battle began. I was paired against Stinger, a girl from France. A girl who I had lived with for the past five years. We weren't close, but we weren't enemies either. At least, not until now.

She made the first move, swinging and knocking me back. I punched her in her face, stunning her for a second, before she came back with a low roundhouse kick. She swept me off my feet, then kicked me repeatedly in the stomach. I'd let her get the drop on me. I couldn't breathe and I knew this was how I was going to die.

Then, out of the corner of my eye, I saw Chin Ho, still standing against the wall, shaking the vial of Gerex. I needed it. I cared about winning the drug more than I did living. And I would do whatever necessary to get it. I grabbed Stinger's foot midkick and yanked it out from under her. She hit the ground hard. I was in too much pain to get up, so instead I snaked over to her, put my forearm against her throat, and pressed all of my weight into her until she stopped breathing.

I jolted upright so fast that my side injuries ached as much as they did when I was thirteen. I wiped the tears out of my eyes and worked on leveling out my heart. That had been my first kill. And that night I had been too high to care.

It was nearly morning, and there was no way I'd sleep after that. I pushed the negative parts of the dream out of my mind and focused on what I could do about it. By the time I was done with KATO, no one would *ever* go through what I had.

I was ready for Scorpion the next morning, but was surprised when I opened my door. Cody stood in front of me with his arms crossed. "What are you doing here?"

"You're mine today, Viper." His voice was cold and aggressive. "I won't have the same restraint Travis does."

I sighed. "The threats are starting to get a little old." I gave him a once-over, taking him in differently from how I had before. He was smaller than Scorpion and, based on everything I'd seen in the gym, he was slower too. I could take him easily, even with a bruised rib. "Where's Scorpion?"

Cody shook his head once. "It's none of your business."

I crossed my arms and leaned against the doorframe, doing my best impression of calm. "He's my designated sparring partner, so I think it's a little bit of my business."

He clenched his teeth. "He's on a mission."

"Good for him," I said. "But what none of you seem to get is that I don't need to be guarded. Scorpion is supposed to help me. If he's not here, I can manage on my own at this point."

His lips pressed into a line. "We don't trust you, Viper. You have to know that. And Travis said that he was supposed to guide you until your first mission. Now, if you don't come with me, I have to believe that you have something to hide. Is that the case?"

My eyes narrowed. I grabbed my notebook and pen and headed down the hall, not giving Cody the satisfaction of an answer.

Cody glared at me through my entire breakfast, and I very pointedly ignored him. When we got to the gym for the morning training session, Nikki tried to grab me but Cody stopped her. "Oh no," he said. "She's mine."

Nikki stepped closer, getting in his face. Rachel stood a step behind, her anger visibly growing by the minute. "Just because Travis isn't here to keep an eye on her doesn't mean you get to be in charge," Nikki said.

He let out a heavy, irritated grunt. "Look, Nikki, I know she's your latest lost cause, but you don't get to protect her. She hasn't earned it."

Nikki tried to argue, but Rachel tugged on her arm. "He's right," she said. "None of us were told we had to be nice to her, and Travis isn't here to enforce anything."

Nikki's eyes widened. It was a safe bet she'd never met quite this much resistance before.

"It's fine," I said to her. "I can handle him." There was a doubtful glint in her eye, but I blew it off. "Don't worry about me."

She didn't seem convinced, but she let Rachel pull her away, leaving Cody and me alone. He stalked off past other agents who had already claimed the more spacious areas, and came to a stop close to the center of the room. It would seem that this was this best chance he was going to get to make a show of putting me in my place. Cody must have talked to Scorpion, because his first hits were to my side, which nearly made me see stars. He took the time to give me a cocky, condescending smirk, which gave me just enough time to recover. Cody was good, but not as good as Scorpion. Even injured, I was able to take him down.

The biggest surprise of my morning came when I was told that *Rachel* of all people would be escorting me to my classes.

"You must have lost a bet or something," I said, once we had made it to the courtyard.

She glared at me, giving me a look so piercing it made my heart skip. "I *hate* you."

"You're not the only one." I couldn't keep the light laugh out of my voice.

"Am I the only person who you gutted and left with two broken legs?" she asked. "Or is there some club I can join?"

"I was only doing a job."

She stopped walking and I turned to look at her. The rage radiated off her. "Are you saying I should just get over it?" Her voice hit a pitch that was clearly out of her control. I stayed quiet. "You don't know what it was like coming back from that. What you did—" She cut herself off and visibly swallowed the emotion. "You don't get to speak to me." She started walking again. "Not a single word."

I wasn't in any position to argue, not that I even wanted to.

I snuck away in between classes to check for KATO's message. They hadn't questioned the information I'd sent them, but they did ask if that was truly everything the IDA had. It made my stomach turn. Not only because I felt like they were questioning me, but also because it seemed as if they wanted to be sure. As if there *was* something for the IDA to know, but KATO wanted to be positive they were in the dark. I told them I'd sent them everything I'd found, but I'd keep looking.

The message stayed in my mind the rest of the day, but I had other problems to deal with more directly. Fortunately, Nikki stole me from Cody when I got to the gym that afternoon. Cody, who was looking for revenge from earlier, wasn't happy about it, but Nikki had let him have his way that morning and she wasn't about to give in twice. She took me outside and spent the rest of the workout time taking me through yoga, which I knew about but had never practiced. It was slow and methodical and didn't strain my side too badly. In fact, when we were done, I felt so relaxed it was as if I had gotten an acupuncture treatment. After, she walked me back to my room, most likely to make sure no one else did, which I was grateful for.

"I'm sorry about Cody," she said as I unlocked my door.

"It's not your fault." I looked everywhere but at her, hoping she'd get the hint to change the subject.

"Still," she said, then she broke off. I looked up at her. She slowly scanned my room, taking everything in, before coming back around to me. "You haven't changed it."

"What do you mean?" I asked.

"Your room." She turned her attention back inside. "It's exactly the same as it was when Simmonds assigned it to you. And I know because I used to live in a room identical to this when I was in school. You didn't change a thing."

I shrugged. "I've never thought about it."

"You've never decorated a room before, have you?" she asked.

I shifted uncomfortably. "It's been a long time since I actually *had* a room."

Nikki's eyes flicked to mine for a half a second, then back to the room. "Okay, then. It looks like we have some work to do."

"You don't have to." I shook my head, feeling anxious at the prospect.

"Oh no," she said, still absorbing every detail of my room. "This is my project now." She smiled at me. "Don't you worry about a thing."

"Nikki, really—"

She started to down the hall, still smiling. "Good night, Jocelyn."

Later that night, I was stretched out on my bed with another round of ice packs strapped to my side. I was almost about to fall asleep when there was a sharp knock at the door. I didn't move, hoping that whoever it was would think I was sleeping and leave. They knocked again. "Viper!" Cody's voice went right through me. "Get your ass to this door or I will break it down!"

I struggled to get up while Cody pounded like he was trying to knock the door off its hinges.

"Give me a minute!" I ripped off the ice packs and pulled on a shirt. Cody's fist never stopped.

I yanked the door open but held on to it, ready to slam it in his face if I had to.

Cody's demeanor changed. He rocked back and forth on his feet, seeming a little shifty. "You need to come with me."

I tightened my fingers around the knob. "I think I've had enough of you today."

He had a biting comment sitting on his tongue, but decided against it. He took a deep breath, and when he spoke it was extremely controlled. "This isn't me asking. Simmonds wants to see you."

I squinted at him, looking for some sign that he was lying.

"You *need* to come with me. Now." He was getting frustrated. "This isn't a trick."

I tilted my head, considering for another second, then looked him in the eye. "It better not be." I started down the hall, with Cody right behind me.

He stayed quiet the entire walk to the director's office, and his muscles were coiled and tight. It couldn't have been more obvious that something was wrong, and a part of me enjoyed it. Every step he took was heavy and purposeful. When we got to the office, he opened the door without knocking. The second he did, we were hit with a wall of yelling.

"You can't possibly be considering this!" an older man shouted. The room was full of people—at least twenty—and I recognized only a handful of them.

"I'm more than considering it," Simmonds shot back. "It's the closest thing we're going to get to a test without risking an agent or assignment. If this works, she'll prove that she can be trusted in the field and we'll get back one of our best agents."

"And if it doesn't?" the first guy asked. "You're willing to risk letting someone that dangerous loose in the world?"

"If that happens, she'll have two spy agencies after her. She won't get far," Simmonds said.

My heart skipped a beat. They were talking about me.

"She's an expertly trained spy," Simmonds continued. "And now she works for us. It's ridiculous to have her here if we're not going to use her. And if it doesn't work out, then we won't have any less than we would have if we'd followed procedure."

"She spent ten years working for KATO," the man said. "I don't care how she got there. She can't be trusted!"

"I happen to know she can be." Simmonds voice was deep and powerful. "I would have had her on active missions a week ago, but *you* want her to prove herself. This is the best way."

Cody cleared his throat, cutting off the argument, and every eye in the room trained itself on me.

Simmonds straightened up. "Jocelyn. Excellent, you have your first assignment."

"Roy—" the man started, but Simmonds cut him off with a glare.

Excitement swirled inside me, like it had been caged and cooped up as much as I had. This was my chance to get back in the field. Simmonds's eyes came back to me. "Agent Elton has been compromised," he said. "He was on an assignment in China and he's been out of contact for over twelve hours."

I stood up straighter, falling into the comfort and exhilaration of a mission. "What do you need from me?"

He looked directly at me. "It's agency policy not to stage rescue missions, as we rarely have enough intel to pull them off successfully. But in this case we're making an exception. We're sending you to China to retrieve Agent Elton."

"This is a bad idea," a woman to his left said. "Especially given the nature of Elton's original mission. And on top of that, we'd be sending her to China, a country with a history of assisting North Korea. The only way we could make it easier for her to pass on information is if we dropped her in KATO's headquarters."

Simmonds spun around to face her. "This is no longer a discussion. Agent Jocelyn Steely is going to China to retrieve Agent Travis

Elton tonight." The room was dead silent. He scanned every face, waiting for someone to challenge him, but no one seemed that stupid. "I need the room. Agent Steely and I have some details to discuss."

The room emptied slowly with disgruntled mumbles that I couldn't completely make out. The only person left was Cody.

"Agent Mathers," Simmonds said, "that means you too."

Cody nodded and turned to me. "If you come back without him, I'll end you."

I took a step closer, drawing myself up to my full height. I knew what it meant to execute a mission. I knew how to be in charge. "The list of people in this place who want to kill me is getting longer by the second, so you're going to have to take a number. But how about you let me do my job while you're waiting for your turn?"

He was readying a comeback, but Simmonds cut him off. "Mathers, *now.*"

Cody's mouth tightened and he backed out of the room. Once he was gone, Simmonds closed the door firmly behind him and sat at his desk. I glanced behind him at the missions map and noticed a red dot on the lower edge of China. I could guess what the color meant.

I sat on the edge of the chair, getting as close to him as I could, trying to contain myself. An agent was hurt—one of their best. It wouldn't look good to seem too excited. "I'm going on a rescue mission."

He nodded and slid a file across the desk. "Elton was sent to a Hong Kong science lab to retrieve data the Chinese stole from KATO about a month ago."

I saw where he was coming from. "You wanted to know if KATO has been working on something without tipping them off." I smiled lightly, appreciating the approach. "And the best way to do that is by taking intel someone else already successfully stole."

"Exactly." He laced his fingers together across the desk and met my eyes. "Elton should have been on his way back hours ago, but he missed his extraction. We don't know what happened to him or if he's even alive, but it's your job to find him and bring him back."

I flipped through the file feeling more relaxed than I had since I first got to the IDA. Preparing for a mission was something I was used to, and being on one was the closest I'd ever come to feeling free. "What do we know?"

"Very little," Simmonds said, "which is why rescue missions are against protocol. We lost control of the security feeds when Elton was in the building, which has never happened before. We were able to regain them, but it was too late. You'll have go back to the initial intel site and try to track him from there."

I nodded a little too eagerly. "I can do that."

Simmonds studied me for a moment. "This is dangerous, Jocelyn."

I rolled my shoulders back, prepared. "I've gone on more dangerous missions with less intel. I'll be fine."

"Dr. March wants to see you before you leave. You're getting on a plane once you're done."

I nodded.

Simmonds opened a desk drawer and pulled out a small earbud. "Here's our comm system. It's also a GPS. It goes deep in your ear. You have to push it to talk, but if you're offline for more than fifteen minutes it kicks on automatically unless we know you're going dark."

I took the earbud from Simmonds and studied it. I'd never had this kind of support from KATO. They were big on their agents being able to handle field situations on their own. As long as they had the drug, they knew we'd come back. "I take it Scorpion doesn't have his anymore?"

He nodded grimly. "According to Walter, it must have been smashed about twelve hours ago."

"Who's Walter?"

"He's our tech expert. You'll be working with him too. He can hack almost any security system or computer." Simmonds leaned in. "Stay in touch and report back what you find. We'll have an extraction team in the air tracking you and waiting for your signal to move in."

"Okay." I kept going through the folder, then I glanced back up at him. "I'm going to have to tell KATO about this. As far as I know they're not tracking me directly, but if they get independent intel that I was in the field, they'll pull me back for not keeping them informed."

Simmonds nodded. "Fine. Find a way to get to a computer and tell them what you have to."

"Okay." I nodded once more. He didn't have to say how important this was. I gathered the file and headed for the door.

"And, Jocelyn." I turned back around to find Simmonds wearing one of his more serious expressions. "Good luck."

I gave him a small smile. "Thank you."

No one had ever said that to me before.

Chapter Ten

MISSION CLEANUP

D r. March was waiting for me when I arrived at the medical wing. She gave me the usual visual inspection. I hadn't thought about my torso since Cody showed up at my door, and now I was trying to keep March from noticing. The adrenaline rush had taken over, and all I could feel was the familiar pre-mission excitement. Some of the happiest moments I had ever had working for KATO were right before a mission. They'd send me out for days at a time with just enough of the drug to hold me over until I got back. No one was looking over my shoulder or checking up on me, and I knew I had the skills to pull off whatever they asked me to. It was a feeling I was getting increasingly desperate for.

"How are you?" Dr. March asked once I was settled into an exam room.

"I'm doing okay," I said.

She looked at me skeptically. "I want to give you a physical and an acupuncture treatment before you go. I'm told this won't take more than a few days, but I want you to be as symptom-free as possible."

She pressed on my side before I was prepared and I winced. Her eyes darted to my face.

"It's fine." I looked her right in the eye, hoping to back my overly insistent tone.

It didn't work. Her eyebrows tightened in concern as she slid my shirt up. "Jocelyn!" I wanted to pull away, but I didn't have anyplace to go. She pressed again, harder, and I clenched my teeth together to hide the pain. "How did this happen?"

I shook my head. "It doesn't matter."

She pursed her lips and leveled her gaze at me. "Lie down."

"They're just bruised. I can handle it."

"I get that this assignment is a big deal, but I'm not signing off on a mission while there's a chance that you're bleeding internally." She was firm. "I won't put you out in the field to die."

I bit my lip and lay back. She pressed on my stomach and ribs, with me cringing slightly, but in the end Dr. March determined that my injuries were superficial and not enough to hold me back.

Afterward, I stretched out, ready for the acupuncture treatment. When I was done, she signed my paperwork and left me to find my way out. I stopped in one of the side offices to let KATO know about the mission. There was also a response to my earlier post, impressing upon me the importance of keeping them updated if the IDA learns anything else about their operations. Now I knew I wasn't paranoid; KATO *was* working on something.

As hard as it was, I did my best to put all of that in the back of my head. I had a more immediate mission to worry about, and KATO couldn't be a priority right now.

There were a few other agents on the trip with me, but no one I knew. Once they gave me the miniature tablet I'd need and showed me what it could do they kept their distance, which was fine with me. I had read over the mission file at least ten times on the plane ride over.

It didn't matter that I was rescuing one of my least favorite people. I barely had the time to appreciate the fact that the golden boy of the IDA managed to get himself in trouble. He was my mission now and that's all that mattered.

After landing close to Hong Kong, I transferred to a helicopter. I had a parachute strapped to my back, the address of Scorpion's last location memorized, and a backpack with everything I'd need around my chest. I leaned out of the chopper's door and pushed off, letting the exhilaration take me to the ground as the hot wind slapped my face.

It was dusk when I dropped over the outside of the city, and landed on top of a building. I hurried to the street and moved between the crowd and buildings, keeping my head down. Speed and agility had always been my greatest strengths, and even though I was out of shape, it wasn't all lost. I pulled a hat out of the backpack and tugged it down to my eyebrows. Walter was supposed to be disabling the cameras as I went, but I wasn't leaving anything to chance.

I stopped across the street from the science and technology skyscraper and pulled out the miniature tablet I'd been given on the plane. "Command, I need the blueprints to the building."

The comm in my ear was quiet, but after a second the screen on the tablet blinked and the blueprints appeared. According to the mission file, the intel Scorpion needed was on the twenty-sixth floor. Since the information in the building was highly sensitive, I had no doubt security was going to be pretty tight. My best chance to get to the twenty-sixth floor undetected was through the elevator shaft.

I pushed my comm in. "Command, can you take the security system and cameras offline for four minutes?"

"Just tell me when, Viper," Walter said, his voice gruff and annoyed.

"What's the weakest point of entry?" I asked.

"The back service entrance." Every answer he gave me was short, to the point, and laced with irritation.

I moved to the side of the building and peered around the corner at the door. It had a camera on it. I set the timer on my watch for four minutes. "Cut the cameras *now*."

"Clear," he said. I started the timer and hurried to the door. It took me seven seconds to pick, and if it weren't such a complex lock I would have been in quicker.

The service elevator was twenty feet away. But first I had to take out the burly security guard who was staring at me. He moved toward his radio, but I was next to him in seconds, twisting his arm behind his back and pinning him to the wall. He started cursing in Cantonese, but I didn't waste time retaliating. He was stronger than I was, and if I gave him a chance to think, I'd never make it out. I took my free hand and drove it into a nerve in the back of his neck. He dropped hard.

I didn't waste another second looking for anyone else. I sprinted down the hall to the service elevator, which got me as far as the third floor. From there I jumped on the regular elevator, and pushed the Chinese figure for twenty-five. I popped the roof hatch and pulled myself up and out onto the top of the car. When it came to a stop, I pried the doors above me open and climbed to the twenty-sixth floor. This way when the system went live again the floor below me would be searched first, buying me some extra time.

I hurried down the hall to the room and pressed on the door

handle, but it was locked. "Command, I need lab 2685 unlocked. It's a key fob entry."

The voice in my ear stayed quiet but the red light flashed green. I threw the door open and ended up in a lab. I glanced at my watch. I had thirty seconds before the system turned back on. The lights in the lab were off, but I stood quietly in the doorway, listening to be sure I was alone.

"Where are the cameras in here?" I asked Walter.

There was a brief pause, and when he spoke I could hear the exasperation in his voice. "To the right of the door. In the corner."

I scanned the room and grabbed a towel, then jumped up on the counter and covered the camera. I needed to be gone before security came to investigate.

I turned on the light. It was a risk, but it also meant I'd get out of the building faster. I took in the situation. Tables were overturned, computer screens cracked, and broken glass sprinkled the floor. Based on the struggle, it looked like Scorpion had made it at least this far, but I had no way of knowing whether he'd managed to get the intel or not. I gave the room another pass. There wasn't any trace of blood, which meant he was either taken or killed off-site. It was strange that the room had been left this way.

"Viper, you've got security on your floor."

I pushed my comm in. "Copy." I hurried to the window, ready to break it, but before I could I noticed a small flashdrive lying on the ground right behind a shelf.

"They're at your door," Walter said.

I crammed the drive into my pocket, hoping Scorpion had transferred the data, then threw a chair out the window to break it. The glass hadn't even hit the ground when I pulled my rappelling rope out of my backpack and locked it into place. I jumped out the window and slid down the building, tugging the rope just as a swarm of security guards surrounded the window.

I booked it away from the building, maneuvering through the busy streets. "Command, the Hong Kong police are going to get an emergency call. If you could make sure it doesn't make it to them, that would be great."

"Goddamn it, Viper!" Walter yelled in my ear.

"Can you do it or not?" I asked as I dove into an alley and behind a Dumpster.

The sound on my comm went quiet for a moment, then Walter tapped back in. "It's taken care of."

I let myself relax against the wall for a moment to get my thoughts together. I didn't get more than ten seconds before Walter interrupted me. "Viper, what did you find?"

I recapped the new intel for him.

"So, you failed the mission," he said.

"I didn't fail," I said, hissing into the comm. "There's more to this."

"Then what's your plan?" He had been brisk and impatient this whole mission, but now it was at its peak. I would have punched him if he were within reach.

I thought for a moment. "Can you send me security footage from right after Scorpion went dark and a copy of the security workers' manifest at that time?"

"What could you possibly need that for?" Walter asked.

"Just send it to my screen," I said. He was sitting on the edge of my patience, but he had the sense not to respond.

When my data screen changed, I did a quick count of the manifest, then flipped through the security feeds and did a head count. The numbers matched. "We don't have any security footage from anywhere around the building at the time, right?" I asked.

"If you've read the file—"

"That plus the fact that all the guards who are supposed to be on shift *were* means that it wasn't an inside job. No one cleaned up that room because no one working there realized they'd had a break-in. Whoever took Scorpion knew he was coming and had the resources to shut down city security." I was thinking out loud for Walter's sake—to make sure he knew how good I was. "I need a list of all buildings in Hong Kong that are owned by the government—either directly or through a shell company. I need addresses, building purposes, everything you can find." Whoever took him wouldn't have taken him far. They didn't have a lot of time to plan, and they'd have to work with what was close.

His annoyed huffing and puffing filled my ear. He didn't trust me, and his hesitance was enough to make me snap. "Everything'll be on your tablet in a few seconds," he said.

"Thank you." He had all of the locations inputted into my GPS map. One was less than four blocks away. According to the list it was purchased by a front company for Chinese intelligence. It hadn't been used in years, and I had no doubt that was where they were keeping him.

I ran the distance to the building, taking back alleys, avoiding the streets, and making sure I stayed away from any route a brave security guard might take if he decided to come after me. I stood across the street from the office building Walter had sent me to. It appeared to have about ten or twelve floors. If it hadn't been used in a while, my guess was the security was probably lacking, but I had Walter check on it anyway.

"It hasn't been updated in years," he said. "But it doesn't matter. From the looks of things there isn't any real power running to it. There's such a low output it's probably from a generator."

"Will they get some kind of alarm if the door to the roof is opened?" I asked.

"Yeah, it looks like the generator is strong enough for the most basic security measures."

Perfect. Now I just needed to be sure I was in the right place.

I found the infrared scanner on my tablet and passed it over the building. The upper floors were completely clean, but the bottom floor was a different story. There was a cluster of five people standing around a door on the first floor. They were huddled toward the edge of the building, most likely standing in a stairwell. The door didn't seem to have a room behind it, which meant it had to lead to the basement. There were only two reasons why five people would be guarding a basement door in a supposedly abandoned building: They were either protecting something or guarding someone.

Scorpion was alive.

Chapter Eleven

GOING IN BLIND

etting into the building was the easy part. The apartment building next door was only a touch taller, and uncomfortably close. I jumped from the roof of the apartment building onto the one I needed to break into, then attached my rope to the roof and rappelled halfway down its side.

I could probably have taken all five guards if I had to, but in this case my best chance to pull this off was to split them up. I hung on to the side and used a glass cutter to cut a hole that was just big enough for me to fit through. Once I was in, I pulled the rope through and left it there. I wanted the break-in to be obvious—it would take longer for the guards to search the building and give me more time to get to the basement. I hurried up five floors to the roof, then pushed open the door, dropped a lock-pick kit, and sprinted back down to the floor I'd come in. I had just shut the door to the stairwell when three guards came flying past. I waited until they were two floors above me before I eased the door open and ran down to the first level. I paused before I rounded the basement corner, preparing myself—two guards I could take, especially if I caught them by surprise.

I flung myself around the corner before either could react. I jumped behind the one closer to me and wrapped my arm around his neck, cutting off his oxygen supply. I was determined not to kill anyone unless I had to.

He had a military-grade weapon strapped across his chest. I held on to it as he slid to the ground, then used the heavy butt of the gun to swipe the second guard near the ear. He dropped in an instant.

I hurried down the steps into the concrete basement. Everything about it was harsh, hard, and empty. Scorpion sat on an old mattress against the wall. It was hot in Hong Kong at this time of year. The basement was a few degrees cooler, but it was still too hot and stuffy to be comfortable and smelled of stale sweat.

He jumped up off the ground when I came down the stairs. I was surprised he wasn't tied up. He backed himself into the corner with his fists balled defensively in front of him, ready to take on anyone. He didn't seem to realize who I was. I moved a few more steps closer and saw that his eyes were red and so swollen they were reduced to slits. I came even closer and he backed himself against the wall, like he was trying to be sure no one would sneak up on him. He looked panicked, which was something I never expected to see.

"Scorpion?" My voice was cautious as I edged closer. He looked startled, and it wasn't until then that I realized that even though his eyes were partially open, he couldn't see a thing. "Travis." I said his name gently, without a hint of mockery.

"Who is it?" He sounded startled and uncertain, and unable to hide it. I had imagined finding him a number of different ways, including dead, but this wasn't something that ever occurred to me.

"It's—Jocelyn." My throat cracked as I stumbled over my own name.

"Viper?" He couldn't believe what he was hearing. His fists got tighter, ready to strike. I stepped even closer so I could get a good look at his eyes. I didn't know what had been done to him, but based on how red and teary they were I was sure he must have been rubbing them. "I knew we couldn't trust you."

"I'm not working for these people," I said. "The IDA sent me."

He shook his head. "That's impossible. We don't do rescue missions." He pressed his back into the wall, trying to get even farther away from me.

"I guess they do for the golden boy," I said.

He rubbed his eyes, frustrated and desperate. "I don't believe you."

"We don't have time for this." I was all too aware that the building was being searched. "There are five guards. I took out two of them, but the other three are going to be back soon. We need to get out of here." I grabbed his wrist and tried to lead him toward the stairs.

"I'm not going anywhere with you!" He pulled away and tried to punch me with his other hand.

I dodged the strike easily and caught his fist. I pressed his arm into his chest so he couldn't attack me again. There was enough tension in him to break a rock. "You can either stay here and let these guys kill you, or you can take a shot with me. If I'm lying, you're dead either way, but if I'm not, then you may make it out of this."

His breath was heaving and angry, but I felt his arms relax. "I don't trust you." There a hint of defeat in his tone that almost made me forget who I was talking to.

"You don't have a choice."

He leaned his head back against the wall, weighing his options, then after a moment he nodded.

I loosened my hold on his wrist and tried to get a plan together. I wasn't expecting him to be so defenseless. It was going to make getting out more complicated. The only thing I had going for me was my training. Failure was never an option. I had learned to be quick and think quicker. "Okay," I said, "here's how this is going to work. You have to go wherever I lead you and you have to do *exactly* what I say, okay? No thinking and no second-guessing. I'm in charge here and we do this my way."

He nodded hesitantly. "Yeah. Okay."

"If I put you someplace, stay there."

He rubbed his eyes and inhaled sharply. "Fine."

"Good. Now, we need to move and we have a lot of stairs coming up." I reached for him again, and this time he gripped my wrist. I led him up the stairs and he stumbled, catching himself on the railing with his free hand. I stopped him when we got to the top of the basement stairs and eased the door open. The two guards were still on the floor where I had left them, and the room was clear. I tried to pull him forward, but he wouldn't move. I glanced back and saw him choking the railing.

"Come on." I tugged him. "We need to go."

But he shook his head. "I can't—I don't—" Trust me. He still didn't trust me.

I tightened my hold on him, trying not to get frustrated. If our roles were reversed, I wouldn't have trusted him to get me this far. "You are my mission." My tone was harsh and confident, leaving no room for doubt. "If nothing else, you know how seriously I take that. I'm not going to leave you behind."

He hesitated and dropped his head. I could see him struggling with all of this. "Promise?"

The uncertainty threw me, and it took me a moment to answer. "I promise," I said. "Do you think you can keep up with me?"

He nodded more confidently than before.

"Okay. Then let's get out of here." I pulled on his arm and he let go of the rail. This time he stayed with me, moving faster than I was expecting. I guided Scorpion around the guards and we hurried up the stairwell, with him faltering only a few times.

We made it to the third floor before we ran into any real problems. The door to the floor opened as we were coming up the steps below it. I stopped quickly and flattened Scorpion against the wall. He moved easily and had enough instincts to stay perfectly still. The door opened out, shielding us from the guard. I crept slowly upward the opening door, letting go of Scorpion and pushing his chest so he'd stay put. He took the hint.

I got close to the door, and waited until the guy started to cross the threshold. Then I slammed it shut, trapping his head. He fell hard, and one of his friends came charging after us. He pushed a button on his radio and told the rest that he had found the intruder. I spun into the floor and ran down the hallway at him. He fired off a few shots. I opened one of the empty office doors and ducked behind it, pulling out my gun and shooting enough rounds to get him to back up. I leaned on my knees, feeling short of breath and more winded than I should have.

But I couldn't afford to wait. I grabbed one last gulp of air, then turned and ran back to the stairwell before he could get his bearings. He would be right on our trail and there was still another guard to worry about. Plus, I'd left Scorpion alone longer than I would've liked.

I kicked the unconscious guard out of the way and hurried back to Scorpion. "Let's go," I said, taking his arm. "They'll be right behind us."

"Did you get hit?" he asked.

I was shocked he cared. "I'm fine." I yanked him harder and we hustled up to the next floor. I pulled him down the hall and into one of the offices. I needed a minute—or even a second—to catch my breath. Everything was quiet.

"What's going on?" he asked. He kept his voice low.

"We just need to wait them out a minute," I said.

"Did you get hit?" he asked, more forceful and serious.

"No." I could barely get the word out.

"I don't have to see you to know you're having a hard time breathing." He was getting angry.

"I'm *fine*." But I wasn't. This had never happened to me in the field. "I only need a minute."

He rubbed his eyes and I could tell he was getting frustrated with me. "You're lying."

My breath started to catch up to me. "Remember how we said you weren't going to second-guess me?"

"You convinced me you had an actual shot at getting me out," he said.

"You're in too deep to back out now," I said. "They will kill you if you don't stick with me."

His jaw flexed.

I stepped in front of him. "I'm *going* to get you out of here. Just stay with me, okay?"

He took a moment before nodding.

I grasped his wrist again and led him out the office, down the hallway, then out the other end into the stairwell on the opposite side of the building. Then guided him back out the door and up the steps. We made it up only one floor—six from the roof—before we ran into more trouble. The guard who had shot at me earlier burst through the door with his gun out. I pushed Scorpion down, then grabbed the railing and windmilled my legs into the guard. It was enough to knock down his gun and stun him momentarily. I dropped back to the ground and grabbed the gun before he could get himself together. I quickly fired two shots, one into each thigh, which would be enough to stop him from getting to us. I pulled Scorpion up. He got on his feet quickly and latched on to my elbow.

I pushed my comm. "I need an immediate rooftop extraction! My location."

I put a floor between us and the latest guard before I tugged Scorpion to a stop. He swiveled his head in my direction, his teary eyes as red as ever. "What is it? Did you get hit this time?"

"Stop asking that," I said. "Listen. There's still one more guard and I don't know where he is. I want you in front of me. Can you handle the steps?"

"Yeah," he said. "I've got the layout."

"If I pull you down, don't fight me."

"I won't."

I nodded, but I still worried. I knew I only had his trust for a limited amount of time, and I was afraid it was running out.

I put him in front of me and pointed him toward the stairs, keeping a hand on his back. He moved a little slower than when I was guiding him, but it was easier to protect him from behind. I'd either get hit or see the attack coming.

With every floor we passed I checked down the hallway, looking for the last guard. We had two floors to go when the door behind me popped open. I pulled Scorpion to the ground just as the guard got off three shots, all of which missed. I fired back and got Scorpion to his feet, pushing him up the stairs. He didn't need much encouragement. He pounded up the stairs at an impressive speed for someone who couldn't see. I fired a few rounds over my shoulder, keeping the guard at bay.

I grabbed a fistful of Scorpion's shirt and yanked him to a stop. "Watch. The door to the roof is right in front of you. Let me by and I'll get you out."

He pressed himself against the wall. I opened the door and flung him outside right as the guard came running up the stairs, bullets flying. I tried to dive out of the way, but a bullet spiraled past me, grazing my forearm.

I took a sharp breath and sprinted out onto the roof. I slammed the door shut and shot a round into the keyhole as the helicopter landed.

I grabbed Scorpion's hand with my good arm and led him to the door. Another agent popped his head out. I pulled Scorpion back in front of me, put my hand on his back, and led him to the door. "Someone's going to help you onto the chopper, okay?"

He nodded. I held him steady as the new guy reached out.

"He can't see." I had to yell over the noise.

The agent nodded and pulled him up. I jumped in the chopper after him and it was off the ground before the door shut.

I collapsed against the seat and the window, panting. I kept my distance as the three medics on board rallied around Scorpion. I was lucky that he trusted me enough to get him out, but I wasn't about to let myself believe that this would change anything.

After a few minutes my heart rate started to return to normal, but it was also when I started to realize how much I wanted Gerex. I breathed deep and rolled forward, resting my head on my knees. This was a trigger I never saw coming, and it was the strongest I ever had. But it made sense. Usually after a mission I was picked up by KATO and desperate for a hit. It was a combination of the last of my drug supply leaving my system and a reward for a job well done. Completing a mission meant getting a high.

"Agent Steely." I looked up at the light-haired medic standing in front of me. "I need to look at your arm."

I shook my head. "It's fine." There was no way a field doctor who didn't know me or my history was coming near me with any kind of "standard treatment" drug.

He sighed heavily, exasperated. "Agent Steely, it's protocol."

I was ready to unravel. "I don't care about protocol!"

The medic stepped back, wide-eyed and confused, but ready to challenge me.

I breathed through my nose, trying to keep my demons under control. I hated what I was about to say. "Tell Simmonds—tell someone to have Dr. March on standby."

The medic raised an eyebrow, and a glint in his eye told me he had more questions. I glared at him like he was the only thing standing between me and Gerex—like I could kill him with my brain.

He nodded slowly and dropped a clean cloth on the seat next to me before backing away. I took the cloth and pressed it over my wound. Then I leaned back into my seat and watched the medics inject Scorpion with something to put him to sleep. I closed my eyes, wishing I could do the same.

Chapter Twelve

NOT ENOUGH

The best high I had ever had was after a mission. The assignment had taken longer than it was supposed to and I was low on Gerex. We had a protocol in place to buy street drugs and alternate between them and the Gerex. The heroin got me through, but it didn't do nearly enough. My handler was on my extraction chopper with a needle. I hadn't been without the drug completely, but my dosage had been so low I was feeling minor withdrawal. The state of bliss I was in when he pushed the Gerex in my vein was so overwhelming I nearly passed out. I was light and free and whole all at once. Nothing could weigh me down.

Dr. March was waiting for me when we landed. She had the field medics move Scorpion while she took me back to the medical wing. I was trying to fight off the symptoms, but I was losing.

"It's a trigger," I said. "After a mission—"

"Okay." She wrapped her arm around my shoulders. "You're going to be okay."

My teeth started chattering as she led me away from the other agents. I didn't even realize she'd put me on a bed until I felt her pulling at my hair, trying to get a clear path to my ear. I couldn't calm down and I couldn't stop shuddering. I wanted a hit more than I ever had since I'd gotten clean. My cheeks felt wet. I didn't know I was crying until Dr. March wiped my face. She pulled a blanket up to my shoulders, and sat with me while we waited for the acupuncture to kick in. It wasn't as immediate as it usually was, and even when I did start to feel something it was only enough to take the edge off.

I gritted my teeth and breathed through my nose. "It's not stopping."

"I know," she said, running a hand over my hair. "It will. You've just got to ride it out." She pushed a few more needles into my ear. I relaxed another fraction, but still not enough to be comfortable.

There was a knock on the door, and one of the field medics stuck her head in. "Dr. March, we need you next door."

"Okay," she said, not taking her eyes off me. "Give me a minute." The door fell shut. "I'll be right back. Just focus on breathing."

The door closed softly and I put all of my energy into each breath. Each minute felt like an eternity. I shut my eyes tight, like I was trying to squeeze the addiction out of me. If I didn't know for a fact that Dr. March didn't keep any drugs in the room I would have raided every cabinet in search of something that would help. I ground my teeth together, hating myself for being weak. Because if there was any possible way I could get a drug into my system I would have done it by now.

I was so locked in I didn't even hear Dr. March come back.

"I'm going to keep you here tonight," she said. "I want to be able to monitor you."

I opened my eyes and swallowed hard. "Is Scorpion going to be okay?"

She smiled lightly. "He was exposed to a chemical that causes irritation and temporary blindness. He should be fine in a few days."

I shivered. I hadn't felt cold flashes since my first detox. I wrapped the blanket tight around my shoulders. Dr. March shined a light in my eyes and put a hand on my forehead. "Cold sweats," she muttered. "We're going to add some aromatherapy. Sit tight for a minute." She went over to a cabinet and fished around for a few small bottles. "I want you to breathe these oils in, okay? Close your eyes and try to relax."

She held one of the small bottles in front of my face and I inhaled. I felt some more tension leave my body. Dr. March kept a steady stream of essential oils flowing under my nose. I breathed as deeply as I could, and after what felt like forever I felt myself calming down. I wrapped the blanket even tighter around me, appreciating the stability. I kept twitching, but the need for the drug had dulled. March left me like that for another twenty minutes before putting her hand on my forehead again. "Good." She wheeled a cart of supplies closer to the bed and pulled out the needles. I sat up as she started cleaning the graze wound on my arm.

I could barely feel the sting of the antiseptic. Then the reality of the mission washed over me. The only thing that scared me more than being overcome with a craving was the way I had faded. I almost didn't want to mention it. But I knew that would be something I'd pay for later. "Something happened in the field—other than the trigger."

Her nose wrinkled in concern as she put the finishing touches on my bandage. "What do you mean?"

"When I was trying to get Scorpion out of the building we had to outrun a few guards," I said. "I couldn't keep up."

Dr. March pulled a chair from the corner and sat down. "That's not so surprising. You've been out of the field for nearly two months. And at least half that time was spent in detox. It would make sense that you'd be a little behind."

I shook my head. "That's not it. I was more than just out of shape. I couldn't *breathe*."

She nodded slowly and I could see in her face that she had a theory. "I think it's because the Gerex is out of your system. This is the first time you were in the field without it and I think the steroid component did more for you than we realized. It got to your senses, your instincts, your reaction time—everything you would need to be a good agent."

I swallowed. "When will I get that back?"

"I don't know if you can completely get everything back to the level you were at, but you should be able to get close. You're going to have to work for it a lot more than you used to."

I nodded, and closed my eyes. I couldn't think about the damage Gerex had done to me. Not while I was still crippled by it.

Dr. March's voice brought me back. "Director Simmonds is outside. If you're up for it, he'd like to see you."

I bit my lip. I didn't want anyone to see me like this. Dr. March seemed to sense my hesitation. "Jocelyn, he already knows what you're going through. You don't have to hide anything."

I rubbed my eyes, defeated, and sat up. "Okay. Sure."

She nodded, went over to the door and silently held it open. Simmonds stepped in, and his eyes held mine for a moment.

"I'm going to check on a few things next door," Dr. March said. She was talking more to me than Simmonds. I nodded. She gave me a final once-over, then left us alone.

Before he could talk, I took the flashdrive out of my pocket and put it on the cart Dr. March had left near the bed. Simmonds looked at it, then back at me with an amazed expression. He lowered himself into the chair March had vacated, and when he spoke his voice was soft, like he was afraid to upset the quiet hum of the room.

"We'll get people working on this right away," he said. He reached for the flashdrive, tapping it on the tray for a moment, as if he were trying to be sure it was real. Then he dropped it in his pocket. "You did an outstanding job." His face was even and absolute.

"Thank you," I said, my voice barely above a whisper.

His serious expression intensified. "What you did was remarkable. You went into a situation blind, and were able to locate and retrieve our operative, and get the information he was sent for, in less than four hours. It is one of the more impressive performances this agency has seen."

I shook my head. Nothing about me felt impressive. "I only completed the mission."

"You did more than that." He leaned closer like he was trying to make me understand. "You won a lot of people over around here—at least on some level."

"What does that mean?" I asked.

"It means that they may not completely trust you, but at the very least they respect you." He paused. "They understand your value."

I laughed. "I'm not even sure *I* understand my value."

He wasn't amused. He looked me hard in the eyes with an intensity that made me understand why other agents were intimidated by him. "There is no one in this agency who could have done what you did tonight. You were trained to survive in a way we can't understand. It means a lot to save a fellow agent, and the history between you and Agent Elton is no secret around here. The way you were able to execute your mission regardless of your feelings may have made you one of our more valuable assets."

I shrugged. "I've got a lot of experience completing missions I want no part of. At least this one was saving someone."

Simmonds's lips strained for a moment, then he pushed on. "Dr. March tells me she's going to monitor you overnight. Before I go, I want to give you an update about the search for you father." I tensed. "We haven't located him yet, but we have narrowed down the list of possible locations. He was careful not to hide anyplace we'd suspect."

"If he doesn't want to be found, then maybe you shouldn't try too hard."

Simmonds leaned in, close enough to make eye contact that was impossible to avoid. "If he'd known you were alive, he'd never have wanted to disappear. Trust me on this."

It didn't make me feel better, but I conceded. "Yes, sir."

He nodded and got up to leave. I started to relax, but then I remembered what I'd found before I left on my mission. "Sir, there's something else." He stopped halfway to the door and turned back to me. I was exhausted, and I didn't feel like dealing with anything else tonight, but it couldn't wait. "Before I left, KATO told me again to make sure I keep them updated on anything the IDA learns about them. It's the second time they asked me that. I think you were right to send Scorpion on this mission. They're up to something, and there's a good chance the reason you haven't had intel lately is because they're working hard to keep it quiet."

His face darkened. "That would explain a lot," he said. "Hopefully whatever's on this flashdrive will give us some kind of lead." He patted the drive his pocket. "But don't worry about it for tonight. Just try and get some rest. I'll contact you when we have something to go on."

I sighed when he left, and couldn't seem to make my brain work any harder. So instead, I took Simmonds's advice, pulling the blanket even tighter around me and allowing its pressure to soothe me to sleep.

Simmonds gave me the week of classes off to get myself back together. I only took a few days. I wasn't looking for special treatment. He also raised my security clearance to the standard level-four-agent status. I took the time off to check in with KATO and report the details of the mission. I kept my report limited to the rescue mission I'd successfully accomplished, leaving out the flashdrive—which the tech team was still working on—altogether. They were very happy to hear I was "endearing" myself to the IDA, and again reminded me to keep them updated on any new intel. It didn't matter that Simmonds knew exactly what I was doing, the more time I spent talking to KATO, the dirtier I felt. I made myself remember that we were on to them, and that eventually this would all be worth it.

I was no longer tied to an IDA guide since I had completed my first assignment. I spent my new freedom actively avoiding as many people as I possibly could. Despite what Simmonds had said, I didn't believe I changed as many minds as he seemed to think. At least, not on the agent level. And with my recent cravings, I wasn't looking to put myself in a position to be agitated.

I did a quick inspection of the gym on my first day back. Scorpion was nowhere to be found, but Cody, Nikki, and Rachel were working out near their usual wall. I knew they saw me the second I walked in, but no one came over to me or bothered me. It wasn't until I got started with the punching bag that Nikki approached.

"Hey," she said. "You want a partner for the day?"

I hesitated, but agreed. I was sure she wanted to know more about what had happened in Hong Kong, and was pleasantly surprised when she didn't bring it up. We stayed focused on the workout, taking turns holding and punching the bag.

I had no idea how long we'd been at it when a buzz started to fill the gym. I glanced out the corner of my eye and saw Scorpion standing in the middle of the room. I hadn't even noticed him come in.

Agents surrounded him in seconds. I could hear everyone dying to know how he was doing and what had happened. He brushed the questions aside with answers like, "I'm good," and "Nothing I couldn't handle." Nikki seemed like she wanted to go to him, but she took one look at me and stayed put. I kept my focus on her, wishing I could block him out. I didn't know how to handle him. We'd had an understanding in Hong Kong. But he'd beaten the shit out of me before he left for his mission, and I hadn't forgotten that.

I saw Scorpion moving toward me. I took a swing at the bag, but he caught my wrist before I could land the punch, putting himself in between me and Nikki.

"What are you doing?" I asked, annoyed.

He let go of my arm and stood with his arms crossed.

"Travis, what the hell?" Nikki stepped next to him, glaring.

"Not now." He didn't even look at her. Nikki wasn't one to let these guys talk to her like that, so there must have been something about his tone that kept her quiet. He gave me a once-over, scrutinizing every inch of me. "What are you up to?"

Now I was confused. "What are you talking about?"

"I'm talking about how you acted in Hong Kong. You made sure nothing happened to me." His eyes constricted like he was trying to read my mind. "After what I did to you, you got me out. That's not normal."

"I told you: You were my mission." I tried to blow him off, but he wasn't having it.

"Bull. It would have been so easy to kill me and make it look like an accident." He shook his head. "I couldn't even *see*. You could have gotten away with it."

"So you think because I did what I was supposed to, it means I'm up to something?" I couldn't win. I didn't expect him to trust me, but I had thought I'd at least earned some room to breathe. Instead he was trying to suffocate me.

"I think you've got a much longer play in mind." He took a step closer. "I'll find out what it is. This isn't a fight in the field. You're in my house, and I *will* catch you."

I clenched my jaw. "There is *no* play."

He stared down at me, getting angrier by the second. Then in one quick movement, he stepped back and punched the bag hard, right at me. I just barely dodged it, falling to the floor to save it from hitting my still-sore side. I stayed down and watched him stalk out of the room. Once he was gone, a hand appeared in front of my face. It was Nikki's. She waited patiently for me to reach up and then pulled me to my feet.

Once I was standing, she gave me a hard, searching look and fixed me with an expression I couldn't read. "Just so you know, I don't think he's right."

"You're the only one."

Nikki shrugged. "I might be. But you really made a statement bringing him back. I don't know what happened in Hong Kong, but Travis stopped just short of saying you saved his life. And if that's true, after everything he's done to you—" She broke off and stared at the path Scorpion had taken out of the gym. "Then you must really want to be here."

"I do." I kept my voice even, afraid to read too much into what she was saying.

She nodded once. "That's what I thought. Though I have to say, he might give you a little more of a shot if he knew what your secret research project was and what it meant to you."

I shook my head hard enough for my side ponytail to swing. "Absolutely not."

"Okay," she said, stepping back behind the bag. "If that's how you want it. But know I'm on your side." I should have known better than to allow the small bubble of hope to grow in my chest. But I didn't have it in me to pop it.

Chapter Thirteen

NOT-SO-SECRET AGENT

Three days had passed since Scorpion's return and he hadn't spoken to me since. But he *was* watching me. Most active agents lived off campus, so even though the gym is open on weekends, it was pretty much used by only the academy kids and me. Scorpion had been there every day that weekend. He kept to himself, doing some form of cardio or another, and he made sure he was facing me at all times. I kept myself focused on my workouts. I couldn't do too much else while I waited for word on the drive, and I had to make up for whatever the Gerex had done. I was starting to feel a little bit stronger, and I hadn't felt short of breath since I'd been back, so I considered it an improvement.

Simmonds finally called me into his office early Monday, about a week after the China mission. I knew it had to be about the drive.

"There are a few layers to this," he said once I had seated myself across from him. "We know all of the intel that came back is about KATO, but the Chinese had put their own decryption on the drive. It took our tech team some time, but they were able to remove it."

I nodded eagerly, trying to keep my impatience at bay. "What did they find?"

"There are two smaller files and one larger folder," Simmonds said. "One file was accessible, while the other is also encrypted, but in a very different way. We think this is KATO's encryption that the Chinese weren't able to crack yet. The folder has a similar encryption, but it's significantly more complicated. Both of those will take time."

"Okay," I said, shifting to the edge of my seat. "What about the file you could access?"

Simmonds gave me a small smile. "I was hoping you could help us with that." He slid a piece of paper in front of me. "According to our translators, it doesn't make even a little bit of sense. It's my best guess that it's coded. I'm sure the Chinese were working on cracking it at the time."

I studied the single line of Korean characters on the paper. "It's more than a simple code. It's a cipher. But I don't think it's one of the more complex ones." I looked up at him. "At least, not if you know what you're looking for. The Chinese probably didn't even know where to start, though."

"How much time do you need?"

"Give me a few hours with it," I said. "There are a few different possibilities I want to run though. I'll check back with you when I have something."

I skipped the morning training session and went back to my room to work on the code instead. A couple hours and several cipher keys later, I had cracked it. It was a date, a time, and coordinates. I had the information to Simmonds before lunch. The date was a little more than a week away, and from what he could tell, the coordinates lined up with a warehouse in Iran. It didn't say what KATO had planned, but he said that was his job to find out. In the meantime, he'd given me some more information to pass on to KATO, hoping that the more I talked to them, the more windows the IDA would have into their system and the better chance we'd have at piecing this all together.

I could feel Scorpion's eyes on me at lunch that day. I sat by myself a few tables away from him, stirring a bowl of soup. I was sure missing the morning training session had ignited a new suspicion in him. He was sitting with Cody and a few agents I didn't know, but it seemed even they couldn't take his attention from me. I still had to make my next contact with KATO and had hoped to avoid ducking out between classes again. I didn't want any of the students or teachers noticing a pattern. But the way Scorpion was watching me, I knew there was no way I'd be able to pull it off outside of that time.

A hand waved in front of my face. "Hello? Anybody in there?"

I blinked back to reality and realized Nikki was sitting in front of me. She had her own plate of food and was looking at me with a curious and concerned expression.

"What?" I asked.

"You find anything new about your parents?" she asked.

"No." I hated that I hadn't been able to give the search much time with everything else going on. I glanced over her shoulder, past the tables full of chattering students and agents, at Scorpion, who scrutinized me with an unreadable expression on his face. "I can't get much done without the hawk hovering."

She turned around and saw who I had been looking at. "I see the ice hasn't thawed between the two of you."

I shrugged. "I get why he doesn't trust me. I just don't know how rescuing him made him *more* suspicious."

I glanced over at Nikki, who looked bewildered that I had said anything. I hadn't meant to. But after last week I found myself genuinely wanting to trust her. She took a moment to recover, then spoke softly enough that no one around could hear us. "You scare him, Jocelyn."

My eyebrows arched, stunned.

She continued. "Hong Kong is one of the few times when he's truly gotten beat. He's had things not work out, but he doesn't get *beat* like that. Unless he's facing you." She sighed. "Hong Kong was a combination of bad luck and bad intel. It was bound to happen to him eventually. But you've taken him out consistently, and you've found more of his weaknesses than anyone else. And now you're here. Every day. And you've seen him in a more vulnerable state than any of us have. He doesn't like you around him or his friends. He's afraid he can't protect us. And he *hates* that I'm talking to you."

I looked back over at him. Now he was laughing at something Cody had said. But it wasn't a real laugh. It fell short of his eyes. A part of me liked that I scared him. It meant he was as uncomfortable as I was. "So when I got him out of Hong Kong—"

"You confused him," she said. "As far as he's concerned, there's no way you could be on our side, which means if you saved him there's a bigger reason for it. And the fact that you saw him so defenseless only added to his concern."

I nodded slowly, taking a moment to digest her words. "How do you know this much about him?"

Nikki shrugged. "He's a year older than me, so we spent some time at the academy together. And we were partners for a while after I graduated two years ago."

"So, you're not partners anymore?"

She shook her head. "We didn't really click. But it was enough for me to join his training group, which was not easy to break into."

"What made it so hard?" I asked.

She leaned a little closer. "Cody and Rachel were seniors when Travis was a freshman, and when they saw he needed a challenge they went out of their way to help him. At the time, they were some of the IDA's top prospects, which made the three of them together a little bit legendary. They kept working out together even after Cody and Rachel became agents. It was just the three of them until I graduated. I've gotten to know all of them pretty well over the last two years."

I fidgeted uncomfortably. I didn't know what it meant to get to know someone. In fact, I went out of my way *not* to get to know the other KATO agents, in case I ever had to kill one.

"Anyway," Nikki said, "you should probably get to class. I'll meet you after. I've got everything we need to decorate your room. That should chase the hawk way for a little while, okay?"

"Yeah." I nodded. "Thanks."

I had to run out of Agent Lee's room to get my message to KATO before my next class. I was a little more practiced with getting into the system by now. I had started typing KATO's spoof proxy before I even sat down and a minute later I was on the board where I needed to be. Simmonds had given me some twisted and skewed details about what I'd been learning at the academy, and I was careful to replicate the wording and punctuation from the file exactly.

I heard a small click of the door opening behind me and hit the post button as fast as I could. I couldn't close out of anything else, because the next thing I knew I was pulled out of my chair and hurled to the floor.

"I knew it!" Scorpion stood over me, so angry the vein popped out of his neck. "I fucking knew it!"

"It's not what you're thinking," I said, struggling to get to the computer. He pushed my shoulder into the ground with his foot. Any harder and he might have dislocated it. I clenched my teeth together, frustrated at how slow I had become without that stupid drug, slow enough to have landed myself in this situation.

He leaned over the computer. "The hell it's not!" He read my post. "You sent them a message! What the fuck were you telling them?" I kept my jaw clenched shut, which seemed to only make him even angrier. He stooped down and pulled me up by my collar, then slammed me into the leg of the table. "Tell me. Now!"

Still I said nothing.

"I could kill you right now, and no one would have a problem with it." There was an uplifting note in his tone.

"Simmonds would," I said with enough conviction to make him pause.

"You really think so." He sat back on his heels, then nodded. "Yeah, let's go see him. When this is all over, I don't want anyone having to question that I did the right thing." He stood up, towering over me. "And Simmonds should know how you played him."

He grabbed my wrists and twisted my hands behind my back. Then he pulled me to my feet so quickly I stumbled trying to walk. He dragged me along after him with so much force I swore he wanted me to fight him. But I wouldn't. I couldn't afford to cause a scene. I still had a lot of work to do here, and I would never get the chance if I started attacking agents in the center of campus. I could still save this mission, I just couldn't make things any worse.

Fortunately, there weren't too many people out and about at this time of day. All the kids were in classes and the other agents were scattered, spending their free time on or off campus as they wanted. I did my best to keep up with Scorpion as he pulled me across the courtyard, hoping if anyone did see us the weirdest thing would be that the two of us were together.

Scorpion didn't even bother to knock when we got to Simmonds's door. He shoved the door open and threw me in. Simmonds wasn't alone. Two other agents—one male and one female—sat in the chairs across from him. The three of them seemed to have been in a deep discussion before we interrupted. I didn't recognize either of the agents, but they appeared to be in their midtwenties.

Simmonds's eyes widened as he took us in, and I shot him an apologetic look. He glanced at the agents across from him. "I'm going to need a minute with them."

The agents agreed easily, but gave both of us curious and questioning looks as they stepped outside.

Simmonds looked between the two of us once the door had closed. "What's going on?"

I put myself on the other side of the room, as far away from Scorpion as I could get. I shook my head at Simmonds. I didn't want to commit to a story until I heard what Scorpion had already worked out. He took the bait.

"I caught KATO's *Viper*"—he spit the word out of his mouth and glared at me—"sending a message back to her agency."

Simmonds's expression didn't change. "I see," he said, then turned to me. "Was it what we discussed?"

"Yes, sir," I said. "But I only had time to post it. I didn't get to log out of anything."

"Then let's handle that first, shall we?" He turned to the laptop on his desk. "What computer were you on?"

"C-six in the Academy Building." I slid my hand under my ponytail, rubbing my burn nervously as Simmonds remotely logged me out of the computer I had been using. Then I risked a glance at Scorpion.

He was looking from me to Simmonds with a stunned look on his face. And I swear the vein in his neck got bigger. "Someone better tell me what is going on." His voice was a quiet anger. He was beyond yelling.

Simmonds fixed me with a disappointed look. We had to tell him something, which neither of us wanted. And it was all my fault.

"I'm sorry, sir," I said, then shrugged halfheartedly. "I guess this is me asking for help." I felt Scorpion's eyes on me.

Simmonds grimaced, but I could tell I had him there. He sighed and leaned his elbow on his desk. I kept my mouth shut, gripping the back of one of the chairs to stay calm.

"You were right," Simmonds said to Scorpion. "Jocelyn was sent here to be a double agent. She told me so the first time we spoke."

"She told you?" Scorpion's forehead wrinkled in confusion and he sunk down into the other chair.

Simmonds nodded. "Everything I said when she first got here was true. Her parents *did* work for this agency and she *was* kidnapped as a child to get back at all of us. The North Koreans took great satisfaction in raising one of our own against us."

Scorpion straightened and tensed. "If she's against us, then why—"

"She isn't against us." Simmonds's voice was calm enough to keep Scorpion in his seat and to keep me being swallowed by my own disappointment. "She confessed her mission the second she got here and KATO has no idea. She's been feeding them exactly what we want them to know."

"So—" I could practically see the wheels turning in Scorpion's head. "So, what she was sending today—"

"Was discussed and agreed upon by myself and the board of directors."

Scorpion slouched back in the chair, still in a state of disbelief. "Then why keep it a secret?" he asked. "Why not just tell us all what's going on?"

I surprised myself by answering. "Because we can't risk KATO finding out." Scorpion's eyes locked on me, like he had forgotten I was in the room. "They have spies everywhere. There's something bigger in play, so I still have to act the part. All of you needed to be suspicious of me at first."

Scorpion ran his hands through his hair. "But how do we know any of this is true?" He looked at Simmonds. "How do you know this isn't just some story she's feeding you?"

I shot Simmonds a pleading look, begging him not to give away any more.

"It's my job to know," Simmonds said, not so much as glancing in my direction.

Scorpion shook his head. "No offense, sir, but when it comes to her I don't take anything for granted."

Simmonds leaned closer to him. "Agent Elton, I think you know by now what my word is worth." They were talking about something else now, and I didn't completely understand what.

Based on Scorpion's expression, it looked like the weight of Simmonds's words hit him. "Of course I know."

"She's proven herself to me," Simmonds said. "If you respect me, you'll respect that."

Scorpion shook his head, like he couldn't wrap his mind around any part of this conversation. His eyes came to rest on me, taking me in. And for the first time, his face wasn't filled with the pure hatred I was accustomed to. It looked more like Nikki's had the first time she came over to me in the gym. He rubbed the back of his neck, still in a state of slight disbelief. "All right, sir. I hear you."

Simmonds relaxed back into his chair. "You can't tell anyone else. This is clearance-level-seven material."

"I understand," Scorpion said. "You know I can keep things to myself."

"I do." He buzzed the other agents back in. "You both can go."

Neither of us needed to be told twice.

I blew past the agent holding open the door and walked briskly down the hall, trying to get away from Scorpion. But he kept pace.

"So," he said, a hint of disbelief still in his voice. "All of that's true? You're *our* double agent?"

"Are you *kidding* me?" I pulled his arm, spinning him around to face me. "You just promised to keep your mouth shut!"

"No one's here," he said gesturing. "And clearance level seven doesn't mean I can't talk about it with you. It only means I can't talk about it with people who don't know. And I won't." He was too calm. "All of this is true?" he asked again.

"*Yes.*" I kept my tone short.

"I guess that'll make our training sessions better." He flashed a smile, clearly thinking he was joking.

Anger burned in me but I pushed it down enough to keep from completely lashing out. "We're not going to do this."

I continued to move down the hall. Out of the corner of my eye, I saw him turn to me. "Do what?"

"You don't get to ask me questions just because Simmonds managed to convince you I'm telling the truth," I said. "We're not friends. And you spent the better part of the past month making sure I knew it."

He looked away from me, and if I didn't know better I would have said he was ashamed. "What do you want from me?"

"I don't want anything from you." I turned, waiting for him to look at me again. "Don't get in my way and I won't get in yours."

He held my eyes, as if he was expecting more. But eventually he nodded. "Fine."

"Good." I pushed open the door and headed to my room without looking back.

Chapter Fourteen

CLASS FROM HELL

I was startled to find Nikki waiting for me when I got to my floor. Then I remembered we had plans after the classes I never made it back to.

"Is everything okay?" she asked, meeting me halfway between the stairs and my door. "I talked to that tech kid Sam and he said you only went to one of your classes."

"It's fine," I said, moving past her to open my room. "Just a minor issue with Scorpion. But he knows more about me now, so I guess it worked out the way you wanted it to."

"What does he know?"

"Nothing I can talk about."

Her lips formed a silent O. "That kind of stuff."

"Yeah."

"I'm sorry," she said.

I shrugged. "It's fine. Simmonds helped fill him in. Maybe he'll at least leave me alone now."

I opened my door and dropped my notebook on the small square table with the rest of my books. Nikki followed, dragging behind her a few big bags that had been sitting outside my room. "Do you still want to decorate?"

I looked at her out of the corner of my eye. "I never *wanted* to decorate. You told me I had to."

She laughed. "Okay, fair enough." She pulled the bags in farther. "I'm taking that as a yes."

I rolled my eyes but didn't stop her when she started pulling off my sheets and unpacking the things she had brought for my bed. She unfolded new sheets and tossed a corner at me, then showed me how to make the bed. I did my best to mirror what she was doing on the other side.

"So," she said as we finished tucking in the fitted sheet. "You didn't have your own room at KATO?" She glanced at me cautiously.

"No," I said. KATO kept me in a dark underground room with anywhere from six to fifteen others. The hard concrete floors and pointlessly thin mats couldn't be compared with the IDA's setup. "I definitely didn't."

Nikki nodded, taking my short answer in stride. "It's not at all surprising that the countries who are responsible for creating child spies are the least equipped to handle it."

I stopped tucking the top sheet to look at her. "What do you mean?"

"Well," she said, as she continued to work, "KATO, and other similar organizations, are basically the reason the IDA exists. They're the ones that started training kids and putting them into the field, which meant they would have younger, stronger, faster, and more experienced operatives, whose careers would last at least twice as long as the average CIA agent's, assuming nothing happened to them."

"So the U.S. was looking for a way to keep up," I said.

"Exactly." Nikki nodded. "The IDA was designed to maintain a balance and combat drastic agencies like KATO." She smoothed the sheets on her side and gave me her full attention. "There are a whole host of practical and ethical issues that come with teen spies—issues countries like North Korea are less concerned with. Training teenagers to be agents in a partly independently funded initiative, but keeping them out of the field until they are legally adults seemed to be the best compromise."

"I never thought about it that way." I knew KATO was radical and self-interested, but I didn't realize what their actions would mean for more responsible agencies.

"Yeah, it's a tough balancing act trying to keep up with the crazies without crossing too many lines." Nikki came around to my side of the bed and tucked in the sheet I had left incomplete. "And from what I've heard, it wasn't easy getting the other countries on board. The U.S. had to agree to supply both the base and the initial recruits, which is why all of the agents we have are American. Once the IDA is considered to be 'successful,' the other countries are supposed to open themselves up to recruiting as well."

"This place has been around for a sixteen years," I said. "I would think that counts as success."

Nikki shrugged. "Governments have a history of moving entirely too slowly." She started rooting through the open bag. "The comforter must be in another bag. Let's get everything else finished and then we can come back."

She dropped the spy talk after that and dove into the task, walking me through hanging curtains, and pictures, and the various other things she had brought. Before long, I found myself surprisingly absorbed in the process. Nikki had gone with a dark blue theme for the curtains, lamp shades, and area rugs. "You can always change it if you want," she said when we had almost everything in place. "But I thought this would be a good place to start. You can adapt it as you figure out what kind of style you like."

I stood in the door, taking it in as Nikki put the finishing touches on the bed by adding the dark blue ruffled bedspread. "No," I said, trying to wrap my mind around the transformation. "I like it."

She beamed. "I thought you might. It seemed very *you*." I didn't know how she could possibly know what *me* was when I didn't even have a clue, but I kept that to myself.

That night, I slept in my bed without a problem for the first time since I got to the IDA.

I was pretty surprised when I showed up at the gym the next morning to find the entire academy class sitting with the older agents on the floor. Fortunately, Nikki ended up next to me at exactly the right moment.

"You look lost," she said.

"What's going on?" I asked her, noticing Cody, Rachel, and Scorpion over her shoulder. Rachel and Cody scowled at me. Scorpion's expression was unreadable.

"It's some mandatory presentation from a CIA agent," she said. "Since the IDA was started by former CIA agents, this happens every once in a while. We even have to sign in." She pointed at the table by the door that Agent Lee was manning. "Which I'm guessing you didn't do."

"I should go handle that," I said. I left Nikki and approached Agent Lee.

She smiled when she saw me. "Jocelyn. Don't worry, I saw you come in and I already have you checked off."

I thanked her and found a seat on the floor by the door. I had no intentions of sitting through this presentation. The rest of the agency was occupied, which made it the perfect chance to sneak up to the computer rooms and see if KATO had responded to my post.

I sat next to the door with my back resting against the wall. I gave the speaker ten minutes to get started before I gently shifted over so I was sitting in front of the swinging door. I put myself as close to the opening as I could get, then pushed back just enough to have room to slide out. I shut the door, slowly and gently, and waited until it was still before getting to my feet. I made it all of five steps before someone stopped me.

"Where exactly do you think you're going, Viper?" It was Agent Harper.

I wasn't afraid or panicked. I was annoyed. "I didn't realize the bathrooms were restricted during special presentations. Then again, this is my first one, so I guess I'm still learning."

He rolled his eyes. "Right. You're just looking for the *bathroom*."

I readied a comeback, but Agent Lee came out of the gym before I could use it. Her eyes moved from me to Harper; her expression remained neutral. "Is there a problem here?" she asked.

"I just caught Viper trying to sneak off," Agent Harper said with a note of triumph. "Given her reputation, I figured that wasn't the best idea."

Lee nodded a few times, digesting this. "I see." She didn't sound at all concerned. "I'll take it from here, Agent Harper."

Harper's victorious smile dropped. "What? No, she needs to pay for this."

"Pay for what?" Lee asked. "Cutting a mandatory assembly isn't something we like, but we usually don't punish people for walking in a hallway, especially when they're full-fledged agents."

Harper fumed, but was clearly outranked. He opened and closed his mouth a few times before storming off down the opposite hall, away from us and the presentation.

"Thank you," I said to Agent Lee.

She nodded in acknowledgment, then considered me. "I think you should know that I'm leading the team tasked with locating your father."

I stopped breathing for a beat, taken off guard. "I didn't know you—did things like that."

"I don't," she said. "But he's an old friend. He'd want to be found for this."

I hadn't done any real research on my parents lately. It didn't feel that pressing, with KATO's threat level rising. Besides, as much as I wanted information on them, I wasn't prepared to deal with the reality of my living, breathing father. I shifted uncomfortably, desperate to change the subject. "Does that mean you've read my file?"

"It does," she said.

I nodded, taking this in. "I guess that explains why you were nice to me on the first day. And why you're covering for me now. Of course, I could just stop getting caught, and do my job." I tugged at my hair in frustration, wanting to disappear so she wouldn't know how much everything in this conversation was bothering me.

She looked me dead in the eye. "You're doing great, Jocelyn. Better than even I expected, and I never doubted you." She tilted toward the second-floor stairs. "Go handle whatever you need to handle. I'll deal with Agent Harper."

She didn't give me the chance to thank her again.

KATO didn't have much to say about my report, though they reminded me yet again to keep them aware of any new intel the IDA might have on them. My chest tightened every time they did. I hadn't heard from Simmonds about what that date from the cipher might mean, and we were getting closer and closer to it. I did my best to keep my attention on my classes to avoid thinking about what it was that KATO could be so intent on keeping secret.

Global Dynamics that day proved to be much more of a distraction than I was looking for. It was the only other class where Sam sat next to me, and I often took comfort that he seemed to have as much hostility for Agent Harper as I did. And that he was so open about it made it even better.

Though not even Sam could help when Harper decided to make an example out of me, which that day he had. And he was out for blood.

"As you know," he said, "we make it a point to study the history of different intelligence agencies." His eyes landed on me for a moment and my guard went up. "One of the best ways to understand an agency is to look at the case file of an individual agent." He sat at the computer, which was attached to an overhead projector, and pulled up an automated presentation. My stomach twisted with anger and anxiety. "Today, we're going to look at the mission history of the KATO agent code-named Viper."

"You can't be serious." I gripped the end of the table. The only person in the room who dared to look at me was Sam, and I couldn't bring myself to meet his eyes.

"What was that, Steely?" Agent Harper asked. "Something you wanted to add?"

I held back my response. I had a feeling this was his way of punishing me for leaving the presentation that morning.

"That's what I thought." He smirked. "As far as we can tell, Viper first came onto the scene four years ago. She was young, like all KATO agents, and raised to be a heartless, cold killer. Something she seemed to have particular talent for."

I breathed as slowly as I possibly could, trying to keep anyone from seeing how affected I was. I knew I did what I had to do to survive at KATO, but I wasn't proud of it. And while I knew my history was no secret to these kids, the last thing I wanted was for them to see the damage I'd done firsthand.

I opened my mouth to say something—anything—to distract from the situation, but Sam got to me first. "Don't," he said. I finally looked at him. "Anything you say is going to make this worse. The best thing you can do is take it."

He was right. I tightened my hold on the chair, squeezing enough to leave an impression deep in my hands. It felt like my insides were being shredded.

"Her first mission," Harper said, changing slides. A picture of an Indian palace filled the screen and I went rigid. "Was in India. She was sent to assassinate the eight-year-old daughter of an Indian prince. She completed the mission in less than six hours."

I closed my eyes and little Nakini's face flashed in my mind.

"Of course," Agent Harper said, "that's nothing compared to the South Korean orphanage."

My eyelids snapped open and I looked at Harper, focusing every piece of anger I had on him. I could feel the rest of the class watching me, waiting to see when I'd reach my limit. And I knew that's what Harper wanted too.

"Don't do it," Sam whispered. "Keep together. He'll get what's coming to him."

Agent Harper pressed the space bar and a picture of a medium-size building popped up. "After a failed invasion attempt, North Korea wanted a message sent. In order to send that message, they sent Viper to burn one of the bigger South Korean orphanages to the ground."

I shifted in my seat, but I couldn't bring myself to look anywhere but at the screen. The orphanage was one of the worst assignments I ever had. Not all of the kids died, but those who survived were homeless. I still didn't let myself think about it completely.

"Steely," Harper said. I shifted my gaze to glare at him. "What do you think it tells us about this agent that she easily completed two missions involving the murder of innocent children?"

I leaned forward, moving my grip to the table. My heart was pounding so hard I might as well have been on an assignment. I couldn't see or think straight. White-hot rage burned in my chest, while guilt and humiliation churned in my stomach. I lifted the table slightly, ready to throw it across the room. Sam shoved it back down.

I looked at him. His face was straight and more serious than I thought him capable. I didn't know why it mattered to him what I did, but I was grateful. I was ready to fly off the handle. "Take a breath and answer the question," he whispered.

I exhaled loudly and heavily, and turned back to Agent Harper. When I spoke, my voice was constricted and barely contained. "It means that the agency doesn't value innocent lives."

An amused smile danced across his lips. "The *agency* doesn't value those lives? Or the *agent*?"

I narrowed my eyes at him, not trusting myself to answer.

"Keep it up," Sam whispered. "You're almost done."

When I stayed silent, Harper finally turned to the rest of the class. "Can anyone else tackle that for me?" No one dared to raise a hand, so Agent Harper pressed on. "Does this mean they raise their agents to be cruel and heartless?" Again, no one made a sound. "Viper couldn't have been more than"—he studied my face intently—"fifteen when she burned down that orphanage, killing dozens of kids under the age of seventeen. Could it also mean that KATO has little or no regard for civilian life when it comes to making a statement?" He scanned the room. "As field agents, you will come up against representatives from this organization and it's important to understand their state of mind." His eyes found me. "It's possible you won't have to wait until you're in the field to encounter this kind of situation."

I glared at him, but he kept his gaze level and meaningful. Then pushed the space bar. "Moving on."

He went through every major mission I'd ever been on. Every

awful thing I'd ever done was splashed in front of my face for the whole class to see. I had never been so close to a full-blown public meltdown. I was shaking with anger and hints of a craving, and struggling to keep it together. When the bell finally rang, I was out the door before anyone else was out of their seat.

I tore down the hall, barely taking the time to register the blur of faces. I made a beeline for the Training Building. I needed to fight off the fury and craving before they controlled me.

I wanted the punching bags, but I only got about three steps in the door before Scorpion was standing in front of me. "Look," he spoke quickly, "I know I promised to leave you alone, but Simmonds still ordered us to train together."

"Not today," I said, trying to step around him.

He wouldn't let me pass. "If you're serious about getting in the field, you need some real competition," he said. "I love Nikki, but she's no match for you."

I balled my fists, trying to keep my emotions in check, but when I spoke I practically growled. "Get out of my way."

His face got more determined. "What's your problem?" My breath hitched as he examined me. I was holding in more than I knew how to hide. "The only emotions I've ever seen from you are determination and anger." He squinted his eyes and surveyed my face. "This is something else."

I pulled away from him and crossed my arms, trying to keep myself steady. "I don't know what you want me to say."

Now he actually looked concerned. "You're upset."

A spark shot through my stomach. "I'm *not*."

"You are." He didn't back down. "You're rattled." Disbelief tinged his voice. "What happened?"

"*Nothing.*" I pulled my elbows in tighter, trying to disappear.

"Bullshit." His eyes narrowed and I could tell he was getting frustrated. Then he got pensive. "You were just in Sidney's class, right? Did he do something?"

My face tightened. "It doesn't matter. It's not your problem."

"What did he do?"

I kept my mouth clamped shut.

He crossed his arms. "I'll find out."

"Then find out," I snapped. "But you're not going to hear it from me." We both stood there, staring each other down, and my hands started to twitch. "Are we done?" I asked.

"Right." He stepped aside. "Sure."

I fought by myself for the rest of the session, and by the end, I found the Gerex craving manageable. But I still wasn't looking forward to showing my face in the academy the next day.

Chapter Fifteen

BUTTON PUSHERS

*T*he fire was bigger than any I'd ever seen. And I was responsible for it. KATO's orders were specific. Lock all the kids and workers in their rooms and start a fire. Leave a trail of gasoline through the orphanage so it spreads quickly. I had done what they asked, but I couldn't handle it. I ran back inside, unlocking all the doors. I didn't know if they'd make it out, but I had to give them a fighting chance. They were kids. Some were even my age. When all the doors were unlocked, I ran for the roof. The fire was contained to the front of the building, so I could escape down the back. There was an awning above the back door. If I landed on it, it would break my fall.

I made it to the extraction point, feeling certain I'd covered my tracks. No one would ever know what I did. But I was wrong. They knew. I don't know how they found out, but when I got back to KATO, Chin Ho strapped me to a table and put a compression cuff around me. He filled it with air, letting it press tighter and tighter around my arm. He didn't stop until I screamed.

I felt the pressure on my arm when I woke up. I pulled my knees to my chest and rubbed my eyes. That wasn't what happened. It wasn't real. It was both what I *wanted* to happen and what I was *afraid* would have happened. I was fifteen, and while I had harbored thoughts of going against KATO since I was twelve, I had never truly considered taking action until the orphanage. I wanted to give those kids a chance to get out, but in the end I had been too weak and too afraid.

In a lot of ways, I still was. And that was what scared me. I was away from them for now, but if it came down to it, I was terrified that they still had power over me.

I was, of course, the center of attention when I got to Lee's class the next day. I kept my head down and avoided eye contact as I found my seat, but I could still feel the disgusted and horrified looks I was getting. I kept to myself until Gwen and Olivia turned around. As always, Gwen did most of the talking.

"I couldn't believe what Agent Harper did to you," she said. "He couldn't have made it any more obvious."

I blinked. This wasn't the reaction I was expecting. "What do you mean?"

"Everyone knows where you're from. And no matter what happened at your last agency, you must have done *something* to win Simmonds over." She rolled her eyes. "Leave it to Harper to try and turn us against you."

"You're saying it didn't work?" I asked.

Gwen shrugged. "We're the kids on campus. We're used to being told something without all the details. The agents don't like it because it makes them feel like kids again, but we trust Simmonds."

"As far as we're concerned, you haven't done anything bad since you've come here," Olivia said, speaking to me for what felt like the first time. She seemed hesitant about it, but she kept going anyway. "Plus, no one likes Agent Harper. He's not that much older than us but he acts like he owns us. It's also not a good thing to be a teacher at his age. He should be in the field, which means he must have done something bad to get assigned to the base for a whole year." I could see why Gwen said Olivia had a good strategic mind. It had never occurred to me that Harper didn't ask to be teaching.

"And I may not be a grifter *yet*," Gwen said, "but there's a reason I want to specialize in it. I get people, and I can read them well. Agent Harper's problem has as much to do with Travis Elton as it does you."

"What do you mean?" I asked, arching an eyebrow.

"Elton and Harper have been enemies since they were in school," she said. "Even then, Elton was the better agent, and Harper was older. He graduated with Cody Mathers."

"So he's three *years* older," I said.

"Exactly." Gwen nodded eagerly. "And everyone knows the history between you and Elton. My theory is that Harper thinks he can be the one to finally put you in your place."

"He's trying to do what Scorpion never could," I said, piecing things together.

"Right," Gwen said, then she gave a one-shouldered shrug. "But like I said, it's just a theory."

"Yeah," I said. "And it's a good one." It would explain why Harper went out of his way to lower my credibility when I was finally starting to look good.

"All you need to remember is that a lot of us are on your side," Olivia said as the bell rang. "Especially if we had to pick between you and Agent Harper."

I gave them a small smile. "That's good to know."

"Okay, everyone," Lee said as Sam walked in. "Sam! Good to see you today."

Sam smiled and nodded. "You too, Agent Lee." She shook her head as he walked to his seat and was about to move on when he pulled out his laptop.

"Sam." She paused until he looked up at her. "Are you kidding me?"

"What?" He was a picture of innocence. "I'm taking notes."

Lee laughed. "Yeah, sure. *You* are taking notes." She came over, and continued laughing as she closed the top of the computer and carried it to the front with her. Then she moved on like nothing had happened.

Next to me Sam shook his head and pulled out his phone. "Damn, she's good." He glanced up at me. "So, KATO girl, how are you doing after yesterday?"

I smirked. For some reason I didn't mind the phrase coming from him. "I'm fine," I said. Which was more or less true since I'd talked to Gwen and Olivia. Plus, I had worked through the worst of my craving, and I was almost back to myself.

"Harper's an asshole," Sam said. Everything about him was casual, but there was a furious flare in his eyes that I didn't miss. "And I'm going to get him."

I shook my head. "I can handle him."

"Oh, trust me," Sam said, "I know. But if you handle things your way, you'll end up in some serious trouble. If I handle things my way, he'll never know what hit him."

I glanced up at Lee, who didn't seem to notice we were talking. "What do you have in mind?"

Sam simply shook his head. "That's going to be my surprise." He smiled deviously and turned back to his phone. "Oh, and by the way,

Elton cornered me this morning." He flicked his eyes back up to me. "He asked about what happened yesterday."

My jaw tensed. "Did you tell him?"

Sam shrugged. "Yeah. I didn't see why not."

I closed my eyes for a moment, trying not to be annoyed. I knew he'd find out; I was somehow hoping it would take some time. "What makes him so special that he gets information so easily?" I asked.

Sam shot me a slightly disbelieving look. "He's *Travis Elton.*" He said Scorpion's name with reverence, and I rolled my eyes. "No one holds more academy records or has moved up through the agency faster." Then the awe faded from Sam's eyes. "At least, that's why most people give him what he wants. I just didn't think it was a big deal."

I smiled lightly at that. "Well, thanks for letting me know."

He put his attention back on his phone, and left me to figure out how to handle Scorpion.

I wanted nothing more than to steer clear of the afternoon training session now that Scorpion knew about Agent Harper's class. But I couldn't. I'd missed the morning one to meet with Simmonds and get the status of intel I'd decoded. We were within two days of the appointed time, and my anxiety level was rising. Simmonds didn't tell me much other than that he was working on it. KATO was too close to something and it was making me crazy not to know the details of whatever Simmonds had planned. But he'd promised me I'd be a part of it when the time came. I needed to be sharp and I couldn't afford to lose a whole day of training.

Scorpion was leaning against the wall when I got to the training room, waiting for me. "I was looking for you this morning," he said.

I turned to face him and shrugged. "I wasn't really feeling it."

He nodded. "I got the story about yesterday."

I sighed. "Did you say you wanted to work out today, or should I go find a punching bag?"

He considered me for a moment, then nodded. "All right," he said, gesturing toward the mats. "Let's go." He led me through the maze of training students and agents, coming to a stop at the corner I usually worked out in.

"What?" I asked. "No private room?"

He shook his head. "No. I figured after last time, we'd be better off in here."

I nodded slowly. I couldn't be certain, but it seemed like this was for my sake. And I was unsure how I felt about that.

I didn't give myself the chance to think about it. I needed the distraction. I made the first move this time. Charging him. He stepped back, narrowly avoiding my fist.

"You know," he said, "when I saw you so upset yesterday, I wasn't expecting it to be about your mission history."

I pulled my arm back and landed a hard punch to his stomach. He groaned and doubled over. I bit back a smile. "If I wanted to talk to you about it, I would have told you what happened."

He forced himself straight. "I'm just saying, I wasn't expecting that."

I wanted to blow him off, but my curiosity was piqued. "And what were you expecting?"

He shrugged. "I don't know. Something about your family—or *anything* else." He bounced on the balls of his feet, backing away from me defensively.

My face locked as I punched harder, trying to make him back off without speaking. His arms blocked most of my assault, but I knew I had to be making my point.

"That wasn't the only thing I heard yesterday," he said, swinging his leg at my knees. I just barely got my feet up in time.

"Really?" I threw a punch that missed. "And what exactly did you hear?"

"Why you were here for a month before we met." He swung his fist at my side, and I was too distracted to block it. "You were in some kind of therapy for something."

I landed a punch to his jaw without thinking twice, not caring that it was off-limits. I was all too aware of the full room and of the other agents working out only a few feet away, who could potentially overhear us. "You don't know what you're talking about."

He shook off the punch and I was surprised to find a smile peeking out of the corners of his mouth. "I think I know *exactly* what I'm talking about. Or at least I'm close to knowing. I'm not too sure what you were in therapy *for*."

I stopped fighting, and he did too. "Okay," I said. "If this is the game you want to play, I think I'll take a turn."

He wrinkled his forehead, confused, so I plowed on.

"When Nikki and I walked in on you in the archives room, you were searching for something," I said. "You closed out of everything before you even knew I was in the room, which means whatever you're looking for, you're keeping a secret from everyone. Want to tell me about that?"

His eyes narrowed. "How did you know I was searching for something?"

I smiled. "You just told me you were."

He glared, but I kept going.

"Whatever you're looking for must be personal or you wouldn't have closed out of it so fast." I tilted my head to study him. "Is it family related?"

He exhaled heavily. "Okay, fine. I'm sorry I asked."

I nodded once. "That's what I thought."

He shook his head in slight disbelief. "You're not what I expected."

I put my fists back up. "Then change your expectations."

He raised his eyebrows and seemed taken aback. "I'm starting to think I'm going to have to."

Chapter Sixteen

PARTNER

I was on my way to the training facility after my classes the next day when Scorpion came up next to me. "There you are." He seemed annoyed with me, though not nearly as much as he had in the past. He stopped walking and I did the same. "Don't you have a pager?"

I shook my head, confused. "No."

"We should get you a pager," he said. "Come on, Simmonds wants to see us."

I arched an eyebrow. "Both of us?"

He nodded once and took a step toward the Operations Building. "That's what it sounded like." This had to be about the Iranian warehouse. There were less than twenty-four hours until the time I had decoded, and Simmonds had promised me he was plotting something. Though I wasn't too thrilled with the idea of Scorpion being involved.

Simmonds's office was empty when we got there. The map behind his desk caught my attention and I noticed a red dot blinking in South America.

"He'll be here once he's handled that," Scorpion said, following my eyes. "The colors indicate how smoothly things are going. Simmonds gets involved when any mission reaches a red level."

"What do the white circles mean?" I asked.

"Mission pending."

My eyes jumped to Iran. There was both a green dot and a white circle around the coordinates I had decoded. I didn't get the chance to analyze this too much. Out of the corner of my eye, I saw the red light turn green before disappearing completely.

A few seconds later, Simmonds entered his office through a door in the back corner that I hadn't noticed before.

"Agents Steely and Elton," Simmonds said. He was calm and collected as he sat down behind his desk. We followed his lead and sat across from him. He pulled some folders out of a drawer and handed one to each of us, not wasting any time. "Here are the details on your assignment. I'm sending the two of you on a mission as partners."

Scorpion looked at me uneasily out the corner of his eye. "Are we sure that's the best idea?"

Simmonds's eyebrows arched. "You're the only person who can be trusted with her. And she's too valuable to keep on the base."

"I don't think we're ready for this," I said. *I* wasn't ready for this. This assignment was about KATO, and it was important. I didn't know if I could focus if I had to worry about him. "We've just gotten to a place where we're not trying to kill each other."

"Now you have to take that a step further," Simmonds said. "The board has been convinced that you can be trusted. I need you to back that. I'm going out on a limb with you two, and I'm asking you to step up."

Scorpion exhaled unsteadily, but nodded. Simmonds was right—his sense of duty was unreal.

"Good," Simmonds said, "because the skills between the two of you make it possible for us to send fewer agents into the field, but ideally end up with superior results."

I nodded too, swallowing my doubts. This was clearly the only way I was going on this mission, and I wasn't about to risk being left behind.

"What's the mission, sir?" Scorpion asked, recovering.

Simmonds opened the folder in front of him, and Scorpion and I did the same with ours. "You'll be a part of a three-team operation in Iran." He met my eyes for a moment before continuing. "We had sent agents to investigate the details of some suspected activity in a warehouse there."

I studied the file carefully as he spoke, waiting to see how this all fit together.

"According to our agents," he said, "a Liberian arms company is attempting to make a sale to the Iranians. The deal itself is taking place in that warehouse, with the weapons held at a second site until the money has been exchanged. Our team on the ground has eyes on the weapons, but we need to handle this delicately. We're sending in two additional teams. One team to keep the buyers from getting to the location, and one to take out the seller, while the current team confiscates the weapons."

Scorpion nodded and leaned back in his chair. "I get it. We knock out the buyers so they think they've been double-crossed, take out the seller so he doesn't know his weapons are being stolen, and take the weapons so he thinks the Iranians stole them. It keeps the sale from happening, and no one knows we were involved." He smiled. "I like it."

"Good," Simmonds said, "because it's *very* important that this mission succeeds. Our agents were able to confirm that this purchase is being made on behalf of KATO." There was the connection I was waiting for.

Scorpion glanced at me, but didn't speak. I inhaled slowly, doing my best to ignore him. "They're gearing up for something."

Simmonds nodded once. "It would appear so."

And it made sense. Whatever they were planning, they were working hard to make as few waves as possible. Paying a third party to make their arms buy wouldn't draw nearly the attention buying direct would.

"What should I tell KATO my mission is?" I asked.

"Say that you're being sent to retrieve scientific intel," Simmonds said to me. "We'll have details for you when you return."

I nodded. "Yes, sir."

"What team are we?" Scorpion asked.

"Team two," Simmonds said. "You've got the seller."

Scorpion raised his eyebrows. "You sure you don't want me with the weapons?"

Simmonds shook his head. "As much as we value your arms expertise, your combat specialty is more important here. The seller is the most likely to expose us."

"How far do you want us to go with him?" I asked.

They both looked at me sharply. I shifted under their critical glares. They understood what I was asking.

"Nothing drastic," Simmonds said. "We avoid that unless there is no other option."

I relaxed into my seat and nodded. "So knock them out, get any weapons around, and get out."

"Exactly," he said, nodding.

"We can go over everything on the plane," Scorpion said.

Simmonds looked relieved. "Excellent. You each are due in medical for your pre-mission physicals. Your plane takes off when you're done."

We got up to leave.

"Oh, and Jocelyn," Simmonds said. I turned around. "Your new code name is Raven."

"What?" I asked.

Simmonds tilted his head knowingly. "It's about time that we retire the old one, don't you think?"

"Yeah." I smiled. "That sounds good."

Scorpion and I sat in the back row of the plane. Each of the other teams on this assignment was comprised of five agents. It didn't take a genius to work out why we were the only team of two. As much as Scorpion was the only person who could be trusted not to kill me, he was probably also the only person who could handle me if I did end up turning on everyone.

Nikki, Rachel, and Cody were on the first team. They all gathered back near us, while the other two members of their team stayed cautiously toward the front of the plane.

"Looks like this noodle keeps drawing the short straw," Cody said, ruffling Scorpion's hair. Scorpion laughed, but it seemed forced. "What did you do to piss Simmonds off?"

"Don't worry about it," Scorpion said. Nikki had taken the seat in front of me, and Rachel was next to her.

"Let's just hope you don't end up with any broken bones," Rachel said, looking pointedly at me.

Nikki flashed me an apologetic look, but I shook my head. She wasn't responsible for the rest of them.

Cody leered at me. "If *anything* happens—"

"All of you need to go," Scorpion said, cutting off Cody completely.

Cody looked astonished. "Dude, what's wrong with you?"

"We have to work *together* on this," he said, meeting their eyes for half a moment. "And we never have before. We need time to prep."

Rachel and Cody stood, seeming put out, but Nikki gave me an upbeat smile. She leaned closer. "Good luck," she said. "Just in case I don't get to see you later."

I nodded and thanked her as she followed the others to the front rows.

Scorpion spread out the mission file on the bench in between us.

"Okay," he said. He got straight to work, not giving his friends another thought. "The only way this is going to work is if we trust each other. So we need to call a truce."

My forehead tightened. "A truce?" I didn't think that was something people like us did.

"Yeah." He looked me right in the eye. "Because if we don't, we won't be able to pull this off."

"You've been after me from the start," I said. "How do I know I can trust *you*?"

He held my gaze for a moment, like he was debating something.

Then said, "Because Simmonds has been very good to me. He's asking me to do this for him, and don't want to let him down."

I bit my lip, considering. "So, I trust you and you trust me?"

He nodded. "That's how it works."

I took a breath, giving myself a chance to weigh my options. I didn't see any better way. And I desperately wanted this to work. KATO couldn't get those weapons. "Okay."

"Good." He leaned his back against the wall of the plane. "Now, let's go through this, and make sure we're on the same page."

"Sure," I said, shifting slightly.

He leaned forward again over the documents, getting down to business. I felt our dynamic shift and then I really understood how a truce worked. "Not only do we have to take the seller down, but we have to make sure we take out him and anyone with him before they alert the people guarding the weapons that there's an attack. We have to be quick and clean."

I nodded. "I'll go after the seller. I'm quick enough to get to him."

He flicked me a cautious glance. "Are you sure?"

I arched an eyebrow. "You know how good I am."

"Yeah," he said, "but that doesn't mean you should handle the seller the first time out."

"I can get the job done." I felt myself getting defensive, and Scorpion must have seen it too.

"All right," he said after a moment. "He's all yours."

"Thank you." I turned back down to the file. "What are our extraction conditions?"

Scorpion pulled the file closer. "The IDA has a car waiting for us on the ground. The keys will be inside. We have to park it near the warehouse before we go in. When we're done we go to a safe house a few miles away. Each team has one staggered around the area."

I nodded. An operation as high profile as this would make getting everyone out of the country right away difficult. We'd be extracted in shifts—probably in the same order we executed our portion of the mission.

Scorpion leaned back in his seat. "We should get some sleep while we can. Once we're on the ground we have to move."

"Sure," I said. He closed his eyes and relaxed into his seat. But there was something I needed him to know before he got too comfortable. "I didn't like it."

His eyes fluttered open. "What?"

"What I did for KATO." I don't know if was the truce or the weight of the mission, but in that moment it seemed important to tell him. "I didn't like it."

A weird expression crossed his face, but I couldn't read him. I couldn't explain why I said anything. It simply felt like the thing to do. I turned away from him before he could ask any questions. I didn't sleep. There was no way I could let my guard down enough in a plane full of agents who hated me. But it wasn't long before Scorpion dozed off. Once I was sure he was asleep, I sat up again and pulled the file back in front of me. I went over every detail, memorized every face, every name—everything that could possibly help me put a dent in KATO's plans. Scorpion didn't wake up until the plane started its descent.

"Did you sleep enough?" he asked.

I hesitated, then nodded. "Sure."

He didn't believe me, but we both knew he couldn't prove it. And he didn't know me nearly well enough to know for sure.

We landed in a small field about five miles from our location. The sun was just starting to rise. Our teams split up into cars. Since Scorpion and I were only a two-person team, we had a sedan, while the other team had an SUV. Scorpion led the way to the car, and it wasn't until we were inside that I realized how tense I was. All of this was so far out of my element.

"We have to stick together here," Scorpion said once we were on our own again. "No matter what happens."

"Okay," I said. "I got it." But I didn't. It felt—pathetic somehow that I had no idea how to work with another person.

We drove to the warehouse and parked a mile away. We were on the outskirts of town, and there were miles of open land behind us. It was dry and desertlike. We moved silently toward the warehouse, and settled behind a lone bush to wait for our signal. Once the first team had the buyers taken out, we would be on.

Our earbuds crackled. "Team Alpha is a go."

Scorpion and I looked at each other. He nodded once and we crept closer to the building, stopping under a window. I felt the rush of adrenaline that always came with the pre-mission jitters. In some ways, I was more relaxed like this. Even now with the IDA, I still felt free.

Scorpion rocked up onto his toes, taking in the situation before he dropped back down. "We've got a problem. You know how we were expecting the seller and three or four guards?"

"Yeah," I said.

"Well, we've got about twice that many."

I popped up to take a look myself. It took only a few seconds for me to get a good idea of the room. The ceilings were high, but there were so many boxes it would be hard for anyone to get away. There were seven guards, plus the seller. I recognized everyone from the file. According to our intel, they almost never brought the whole security team, which was why this was unexpected. From what I could tell, most of the guards had guns, but not all of them. I had no doubt they could land a few punches, but they weren't overly trained. I could take them out. They were spread out around the room, waiting for the buyers to show up. The only way we were going to get this done was with a little surprise. Scorpion tugged me back down. "We need a new plan."

Our earbuds crackled again. "Team Alpha has confirmation. Beta clear to move in."

There was no way I was letting KATO get those weapons. I pressed my comm. "Team Beta is a go."

Scorpion's eyes widened. "What are you doing?"

"The mission is the same. We don't need a new plan, we just need to be faster." I jumped off the ground and charged the warehouse.

"Raven, stand down!" Scorpion hissed. But I didn't listen. We didn't have time. The mission had to come first.

I kicked down the door and shot the two guys closest to me, who had both pulled their guns. I was careful not to kill them. Scorpion was right behind me. We split up the remaining five guards. I took on the three closest to the seller, while Scorpion handled the other two. The seller was a balding man in a suit and the first thing he did was pull out a phone. I landed a kick to his head, forcing him to stagger and drop the phone before he could make a call. Then I crushed it with my foot.

I turned my attention back to the three guards. I jumped and scissor-kicked the guns out of the hands of the two closest to me, then pulled one of the disarmed guards toward me, shielding me from the third. I shoved him at the last guard, who swayed. I took the opportunity to disarm him, but he did the same to me. The guard I threw down was just starting to get up. I kicked the heel of my boot into the base of his neck—which knocked him out—and focused on the last guard. I swallowed hard, trying to catch my breath, but I was struggling. Despite this, I knew I'd find a way to win. After everything I'd been through, I wasn't about to give KATO the upper hand.

A quick glance behind told me Scorpion was busy with his two guards, so I was on my own. I sparred with the guard closest to me. I got a punch to his head, and he went at my side. I kept moving fast and throwing punches. I was right about to take him down when he pulled a knife at the last minute. I wasn't prepared. He slashed wildly and the blade caught the curve of my neck. It stung and I knew he'd cut fairly deep. I just hoped it didn't tear any muscle. I refused to let myself feel the pain. I grabbed the hand holding the knife and twisted it behind the guy's back, snapping his arm in half. He struggled as I lowered him to the ground. I kicked behind his knees, pressing him down. Then, once he was hurt enough, I took the knife out of his hand and knocked him out.

Scorpion was finishing off his men, and I turned back to the seller, who was still on the ground. I pointed the knife at him and he froze. I looked him in the eye, reveling in the fact that I didn't have to kill him. I leaned closer, then raised the knife, using the hilt to knock him unconscious. Once I was sure everyone was down I leaned over and put my hands on my knees, panting, breathing so hard it hurt. I could feel the blood from my neck spreading through my shirt. But in that moment, none of that mattered. I won. Mission accomplished. I had done my part to keep weapons out of KATO's hands, and it was my first mission for the IDA that wasn't considered a test.

I felt my heart rate slowing down and I gave Scorpion a small smile, but he didn't return it. He just stared at me, his stance stiff and face tight. If I was reading him right, there was an anger behind his eyes that I didn't understand.

He pushed his comm. "Beta team confirmed. Gamma team clear."

He still didn't take his eyes off me. I straightened up and opened my mouth to ask what was wrong, but he didn't give me the chance.

"We need to move." His voice had a strained edge and he turned without waiting for a reaction, leaving me to follow him out.

Chapter Seventeen

AFTERMATH

Scorpion strutted across the desert, making sure to stay a yard in front of me. When we got in the car he reached into the backseat, grabbed a white towel, and threw it at my shoulder. It was so harsh that the impact made my gash ache even more. I pressed the towel into the curve of my neck, trying not to cringe.

Scorpion's mood didn't change the whole ride, and he didn't even glance in my direction. His grip on the steering wheel kept tightening and shifting, and the drive—which was probably only a few minutes—felt as if it were at least an hour. I jumped out of the car when Scorpion stopped in front of the safe house. The adrenaline rush was wearing off and I was starting to feel the craving trigger kicking in. I was prepared for it. I breathed hard through my nose and pushed it aside. I was determined not to let it get to me this time. The number of other things I had to distract myself with would help.

The safe house was compact and blended in perfectly with the surrounding structures. Inside, there was a couch, a table, a small kitchen, and a door that probably led to a bedroom. The whole place was a little run-down, but it was still nicer than any of the houses KATO had put me up in. Scorpion was right behind me with the bag from the backseat of the car over his shoulder. He dropped it on the floor the second we crossed the threshold and slammed the door so hard I jumped.

I looked up at his face, and the fury I had seen festering just below the surface now couldn't be more apparent. When he spoke, it was with enough hostility to scare a lion. "Don't you *ever* fucking do that again!"

"What are you talking about?" I had no idea he was angry because of something *I* did.

"What do you think I'm talking about? You charged into that warehouse without thinking twice. I told you we needed a new plan, and you just *decided* we didn't. You put both of our lives in danger." His arms flailed in big, pointed gestures. "How could you be so reckless? We talked about being on the same page, and looking out for each other. And you did *everything* but that!"

"'Reckless'?" I yelled back, pressing the towel harder into my neck. "I did what I needed to do to pull off the mission. You wanted to stand around and talk about it. What was I supposed to do? We had a job!"

"You *never* attempt to execute a mission at the expense of an agent," he fired back. "You could have gotten us both killed, and you nearly *did* kill yourself!"

"This isn't about me. It's about the mission."

If he wasn't angry enough, I had just sent him over the edge. The vein in his neck throbbed and his face started to turn red. "Of *course* it's about you." His voice got louder. "You can't help the agency if you're dead! Agent safety always matters!"

"Well, KATO never worked that way!" He opened his mouth, but then what I said hit him and seemed to quiet him. My voice dropped.

"That's not—I don't know any other way. And this was too important." I could feel my hands starting to shake, craving the Gerex. I swallowed hard, refusing to give in. The impulse softened.

Scorpion clamped his jaw shut. He was still furious, but he seemed to be trying to control it. "Nearly *every* other agency puts its agents first. Nothing is more important than that."

I looked at the ground, completely at a loss.

Scorpion let out a long, exasperated sigh, and I looked up. "All right," he said, forcing himself calm. "Let me see your neck. If you need stitches, which I'm guessing you do, you won't be able to wait until we get back to base."

He stepped forward, and I backed away. "It's okay," I said.

His muscles tightened. "I'm *trying* to show you how to be a partner. Would you just work with me?"

I didn't answer, but I stopped moving. He came toward me, slowly, until he was right behind me. He peeled the towel off my shoulder. The threads got stuck in the blood and pulled at the wound. I hissed but he didn't apologize.

"Sit down," he said, before turning to get the bag by the door.

"Why?" I shifted away. "What are you going to do?"

He put his bag at my feet. "Like I said, you need stitches." I opened my mouth to argue, but he shook his head. "I'm not asking." His voice was stern. "Sit down." He stared at me until I caved and lowered myself onto the couch I'd been standing in front of.

He sat down behind me and started riffling through the bag. He came up with sutures and pills. "Here." He held out the pills. "Take these. I don't have anything else to numb the area."

I shook my head. I had been successfully fighting off the craving, and I wasn't about to jeopardize that. "I'll be fine. Just stitch me up."

He rolled his eyes. "You don't have to prove anything to me."

I shook my head. "I don't need them. Just do it."

"I'm not threading a needle through you without a painkiller." I could hear the irritation building in his voice. "You're not going to gain anything by suffering."

"I said I don't need it!" I was sharp and insistent. The more he pushed, the harder it was to hold back.

"Jesus Christ!" he said. "Why does everything have to be so difficult with you? You don't need to be a hero."

I spun around. "I'm a fucking drug addict, okay?" His face dropped. I'd stunned him. "Get. Them. Away from me."

He studied my face, and I knew he was trying to see if I was playing him. "You're serious."

Now I was the one getting angry. "*Yes.*"

He dropped his head to put the pills back in the bag, and when he straightened up, he wouldn't look me in the eye. "I'll stitch it up cold. As long as you can handle it."

I turned back around so he could get to work. "Don't worry, Scorpion. I'll be fine."

He pulled my ponytail out of the way, his fingers brushing against my burn scar. I bit my lip as the needle broke my skin, trying to avoid associating it too closely with an injection. I exhaled evenly to keep myself steady.

"I'm sorry." He wasn't talking about the stitches.

"I didn't choose to be like this," I said.

"You don't need to tell me."

"I do." I wanted to. I was trying to be a partner. He paused and I could see him glance up at me out the corner of my eye. I closed my eyes for a moment, preparing myself. "KATO engineered this drug called Gerex. According to Dr. March it's one of the most painfully addictive drugs she's ever seen. The first time they shot me up I was ten. I was addicted after one hit."

"That's how they kept you in line, wasn't it?" Scorpion asked.

"Yeah," I said, grimacing as he threaded another stitch through my skin. "I could only get the drug from them. Anything I bought on the street would take the edge off, but it wouldn't get the job done."

"They put you in a position to need them." The poison in his voice surprised me.

"They used it for everything. Every time we sparred each other in training, we were fighting for Gerex. Every time we didn't complete a mission to their liking, they would keep it from us." I swallowed. "Going without it—" I shook my head. "I don't know what they put in it, but going without it is painful. It's like your insides are on fire and it's all you can do to keep from burning from the inside out. Every muscle aches, and every nerve screams. It goes away, eventually, but until it does—"

Scorpion stopped stitching right as a shiver shot through me. He put a hand on my back to steady me. "You're all done," he said, rubbing some antibiotic cream on the sutures and covering them with a bandage. I twisted so I could sink back into the couch. "How did you finally get off it?"

I closed my eyes briefly. Now that I was talking, answering his questions seemed easier. "Dr. March."

Realization dawned on Scorpion's face. "*That's* why you were here a month before anyone knew about you."

I nodded. "If living in KATO for ten years was hell, the month of detox was just as bad. The drug was so powerful and so specifically designed, March was afraid to give me anything to help with the process."

His face got even more serious. "So, you're telling me you had a cold detox from a drug more powerful than heroin."

I nodded.

"Jesus."

My arms twitched and I pulled them across my chest to control it before it spread to the rest of my body. I exhaled slowly and looked back to Scorpion. He was inspecting me and I saw the question in his eyes. "I get cravings sometimes. When I'm stressed or when certain—*events* trigger the familiarity. I'm getting better with it."

"Which is this?" he asked.

I bit my lip, trying to keep myself under control, and told him what things were like at the end of the mission. I looked him in the eye. "If this had been a KATO mission, I'd be extracted and high by now."

Scorpion kept his expression even, but his control seemed forced. "So you're basically programmed to want it now that the job is done?"

I nodded and looked at the table in front of us. I couldn't handle his reaction.

"You worked for one of the most careless agencies in the world. And you killed for them so easily. I never thought it was because you didn't have a choice." He laughed a little and shook his head disbelievingly. "You were fighting for your life, every time. I never stood a chance."

I pulled a smirk across my lips. "You never would have stood a chance anyway."

He didn't smile, and his expression had evolved to one of disbelief. "No one should be controlled liked that." He shook his head. "This life—it's bad enough when I *have* to kill someone, but it's part of the job, and I chose to do it. You never had a choice."

I shrugged. "It doesn't matter." I shifted uncomfortably, suddenly regretting everything I'd said.

"Yes." He was deadly serious. "It does. *No one* should have been forced into that, let alone at the age you were when you started." His jaw locked. "The things you did—"

"That's why it was so important to stop that sale today," I said. "They couldn't get those weapons. The damage KATO would do—"

"Well, we made sure they didn't." He tilted his head to the side. "Though we're definitely going to have to talk about a new approach."

I smiled lightly. It felt so strange to be talking with him like this. Something about the moment reminded me of a conversation I'd had with Nikki. I glanced up at Scorpion. "Do I scare you?"

He looked surprised by the question. "What makes you think that?"

"I just a thought I might." I watched him, waiting, but he struggled to find the words. "Because you scare me."

He was ready to say something, but before he could a sharp chirp interrupted us. The phone in the pack was ringing. He held my gaze for another moment, then leaned back to get the phone. I pulled my arms to my chest and gripped my biceps. The call took only a few seconds.

"We need to move," he said when he hung up. "There's a field half a block away. Our extraction chopper is picking us up in ten minutes. They're taking us to an air force base to get a plane home."

We both stood up, and I followed him out the door, leaving the conversation behind. We had to run between buildings to get to the field, which put me back in mission mode. We waited on the edge of the field, not speaking. We were there a minute before we heard the chopper. We jogged toward it before it landed. I jumped through the open door, with Scorpion following. We were back in the air in under thirty seconds.

When we were safely on board, I made a beeline to the back corner. I did the same thing when we transferred to the plane. I needed to be alone if I had any hope of keeping it together until I got to Dr. March.

No one bothered me.

Chapter Eighteen

DYNAMICS

I found my way to the medical wing when we got back. I must have fallen asleep after my treatment because the next thing I knew I was opening my eyes. I relaxed on my back and tried not to think of how stupid I had been. I shouldn't have told Scorpion as much as I did. I shouldn't have trusted him. I got caught up in the mission—in the idea of a partnership.

The door to my room opened before I could dwell on things for too long. "You're up," Dr. March said. "How are you feeling?"

"Good." I sat up. "Better."

She smiled as she put on a pair of gloves. "Glad to hear it. I need to check your stitches."

I rubbed the wound on my neck, which was throbbing. I leaned forward so she could get a good look, wincing as she peeled back the bandage. "Elton did a good job with this." She sounded impressed. "There shouldn't be too much of a scar."

"That's good," I said.

"How did it happen?" she asked, applying antiseptic cream and replacing the bandage.

"I was too slow," I said, shaking my head frustrated. "I've been working to get my speed back, but I just—can't."

Dr. March squeezed my shoulder. "You're not that far removed from the drug. What you're going through isn't easy. It will take some time."

I nodded, still feeling unsure.

"You're free to go whenever you're comfortable," she said.

"I don't have to stay the night?" I tried not to sound too excited.

"Not this time," she said with a smile. "You're stable enough that I'm okay with letting you leave—unless you're not."

"No," I said, popping off the bed. "I'm good."

"Okay, then. You can head out when you're ready. Director Simmonds needs to debrief you and I'll need to see you in about five days to get the stitches out."

Simmonds was waiting for me when I got to his office. From what I could gather, being debriefed by the head of the agency wasn't something that happened often. I didn't know if it was because of the way I'd acted or because of who I was, but I wasn't complaining. I'd rather talk to him than anyone else.

I was happy with the overall outcome of the mission, but we needed to see what KATO wanted with those weapons. The only thing we had to go on at the moment was the flashdrive from China. I asked Simmonds about the other encrypted files. He said the tech team felt they were close to breaking through the weaker decryption, and handed me a pager, promising to let me know when it came down. He also gave me the details of my cover mission to pass on to KATO.

I stepped out of the office when I was done and found Scorpion leaning against the wall across from the door. I hesitated, both because he'd surprised me and because I was a little unsure of what to expect from him.

"Hey," he said, studying me cautiously.

"Hi, Scorpion," I said, trying not to shy away.

"How did your debrief go?"

"It was fine." I started walking down the hall and he fell into step next to me.

He glanced at me out of the corner of his eye. "And how is— everything else?"

I turned away. "It's good." I felt a weight on my chest. I didn't want to talk to him. Not now.

He tugged my arm and forced me to stop. I looked him in the eye for the first time that day, but only for a second. I felt my face flush and dropped my gaze to the floor.

"What is with you?" he asked.

"Nothing." When he didn't say anything I looked back up. He was staring down at me, his eyes wide with disbelief. I sighed and then I started talking fast. "I shouldn't have told you what I did, and I shouldn't have let my guard down. I didn't mean to say that much." I looked back to the ground. "No one should see me like that."

Silence followed until Scorpion found his voice. "Oh my God." He sounded astonished. "You're embarrassed."

"What?" My neck snapped up, straining my stitches. "No I'm not!"

"Yes." He was so sure. "You are."

My face burned hotter and I stepped around him.

"Hey, now." He grabbed my wrist before I could get too far away and pulled me back in front of him. "Jocelyn, look at me."

I tilted my head up and glared. "I'm not embarrassed."

A small smile spread across his lips. "All right, fine," he said. "You're clearly not embarrassed. I don't know what I was thinking." When I didn't laugh he got serious. "You asked me something before the extraction."

I shook my head. I didn't want to hear this. "Don't," I said. "It's fine."

"You *did* scare me," he said. I froze, not knowing how to respond. "But you don't anymore. And you shouldn't be afraid of me either."

I rocked on my feet uncertainly, and Scorpion watched me, waiting. "I know I'm unpredictable," I said.

He snorted. "That's an understatement."

I glared at him, but kept talking. "You should know I would never go back to KATO. I have too much at stake."

His smile faded and his expression went stern. "I believe you."

My eyes locked on him. "Are you serious?"

He tilted his head, as if he could barely believe the words that were about to come out of his mouth. "Jocelyn, after this mission, I'm going to believe you until give me a reason not to."

I stared at him, shocked. "I don't entirely know what to do with that."

A full smile broke out on his face. "Just sit with it. Take a few days to get used to the idea." He rubbed his chin. "And something else you can think about—when we're off comms, partners don't usually call each other by their code names."

I blinked, taken aback. "Yeah," I said. "I'll work on that."

. . .

I waited until the last possible minute to get to Global Dynamics. Interrupting KATO's plans had given me a renewed focus, and I was more determined than ever to keep my cool with Agent Harper. Limiting my exposure played a big role in that.

I breezed into the room just ahead of Sam. I tried to get to my seat without an incident, but Harper had other ideas.

"Well," he said, stopping the two of us. "It's nice of our problem children to show up."

I bit my tongue, which was not what Agent Harper wanted.

"Kill anyone lately, Viper?" he asked. He refused to let my old name go.

My temper flared. I couldn't take it anymore. I took a step forward to fight him, but Sam kicked me. I whirled around to face him.

Sam shook his head. "Keep walking, Steely."

My jaw locked, and when I didn't move, he turned me around himself. He kept his hands on my shoulders, guiding me back to my seat. "I have a plan," he whispered.

I arched an eyebrow, but eased into my chair, keeping my mouth shut.

Agent Harper looked from me to Sam. "Is there something you want to share with the rest of us?"

Sam shook his head. "Nope. I'm good."

Harper looked suspicious. Sam was never one to hold back. It was enough to make the whole class curious. Agent Harper turned back to his computer and pulled up his presentation for the day. Sam smirked. From the look of things, Harper was playing right into his hands.

The presentation was on the recent history of Russian espionage. Sam took out his phone. He held his pen in one hand, pretending to take notes, while he typed on his phone with the other. I kept my eyes on his screen next to me, watching as computer code ran itself across the phone. The screen changed and a small compact version of Agent Harper's computer screen appeared in Sam's hand.

I glanced up at him, and he smiled mischievously. He then opened a version of the presentation, flipped to the second page, erased the content, and dropped a video file into the slide. He made a few more tweaks to the presentation, then saved it. Once he was done, he went back to Agent Harper's computer screen and reopened the file so the changes were included. The screen in front of the room blinked. If anyone noticed the change, they pretended not to.

Sam kept Harper's screen in the palm of his hand, while I held my breath and waited. Then, when Agent Harper finally flipped the slide, I had to force my face to stay neutral. A giant black video square filled the screen with a triangle play icon in the middle. Most people in the room kept it together, but a few whispers made Agent Harper look back at the screen. "What the—"

Sam pressed the play button before he could finish his sentence.

It was a fight. Actually, it was a series of fights between Harper and Cody, and Harper and Travis. As strange as it was to call Travis by his first name, it was even stranger to see him so young. All of the fights seemed to be filmed on phones and Agent Harper lost every single time.

Real-life Harper's eyes widened when he realized what was playing. He started hitting keys, frantically doing anything he could to get the video off the screen. But whatever Sam had done, he'd made sure we would be watching the entire show.

Each time, Agent Harper hit the mat hard. The fights were pretty embarrassing on their own, but together it was downright humiliating—especially coming from someone with as much pride as Agent Harper seemed to have. The worst of them all was the last one. Harper eyed Travis up and down, exuding confidence to the point of cockiness. From what I could tell, they were both still students. They were in the training room, and the entire facility had come to a stop to watch them go at it.

Travis's eyes were narrowed and his face was set. He moved slowly to the center of the mat, ready for a fight. Agent Harper met him there with a smirk.

I glanced back at the real-life Agent Harper at the front of the room. His back was to us, his hands balled into tight fists pressing into the top of the wooden desk. If it were anyone else I would have felt sorry for him.

On the screen, Agent Harper took the first swing at Travis. He threw three hard punches to his gut, which made Travis double over into a defensive position. But he recovered quickly and used his hunched angle to land a punch in Harper's throat. It stunned him long enough for Travis to kick Harper's legs out from under him. He slammed into the mat.

Agent Harper tried to push himself up, but Travis stuck out his arm and knocked him down again. Then Travis jumped on top of him and threw punch after punch at Harper's skull. He kept hitting him long after he should have. It was beyond defeat. It was beyond the point of embarrassment. The clip ended with Travis being dragged off Agent Harper by Cody and another agent.

When the screen went black again, the room was dead silent. Agent Harper stood frozen with his back to us, but he was so angry I could see his shoulders shaking from the back of the room. No one dared to make a sound.

"Samuel Lewis," Agent Harper roared. "Get. Out. Of my room."

Sam shot me a victorious smile, grabbed his bag, and sauntered out of the classroom. He didn't even act sorry.

And I kind of loved him for it.

Chapter Nineteen

CODED

Simmonds asked to see me before classes the next day. He was standing in the corner of his office when I got there, pulling a page out of the printer.

"We got into the next file on the drive," he said, handing the paper to me. It was similar to the last one. A single line of Korean, though this one was longer.

"It's another cipher." I didn't need to see it for more than a moment.

"The fact that the Chinese didn't decrypt it probably means they couldn't," Simmonds said. "And if it is more protected than the other one, there's a very good chance it's going to be a more sophisticated cipher."

I flicked my eyes up to him. I hadn't considered that. "If it is, I'm not sure I can crack it," I said. "The last one was a simple cipher. The kind KATO would have sent if they had to get a message to someone like me while we were out in the field. I know the more complex ones are layered, but they never taught them to agents at my level."

"Jocelyn." His voice was pointed and strong, demanding my full attention. "We both know you were more rebellious than they ever realized. It's the reason you got this far. You know more about their facility and their operations than they ever intended. I have no doubt you know something that will help."

I nodded. I still wasn't convinced I could pull this off, but he was right—I *did* know more than I was supposed to. "I'll see what I can do."

My mind was running through every KATO meeting I had overheard, trying to piece together a technique. I remembered something from about a year ago about moving through multiple codes. It didn't mean too much to me at the time, but now I was pretty sure that was exactly what I needed. And it would make sense that for highly sensitive information, agents would have to put the phrase though one cipher key, then put that result through another and another until the phrase had been through enough keys to crack the ultimate code.

I was tempted to skip my classes and get started, but I didn't want to draw any more attention to the situation than I had to. I went straight to Agent Lee's room. I was early, but it meant I would have the room to myself for a little bit to play with the code.

The class had filled in while I was working, and Agent Lee had started teaching, but I was too consumed by the cipher to pay attention.

"I think I might be a bad influence," Sam said, flopping into his seat next to me, staring pointedly at my paper.

I flipped the page over and stuffed it in the back of my notebook. "How much trouble are you in?" I asked, not giving him a chance to question what I was up to.

"What, for the Harper thing?" He shrugged. "Not too much."

I arched my eyebrow. "How much is 'not too much'?"

"I'm suspended from the tech lab for a week. It would have been worse if Agent Harper had the guts to tell Lee what the video was."

Agent Lee was in charge of the day-to-day operations of the school, which included disciplinary actions.

"How did you even get a hold of that video?" I asked.

Sam smirked, arching his lip enough to show a few of his teeth. "I have my ways."

I rolled my eyes. "Okay, fine. How did you know to use it?"

Sam shrugged. "Everyone knows about the history between Travis, Harper, and Cody. It's passed down from one spy class to the next. And that fight was legendary. Everyone said that Agent Harper had a black eye and a bruised jaw for the rest of the year. He even had to go to graduation that way. He spent the rest of Travis's high school career trying to take him out in any way he could, but Travis always outsmarted him. Not that it was really that hard to do."

"Have you ever done anything like that before?" I asked.

"What, you mean like the PowerPoint hack?"

I nodded.

"Nope," Sam said, smiling. "It worked out better than I ever could have imagined."

Lee cleared her throat at us, and Sam pulled out his phone. We both got quiet for a moment.

Once Lee looked away I turned back to Sam. "You know I don't need you to stand up for me."

He snorted. "Trust me, it wasn't only for you. He's been an asshole to all of us at one point or another. He deserved it."

"How do you know *I* don't deserve it?" I asked.

Sam watched me for a moment, then shrugged. "I have a feeling."

I smiled at him, and was about to turn away when I realized something. With everything KATO was up to, I didn't have the time to look into my mom like I wanted to. But I was staring at the person who had proven to be the best at digging up details other people didn't want found. My smile widened. "Does that mean you would help me out with something?"

His eyebrows knitted together. "What did you have in mind?"

I brought him up to speed about my parents and where I was in the search—which wasn't very far. His face got more and more serious as I went on. "You think Simmonds is keeping something from you?"

I shrugged. "I think he's told me all he's allowed to, but there's a major piece missing. My mom did more here than just fieldwork. She was involved in some level of development."

"And you think that's connected to how she died?"

I nodded.

"Okay," he said. "I'll look into things."

"Thanks," I said. "And thanks for the video. Even if I didn't need it."

He flashed his mischievous smile. "Oh, that was my pleasure. And let me know if you ever want to fill me in on the rest of your story." He tapped his pen on the back of the cipher. "It'll be nice to see how right my gut is."

I rolled my eyes. "I'll keep that in mind."

Chapter Twenty

SAME PAGE

M y stitches kept me out of the afternoon workout that day, so instead I went back to my room after classes to work more on the cipher. I had been at it for hours, randomly trying different cipher keys, before a memory triggered. At the same meeting where I had first learned about the cipher combinations, three names were mentioned—names that I believed were code for various combinations. I wrote down the names along the bottom of the page.

I stared at them, and then felt the spark of an idea. I did a quick count of the letters in each name. Each was six letters long—so it would make sense if this meant to put the phrase through six different cipher keys. Each individual cipher key that KATO used had a code name. They had to have made up the combination name with the first letter of each key's name. I worked the code through each of the combinations, and after the third one, the message made sense— or at the very least, it was something I could read.

The snake is hidden in the frozen forest. The job is nearly complete.

I studied the message, but I only understood half of it. The *frozen forest* is the code KATO commonly used for Russia. So, whatever the snake is, they're keeping it somewhere in Russia. I pulled at my hair in frustration. I needed to figure out what the snake could be, or this whole message was meaningless.

A knock at the door pulled me out of my thoughts. The last time anybody knocked it was because Travis was in trouble. This time, he was the one standing on the other side.

"Hi," he said. He had a plastic bag in his hand and looked a little breathless. The tension in his face told me something was off.

I squeezed the doorknob. "Is everything okay?"

"I don't know," he said, sounding stressed about something. He glanced around my room. "Your room's different."

"Yeah," I said. "Nikki helped me."

He nodded, a little impressed. "It looks good. Better than sleeping on the floor." He gave me a pointed look.

"I'm getting used to it," I said with a small smile. "What's going on?"

He rubbed the back of his neck uncomfortably. "Can I come in? I need your help with something." He held the bag up. "I brought dinner."

I gave him a curious look, but stepped aside to let him pass. He gave me a nod of thanks and crossed the threshold. I moved my books off the table so Travis could set the food down, then sat down across from him. Travis busied himself with unpacking the bag, but the tension radiated off him.

"I didn't know what you liked," he said, putting a Styrofoam container in front of me. "But I figured I couldn't go wrong with some American classics." He opened the box to reveal a big juicy cheeseburger. My mouth watered from the smell alone.

"Burgers used to be my favorite," I said. "I can't even remember the last time I had one." I knew it was before I was taken, but I couldn't place the exact moment. And I was sure I didn't appreciate it like I should have.

Travis smiled and opened the other three boxes. One held his cheeseburger, and another had chicken fingers. "Just in case cheeseburgers weren't your thing," he said. "We can share them." But it was the fourth box I couldn't take my eyes off.

"Are those fries covered in cheese?" I asked. I glanced away just long enough to see him nod. "I've never had those before."

Travis looked astonished. "How is that possible?"

I shrugged. "I spent ten years in North Korea with missions focused mainly in Eastern Europe and Asia."

"But you were a kid in America before that, right?" He couldn't seem to wrap his mind around the idea.

"And at no point during that time did anyone put cheese-covered fries in front of me," I said.

He shook his head, still in a slight state of disbelief. "Well, here's your chance to fix that." He took a seat and pushed the container of fries closer to me. "They're called cheesy fries, and they'll change your life."

He was right. It was easily one of the most satisfying experiences I'd ever had.

"What did you want to talk about?" I asked, finally taking a bite of the cheeseburger. It was even better than I remembered.

He shook his head. "We'll get to that soon enough. For now, just worry about eating."

I savored another taste, and it was nothing short of heavenly. "Where did all this come from?"

"A diner near campus," he said, finally digging into his own. "It was one of the first places I found when I started at the academy."

"How do you even end up in a school like this?" I knew how KATO got its agents, but the IDA undoubtedly had a very different approach.

"I got recruited like everyone else," he said, grabbing a chicken finger. "The IDA has access to every major educational testing company in the country. They find the scores and skill sets they want and then send a recruitment agent to judge how likely the student would be to come to the IDA if offered the chance. Parents are told their child is being given the opportunity to spend high school at an elite boarding school. Most can't say yes fast enough. The students aren't told the truth until they agree to come, but can change their mind if it's a deal breaker."

"What happens if you go through the academy and you don't want to be an agent anymore?" I asked. "You're stuck because of a choice you made when you were a kid?"

He shook his head. "Absolutely not. You can opt out at any point and go back to your old school. I'm sure you'd have to sign a bunch of confidentiality agreements, but you're never stuck here. The IDA doesn't want agents who don't want to be here." He rubbed his jaw, thinking. "Though, most people end up sticking it out, so I wouldn't be surprised if the recruitment tests considered that too." He looked down at my takeout box and saw my burger was gone. He nudged the fries closer to me. "Don't hold back on my account."

I didn't need any more convincing. And when I was done, I had eaten more food than my stomach could hold. I leaned into the back of my chair, shifting to find a position that would make me feel less full.

"You okay there?" Travis asked, laughing.

"I didn't know it was possible to be this stuffed." I shifted again. Travis surveyed me hesitantly, and I could see the question in his eyes. "Whatever it is," I said, "just ask."

He held back for a moment, then squinted, the uncertainty more apparent than ever. "Did they starve you?" His face was curious but sympathetic, and his voice was soft.

I shook my head. "No, they didn't starve me. They fed me enough to keep me alive and strong, but none of it tasted like anything. I forgot food even *had* taste." I lapsed deep into thought remembering everything. All ten years. The scars and burns and murders and missions played in my head, and I almost forgot his eyes were on me.

"You came here for a reason," I said. "And I know it has nothing to do with introducing me to cheesy fries."

He sobered even more. "I'm going to tell you something, and I need you to listen before you say anything, okay?"

I sat up straighter. He was just cryptic enough to worry me. "Sure."

He took a deep breath, preparing himself, then he leaned forward. He kept his voice low even though we were alone. "About a year ago, there was a scientist in England, Dr. Craig Foster, who specialized in a certain kind of nuclear alternative chemistry. I don't know the exact science behind it, but the point is, he was one of a handful of people who could revolutionize warfare. His device would make it possible to stage an attack that would take out a small target, but release a gas that would kill anyone who was in a given radius. This means it would be feasible to conquer a country without having to completely rebuild."

I nodded, following him. "Because targeting leaders and military officials would be easier than ever."

"Right," he said. "At least, that was Foster's theory. As far as I know, he hadn't started building or testing anything yet. He kept his research private—his government didn't even know all the details. The only reason he was conducting it at all was in case there was a threat."

I grimaced. Some of the most destructive plans started out that way.

Travis continued. "KATO found out about him." My esophagus felt like it got a little smaller. "They wanted him to use his research and threatened his two daughters to get him on board. He was ready to do whatever they wanted when the IDA got wind of it and stepped in."

"I remember this," I said, struggling to find my voice.

His eyes sharpened. "Were you involved?"

"I didn't get the chance." I couldn't look him in the eye. I remembered being disappointed. It would have been one of my few assignments west of Russia. "I was supposed to kidnap him if he resisted, but I wasn't needed."

Travis held my gaze for a moment before pushing on. "We sent three teams into the field—one to track KATO, one to watch Foster, and one to guard his daughters."

"Which team were you on?" I asked.

"The daughters'." He shifted in his seat. "They were the key to all of this. Foster wouldn't cave as long as we could protect them."

"But he must have."

His eyes darkened. "Let me finish." I backed away from him a little and nodded. He took another deep breath before continuing. "We had a team securing the safe house we were keeping them in. Abby, the older one, was sixteen. She put on a brave face to keep her sister, Eliza, calm, but I could tell she was scared." A shadow of a smile crossed his lips. "I was pretty sure Eliza knew too. She was only two years younger. But she never said anything." He spaced out for a minute, completely lost in thought.

"Travis." It was barely more than a whisper but it jarred him back.

"Sorry," he said. "They were asleep one night, and I was their primary guard. We got ambushed. But it wasn't by KATO. It was the Chinese. We figured they had to want Foster for the same reason. We hadn't heard any reports about China looking to build up their chemical weapons program but they couldn't have been there for anything else."

He closed his eyes tight for a moment and swallowed. "I knew if they managed to get into the building, it was because they either killed or disabled the other agents. There was no way I'd be able to take all of them, and the only thing I could think of was the damage that would happen if anyone got a hold of those girls. So I tried to keep that from happening."

"What did you do?" I asked, finding my voice.

The guilt and hurt was building in his eyes. He looked down at a napkin on the table, flipping the edge with his thumb. He was emotionally defenseless tonight and he knew it. "The only thing that made sense to me at the time was that if they weren't alive to kidnap, then Dr. Foster wouldn't do what KATO wanted."

In that moment, I stopped breathing. He couldn't be saying what I thought he was saying.

"They had both woken up and Abby was closer. I—got her." He paused, giving himself a minute. "The Chinese knocked me out before I could get to Eliza." He leaned back into his chair and finally turned his eyes back to me. "How's that for irony? There *is* a cold killer at this table. It just isn't you."

I didn't smile or blink or give any kind of sign that I had heard that last part. He had a good reason for what he did. A better reason than I had ever killed for. But I knew more than anyone that a reason doesn't make it right. "Who else knows this?"

"Aside from Simmonds, only Cody, Nikki, Rachel, and a handful of others who were on the team, but they think it was an accident— that I was aiming for the intruders and missed," he said. "The file was sealed, and no one is allowed to talk about it."

"Then why are you telling *me*?"

He shifted back over the table. "When a mission goes sideways, agents aren't allowed to keep investigating. We have too many jobs to get hung up on the ones that don't work out. But Simmonds made an exception. After that night, Foster and Eliza disappeared. It's the biggest mistake I've ever made, and only Simmonds knows the whole story. He knew I wouldn't let it go, and he said I could use the IDA's resources as long as no one else found out. And if anyone did, my investigation would be over."

I tilted my head. "You're taking a pretty big risk talking to me."

"He approved it." Travis took a piece of paper out of his pocket and pushed it to me. "It's been a year and I haven't come up with anything concrete. Then today I found this. About a week ago, the IDA learned of a meet between Chinese and Russian agents. They're known allies, so in cases like this the IDA sends an agent to listen in, with the hopes that they'll reveal something to each other in person that they wouldn't through another form of communication. This is the report that agent filed."

I scanned the document. It wasn't all that interesting until about halfway through the conversation. Apparently the Chinese agent referenced the incident in England and implied that China had performed a kidnapping for North Korea. I looked back up at Travis, who wore an eagerly curious expression. "Have you heard anything about this?"

"No," I said, thinking back to a year ago. "I can't think of—" Then it hit me. "How old did you say Eliza was?"

"Fourteen." He searched my face, trying to read my mind but failing. "What is it?"

"I found a way to crawl through the vents at KATO. It was my own way of rebelling. I couldn't leave because of the drug, but I could know more about the agency than they wanted me to." I put my elbow on the table and rubbed my forehead, trying to remember the conversation. "About a year ago I found my way to the director's office. He was having a meeting about what to do with the girl the Chinese were turning over. They said something about a treaty, but they didn't talk about the details." Everything was starting to add up. This was something else KATO had got a third party to do for them. "They said the girl was fourteen. And—" I stopped short when I remember the next part.

"And what?" He leaned closer to me, desperate. "Tell me."

"They said 'the other one' was killed."

His teeth clenched.

I kept talking. "They said she was coming into headquarters for a debrief, then was reassigned to a satellite training facility. I never saw her and I don't know where they sent her."

"But she's in KATO?" he asked, eager.

"Yes," I said, "but they have stations and safe houses all across the world. She could be anywhere." A plan was starting to come together in my mind.

He nodded. "At least now I have a place to start."

"*We* have a place to start." My voice was so sharp and sure it threw even me.

Travis was already shaking his head. "That's not why I told you about this. I just needed to know if you had intel I didn't. This is my problem. I'm not asking you to get any more involved than you are right now."

I grabbed his arm resting on the table and squeezed. "This is bigger than us." He tilted his head doubtfully. "KATO's been working on something. First they send me here, and they repeatedly ask me to keep them posted on any new intel the IDA gets about them. Then we find out they're attempting to load up on weapons, and now we know they have someone capable of giving them a weapon designed to take over a country." His eyes darkened, and I hurried on. "If Eliza is the key to Foster's cooperation, then finding her would give Foster a reason to stop."

Travis eyed me hesitantly. As if he wanted to believe me, but was afraid to. "How would we let him know we have his daughter?"

I bit my lip, thinking. "I don't know," I said after a moment. "But we can worry about that once we find her. She needs to be out of

KATO's hands, and not just because of what she means to their plan." I took a slow, deep breath to give myself a moment. "I know what they're doing to her, because they did it to *me*. So I can't know about this and not help."

Then something happened. The doubt, guilt, hurt and anger melted from his face, and was replaced with worry and a concern so deep it cut me. "What exactly did they do?"

I blinked and refocused on him. His eyebrows were compressed and his face was hard, but his eyes were so open they scared me. I'd never talked about this before—not even with Dr. March, who knew more details than anyone—but no one had ever asked quite like him. "They did a lot," I said, keeping my voice detached. "More than we have time for."

"Come on," he said. "Give me something."

I sighed. "Is this only because you want to know what they're doing to Eliza?"

"No." His eyes got more intense. "It's because I've treated you like shit my entire career. And now you're ready to dive into this without thinking twice."

I picked at the Styrofoam box in front of me, so I'd have something to do. "This isn't just for you."

He didn't care. "Jocelyn, please." He was practically begging, and it made me look up. If it was possible, the concern in his face got even deeper.

I nodded, still not quite sure how to talk to someone who cared. I wasn't about to tell him everything, but I had a compromise in mind. "You have to have heard enough by now to have questions. You can ask *one*."

He leaned back in his seat, taking me in, considering carefully. His eyes started at my head and moved slowly down my face. He got as far as my neck, then his eyes flicked back to mine. "How did you get that scar near your ear?"

I inhaled slowly, subconsciously rubbing the red welt under my hairline. I hesitated, wishing I had given his question more conditions. But after everything he told me tonight, I had to answer. "That happened when I was twelve. One thing KATO values highly is their secrets. They wanted us to be able to keep their secrets no matter what." Travis's eyes darkened and I knew he could see where I was going with this. I pressed on. "Every day for a week my handler burned me with a hot poker to build up my pain tolerance. The first day it was five seconds, the next ten. They added five seconds each day until I could tolerate half a minute."

Travis looked like he was about to be sick. "*Tolerate?*" His voice was hoarse. "There wasn't even a reason?"

I didn't move. I just looked him dead in the eye.

He reached his hand out for me and motioned me forward. "Come here." I scooted to the edge of the seat and leaned over the table. Travis slid his hand under my ponytail and cupped my neck. His fingers ran along the burn, then he stood to get a closer look. "It looks more recent than six years old."

I pulled away and looked at him, shocked. "How do you know?"

His eyes narrowed and his tone was harsh. "I know."

I swallowed. "They did a tolerance check once a year by burning the same spot. My last one was three months ago."

I could see Travis getting angry, and I was taken aback to find a part of me was happy about it. He cared that I'd been hurt.

I sat back in my chair. "I'm helping you with this."

"Yeah." He nodded slowly. "Okay."

"Do you have any kind of plan?" I asked.

He shook his head. "Nothing too specific right now, but we can start in the library's computer rooms. They're tapped into some of the most extensive databases on campus."

I nodded. "We should also tell Simmonds. He should know KATO has Foster."

"Yeah, you're right." Travis sighed and glanced at his watch. "I should get going, but we can meet with him first thing in the morning."

Chapter Twenty-One

GERMANY

Travis got to campus early the next morning and the two of us were at Simmonds's office door before he even arrived. We didn't talk too much, but things had changed. We were *comfortable* around each other, which was something I never expected would happen when Travis had pulled that gun on me a month earlier.

Simmonds's eyes widened when he saw us waiting for him, but he didn't ask any questions until we were inside. "I take it this is about your meeting last night?" He leaned casually against his desk while Travis and I stood in front of him.

"Yes, sir," Travis said. He glanced at me, and the two of us took turns relaying the story.

"So you're telling me," Simmonds said when we had finished, "that you can confirm that KATO has Craig Foster?"

I nodded. "As of three months ago, yes," I said.

Simmonds rubbed his chin. "A lot can happen in three months."

I tilted my head to the side, understanding what he was getting at. "Sir, this is KATO. Unless you found a body, they still have him."

He grimaced. "That's a very good point." He looked to me. "You think this is what they've been planning?"

"It makes sense," I said. "Something this big they would want to keep quiet until everything is in place."

"Jocelyn thinks we need to see if we can track down his daughter," Travis said. "If we can get to her, and find some way to get a message to Foster that he doesn't have to cooperate with KATO anymore, it could complicate their agenda."

Simmonds nodded. "I'm not sure how easy that will be, but it's a place to start. It'll take some time, though."

"That's the only downside," I said. "But Travis said Foster hadn't started to build or test his device when he was taken. He still had a lot of work ahead of him. We may be running out of time, but I still think we have some."

"It's worth a shot," Simmonds said. "How's that code coming?"

"I cracked it, but it isn't enough." I gave him a halfhearted shrug and told him what I'd worked out. "There's another layer to it that I just don't know."

"Very well." Simmonds drew a slow breath, taking everything in.

"What about the last folder on the drive?" I asked. "Maybe something in there could either give us more information on their plan or give us some clue about where to find Eliza."

"We don't know anything on that front yet, but we need to start moving things along," Simmonds said. "Have your pagers near you today." He met our eyes pointedly.

My whole body lifted. He had a plan. "You'll have something ready that fast?"

His expression didn't give anything away. "Just be ready if I need you."

I spent the rest of the day compulsively looking at my pager, waiting for it to go off. It finally happened shortly after lunch. I made it to Simmonds's office in record time, barely beating Travis, who was right behind me.

"We're making a move?" I asked the second we walked in the door.

"We are," he said. "We've been working on this for some time, but I had wanted to wait until all of our internal resources were exhausted. Everything you two told me this morning changed the situation." Simmonds pushed two files across the desk. "Here's your next assignment."

I flipped the folder open. "Germany?"

"There's a gala at the Russian embassy," Travis read. "We're copying a decryption device?"

Simmonds nodded. "It belongs to the Russian ambassador to Germany, who is the former head of the SVR. Our tech department is still working to decrypt the rest of the flashdrive from China, but they're not optimistic that we have the capabilities to do so."

"But this device can do it?" I asked.

"It will be able to handle this and many other files like it," Simmonds said, his excitement evident.

"KATO's going to want something," I said, gripping the back of my neck. "As far as they know, when I went to China I went for Travis. They don't know I got the drive."

"We'll come up with something to give them," Simmonds said. "For now just tell them you're on a data-retrieval mission."

I nodded and scanned the documents in the file. "Are these our covers?" According to this, Travis would be posing as a German businessman, and I would be his date. My heart rate spiked. The cover story made me uneasy. I ignored the feeling. We needed to get this device.

"Yes," Simmonds said. "We had Walter build a complete profile for each of you, including Internet backgrounds. If anyone tries to look you up while you're there, they'll find exactly what we want them to."

I nodded, pushing my uncertainties aside. "Do we leave now?"

"Dr. March needs to see you both, but after that, you're good to go," Simmonds said. We nodded and filed out.

Since we had cover stories, we flew commercially into Germany. "I know I probably don't have to say this, but I'm going to anyway," Travis said once we were seated in first class. He waited a beat to be sure I was listening. "Promise me that you aren't going to take any unnecessary risks."

I glanced at him out of the corner of my eye, trying not to be annoyed. It was fair. "I won't. I learned that lesson last time."

He nodded once. "Good."

I sat back in my seat and stared out the window. I didn't feel like talking.

After a while Travis turned away from me and closed his eyes. He fell asleep pretty easily. Once he did, I pulled out my tablet and used the plane's Wi-Fi and the proxy to get to the KATO message boards so I could fill them in on my new mission. I logged off as quickly as I could, then I leaned back into my seat and did my best to relax.

We checked into a hotel for the night to help maintain our cover. There was an extraction team on standby, so we weren't supposed to actually stay overnight unless we ran into a problem getting away. I'd worry about the logistics that would come with that if I had to, but for now we were primarily using the room to get ready for the gala.

Galas were fancy, formal affairs, which meant this mission came with a dress. I looked at myself in the mirror. The dress was blue and shimmery and fit me perfectly. I almost threw up on the spot. Every time I had to look like this with KATO it was because they were sending me on a more *personal* mission. The killing missions made me feel dead inside, but the sexual ones were worse. They made me wish someone would kill *me*. My survival instinct was the only thing that kept me alive in KATO, but the few times I almost gave up were after missions like those. It was the most powerless feeling in the world.

I took great care with my makeup, somehow hoping if I focused on my face and hair it would distract from what was eating at me. Of course it didn't. It only made it worse. I put the last pin in my hair so it was half up, yet still flowing down my back. I stood in front of the long mirror on the wall, feeling a little light-headed.

"Wow."

I spun around. Travis was leaning against the bathroom doorframe, staring at me like so many others had when I looked like this. Like so many marks had. It was supposed to be a compliment. My brain knew that, but I couldn't seem to convince my heart, which was pounding furiously.

I squeezed my eyes shut and shook my head. "Don't."

"What's wrong?" His tone shifted, and I could hear the surprise and apprehension.

I took a breath to calm down and remind myself how important this mission was, then opened my eyes. "Nothing." I grabbed my coat off the bed. "Sorry. Let's just go."

His eyes followed me around the room. "Okay." He sounded a little skeptical, but he didn't ask any questions. "Here's your comm." He dropped the small earpiece in my hand.

"So, how exactly does this work?" I asked, putting the piece in my ear, trying to focus.

"What do you mean?" Travis asked, confused.

"Last mission with you was my first mission with a partner. I've never worked with someone in this type of situation," I said. "Where you're in one place and I'm in another."

He blinked a few times and got that perplexed, sympathetic look he got whenever I told him something about KATO. But he moved on quickly. "I tell you what I'm up to and how long you need to provide a distraction. Then I'll tell you when I'm done and we'll meet at the extraction point."

I exhaled, doing my best to focus on the tactical part of the mission. "And if I need you for anything?"

"Get away from the crowd and tell me through the comms, otherwise we assume everything is going as planned unless the comms kick in. They won't stay off-line for more than fifteen minutes. So if either of us ends up in a bad situation the other will know."

"Okay." I nodded once and steeled myself. "We should probably get going."

The valet took the keys when we pulled up to the embassy, and Travis offered me his arm as I got out of the car. It was weird to have this dynamic with him, but I was determined to use it to get me through this mission. I gripped his forearm tight—tighter than I normally would have. It was as if I was using him as an anchor. If he noticed, he didn't comment. He led me through the embassy's tall doors and handed the security guard our invitations. The IDA sent an advanced team in to station weapons around the room. We would pick them up when we were inside.

Once we passed the security checkpoint we entered a large rectangular ballroom, extravagantly decorated and fit for any high-society party. Windows lined the back wall, so tall they practically stretched from the floor to the ceiling. The chandeliers were crystal and hung at three different points across the hall.

"You take the gun by the window, I'll get the one by the door," Travis said.

I scanned the room, taking in every detail, and pausing for a moment on the place where the hiding spot was supposed to be.

"I see Popov," I said, spotting the middle-aged security member on the other side of the ballroom. Ivan Popov had been on the ambassador's security team since this particular ambassador took up residence in the embassy. He was former Russian military, and this assignment was his idea of retirement. The IDA's intel said he didn't take the job nearly as seriously as he should and had a habit of getting distracted at parties. The only reason he was still on the detail at all was because he was one of the ambassador's closest friends.

I glanced at Travis and saw he had spotted Popov standing in front of a narrow alcove. Inside that alcove was a small staircase, which was a design flaw in the building. At one point the ballroom was intended to be a kitchen, so the stairs were built for housekeepers and staff. It was common for the ambassador to station a single guard in front of the stairs to keep people from wandering to the upper levels. Popov, who enjoyed being a part of the party, was the one most commonly selected for this task. And since most people didn't even know about the staircase, he saw it as a pretty casual assignment.

"All right," Travis said. "You know what you have to do."

I nodded and my heart sped up. I tried not to think about how much this reminded me of KATO and focused on the fact that it wasn't. And that in the end, I wouldn't have to leave this room with anyone but Travis. "Let me know when you're out," I said, convincing myself to pull away from him.

I moved around the edge of the room, pausing near the window to get a drink and pick up the gun stuck in a nearby flowerpot. I used my purse to shield the room, then snuck it inside and continued maneuvering my way to Popov. I fought the urge to down the drink in one gulp. If I did I'd want more, and in the end it would barely have any impact. But if there was something stronger I could get my hands on, I wasn't so sure I'd be able to show the same restraint.

Travis took a different path to the staircase, opting to weave across the room and blend into the crowd. We wanted to pull this off as quickly as possible. Travis's job was to get to the ambassador's second-floor office and plug a replica of the ambassador's decryption device into the real thing. The tech team had programmed the replica to copy what was needed on its own. Travis just had to wait until the device was fully cloned.

In order for Travis to get to the office, I had to distract the man guarding the stairs and keep him out of the way. The best way to do that was to make sure his attention stayed on me.

I came at Popov from the side, giving myself some extra time to assess the situation. His eyes moved across the room, and I noticed his attention hovered on the women. I swallowed and forced myself in front of him.

"You must be *very* good at your job to end up in such an esteemed position," I said in perfect Russian.

Popov turned and examined me. His eyes lingered just a little too long in all the right places, and I knew I had him. It made my skin crawl.

"I do not believe I have seen you at any previous functions," Popov said.

I smiled and extended a hand. "Mika Stromberg."

It was pretty clear he couldn't have possibly cared less what my name was. He took my hand, kissed it, and started flirting with me almost instantly. "I am Ivan."

"I know who you are." I dipped my head and looked at him through my eyelashes. He still hadn't let go of my hand, and I shifted enough to angle him away from the alcove. Travis took the opportunity to disappear behind him. "You have a *reputation* I was hoping to experience firsthand."

That was all it took. He gave my arm a tug and pulled me closer to him. Then he took my drink from me and passed it off to a nearby server, before gently backing me into the wall. When he finally let go of me, it was only to brace himself, so he was hovering over me, while his other hand came to a stop on my waist. "I think that's something that can be arranged."

I felt the bile rising in my stomach, but I swallowed it back down. I sank against the wall and blinked up at him, which he took as an invitation to come even closer. I was having a hard time breathing.

"Now, tell me," he said. "What is a pretty thing like you doing wandering around here unattended?"

I smiled. His thumb rubbed up and down my side. I fought off a shiver. "My date wasn't paying much attention to me. He has a little bit of a wandering eye."

"How can any eyes wander when you're in the room?" His voice was supposed to be seductive, but it was anything but. I forced a laugh and leaned closer, feeling more powerless by the second. We kept talking, and he kept touching me more and more inappropriately. I let him—I didn't have a choice.

I giggled while I looked around the room for something to distract me, but nothing held my attention. I took in the crowd and couldn't help but think that anyone here could be a KATO agent. It would be so easy for them to get to me if they suspected me of anything. I swallowed, fighting the paranoia.

I spotted two people meeting in a corner, near a door so small it probably went unnoticed by everybody else in the room. The man was on the shorter side and had been standing there for ten minutes when a woman in a black dress walked up to him. They talked quietly and kept glancing around. Amateurs. They couldn't be any more obvious that they were up to something. After a moment, the man nodded, opened the door a crack, and they both slid inside. The woman snuck back out in less than two minutes.

My heart started racing with excitement and dread. I knew what had happened in that room. I knew the signs of a drug deal anywhere. I'd made enough of them when I was in the field and afraid of running out of Gerex. Alcohol may not have been worth it, but if there was a strong opiate in that room—

"I'll be done in five minutes." Travis's voice jolted me back to reality. "I have another way out, so I'll meet you at the extraction point."

I smiled at Popov and he continued to lay it on thick, but I kept my eyes on the door in the corner, letting the memories of being high take over. I had *never* wanted it so bad. I could feel it. And I *needed* it back in my bloodstream. Even if it wasn't Gerex, I needed to feel something close.

A long rough finger on my face drew me back to Popov. He was staring at me, with a cocky smile like he knew I was his. Then I remembered the mission. I couldn't think about anything else. Only the mission. I had to exit the conversation in a way that wouldn't arouse his suspicion.

"You should step away from me," I said, glancing behind him.

He gave me a questioning look.

I leaned in to whisper in his ear. "I see my date looking for me," I said. "And while he may have a wandering eye, he doesn't like it when I have one. He tends to get jealous."

"Ah, I see." He gave me a knowing look, and stepped back. Though he was still too close for comfort. "I will meet you after the party, yes?"

I beamed at him. "Of course."

He relaxed a little, and I smiled at him one last time before I stepped away. I had done my part of the assignment. Now that Travis had what he needed, the only thing I was supposed to do was get out. But instead my eyes stayed on the small door in the corner. The woman, who had to be the buyer, had left almost as soon as she got there. But the door hadn't opened again since—and I'd barely taken my eye off it. The dealer was still inside.

Chapter Twenty-Two

CHANGE OF PLANS

I ground my teeth together, keeping my attention on the door. If he came out I wouldn't be able to approach him. Not with a roomful of people who I needed to buy my cover. But if I were to go to him it would be a different story.

I swallowed hard. I couldn't do this. Not on a job. And even if I did, the strongest street drug wouldn't come close to doing what I needed it to do. But when I looked down at my blue sparkling dress and heard Popov's words echoing in my head, I didn't care. I needed something, *anything* in my system. The overwhelming need to get high refused to let go. I had time before I was supposed to meet Travis at the extraction point. I could make this happen.

I slipped into the room so effortlessly it took the dealer by surprise.

He jumped when I shut the door, but got over it quickly. "Can I help you?" His voice was deep and scratchy.

"I'm pretty sure you can," I said. "What are you dealing?" Whatever it was, it was feet away from me.

He gave me a hard look. "I don't know what you're talking about."

I smirked and pulled out a roll of IDA in-case-of-emergency money from my purse and dropped it on the table. He looked surprised. I arched my eyebrow. "Do you know what I'm talking about now?"

He looked down at the money, then up at me. "Heroin." He dropped a packet of white powder on the table.

I picked it up and examined it closely. It was hard to tell how pure it was, but I was sure it would be enough. I dropped the pouch into my purse without another word. I clutched the blue bag, all too aware of the drug resting against my gun. The dealer watched me wordlessly, waiting for me to make the next move. I stepped back into the ballroom, and I felt my control slipping. The shaking that I had been able to repress started to intensify. I'd never felt like a bigger failure, and it didn't seem to matter.

I ducked out of the main ballroom, found a bathroom out of the way, and locked myself inside. I threw water on my face and breathed deep. I couldn't think straight. The only thing I saw was the white powder.

I looked at myself in the mirror and the blue dress stared back at me. I picked up the packet and slid down the wall, pulling my knees to my chest. I held the drug out in front of my face and studied it. Guilt ate at my stomach for spending the IDA's money like this, but it was done.

Now that the money had been spent, it seemed like a shame to waste it. I opened the bag, dipped my fingers in, and rolled them in the powder, then dusted them off and smelled the residue. I was close to giving in, and I was so, *so* tired of fighting it. I'd held out for so long—months without anything. Just this once I wanted to give myself what I needed.

I closed the toilet seat next to me and spread some of the heroin on top of it. I would rather have injected it, but I didn't have all the tools. I leaned over the toilet, ready to snort.

Then my comm clicked on.

"Seriously," Travis was saying, "it doesn't matter what you do, you're not going to find out who I'm working for or what I have."

"You will break," a Russian voice said. "And you will give us everything we want."

I sat up straight. He'd been caught. I hadn't even realized that it had been fifteen minutes since we'd last signed off. The comms had kicked in on their own.

There was a condescending tone to Travis's voice. "That's going to be harder than you think it is."

I dusted the drug off the toilet and tucked the rest of the packet in my purse. I splashed more water on my face. I had to pull myself together. The job wasn't done, and I was jeopardizing everything.

I tore out of the bathroom and fought through the craving, desperately focusing on Travis. He must have been caught after he left the office, and if I had to guess, it was probably before he got off the floor. I glanced back to the alcove and saw Popov was gone. I let the adrenaline of the mission replace my need for the drug. I crept to the next floor and found a closet that had an air duct, well away from any security cameras. I strapped my purse to my thigh—there was no way I was leaving it behind—then I popped out the vent and lifted myself up into it.

Once I was out of the way, I pulled out my tablet and looked at the blueprint. I quickly found the office Travis had broken into. Then I crept along the ducts, listening for any sign of a confrontation. If Travis had been caught on this floor, they probably wouldn't have taken him too far away.

I was dead-on. I'd moved only a few feet when I heard voices coming from the first offshoot. I pulled myself down and found that I was looking into an elaborate library. The vent was in the ceiling, and I could see the whole room perfectly. Travis's back faced a stained-glass window, and four guys with guns stood between him and the door. Popov was one of them.

I scanned the room from my bird's-eye vantage point, trying to come up with a way to get him out. Usually I could handle four guys, but I was still shaky from the near relapse. It would be too much of a risk.

My eyes fell on the window behind Travis, and I knew what I needed to do.

I pushed myself backward through the vent, and back to the closet.

I pressed my comm in. "I've got a plan. Stand by and I'll get you out." He couldn't answer me, but I wanted him to be ready.

I found the steps and sprinted up a level to the top floor of the embassy. Then I used the blueprints to find the room right above the library. It was a bedroom. Fortunately, the house was uniform and the windows lined up perfectly. I had found some rope in the supply closet I had been in. I opened the bottom window and tied the rope tightly around the radiator underneath it, then dropped the rest through the opening. It would be perfectly hidden behind the stained glass.

I went back downstairs and through the vents. I hovered above the room, looking around. There were two guys right below me, and one of them was Popov. I could take them out easily, even in my current state. It was the other two I would have a problem with. The only way I was going to get past them was by catching them off guard.

"Be ready to grab the rope," I said to Travis. I watched his face.

There was absolutely no sign of recognition, but he had to have heard me.

I pushed myself up so I was practically doing a bent-knee push-up with my feet resting on the grate. Then I lifted my hips, supporting my weight on my hands, and slammed my feet into the vent, knocking it to the floor. I dropped down and held on to the duct while I swung my legs at Popov and the other guard closest to me. I hit my targets right below their skulls and they fell to the ground. The other two guards had their guns out, firing at me. It gave Travis the chance to attack them from behind. He stunned them enough to knock their guns down and I didn't give them a chance to recover. I grabbed Travis's arm, pulled him toward the window and jumped through it. Glass shattered around me, but I grabbed the rope easily. Fortunately, Travis was right behind me. We slid down the building and hit the ground running. I pushed my comm. "This is Raven. We need an immediate extraction at our location!"

My earbud crackled. "Extraction en route. Twenty seconds out. The street intersects fifty feet from you."

Travis and I ran hard to the intersection. Our ride was already waiting for us when we got there. We both jumped in without bothering to slow down.

The car took off and we collapsed against the seat, panting.

"How—" Travis said between breaths. "How did you know to do that?"

I shook my head. It wasn't the first time I'd had to get out of a building that way, but I didn't want to get into it.

"Are you okay?" I asked.

He nodded. "They caught me coming out of the office, but they didn't do anything more than point their guns at me." He peered at me. "Are *you* okay?" He pulled my arms forward. "The glass cut you up pretty good."

I looked down, noticing the small shallow cuts that lined my arms. If I had to guess, my face probably looked the same. I swallowed hard and pulled my arms back. "Did you get what we need?" I asked.

He shot me an incredulous look, like he couldn't believe I asked, then reached into his boot. He pulled out the thin, wide device. "They searched me, but couldn't find anything other than my gun." He laughed. "I'm pretty sure I was about to get strip-searched when you showed up, so your timing couldn't have been better."

I smiled lightly, then leaned into the seat behind me, finally catching my breath.

We transferred to a plane shortly after that. I tried to get settled, but my hand brushed my thigh where my purse was strapped. Now that the adrenaline was wearing off I found myself falling back into the intensely desperate need I had back in the bathroom. I unstrapped the bag and slipped it out from underneath my dress. I fingered the silver beading, feeling like I was holding one of the most valuable things I'd ever touched. I should have ditched it back at the scene, but I—couldn't. I had come so close to giving in that I couldn't let it go. The idea that I could still get high once I got back to the IDA was the only thing that got me through.

"Jocelyn?"

I looked up at Travis, who was watching me cautiously. "I just said your name three times," he said. He knew something was off. I hated how well my former enemy had come to know me.

"Sorry," I said, running my hand through my hair, pulling the pins out. I wore it down so rarely I'd forgotten what it felt like to have it hanging around my neck.

He was still staring at me. "What's wrong?"

I was tense but I wasn't shaking. The little adrenaline I had left was keeping the craving at bay, but the more it wore off, the more agitated I felt. I didn't know if I could handle when it did—I didn't know what I would do. "I'm—sorry," I said. "I should have noticed the guard was gone."

"That wasn't your fault," Travis said, shaking his head. "I told you I had a way out." He was quiet for a moment and I kept focused on my breathing. "There's something else going on here."

I squeezed my bag tight and looked up at him. "No, there's not," I said. I couldn't tell him about the drugs in my purse any more than I could tell him about the reason I'd bought them. It was beyond weakness. It was the part of KATO that was more humiliating than I could stand. I exhaled. "I just need to see Dr. March when we get back."

This was deeper than a craving. Every part of me wanted the drug. If I weren't on a plane surrounded by agents, I would be high already.

I tried to turn away from him, but I couldn't. He was giving me one of his hard, searching looks, like he was trying to x-ray my soul. Then after a moment he sat back, defeated. "You still don't trust me."

"What?" I asked. "Yes, I do." And I did. But I was just starting to win him over and this would change everything. "You need to trust *me*. I'm fine."

"This isn't about me," he said, edging closer.

"Well, it's not about me either," I snapped.

He got even more serious. "Every time you get shifty on me,

you're holding something back. What is this time?" he asked. "How worried do I need to be?"

"I don't need you to worry about me!" He was wearing me down. I had to get him to go away. I needed to be left alone. I leaned in close to him and when I spoke it was in a hiss so sharp and quiet, only he could hear it. "Stop pretending to care. You can't help me any more than you could help Eliza." He looked as if he'd been slapped, but I kept going. "I've been around a lot of heartless agents, and I'm not fooled. You're just as bad as any I've come across." I kept my glare even and intense. "So, back off."

He stared at me with an expression of horror and betrayal etched so deeply into his face it hurt to look at. "Fine," he said, his voice barely audible. He turned and left me alone.

I closed my eyes, hating myself, and leaned my head against the seat behind me. I held my purse close to my chest, wishing the drugs could numb every emotion inside me.

Chapter Twenty-Three

TRAPPED BY THE TRUTH

ravis didn't talk to me the entire ride back to the base. He didn't even look up when I changed in front of him, and I wanted out of that dress so desperately I didn't care who was watching. He was off the plane before I could stand.

I went right to Dr. March's office. I forced myself to breathe easy, and tried not to think that I was holding a temporary solution in my hand.

Someone must have told Dr. March when we were getting back, because she was waiting for me in the lobby. She gave me her usual once-over. "You look better than I was expecting," she said.

I exhaled heavily and shook my head. "I'm not."

Dr. March stiffened. I knew merely admitting that would tell her how bad off I was.

I clutched my purse tightly. I'd left the dress on the plane, but there was no way I was leaving this behind.

Dr. March led me to the back offices, shooting me some of the most concerned looks I had ever got from her, which made me even more anxious. When we got to one of the exam rooms, she held the door open for me and sat me down on one of the beds. "What's going on?"

I opened my mouth to tell her, but I couldn't. Instead, I held my bag out to her. She looked at me hesitantly for a second, then tried to take it. I clutched the purse with a death grip, and Dr. March had to pull to get it out of my hands.

I felt my arms start to shake the second she took it, and gripped the bed to keep her from seeing. She eyed me carefully over the top of the purse, then flicked the triangle clasp open. I looked at the ground so I didn't have to see her reaction.

"Where did you get this?" Her voice was rigid.

"At the embassy." I had to force the words through my dry and raspy throat. "There was a dealer."

She nodded somberly. "Did you take any?"

I shook my head hard. "No. But I almost did. Travis needed me— so I didn't."

She nodded again. "You know better than anyone that this isn't really going to get it done for you. So, what made you this desperate?"

I stared at her blankly for a moment. I should have had an answer prepared, but I didn't. I blinked. "It was the mission." I waited a beat. She didn't move. "I knew how I'd feel after, and I didn't want to feel that way."

She stayed frozen for another moment, then shook her head. "You've never lied to me before. You've kept things from me, you've downplayed, but you've never lied."

I rubbed my sweaty palms against the sheets. "I'm not lying."

She stayed quiet, thinking. "Here's what we're going to do. I'm going to give you an acupuncture treatment, then you're going to get some rest. We can talk about this some more in the morning."

"There's nothing to talk about," I said, my frustration giving way to anger. "And I don't need to stay here. I can go to my room."

"You're not going anywhere until I can determine how at risk you are for a relapse." Her tone was firm. "And I can't do that until I know what pushed you into buying, and almost using, heroin."

I put my head in my hands, tugged at my hair. "It was only the mission."

"No, it wasn't." She didn't believe even a small part of what I was saying. "Now, lie down. I'm going to get rid of this." She waved the pouch.

I sunk into the pillow when the door shut. She gave me my acupuncture treatment when she came back and, after that, a melatonin tablet to help me sleep. It was the only thing that made my mind turn off.

My eyes were heavy when I woke up. So heavy that I didn't even think about where I was or what had happened the day before. When I could finally lift my lids and blink, I found Travis sitting in a chair against the wall. Then it all came screaming back to me. I closed my eyes again and rolled over, putting my back to him.

"Oh no." The chair scraped against the floor and I knew he'd slid closer. "You're not getting away that easily."

I squeezed my eyes shut tighter. "*Please.* Leave me alone."

"I'm not going anywhere until you talk to me." His voice was tinged with frustration and determination.

I sighed and rolled over. I could only imagine what I looked like; makeup rings around my bloodshot eyes, hair that had been perfectly curled hanging loosely.

He watched me, taking all of this in. "Jocelyn, what happened yesterday?"

"Why would you even care after what I said?" I asked, hoping that if I reminded him, he'd go away.

"Because now I know there was a lot more to it." He tilted his head to the side. "Something happened on that mission that made you want to buy drugs. You put both of our lives at risk, and I want to know *why*." My eyes locked on his. He was angry and he had every right to be, but there was some curiosity too. "We fought against each other for *years* and we shouldn't have. So, I'm giving you a chance to explain."

I didn't answer. I couldn't. I didn't know how.

"Who—who told you?" I pulled myself into a sitting position and tucked my knees to my chest, leaning with my back against the pillows.

He arched his eyebrows. "Who do you think?"

I shook my head. "She shouldn't have said anything. She's my doctor."

"She's worried about you," he said. "She said you wouldn't even tell *her* what caused this." I looked down at the end of my bed, trying to count the rungs on the footboard to avoid facing him. He leaned in closer to stay in my range of vision. "I could kill you right now, but you owe me an explanation."

I blinked, but this time I didn't look away. "I don't—I don't think I know how."

He sat back a little, and I could see his curiosity outweighing his anger. I wanted to tell him. After what I said to him—he was right, I *did* owe him. I opened my mouth, but the words never came. I shook my head and looked away again.

"Come on, Jocelyn." Travis let out a grunt of frustration, pushed himself out of the chair, and started pacing at the foot of my bed. "Talk to me!"

"I've never talked about this with anyone before!" I said, matching his frustration. He pivoted to a stop in front of the bed. I had his attention. I held his gaze, taking a moment to breathe. "Not March, not Simmonds, and not anyone at KATO who didn't make me."

I curled into myself even more. He stretched out his arms, gripping each end of the footboard rail, preparing himself. "Just *try*. That's all I'm asking."

I looked away for a minute, weighing my options. My stomach rolled and my muscles were tight enough to break a ship in half. But he was more than willing to camp out there until I finally cracked. On some level, that alone made it a little easier.

"It was the dress," I said, looking up at him. He seemed surprised that I was actually talking. "The only missions KATO put me in a dress for were more—*personal* than stealing or killing." I couldn't say what they made me do.

I watched Travis closely, gauging his reaction. "They made you sleep with the mark?" His voice was rigid, and on the edge of control. "How old were you?" His fingers squeezed the rail so tightly I was afraid his knuckles might cut through the skin.

I swallowed, remembering. "Fourteen the first time."

He exhaled heavily and looked at the ground. "How many times?"

"Six." I kept my voice even. "I was lucky."

His head snapped up. "*Lucky*?" he growled.

I nodded. "I was better at retrieval and assassination. They only needed me for—*that*—if there was more to the mission than other agents could handle."

"You never said anything about that kind of assignment before," he said. "You never even *hinted*."

I uncoiled slightly. "I'm not exactly proud of it." Travis's eyebrows shot up and I rolled my eyes. "I mean, I'm not proud of *anything* I did for them, but the other stuff—the guilt I can handle. At least in those situations I was in control of what happened to me." He watched me steadily, and I scooted halfway down the bed, somehow feeling like I needed to be closer for him to understand. "Everything I did for KATO makes me sick. The things I stole for them, the people I killed—all of it. But nothing made me feel more like property— more weak and dirty—than having to trade myself for the sake of an assignment."

Travis pursed his lips and nodded. He was still angry, but it wasn't at me anymore. "And that's exactly what we made you do."

I shook my head. "But it wasn't the same—or, it shouldn't have been. I knew this mission wouldn't end up the same way, I just didn't expect to have the reaction that I did. It wasn't until the dress."

He shook his head, disgusted. "If I had known you were one of ours—all those times we fought. I could have grabbed you. I could have brought you back."

He was so genuine that it tugged at my heart in a way I didn't know was possible—in a way I couldn't handle. So instead I smirked. "You would have had to beat me first."

It took him a moment, but eventually he smiled too. "I beat you the first time."

My smile widened. "And I shot you for that later."

Then he got serious again. "You could have killed me that time," he said slowly, like he was trying to work something out. "When we were both after the Project Pegasus files. You had the shot."

I took a slow breath through my nose. "You weren't a required target."

He looked me dead in the eyes. "I would have killed *you* if I had gotten the chance."

I swallowed. "I know."

He nodded, considering me. "You have a good heart."

I rolled my eyes. "I don't—"

"You *do*." He was fierce and firm, and it clearly wasn't up for debate. I clamped my jaw shut even though I didn't completely believe him.

Everything I'd done for KATO settled on the surface of my memories, which made it hard for him to be right. I twisted my hair off my neck, feeling suddenly overheated. Travis's face scrunched as he studied me. Something had caught his eye. I let my hair fall and it seemed to bring him back to reality.

"What?" I asked.

"Your scar," he said. "Did the same person who did that put you on those jobs?"

I subconsciously brushed my hair over the scar, not used to having it exposed. "It doesn't matter."

"Joss, please." I startled at the nickname. I hadn't been called that since before I was kidnapped. "We're talking about this. Just answer my questions so we don't have to ever again."

At first I didn't say anything, but after a moment I nodded. "It was the same person—more or less. It was my handler. A guy named Chin Ho. He was in charge of me from the time I was kidnapped. The missions came from higher up, but he had to sign off on all of them. He also trained me and drugged me and, if it was necessary, he would have killed me." I paused. "If they catch me, he *will* be the one to kill me."

"That's not going to happen." He dismissed the thought so casually, it was as if there was absolutely no possibility. I ran my hand through my hair and slid away from him. He was wrong. And he had to know he was wrong. But I was too tired to argue.

He straightened up and finally released the rail. "You should get some sleep." Then he considered me for a moment. "Dr. March is going to need to know what you told me. Do you want to tell her or do you want me to?"

I swallowed hard. I had never been someone to let other people do the hard job. But I had also never had the choice not to. And the truth was, I shuddered at the thought of telling anyone else that story. I bit my lip. "I don't want to do it again."

He nodded, his eyes level and understanding. "I'll take care of it." He moved to the door.

"Travis," I said before he could leave. "You're not—" He stopped short of the door, waiting patiently for me to find the right words. "You're not heartless. I didn't mean—I shouldn't have—"

"It's okay," he said, mercifully cutting me off. "I get it. But thank you." I nodded and he smiled. "Get some sleep."

I fell almost instantly into the soundest sleep I had ever had.

Chapter Twenty-Four

SCIENCE

D r. March cleared me the next day. We talked about the mission a little bit, but she didn't push, which I was grateful for.

I went late to the training room my first day back. The agents-only gym time was over and I had the place to myself, which is why I was surprised when the door opened and Sam walked in.

I stopped punching the bag and turned around. "What are you doing here?" I asked.

He had his backpack on with the straps loosened so that it hung low. He sauntered over toward me, like he owned the room. "I got kicked out of combat training," he said with a careless shrug.

I shook my head, but I had to smile. Most of the morning classes were taught by the same agents who teach the afternoon classes. "Did you piss off Harper again?"

"I might have." He dropped his backpack and leaned against the wall. "I'm supposed to go find Agent Lee, but I'm going to be in pretty big trouble, so I'm not in a rush."

I started hitting the punching bag again. "Like you would get in trouble with her."

He laughed. "Are you kidding me? I'm in trouble with her more than I am anyone in the building. I'm late to almost *every* class. Just because she doesn't give me a hard time about it doesn't mean I don't end up in detention."

I stared at him, astonished. "Then why are you late every day?"

"Because I have access to the agent-prep rooms, which I can only use when no one else is in there." He flashed a proud smile. "So, it's more than a fair trade-off."

"You've really got this place wired, don't you?" I asked.

He laughed. "Jocelyn, you have no idea." He started digging through his backpack. "Anyway, I'm glad I found you. I did some investigating on your mom while you were away."

I couldn't help the way my heart tensed. "What did you find?" I kept my voice calm and curious.

He pulled a file folder out of his bag and handed it to me. "These are some of the projects she worked on." Inside were pages and pages of weapons plans. My stomach roiled. From jewelry with built-in tranquilizers to nerve-gas grenades, my mom seemed to have been involved in it all.

"I don't know what her role was in these projects yet," Sam said, snapping me out of my trance. "All I could come up with so far is that she was involved with them, but I'll keep looking."

I nodded, trying to ignore the twisted feeling in my chest. "Thanks, Sam," I said, tearing my eyes away from the pages. "Really."

"Don't mention it," he said, zipping up his backpack. "I should get going. Agent Lee isn't going to be happy if she has to come looking for me."

"What exactly did you do to Agent Harper anyway?" I asked.

"That's the thing," Sam said. "I don't even know."

I arched an eyebrow at him. "Yeah, right."

He smiled. "Okay, fine. It might have had something to do with the punch I landed to his face when we were doing a hand-to-hand punching drill." My stress faded away and I laughed. Sam shrugged again. "Harper was walking by and my hand just—slipped."

"Did it at least feel good?" I asked.

Sam's face lit up. "Oh, better than you can even imagine." He put his backpack over his shoulders. "See you later, KATO girl. I'll let you know if I come up with anything else."

Later that night I flipped through the file Sam gave me again, but I couldn't stomach any more than that. At least, not until I knew more details. And it wasn't long before Travis gave me something new to think about. The first time I saw him after the medical wing had been when we crossed paths early Monday morning, three days after I was released. I could tell he wanted to say something, but I wouldn't give him the chance. Instead I asked him about when we were going start working on finding Eliza. We made plans to skip the afternoon training session and meet in the library when I was done with my classes.

I knew the library was on the top floor of the tech and training facility, but I'd never had a reason to go until now. It was expansive. Tables filled the front portion of the room, and behind that were shelves and shelves of books. Travis said there were some private rooms in the back that had access to the library's inventory along with the IDA's databases. Most of the tables were taken by either students studying or by agents who seemed to be flipping pages with intense concentration. I saw Gwen and Olivia working at a table nearby, and asked them to point me in the right direction. I started moving through the stacks, walking slowly, taking in each section until a voice stopped me.

"Are you kidding me?" I turned into one of the aisles to see Rachel glaring at me. "You've taken over every other place on campus. You had to come *here* too?"

I rolled my eyes. She had every right to hate me, but she didn't own the campus. "It's not *your* library," I said.

She stepped toward me. "All of this is mine." She was much closer than I was comfortable with, cornering me against the bookcase. "*You* don't belong here."

I met her eyes. She was trying to bait me. "You need to step back."

Instead she stepped closer. "You going to kill me if I don't? That's what you do, right? You didn't get me before so you have to finish what you started?"

"If that's what I wanted, you wouldn't have to ask." The more she invaded my personal space, the less patience I had.

She shoved me into the books. "You need to pay for the damage you've done. No one's made you!"

I pushed her off me, but I didn't attack. It was what she wanted. Though, apparently a push was all it took. She tried to punch me, but I dodged it and stepped back, putting some space between us. She moved for another hit, but we were interrupted before she could.

"What's going on here?" Travis asked, strolling casually in front of me, effectively forcing Rachel to keep her distance. He faced Rachel with his arms crossed, making it clear who he thought was responsible.

"You're defending *her*?" She was stunned. "You're picking the cold killer over *me*?"

I couldn't see his face, but his stance and voice were rigid. "You can go now."

The hurt in her eyes deepened. "I can't *believe* you!"

Travis didn't move a muscle. And after it became clear that he wasn't changing his mind, Rachel turned away from him and stormed out of the library. Travis didn't move even after she was gone. He stood eyeing the doors until he was sure she wasn't coming back. Then when he turned to me, it was with this mixed expression—like he didn't quite know what to make of me. "This way," he said, leading me back down the aisle. I was surprised he didn't have more questions, but when I looked back I saw that the handful of people in the room were watching, Gwen and Olivia included. We stalked to the back of the library where a row of doors lined the back wall. He found an empty room and didn't speak until the door was shut.

"Why did you let that happen?" he asked.

"*Let*?" He was blaming *me*? "*She* attacked me!"

"I saw." He was fairly calm, given the situation. "And you did nothing to stop her. So, why not?"

I glanced up at him. It was getting easier to tell him the truth. "Because I've hurt her enough."

His face softened. "You've never taken any of her shit before."

"If she says something to me, I'll say something back," I said. "But this was different."

I leaned against the table in the room and Travis came next to me. "You were in an impossible situation."

"I know," I said, nodding. "I wouldn't do things any differently. I did what I had to do. But that doesn't make it okay."

"Have you tried apologizing?" he asked.

I snorted. "How is an apology from me going to mean anything?"

He shook his head. "I don't know. But Rachel doesn't forget easily."

"Yeah," I said. "I figured that out."

"Look," he said. "I know this is none of my business, but have you ever talked to someone about—*everything* that's happened to you?"

I tilted my head, confused. "What do you mean?"

"I mean someone who can help you work through all of this."

I shook my head. "I don't want to work through it."

"Joss—"

"No." I was firm. "I don't want to get past any of this. Not while I can still end up back there."

"You won't." His face was sympathetic.

"I could." I looked right into his eyes, trying to make him understand. "I need to remember what they can do. I need to remember what's at stake and I need to use all of it to hurt them. I won't be able to do any of that if I get *past* it. I need to hold on to it for a little while longer."

He held my gaze, but his face didn't change. Then I pushed myself away from the table. "We have bigger things to worry about for now," I said.

"Right." He straightened up and gestured to the row of four computers along the back wall. "*These* are what we came here for. They have access to every file the IDA has. You need a level-six clearance to access the least secure files, which because of my special research project, I have." He logged on to a computer. "I got Simmonds to give you access too."

"Okay," I said, taking a seat next to him. "You look for anything science related. I'll go back through everything on KATO and see if I can pick out a connection you might have overlooked."

"Good plan." He started typing. "You want to look for the Cole database."

I pulled up the database while I told him everything I knew about KATO's scientific interests. It wasn't much, but neither of us knew what would be relevant. We'd gotten into a pattern of a few frantic keystrokes, followed by a minute of silence, then more typing. About an hour in, I noticed Travis had been quiet for five minutes. I glanced over and saw he was completely engrossed in something.

"What did you find?" I asked.

He jumped and turned to me, startled. Like he had forgotten about me. "Joss—did your—" He broke off, swallowed, then tried again. "Did your mom develop anything KATO would have an interest in?"

My head snapped in his direction. "What are you looking at?"

"I tried the scientific angle, like you said." He leaned back so I could get a better look. "And your mom came up."

After what Sam had given me I wasn't surprised that her name popped up, but I didn't expect to see it tied to science. I filled in Travis on everything I knew about my mom. It didn't seem directly relevant until now.

"So you think they killed her because—"

"They were done with her." I swallowed. "I've been trying to fig-ure out what weapon KATO made her build, but now it seems like I should be wondering how many she had a hand in." I rubbed the back of my neck.

"Stop," Travis said, sliding a hair closer. "We don't know enough about her work to try and guess. And as far as our records go, there wasn't any kind of advanced weapon development during your first five years at KATO."

I exhaled heavily. "But that doesn't make any sense," I said. "If she was good enough to hold on to for three years, she must have been useful to them. They wouldn't have gotten rid of her until she gave them what they wanted."

"We'll figure out how this all fits together," he said. "If her job was science related, it may even help us. Whatever your mom was working on is probably very different from what Dr. Foster's doing, but the one thing they both have in common is that neither of them wanted to be doing the work. Which means they were both likely to draw the process out as much as possible. If we can find out what your mom was doing and how much work she had done coming in, we might have a little bit of a better idea how patient KATO is willing to be."

I nodded. "And from there, we can figure out what kind of a time-table we're looking at for Dr. Foster."

"Exactly," he said. "We need to find out what your mom's job was at the IDA. Then we can see exactly how different or similar it is to Foster's."

"Sam seemed close to finding something out," I said, wheeling back over to my computer. "But for now let's see what else we can come up with on our own."

Travis and I hadn't found anything else helpful, but I didn't feel defeated. While we were researching, Simmonds had the tech team working on decrypting the drive with the new tech we'd brought back from Germany. Hopefully between the three of us we would end up with a more solid idea of where we should be looking.

I was so lost in thought, I hadn't realized Sam had shown up surprisingly early to Lee's class until he'd waved his hand in front of my face. I blinked a few times. "Oh," I said. "Hi."

He smirked. "Those deep thoughts wouldn't have to do with an interesting article you found yesterday, would they?"

The article. I quirked an eyebrow at him. "Seriously, how do you know these things?"

Sam smiled. "Trade secrets."

I rolled my eyes. "Of course. Do you need me to give you any kind of background?"

He waved me off. "I think I've pretty much got it figured out."

"How close are you to getting access to her job description?" I asked.

"I'm still couple clearance levels away, but I'm getting there."

"Is there any way you could put a rush on it?"

"Consider it done," he said. Then he got quiet for a moment. I could tell there was something else he wanted to say, but it took him a moment to work up the courage. "I know you didn't ask about this, but I've been looking into your father on the side. The search team isn't moving as fast as they'd like."

"That's fine," I said, my tone harsh.

"If you wanted I could get into it. See if I can find something—"

"Sam." I kept the anger out of my voice. He was only trying to help. "I need you to focus on my mom, okay? That's it."

He studied me, debating something, then shrugged. "Okay. Let me know if you change your mind."

"Thank you."

"Don't mention it," he said, pulling out his phone as Agent Lee took her place at the front of the room.

She looked at our corner and seemed startled. "Sam?" *Astonished* was actually a better word. "Samuel Lewis? Is it really you? You're early?"

Sam smirked. "Don't get too used to it, Agent Lee."

But Lee beamed. "Sam, this is the best day of my teaching career. If it never happens again, I can be satisfied knowing that, just once, Samuel Michael Lewis was on time for my class."

Sam smiled wider. "I'm so glad I could make you happy."

Lee laughed lightly. "You have no idea how much."

Agent Lee started her lesson and Sam turned back to his game.

"Why *are* you early, anyway?" I asked.

"The prep lab was booked a half hour before our class started, so I had to be out." He hadn't even looked up from his phone.

I tried to pay attention when Lee started teaching but my thoughts stayed with Sam and my mom. If anyone could find specifics about my mom it was him. And if we could do that, then just maybe we stood a real chance of getting to Eliza in time.

Chapter Twenty-Five

FIELD TRIP

I hadn't heard anything new from Simmonds the rest of the week, and it was taking everything I had not to check in with him regularly. Travis and I kept busy trying to find information on anything that would lead us to Eliza—including details about what my mom may have done for KATO. She was the only other person we knew of who had been taken like Dr. Foster had. Learning about her work could give us some idea of how much time we had to get to Eliza before KATO did anything with Foster's research. But we weren't having any success. At least, we weren't until Sam joined Travis, Nikki, and me at lunch on Monday.

"I was hoping I'd find you guys here," he said, making himself comfortable. He clearly had an agenda, not even bothering with hello. "I did some more digging into your mom's background." He spoke only to me as he spread out the folder he'd brought with him. "I tried looking off campus, through some more public records." He pulled out a tax return from twenty-three years ago. "It turns out she worked at Spencer Industries."

He gave me this pointed look, like this was supposed to be some big revelation. "I don't know what that means," I said.

Nikki stepped in to explain. "Spencer is one of the biggest scientific and industrial development companies in the country."

"I tried to hack their servers," Sam said, "but it looks like your mom's files are too old to be stored digitally."

"They're based in Wilmington," Nikki said, glancing from me to Travis.

I was starting to get it. "So we can go there and find out what she did for them?"

Travis nodded. "Yeah, we can."

I stuck a fork in my chicken. "I'll go to Simmonds."

"We'll come up with a plan and meet you in the atrium of the Operations Building," Nikki said. There was no question that they were coming with me.

I took the file from Sam and thanked him as I hurried out of the cafeteria.

I had to wait only a few minutes when I got to Simmonds's door. Once I was inside, I spelled out everything we had on my mom and what Travis and I were trying to do with the information.

Simmonds sighed when I finished. "I don't know anything for sure," he said. "But knowing what your mother did for us, I can guess what she did for KATO. And if I'm right, she started the entire project after she was taken."

I met his eyes evenly. "You know I need more than that."

"I do," he said. "But, if it's what I think it is, you're not going to like what you learn."

I forced my expression to stay neutral, ignoring the new weight that settled into my stomach. "I don't care." I was too close to walk away.

"Be that as it may, I've given you the relevant information, and your other motives for this are purely personal. This isn't a mission

I can authorize." I felt a knot twisting in my chest, but Simmonds continued before I could snap. "However, I think you're forgetting that you are not a prisoner here. You're an eighteen-year-old agent who has earned the right to leave campus if she wants to." He gave me a pointed look.

"Right," I said, understanding what he was getting at. "Thank you, sir." I ducked out of his office without another word.

"Did he sign off?" Travis asked when he saw me round the corner into the atrium.

"Unofficially, but yeah," I said. "Do we have a plan?"

"Not only do we have a plan, but we have everything we need to pull it off," Nikki said. According to Sam's file, we'd need to meet with a Dr. Rollins, who was my mom's supervisor at the time. We would pretend to be scientists interested in her work. It would give us the in we needed and a reason to ask specific questions about my mom. Travis and Nikki had already changed and Nikki had a shirt and blazer for me to throw on.

"I'm driving," Travis said, leading the way out. When we reached the parking lot behind the Operations Building, we found a surprise waiting for us. Sam was sitting in the backseat of Travis's locked car.

"What are you doing here?" I asked once Travis had gotten the door open.

"How did you even get in there?" Travis asked. His voice was laced with amazed indignation. "Did you hack my car?"

Sam smiled and twirled his phone in his hand. "Absolutely not, Agent Elton. I would never do something like that."

Nikki snorted and Travis's jaw tensed in agitation. I didn't try to hide my laugh.

"You're not coming with us," he said to Sam.

Sam turned to face him fully. "After all the work I put into this, do you think I'm going to stay here while you guys get the big reveal?"

Nikki gave him a one-shouldered shrug. "You *do* have classes."

"So does she," he said, pointing at me.

"She's already an agent," Travis said, crossing his arms. "She can get away with it."

"Just let him come," I said. "It's not like he'd pay attention in class anyway."

"And I can help you," Sam said. "I can get you in the building."

Travis arched his eyebrows. "We can get ourselves in."

"Anything you do without me is going to come with questions." He looked at each of us. "I can get you on Dr. Rollins's schedule and the building's security guest list."

I glanced at Nikki and Travis. "It *would* make things easier."

Travis eyed Sam, considering. "Fine," he said after a moment. "But if you get in trouble, none of us were involved."

"Of course not," Sam said, sinking back into his seat. He turned his attention back to his phone as the rest of us piled in. Nikki took the backseat, leaving the passenger seat for me.

"So," Sam said as Travis pulled out of the parking lot. "What kind of music do you have here?" I glanced back and saw him on his phone, scrolling through what I assumed was Travis's music collection.

Travis's eyes jumped to Sam in the mirror. "Stay away from my music."

The speakers filled with light rock music, and Travis's glare to the backseat intensified. Sam just sat there with the same cocky smile, his eyes twinkling. I couldn't help but laugh.

. . .

Despite the fun Sam had on the way over, he was all business when we pulled up to Spencer Industries. He had access to their system in less than a minute. "Do you have aliases you want to use?" he asked.

"Yeah," Travis said, handing over three ID cards.

I leaned closer. "Where did you get these?"

He shifted uncomfortably. "I had them made while you were talking to Simmonds."

"Without him signing off?"

He shook his head once. "Don't ask."

I glanced at Nikki, who rolled her eyes. "You don't want to know."

"You guys are good to go," Sam said, passing the IDs around. "Keep your phones on you. You have my number if you need me for anything."

"Oh, do we?" I couldn't keep the amusement out of my voice. He hadn't touched any of our devices.

Sam only smirked and sent us on our way.

Getting into the building was as easy as Sam said it would be. Once we were in, it wasn't any harder to get to the chemical engineering floor, which Dr. Rollins was apparently in charge of. My heart started to pound as I thought of all the chemical weapons my mom could have developed for KATO. The damage that could have been done. I pushed the thoughts away and focused on what we had to do.

Before long, we were standing outside Dr. Rollins's door.

"Nikki, you take notes," Travis said. "Get everything down so we can sort through it later." She nodded and pulled out a notebook. "Joss, you and I will ask the questions. We need to do everything we can to steer the conversation toward the specifics of your mom's research."

I took a deep breath. I'd been on research assignments like this before. Assignments on which I had to get information out of someone as casually as I could. But I never had this fluttering feeling in my stomach.

Travis knocked on the door. It opened quickly. Dr. Rollins was a gray-haired man who was probably close to retiring. He was flustered at first, since he had no memory of setting an appointment with us. But he was quick to recover and invite us inside, offering to do anything he could to help. He was patient, and seemed genuinely interested in helping us.

"So, you're looking to get in touch with Lexi Steely?" he asked.

"Yes," Travis said. "We came across some research she did while she was here and wanted to follow up. We're having a hard time tracking her down, though."

"I'm afraid I can't be too much help with that." He rubbed his jaw, thoughtfully. "Lexi was a very talented scientist. She'd look at a problem, see how everyone else was attacking it, and find a different approach. But unfortunately I haven't heard from her since she left."

I wasn't used to hearing about my parents like this. A sick, sad feeling settled in my stomach. I inhaled sharply. This was a mission, just like anything else, and it was time I started acting like it.

"Can you tell us anything about the work Lexi did while she was here?" I asked.

His brow furrowed, pensive. "She started working here about twenty-five years ago. She wasn't here long—I think it might have been only a year—but the work she did was incredibly impressive. She started with a few smaller projects, but it wasn't long before she was assigned to the bigger development teams. She set herself apart quite easily."

"What type of chemical engineering was her specialty?" I asked.

"She coordinated across a couple different labs, but her strength was definitely in pharmaceutical development," he said. My stomach plummeted.

"Drug development?" Nikki asked, looking up from her notebook. "Really?"

"Oh, absolutely," Dr. Rollins said with a nod. "She was on the verge of a major breakthrough on a cancer treatment drug when she left. In fact, I assumed that was why you were here. We used her work as a basis for most of our advancements in that area for several years after."

He kept talking, but I had stopped listening. I was too busy fighting the urge the throw up. If drug development was my mom's strength, I had no doubt what KATO had used her for.

Travis met my eyes, and I knew he had put the pieces together too. He wrapped up the meeting as quickly as he could after that, thanking Dr. Rollins profusely for his time. I followed Nikki down the hallway, and Travis fell into step next to me, keeping a cautious eye in my direction. Despite the way everything was turning inside of me, I knew, this time, no one could tell by looking at me. This was a secret I desperately wanted to keep.

Sam peppered us with questions the whole ride back, while Nikki and Travis took turns answering or deflecting, depending on the question. But I barely noticed. Everything around me was a muted haze. It was all I could do to keep myself together.

. . .

Our group dispersed when we got back to campus. Sam hurried to make up for lost time in the agent prep labs, and Nikki ran off to the training session. It took me a minute to even consider the fact that I had to get out of the car. I reached for the door, but Travis grabbed my other arm.

"Hey," he said. "Are you okay?"

I nodded.

He shifted in his seat, angling himself so he was facing me better. "I'm not just talking about how you're feeling. I'm talking about your—cravings."

Cravings for a drug that my *mom* created. I looked away, balling my fists to keep my hands from shaking.

"Jocelyn." I turned back to him. His expression was intensely puzzled and concerned.

I shook my head. "Don't be nice to me."

"What?" His forehead creased. "Why not?"

I looked him dead in the eyes. "Because if you're nice to me, I might lose it."

His face softened. "Maybe you need to."

I drew a tight, shaky breath. "*Please.* Don't be nice to me."

He was quiet for a long moment, then said, "Okay."

Neither of us moved. And after a minute, I couldn't take the silence. "I'm just so—*angry*," I said. "For years the thought of my parents was what got me through KATO. Knowing that they worked for the IDA meant that if I could just get out, then there might be someplace safe to go. I thought they saved me." I raked my hand across my scalp. "But my mom—she did this. She was supposed to—she wasn't supposed to put something like that in me. And I hate her for it."

I stared out the windshield at the brick wall ahead of us. He didn't say anything until he was sure I was finished. When he did, his voice was soft. Almost as if he were afraid he might scare me away. "You have to be realistic, though. She probably had no idea it would be used on you. And from what you've said, I bet they'd threatened to kill you if she didn't develop it. Exactly like they did to Dr. Foster." I finally looked at him. "Not only that, but that drug was the only way KATO could control you. What would they have done to you if they couldn't?"

I swallowed hard. "They would have killed me."

Travis nodded "She saved you. It may not have been pretty or ideal, but you're alive. Now you have a chance to do something about it."

I took deep breath, letting his words sink in, then I found myself nodding. "Okay."

His eyebrows shot up. "Yeah?"

"Yeah." I felt myself relax a fraction. I didn't know whether I believed what he was saying or whether I just wanted to.

Both of our pagers chirped before either of us could say anything else.

"Simmonds wants to see us," Travis said, glancing at his.

I looked to my own pager. This had to be about the files. I couldn't think of anything else that would need our attention. A short surge of anticipation forced everything else to the background. "All right." I pushed my door open with a renewed sense of purpose. "Let's see what he's got for us."

Chapter Twenty-Six

SECRETS

gents," Simmonds said, nodding at each of us as we walked through the door. "Did you find what you were looking for?" he asked me.

I nodded once. "We did." He gave me a hard, sympathetic look, but I didn't want to talk about it anymore. "What did you need us for?" I asked.

He took the hint and moved on. "The tech team decrypted the rest of the drive. I haven't had a chance to look at the data yet, but it's being uploaded to my computer as we speak."

I drew a sharp breath, hoping this would give us everything we needed. Travis and I both stood in front of the chairs by the desk, waiting. I drummed my hand against my thigh, finding it impossible to keep still.

Simmonds started typing on his computer, sending the files to the empty screens behind him as he opened them. I scanned the documents quickly. They were too big for a cipher, and had already been translated to English. "These are mission files," I said. My old code name caught my eye. "And some of them are mine?"

"It looks like it," Travis said, taking a step closer to me.

Simmonds clicked on one of my files. It was a mission that I'd been on within the last year to a research lab in India. I'd had to get a specific type of titanium.

I swallowed hard. I had a guess where this was going. "Were all of these missions retrievals?"

Simmonds flipped through a few files. "It looks like they were."

Most of it was a mix of chemicals and metals that could be expected to come together for some kind of explosive, but then there were random things as well. Produce from specific fields in specific counties, minerals from specific mines, sand from a specific beach, and everyday chemicals that shouldn't play too much of a role compared with the more combustible elements.

"These have to be for Foster's weapon," I said.

"I would say you're correct," Simmonds said, staring at his computer. His eyes met ours for half a moment before he sent the image to the screen behind his desk. "I believe we've found out what KATO intends to do with Dr. Foster's research."

It was plans for a missile. The bottom corner had a date that was six months old. "How long would it take to build something like this?" I asked.

Simmonds shook his head. "We really have no way of knowing."

"But I would think if there are plans for a missile, and a record of these retrievals, it would mean that Foster's close to getting the components of his weapon together," Travis said.

"I guess now we have a better idea of their timeline," I said, letting my bitterness seep out.

"Their target has to be South Korea, right?" Travis turned to me for confirmation.

"Absolutely," I said, nodding. "But they still need a way to move an army across the DMZ." The land between the two Koreas was littered with land mines and explosives. It was called the Demilitarized Zone—or the DMZ. "They'd use the missile to take out the South's army and leaders, which would disrupt their defense system, then the North would send their people across the DMZ to complete the invasion. They can't move on any of this until they have a way across."

Simmonds eyed me steadily. I didn't know what he was thinking, but I was sure I wasn't going to like it.

"What is it?" I asked. I couldn't handle that look.

He sighed. "A little over a year ago, a Japanese research lab was doing testing on hovercraft technology." He paused for a beat, and seemed to be bracing himself. "It was referred to as Project Pegasus."

My limbs went numb and my stomach dropped to my feet. I had stolen the plans for KATO, shooting Travis in the process. I met Travis's eyes, an expression of devastating understanding crossed his face.

I lowered into one of the chairs as the reality sank in. "I did this," I said. I hunched over, putting my head in my hands. "If this works and they get a hold of South Korea, they'll pick another country to target. This could effectively start World War III and *I* gave them the technology."

"You did what you had to at the time," Travis said, his voice so quiet I was sure only I could hear it.

I tilted my head enough to see him through my fingers. "That really doesn't help."

Travis pinched the bridge of his nose and turned back to Simmonds. "Sir, what do we do about this?"

"We need to split our resources between working out a plan to put a stop to KATO, and detecting any kind of weaponized attack coming out of North Korea."

I straightened up, my eyes widened. "Detecting an attack? By the time that happens it'll be too late."

"We don't have a choice," Simmonds said. "They have all the tools they need to pull this off, and they've done an exceptional job keeping it quiet. At this stage, the only way we'd find out anything for sure is if we put people inside that agency. If there was any chance at success I might take that risk, but it's a suicide job."

I stood up, pacing, trying to think of a solution. "I can find out," I said. Just saying the words sent a rush of fear through me. But I had to do this. "I'll get in touch with them or—something. I'll find a way to get what we need."

"How can you possibly get that information without tipping off that you're on our side?" Travis asked.

I bit my lip. "I don't know," I said. "But I did this, so I have to fix it. I'm the only person who has a shot."

"Except there's every chance that it won't work out," Travis said. "And then they'll come after *you*."

"I don't care." And right then I didn't. This was my fault and I had to do something. I was too afraid to think about what it could mean. "They used me to make this happen. I can't just sit here and watch."

"Jocelyn," Simmonds said. "I *promise* you we will find a way to handle this. We simply need some time."

"And what if we don't have it?" I asked. "For all we know, Foster's putting the finishing touches on the missile right now."

Travis glanced at me out of the corner of his eye and shook his head. "No. You're not doing this."

I rounded on him. This was about so much more than me. "I came here to hurt KATO. Now, this wasn't exactly what I planned, but this is how it's happening. I'm the only person in this agency that KATO thinks they can trust. I can come up with some cover story. Something to make it seem like their information is important to my assignment."

"They'll know something is up the second you start asking questions," Simmonds said. "And we'll lose any chance at building our access to their internal database."

"And what good has that done?" I asked. "We know, what? Five side operations? Have you gotten *anything* relevant?" He stared at me silently, as if I were someone he'd never met. "That's what I thought."

"*Jocelyn*—" Travis was angry, but I didn't care.

"No!" I snapped. "I'm doing this."

I left the office, ignoring Travis, who was trying to negotiate with me. I needed to get away. I needed to think and come up with some kind of plan. I was terrified, but my determination kept moving me forward. I needed to act before I lost that. I had made it downstairs, and a hallway away from the building's door, when I heard Travis calling after me. "Jocelyn!"

I didn't respond. I was about to round the corner into the atrium when he tried again.

"Goddamn it, Jocelyn!" He must have sprinted to catch up to me, because the next thing I knew he had a hand on my arm, pulling me to a stop. "Do you even realize what you're risking?"

I tried to tug away from him, but his grip was too firm. "Let me go."

"No!" The vein in his neck throbbed and I knew he was at his breaking point. "If you try and get more information from KATO they're going to know you're not working for them anymore. Do you get that? Do you *want* to end up back in their facility with a needle in your arm? Because that's where you're headed!"

"I don't need to be told what could happen to me." I yanked my arm away from him. "This is *my* call, not yours."

"Joss—"

I rounded the corner before he could say another word and came very quickly to a stop. We weren't alone. There were about a dozen agents gathered in the atrium. Nikki, Cody, and Rachel were among them. Travis's outburst hadn't been quiet, and judging from looks on their faces they had heard the whole thing. I felt Travis next to me and pivoted to face him, breathing heavily.

For the first time at the IDA I made no attempt to hide what I was feeling. I felt the anger and betrayal sprawled all over my face and I didn't care. All of the uncertainty about KATO made this feel so much worse. I was supposed to be able to count on him like I never could on anyone else.

Travis started at me, his eyes wide and apologetic. He opened his mouth to say something, but I didn't want to hear it. I turned my back on him and walked out the doors, moving as quickly as I could across the courtyard without running. Travis hurried after me. "Jocelyn."

I kept moving.

"Jocelyn, I am *so* sorry." He stepped in front of me.

"Get out of my way." I wouldn't look him in the eye. I couldn't.

"Joss, *please*."

I tried to push past him, but he grabbed my arms, and I reacted. I kneed him in the stomach and twisted him to the ground, putting him behind me and out of my way. He didn't try to get up. He just looked at me with one of the saddest expressions I had ever seen. I turned on my heel and left him there.

Chapter Twenty-Seven

UNWELCOME PERSISTENCE

I paced my room for fifteen minutes after I had stormed out of the Operations Building. I needed to calm down enough to think, but I couldn't. I had never trusted *anyone* like I had trusted Travis, and he had managed to not only blow my cover but spill one of my biggest secrets. It didn't matter that it wasn't intentional. I exhaled steadily and made myself shift gears. It felt better to focus on what I could do to get to KATO.

There was no way I could let KATO know the IDA had the missile plans, but maybe if I hinted that the IDA knew something and asked a few follow-up questions, they might give me a clue about their timetable. It wasn't any kind of a solid plan, but it would mean I was *doing* something, which at that point was what I needed. I had yanked open my door, prepared to head out and get to a computer, when I found myself face-to-face with Simmonds.

His eyes narrowed. "I think it would be best if we talked before you went anywhere."

I looked away from him, doing my best to bite my tongue. I knew he was planning to hold me back, so I really wasn't all that interested in what he had to say. But he didn't give me an option.

"Inside," he said, gesturing to the room behind me.

I took a step back, defeated, and he followed me in.

"You cannot expect me to do nothing here," I said, before he had the chance to talk. "Not when I'm the only one in a position to act." I swallowed. "And not when I'm responsible."

"You *aren't* responsible." His face was tight, and his words strong, as if he were willing me to believe him. "If you didn't get those plans, they would have sent someone else."

"But Travis would have beaten that person."

"You don't know that," he said. "Ultimately, you are not at fault for the actions of irresponsible people. What they are choosing to use these plans for is out of your control."

I shifted back on my heels. I didn't agree with him, but I didn't want to fight about it. "I *have* to do something."

"And I need you to wait." I opened my mouth to argue, but Simmonds talked over me. "This is a major threat, Jocelyn. You are not equipped to handle it on your own. This isn't even something the IDA normally deals with. Traditionally I would pass it over to CIA or another agency."

"Then why don't you—?"

"Because we *can't*." His tone was sharp and final enough to force me quiet. "The only reason we know this is really happening is because of *you*." He held my eyes for a moment. "Dr. Foster's research was never published, which means no one really knows what it entails. And that man is so revolutionary, I'm not even sure another scientist would understand the concepts without Foster there to explain them. So those plans and that list of retrievals don't add up to a definitive threat on their own."

I pinched the bridge of my nose trying to process this, but Simmonds continued. "To anyone else, North Korea is merely building a missile, which isn't good, but it also wouldn't be their first. Nothing about this shows any sign of being an immediate issue without Foster, and as far as most of the world is concerned, he's been taken by the Chinese. You're the only person who is in a position to tell us otherwise. And while your word is enough for me, it isn't going to be enough for any government official in *any* country to risk people and resources without more concrete intel. Not with your history. Which means this is up to us."

I felt my resolve wearing down. He was making too much sense. "Then what are we going to do?"

"Right now, I need some time." He paused briefly, and this time I didn't try to interrupt. "We've only ever had four missions into North Korea in the history of the IDA. We contain them from the outside because getting in and out is so challenging. And while I agree that this time it's worth it, we are not moving in until we have a *solid* plan. If we don't, they'll win anyway, and if that happens we'll lose some of our best people. People I will need to prevent this from spreading beyond South Korea."

I exhaled heavily. "How much time do you need?"

"Give me forty-eight hours," he said. "If I don't have something feasible by then, we can reevaluate our strategy."

I bit my lip. I hated the thought of waiting, but Simmonds was right. This was bigger than I could take on with the situation as it was. "Okay," I said, nodding. "Forty-eight hours."

Simmonds gave me a nod of thanks, and then left me to simmer in peace.

· · ·

I couldn't sleep that night. I intended to stick to my forty-eight-hour promise, but that didn't make it any easier to turn my mind away from all of the new developments.

My alarm went off at seven the next morning and I silenced it after the second beep. I closed my eyes for the first time all night and tried to find the strength to get out of bed. When I finally did get up, I took as long as possible getting ready, as if it would somehow make time move slower. I was hoping to avoid everyone, so I didn't get to breakfast until after the morning workout and classes had started. But I wasn't that lucky. I had just gotten my food when I saw Travis out of the corner of my eye moving in my direction. Fortunately the cafeteria was practically empty.

"I need to talk to you," he said, coming to a stop on my right.

I gripped my tray tighter, moving purposefully toward a table. I couldn't deal with this now. Not when KATO could be shooting off a missile at any second.

"I know you can hear me." His voice had an edge to it. One that I was pretty sure he didn't have a right to.

"Then take the hint," I said through gritted teeth.

"Jocelyn—"

"No!" I slammed my tray down on the table "You don't get to say my name like that." I looked him in the eye for the first time since yesterday. "I *trusted* you."

"I know." I heard the regret in his voice, but it didn't affect me. "But it's going to be fine. We can still protect your cover, and no one cares about the other—"

I nearly dropped him again. "Don't give me that. It was *my* secret. Not yours."

A door opened behind Travis, and I saw Cody, Rachel, and Nikki fall in behind him. I wasn't sure how much they had heard, but I knew it was more than I wanted them to.

Travis started to speak again, but I turned away from him before he could get a word out.

"You need to get away from me," I said. He didn't move. "*Now.*"

I watched him, staring him down until he finally left the room.

"So," Cody said, coming closer. "What he said yesterday was true?"

I glared at him over my food. "What, were you all waiting for me?"

"More like waiting for him," Cody said. "For what it's worth, he feels like shit about it. I tried to get more out of him, but he wouldn't give anything else up. It didn't even matter that he already let things slip. And Simmonds benched him until further notice."

I bit my lip and turned away. "That doesn't make me feel any better."

"Yeah," he said. "I figured it wouldn't." He sighed. "I doubt this will mean much to you either, but I'm sorry for everything. You really hurt Rachel, and I wanted to have her back. But I should have known what it meant for Travis to have yours. So, I'm sorry I didn't listen to him. Or to you."

I swallowed hard and nodded. Cody left after that and Rachel followed him.

Nikki lingered behind. She waited for me to acknowledge her, but I started eating instead, not at all in the mood to talk. She only let herself be ignored for so long. She sat down across from me and pulled my tray right out from underneath me. I tugged it back, but she didn't let go. "Nikki, come on."

"No," she said. "*You* come on." Her face was angry and set. "I get that there are some things you had to keep secret, but now that it's out there, you're hiding from me? From *me*?" She paused, giving me a chance to talk, but I didn't have any words. "I've given you a lot of slack because you needed *someone* to. And because I believed you were a good person, regardless of what anyone thought. You owe me."

I looked away for a moment. She was right about all of it. "This isn't really something I want to talk about."

Nikki leaned closer. "But it's something *I* want to talk about it." I met her eyes. "You're my friend, and I want to know what happened to you."

I sighed. She was begging for some kind of explanation, and she deserved that much. "You heard the basics," I said. "KATO made me strong so they could use me, and then they weakened me so no one else could. They drugged me so I'd *need* them." I took a breath. "I *hated* that I needed them so much."

She grabbed my hand. "But you beat them," she said. "Why was this such a big secret?"

"I haven't beaten anyone yet," I said. "I'm working on something bigger, and there's a lot at stake."

She didn't fish for any more details. "I hope I don't even have to say this," she said. "But just so you know, if you're working on any kind of plan, you can count me in."

I blinked, surprised, but nodded. Things were still up in the air with Simmonds, but that wasn't going to last for too much longer. And if he didn't have a plan, I'd need one of my own.

. . .

By the time I'd gotten to Lee's class, I'd had my fill of pity. Since she had already known the truth it made my first class a little bit easier. It also helped that the kids didn't know anything, with Sam, of course, the exception.

He slipped into his seat just a few minutes late as always. "I guess you've had an interesting twenty-four hours." He took his phone out, only bothering to give me half a glance.

I didn't even question how he knew. "That's one way to put it."

He nodded, but still didn't look up. "Well, just so you know, I meant what I said earlier. If you need help with—*anything*—let me know."

"You're the second person who's told me that today," I said.

He flashed me a knowing, wicked smile. "Nikki and I might have talked."

I sighed. "We're in a little bit of a holding pattern right now."

He shrugged. "Okay. But if it's the upper management you're worried about, I can help you out. I know a few backdoor tricks to keep people off your scent long enough to get you into the field. At least in theory. I've never had the chance to try them out."

I wasn't quite thinking anything that big, but it was nice to have options. "Are you ready for that kind of mission?"

Sam leaned back, finally making eye contact. "Honestly? I have no idea. But you're better off with me than with no one."

"Thanks, Sam." I bit my lip to hide a smile. "I'll let you know."

He gave me a one-shouldered shrug, slid back into his chair, and put his attention back on his phone. I did my best to listen to Agent Lee, who was explaining the basics of aerial assessments, but the only thing in my mind was KATO. If Simmonds couldn't come up with anything new in two days I was, at the very least, making contact—regardless of the risks.

Shockingly, my classes had ended up being the relaxing part of my day. If the other teachers had learned the truth, they didn't show it. Agent Reynolds still seemed to think I was up to something, and Agent Scott ignored me as he always did. And at this point I was pretty sure I could end world hunger and I would still be on Agent Harper's shit list. It wasn't until the afternoon training session that I faced any kind of challenge.

Nikki had offered to work out with me, but I wasn't looking to hold back. My thoughts kept coming back to KATO, and Travis, and I wanted to pound something without having to be careful. I took to my corner with a punching bag and did my best to turn off my mind.

I saw Travis on the other side of the room watching me. We made eye contact for the briefest of moments, and then I turned back to my bag, hitting it so hard my hands stung. Travis took a step in my direction, but Cody stopped him with a hand on his chest. They were too far away for me to hear exactly what was being said, but I could imagine it had something to do with me. From what I could tell, Cody was trying to talk Travis out of something, but Travis's face was set.

I shook my head and tried to focus on what I was doing, but it was getting harder and harder to keep my attention where it needed to be. And then Travis grabbed my bag. I punched it hard one more time, pushing it into him. He grunted and glared at me, but he was smart enough to keep his mouth shut.

"When are you going to get it?" I asked. "There's nothing I want to say to you."

His jaw tightened. "You're going to have to talk to me eventually."

"You want to bet?" I punched the bag again, and again he grunted.

"I'm sorry, okay?" He dropped his voice so I was the only one who could hear him. The emotion in his eyes was so raw it startled me.

I shook my head hard. "No," I said. "I can't do this." It was more a reminder to myself than it was to him, but he wasn't deterred regardless.

"Jocelyn—"

I punched the bag one more time. Harder than I had punched it all day. Hard enough that he couldn't keep the pain to himself anymore.

"Goddamn it!"

He let the bag go and hunched over, but I didn't care. I spun away from him and found another punching bag. Travis didn't interrupt me again.

Chapter Twenty-Eight

NEW REQUEST

I met with Simmonds after my classes the following day. He still had few more hours on the clock, but his time was almost up. He told me he didn't have anything he was ready to share yet, but stressed that he was close. "In the meantime," he said, "I think it's time for you to reach out to KATO."

I froze, not convinced I'd heard him right. "You're sure?"

"Yes." He eyed me steadily. "But I don't want you to say anything that might give you away. Just feel them out and see what you can learn."

"Yes, sir." I rubbed my sweaty palms on my thighs and tried to keep the emotion out of my voice.

"I want to see what you're planning on telling them before you send it." He seemed to sense how eager I was. I agreed quickly and hurried out of his office to get to work.

It took longer than I would have liked to get my message together, but when I went back to Simmonds an hour later, he only made a few modifications before signing off.

The IDA has vague details that something big is coming out of our headquarters in the near future. They are turning to me for intel and answers. What should they be told? Is there anything I need to know?

The goal was to gently probe for information under the guise of relaying newly uncovered intel. Even if I only learned what KATO wanted the IDA to think, we would have something to go on. Ideally their response would even give me a window to ask some follow-up questions. But first, I needed them to buy this enough to answer me at all.

I found it hard to breathe when I finally sat down in front of the computer, but I did everything I could to focus on my determination and ignore the fear. I knew I was doing the right thing, but the prospect of ever ending up back in KATO was more terrifying than I typically allowed myself to acknowledge. And now it felt entirely too close.

My hands were numb when I logged on. It was all I could do to find the right website. First I checked for any messages KATO might have sent me. What I found made my blood ice.

I had to reread it five times to process what they were asking. When my heart finally caught up to my brain it was pounding. I logged off the computer and raced back to Simmonds's office, pushing open the door without bothering to buzz. Nikki was in there with him and they both looked up abruptly when I entered.

"Agent Steely—" Simmonds started.

"KATO wants me back." They both stared at me. Simmonds kept his face calm, but his eyes were intense. Nikki, on the other hand, looked horrified.

"You can't go," she said.

"If I don't, they'll know I've turned." I may have been willing to risk them finding out, but now it felt like there was no way out of this without them learning the truth.

"Why do they want you?" Simmonds asked.

"They didn't give a reason," I said. "But they seemed to think I'd be coming back here. So it's something big enough to risk pulling me out, and it's also something that has them sure they'll need me as their double agent once this is over."

I looked only at Simmonds. His face was set. "I don't like where this is going."

"This is my in," I said. I gripped the back of one of the chairs. "I'll come up with a plan." He still didn't seem convinced. "If I don't go back, my cover will be blown. You wouldn't agree to this before because it would give me away. Now it'll maintain my cover *and* put me in a position to stop this from the inside."

"And what if you can't stop it?" Simmonds asked.

I took a deep breath. "Then I'll stay there until they send me back."

"*What?*" Nikki leaned in, trying to meet my eyes, but I refused. I knew what it would mean to stay at KATO, but it was the best move.

"If they need me there now, but are planning to return me, then we can assume this will be while they take over South Korea," I said. "They'll win that battle, but while I'm there I can find out the rest of their plan. Then, when they send me back I'll know everything we need to stop them from growing. I can bring back proof—something you can pass on."

Simmonds stayed quiet, studying me, and I could tell he was seriously considering my idea. Nikki noticed too.

"No," she said. "Absolutely not. This is *crazy*."

After a moment, Simmonds spoke. "I'm not agreeing to this yet, but come up with a detailed plan and we can discuss it."

I nodded quickly, again focusing my energy on my determination. "Thank you, sir." I headed out of the office, but stopped short of the door and turned back to Nikki. "Don't say a word to Travis."

Her eyes hardened, and I hurried out to work on a plan.

I had a plan mostly put together by the time I went to bed. Once I was back at KATO, I could use the vents to get the intel and access I needed to shut down their operation. If I played it right, KATO would think it was a system malfunction and send me back to the IDA while they work on a fix. From there, the IDA will have the intel to contain the situation. I contemplated going right to Simmonds with this, but I wanted to go over everything a few times before I did. I needed every detail completely set if I wanted him to sign off. I was tempted to stay up and iron things out, but I needed my mind sharp.

Of course, that didn't mean my brain would turn off just because I wanted it to. I had another dream. This one was about what would happen if they caught me while I was back inside. My handler, Chin Ho, filled me with Gerex again, and tied me to a chair. He burned me, but this time it was for longer than I was trained for. He was pulling my fingernails out when I woke up.

It was still pretty early in the night, and I couldn't fall back asleep after that. I went over to the training facility to try and work off some energy. I beat the bag until my knuckles ached so much that I was surprised they didn't bleed through the wrapping. I was so locked in I didn't hear the training room door open.

"I've been looking for you everywhere." I spun around to find Travis standing at the threshold. "I never would have thought you could possibly be this stupid." Judging by the look on his face, Nikki had told him everything. He closed in on me quickly, and I was pretty sure it was because he knew I was going to run. I tried to get away from him, but he matched my every step. He was more determined than I'd ever seen him on any mission or training session.

"*Stop,*" I said, trying to maneuver around him.

He shook his head. "Not this time."

I stopped moving and he did the same. He rocked on the balls of his feet, ready and waiting for me to make the next move. I faked to the left and charged to the right, but he didn't fall for it. He caught my upper arms and backed me all the way into the corner, pinning me to the wall. I lifted my back, and tried to head-butt him, but he dodged it. I struggled against him, desperate to get away. I knew I didn't really have a shot, but it didn't matter.

"Knock it off." He kicked my instep, pushing his toes into my feet and pressing them flat against the wall. He dug his knees into mine with enough force to make me cry out, but I still didn't quit. I balled my fists and used the limited movement I had to punch him in the gut.

"*Fuck.*" Instead of making him move away, the pain forced him to lean in even farther toward me. His face was in my neck and his grip was even tighter than it had been. "*Stop fighting me.*" He grunted and forced himself straight so he could look me in the eye. "I'm not going anywhere until I say what I came here to say."

I stopped moving and squared my jaw. "I don't want to hear it."

"I don't care." He loosened his grip slightly, but kept my feet pinned just as tight. "You need to."

I squirmed again and he tightened his hands, pressing me back into the wall hard enough to make me grunt.

"I'm not leaving, and I'm not letting you go until you hear me out." He wasn't being mean, but the determined desperation in his face made it clear that he wasn't about to back down.

I closed my eyes and let out a deep breath. I was still tense, and my heart was pounding angry and hard, but I stopped struggling. He eased up on the tension in my legs and, after he was sure I wasn't going to run, he freed my arms. He still didn't have a ton of confidence in me, though. Only enough to press his palms into the wall next to my biceps, caging me in. He was much closer than I was comfortable with.

"Then talk," I said. My voice was so soft and hoarse I almost didn't recognize it.

He kept his face even for a moment, and when he spoke, it was with more genuine emotion than I could understand. "First of all, I am *so* sorry I let your secret out." I swallowed, and after giving me a moment to sit with that, he continued. "I thought we were alone and I was louder than I should have been. You just had that same reckless look that you had on our first mission and I knew you were driven enough to risk yourself." He glanced away. "You took off so fast. The *only* thing on my mind was getting through to you."

"Well," I said, "you definitely got my attention."

He sighed and dropped one of his arms. "I never meant to do it that way. But you're my partner, and I take that seriously. It's my job to keep you safe in and out of the field." He paused and met my eyes. "You've saved me twice now, so I owe you that much."

I crossed my arms. "You didn't tell anyone anything else, right?" His eyebrows knitted together, confused. "About the *other* things I had to do?"

His eyes hardened. "How could you think I would tell someone that?"

"You promised not to tell anyone about the Gerex or my double-agent status either," I said. "I didn't know what you'd say now that the secret's out."

I couldn't handle looking at the hurt on his face. I focused on the worn blue mat and his black sneakers, feeling ashamed for even asking.

"Jocelyn."

I stared intently at the ground, waiting for him to continue.

"Look at me." His voice was so soft it made my stomach flutter.

I lifted my head and met his eyes. They were so open that they completely drew me in, and wouldn't let go. "I would *never* tell anyone about that. It's not even close to being the same thing."

I exhaled slowly. "I didn't think you would. But after what happened I couldn't be sure."

"Be sure." He waited for me to nod. "Now," he said. "About your latest suicide mission to North Korea."

I shook my head. "Nikki shouldn't have said anything."

"She absolutely should have." He lowered his arm and stepped back, giving me a little bit of room. "I would have killed you both."

"I have to go back," I said. "This is our in. Besides, they'll know I've turned if I don't. Wasn't that your point before? I shouldn't do anything that would blow my cover?"

"It's entirely different and you know it." His jaw tensed. "It's one thing to take on a risky assignment. It's another when maintaining your cover means putting yourself in front of them, let alone the fact that you're considering staying." He shook his head. "The number of ways they can figure out you've turned is more than I can list. And even if they don't, what if they decide not to let you come back to us?"

"Do you think I *want* to go back there?" I asked. He didn't say anything. "The idea that they'll pull me back in—that I'll end up back under their control, shot up with Gerex, scares me so much that I can't get it out of my head." I felt the emotion bubbling in the back of my throat and I had to pause to get myself together. Travis noticed and stepped back, letting me get some air. I pressed on. "And all of that is nothing compared with how afraid I am of what they'll do if they work out that I've been lying to them. I've been dreaming about them since I got here and about what would happen to me. About what *has* happened to me. They're in my mind *constantly*." I swallowed. "But I can't let them conquer a country using intel I collected for them, and do *nothing* to stop it."

He watched me, taking all of this in. "I didn't know you've had dreams."

"I didn't want you to," I said. "I didn't want *anyone* to."

"You know this isn't your fault," he said. "No one around here blames you."

"That doesn't matter, even if it were true." I looked him square in the eyes. "I blame me."

He didn't move for a moment, then he let out a deep sigh. "I'm not talking you out of this, am I?"

I shook my head. "I need to do this."

He inhaled slowly and nodded. "Fine. But you're not staying with them. I'm leading your rescue team."

My eyes locked on him. "What? No, you can't—"

He tipped his head. "You can't seriously think, after the number of times you saved my ass, that I'm letting you go back in there without making sure that you're coming out. If you don't let me do that much, I'll do everything I can to keep you here."

I blinked a few times, trying to adjust to the idea. Something in my chest loosened at the prospect of knowing I had a chance to make it out. Though I still had my share of concerns. "It won't work," I said. There were too many complications. "And besides, aren't you benched?"

"I don't care. This isn't happening any other way," he said. "Let's go. Simmonds is still here." He stalked over to the door without another word. I stayed stuck in place, trying to catch up to the conversation. Travis turned back around when he got to the exit. "Are you coming?"

"Right." I hurried after him. I didn't like the idea of involving anyone else in this, but the relief of not going into this alone overpowered everything else.

Chapter Twenty-Nine

GEARING UP

The walk over to Simmonds's office had pushed my nerves. Strangely, Simmonds didn't seem surprised to see us.

"We have a plan," I said.

He looked back and forth at the two of us, his eyes resting on Travis for half a second longer. "Okay," he said. "Let's hear it."

We sat across from him, leaning eagerly over his desk. "I'm going back into KATO," I said.

"And I'm leading her rescue team," Travis said.

"You're suspended," Simmonds said.

"I have more experience with KATO than any other agent in this place," Travis said. "When this is over, you can order me to move back on campus and monitor me around the clock if you want, but there's no way I'm staying behind on this."

Simmonds tapped a pen on the top of his desk. "Let's just hear this plan of yours before we get ahead of ourselves." As I started to talk, he listened, intrigued, and then began taking notes.

"I'm going to do everything I can to destroy the missile or the hovercrafts—or both. I'll do my best to shut their operation down enough to delay them, and bring back hard evidence that you can pass on to another agency." I was sure I sounded more confident than I felt, but that was fine. I needed him to believe I could do this.

"And if you can't shut it down?" Simmonds asked.

"Then at the very least, I'll get information on their plan and some evidence," I said. "And I'll see what I can find out about Eliza and Dr. Foster, since they're the keys to this. Once we have that, we can figure out a way to use that to our advantage."

Simmonds gave away nothing as he studied us. "Elton, as the self-proclaimed leader of the rescue team, who did you have in mind for this mission?"

"Cody, Nikki, and Rachel."

I arched an eyebrow. "Really? You think that'll work out?"

"They've come around," he said, giving me a sympathetic look. "And I wouldn't risk this with anyone else."

I wasn't sure I agreed, but I trusted him, so I nodded anyway.

"What's your timetable?" Simmonds asked.

Travis deferred to me.

"KATO didn't say how long they'd need me," I said. "But—" I hesitated, afraid if I said too much it would squash the whole mission.

"Joss, what is it?" Travis asked.

I glanced at him. "If I'm in there for more than a day, they're going to try to give me Gerex."

Travis's eyes hardened, and I was afraid he was going to back out. "How can you be sure you'll have that much time?"

"Because I'll tell them I shot up right before they got me. They won't suspect I'm lying to avoid an injection. The only reason they'd give me one early is as a reward, and they're not going to hand those out yet. Not if they're in the middle of their big plan. Rewards will come after." I looked from Simmonds to Travis. "Trust me. I know what I'm talking about."

"How are you supposed to get to them?" Simmonds asked.

"They're going to stage a kidnapping. Once I get in touch with them, they'll give me the details."

Travis was still, thinking for a moment. Then he nodded. "You've got twenty-three hours from the moment they take you to do what you can, then we're coming in. It'll look like a rescue operation, because it *will* be one, only you'll know we're on our way. And we'll do our best to disrupt their plans while we're there."

I relaxed slightly. "Okay."

"Can you put all of us on a decoy mission to get us closer to North Korea?" Travis asked. "It'll give her more time inside."

"We can arrange that," Simmonds said, then turned to me. "I know you're familiar with the facility."

"Oh yeah," I said. "I know my way around every part of KATO. I can do this." My insides were twisting themselves into knots so big I was surprised I couldn't feel them through my skin, but the more I told myself I could pull this off, the more I started to believe it.

Simmonds considered us. "If you can get your team in and out of KATO, I'll arrange for a safe house and we'll come up with an extraction plan."

"You're signing off?" I asked, my heart pounding both out of fear and eagerness. "On both of us?"

Simmonds nodded a fraction. "I am. But, Elton, don't think you're off the hook."

"Of course not, sir," Travis said. "When do we leave?"

"I'll work on a mission profile and have you dispatched to south-eastern Russia within the next six hours."

"I'll contact KATO and let them know they'll have an opportunity," I said.

"Mission folders will be sent to you once they're fully prepared," Simmonds said. I looked to the mission map. We weren't the only active assignment, but I was sure we were the most important. "Is there anything else you need from me?"

I thought for a moment. "If we end up using tech support, I want Sam Lewis on comms."

Simmonds's eyebrows knitted. "Walter is our best tech, and Sam's only a student."

"I realize that," I said. "But Walter doesn't hide how much he hates me. And I can't be worried about him while I'm inside KATO."

He turned to Travis, still not convinced.

Travis shrugged. "She trusts Sam."

Simmonds nodded in concession. "I'll allow it. But he won't have full control, and he will be monitored closely. He may just be the person relaying information."

"All I care about is getting the intel I need as easily as possible."

Simmonds nodded. "That's something I can agree to." He closed his notebook. "Elton, you can assemble your team. I'll have Sam meet you in the prep lab."

I thanked him and led the way out of the room.

I walked briskly down the hall, my pace quickening as the list of things we had to do before we left got longer and longer.

"We need to go over the facility," I said. "If you're coming in, you'll need to know the layout. We also need to go over their intruder protocol. And there are some backdoor ways in that you should know about. We need satellite photos—"

"Whoa." Travis took my arm and pulled me over to the side of the hall. "Slow down."

"We don't have time," I said. "There's so much we have to go over if we're going to pull this off without getting caught. There are blueprints you need to see, security measures you need to know how to avoid, and all of this depends on them not having changed anything too drastically—"

He put his hand on my mouth to shut me up. "Stop talking," he said, then held it there for another moment, driving home his point.

"Okay." He lowered his arm to hold my shoulders. "Now, are you sure you're going to be okay with this?"

I shook my head and tried to step around him. "That's not important. There are other things—"

"It *is* important!" He tightened his grip, and it was enough to keep me in place. "When are you going to get that?"

I looked up at him evenly. "I don't need you to take care of me. I've had a lot of practice doing it on my own."

He stared down at me, holding my gaze. "Well, right now, you're doing a really shitty job."

There was a fire in his eyes that finally made me pause. I took in a long breath through my nose and blew it out through my mouth. Then I nodded. "Okay."

"Now. Let's try this again." He let go of me and crossed his arms. "We're going into KATO. A place that held you captive for ten years. Are you going to be okay with that?"

I had a yes sitting on the tip of my tongue, but I swallowed it. "I don't know." My voice broke. "Yes. I need to be."

"I'm not leaving you there," he said. "We'll make the rescue look good. They'll never know it was staged."

I pinched the bridge of my nose, willing his words to be true.

"You'll have surprise on your side," he said. "They underestimated you. They never even considered the possibility that you could be strong enough to stand on your own."

"Right." I nodded. "You're right."

He smiled. "I know."

"But there's something I need from you," I said.

"Name it."

"I know you're leading the team, but I need to be in charge until they take me." I bit my lip. "I need to make sure you know everything I need you to know, and I need everyone else to listen to me."

"Done," he said. "And they will."

I breathed through my nose, gathering my strength, then nodded. "Okay," I said. "We should get to work."

Sam was already in the mission prep room by the time we got there, bouncing around wide-eyed. He didn't look at all like he had just been dragged out of bed. "What did you do to get me this gig?" he asked. I moved from computer to computer, starting them up. Sam was right behind me every step. "No one at my level has *ever* had point on something like this!"

"You don't have point," I said. "You're just the person I'd rather talk to."

He gave me a self-assured look. "If I've got the comm, I've got point."

I smiled. "But you're not really in charge. You have to run everything through the tech team."

Sam rolled his eyes. "How did you get me in on this?"

I turned to face him. "I asked for you. You've never questioned me. And the last time I had operational support on a mission I didn't completely trust the information I was getting. I can't afford to second-guess anything here."

"Because it's KATO?" he asked; his eyes got just a little bit bigger.

I tensed and held his gaze for a moment. "I need to trust the person I'm talking to."

He nodded, his expression serious. "I'll get you what you need." He spoke with more confidence than someone in his position should. I had a feeling he would take out anyone who tried to get in his way. "What do you need from me now?"

"Get together any kind of satellite footage you can. I need to see a current view of North Korea before we land."

He opened his laptop. "I'm on it."

We were waiting for the others to arrive. Simmonds was supposed to meet with the three of them when they got in, then send them to us. I took the time to get in touch with KATO, telling them they'd have the perfect opportunity to get me in Russia.

It was another fifteen minutes before the prep room door opened, and Nikki, Rachel, and Cody came in.

"Shh," Cody said. "I'm not awake enough for the two of you."

Rachel rolled her eyes. "Now who's being a noodle?"

"Hey, I am *not* a noodle." He glared at her. "*I* made it up. I get to determine if I'm a noodle, so I'm not."

"Of course," Rachel said. "You always change the rules so they work for you."

"I'm not changing the rules." He was bordering on whining. "These *are* the rules."

"Have you guys been briefed?" Travis asked, interrupting them.

"Yes," Cody said, jumping at the chance to change the subject. "We've got a fake mission to Russia to cover our real mission in North Korea." Then he turned to me. "Where do we start?"

I was almost startled by how direct and pointed he was with me, but I got over it quickly. "How much do you already know about KATO?" I asked.

Travis crossed the room and started typing on a computer. "Here's everything we have on their facilities," he said, sending a map of North Korea to one of the three monitors that hung on the wall in front of us. "According to our intel, this"—he pointed the cursor to a spot outside of Pyongyang—"is their headquarters."

I took the mouse from him and zoomed in on the capital and the area surrounding it. "Most of the facility is underground." I studied the map for a moment. "I can't get a good shot of the entrances from this."

Travis's eyes flicked up to me. "Is this where they kept you?"

I nodded. "Yeah. They wanted my division as far underground as they could get us."

"Sam." Travis kept his attention on me even while he talked to Sam. "Can you get images of the suburbs to the west of Pyongyang and send them to Cody's computer?"

Cody nodded and sat down at a computer right behind him.

"Sure." Sam's fingers were already moving across the keyboard. "Give me a second."

I fidgeted with a pencil on the table.

"They're on your screen," Sam said.

Cody sent the picture to the second monitor. "So, how do we get in?"

"There are four different secured entrances." I took over at Cody's computer and pointed out the four houses staggered about a quarter mile away from the edge of the field.

"Underground tunnel?" Nikki guessed.

"Exactly," I said. "But I know another way in." I panned out again. "There are three ventilation shafts at different points on the edge of the field. They're designed for an emergency evacuation of essential personnel. I know where two of them are."

Nikki raised an eyebrow. "How did you find them?"

I didn't look at her. "I did some snooping. Overheard a few conversations."

"You got away with that?" Rachel asked. It was the first time she had ever said something to me that wasn't meant to be cruel. But I could still hear an edge to her voice.

I kept my eyes on the map. "No." I felt all of them look at me and forced a smirk. "But they didn't realize how much I heard."

Travis shifted so he was in my range of vision. He shot me a harsh look, and his mouth formed a thin line.

"What else do we need to know?" Nikki asked, pushing things along before anyone could ask questions.

"Are there blueprints of the interior?" I asked. Travis, still tense, went back to his computer and pulled up schematics for both levels of the complex within seconds. I was pretty sure these were the plans I had given Simmonds when I arrived. "There are two floors," I said. "The upper level is operations and the lower is training."

They listened intently, taking in my direction.

"There's a main entry hall here," I said. There were five hallways that branched off. I pulled the cursor toward one of the halls. "This is the biggest room they have. I'm sure that's where the hovercrafts will be, and if the missile is still in production, it'll probably be there too."

I dragged the mouse back through the main entry hall, and down one of the opposite corridors. At the end, the hall widened into a second smaller atrium. I pointed to the room along the back wall. "That's the control room. If we need to shut anything down, it'll have to come from here."

"Where will you be?" Travis asked.

I met his eyes for half a second, then pointed at the second floor. "They keep recruits and agents in these wings," I said, running the cursor down three of the lower halls. "And prisoners here." I moved the mouse in circles over the two remaining halls.

"Why would we find you there?" Rachel asked.

I looked up at her sharply, expecting to see some kind of smug or cocky look on her face, but instead there was a genuine question. I stared at her for a moment. Then Cody leaned in and whispered something in her ear. Her eyes widened, and I knew she understood.

"We still have a few things to go over," I said, and I started handing out other tips and tricks on navigating KATO. After three hours, I couldn't think of anything else to say. Sam had disappeared halfway through to get familiar with the operations center.

"Is that everything?" Cody asked. He'd taken in every word I'd said. I was expecting some kind of resistance from him and Rachel, but I never got it. Rachel still clearly hated me, but she was completely on board.

I sat at the monitors in front of us, double-checking everything. "I think so."

Cody turned to Travis. "We should plan for our part."

Travis nodded. "We will. We'll have a day to prep in Russia."

I felt a strange peace come over me when he said that. I knew what I would be doing while they were prepping and I felt—calm. I could do this. I could handle being inside KATO. I just had to be the old me.

Chapter Thirty

KIDNAPPED

The plane we took to Russia was a small one—only big enough to fit twelve people. I sat alone with my eyes closed, putting myself in the right frame of mind. I shut out every other sound—the engine, the chatter—and tried to focus. I was so caught up in my own world I didn't realize Travis had sat down next to me until he touched my shoulder. I opened my eyes and blinked a few times, focusing on him. A slim smile spread across his lips.

"What?" I asked.

He shook his head, and his smile got a little bit wider. "A couple months ago, you never would have let your guard down enough for someone to sit down next to you without you knowing."

"Well," I said, trying to meet his smile but coming up short, "I guess I've got other things on my mind."

He got more serious. "You doing okay?"

I nodded slowly. "Yeah, I think I am."

He tilted his head to the side, surprised. "What changed from earlier?"

I shrugged. "I realized that I've been doing this for years. Like you said, I've never been the brainwashed agent they thought I was. I've been playing this spy-double-agent game since I found out my parents were IDA, and I've spent the past year actively trying to get away from them. I've been a traitor and they had no idea. The only difference is now I have another agency—I have an out. It'll be worse if they catch me, but they haven't caught me so far. I just have to keep it up."

Travis nodded. "And you only need to keep it up for twenty-three hours."

"Right." That's what I had to remember.

"And listen." He tipped his head closer to me. "I know you're planning on taking care of most of this before we get in there, but keep in mind that we need to be able to find you. Don't do anything that's going to make our job harder. If you need to wait for us to do any real damage, then that's what we need you to do."

I inhaled through my nose, and agreed. I believed him when he said he wouldn't leave me in there, and the last thing I wanted was for him to get caught trying to find me.

"Try and keep my cover," I said, even though I didn't need to.

"Don't worry," Travis said. "We'll do everything we can. If it goes well, they'll think you're doing a really good job and that we believe you're one of our own. Once we're in we can pretend we've just stumbled on to their bigger operation."

I nodded and leaned back, closing my eyes again. He lingered for another moment, then gave my knee a squeeze and left me alone.

I had the bench to myself for about an hour before I felt someone else sit down. I wasn't looking for company, so I kept my eyes shut, hoping whoever it was would think I was sleeping.

"Oh, knock it off," Nikki said. "I know you're awake."

I smirked and opened my eyes. "Did Travis send you over here to check on me?"

"No," she said. "I sent myself over."

"I don't need to be checked on," I said.

She shrugged. "Maybe not. But I'm bored and you're my friend."

I smiled. "So I'm supposed to entertain you now?"

"Not quite." She reached into the pocket of the chair in front of her and came out with a stack of cards. "Ever play Uno?"

I squinted at the cards. "Not since I was really little," I said.

She gleefully launched into an overview of the game, giving me enough to refresh my memory. It was exactly what I needed to keep my mind off things. We played for hours, until I felt my eyes start to get heavy. Nikki noticed and collected the cards. "You should sleep," she said.

I shook my head. "I'm fine."

"You've got a long day ahead of you," she said. "You should sleep while you can."

I wanted to argue with her. Despite what Travis seemed to think, I still wasn't sure I was comfortable enough to sleep on a plane with other people. But Nikki made a good point, and I figured it couldn't hurt to try. I leaned my head against the window and let my eyes drop shut.

A hand on my shoulder startled me awake.

"Whoa." It was Travis. "Sorry," he said. "I said your name a few times, but you were out."

"It's okay," I said. "Are we there?"

"Just landed. The others are pulling the equipment out of the lower level. We've got an old hotel we're using as our home base here, and the IDA is getting a location for a safe house in Pyongyang," he said.

I rubbed my eyes and sat up straighter. "I have to get in touch with KATO. Is there anyplace we can say we're going to be? Someplace they can get to me without giving up your base?"

He nodded. "We'll find something and come up with a reason why on the way."

The IDA had a car waiting for us. We passed what looked like an abandoned warehouse on the way to the hotel. I could tell KATO I was checking it out as a possible location to set up a mark. The details wouldn't matter too much. Their plans were big enough for them to ask me back here, which could, as far as they knew, blow my IDA cover. They had bigger concerns than my trivial IDA mission.

I contacted KATO once we agreed on the time and location. We'd given ourselves an hour in Russia before the meet. I was ready, but I still felt like I was about to walk into an explosion.

"Okay," Travis said once we were all settled in the hotel lobby. "In an hour, Joss and I are going to go back to that warehouse, then the rest of us have to prep a rescue mission."

"Hold on," I said, raising my hand to get his attention. "*You're* not going to the warehouse. Who knows what they'd do to you."

"I told you we're going to do everything we can to keep from blowing your cover," he said. "That starts now. If this were a real IDA assignment, you wouldn't be sent to scout a location by yourself, and there's a really good chance they know that."

I opened my mouth to argue, but Nikki's voice overpowered mine. "But she's right. It can't be you." Travis's eyes narrowed, but Nikki pushed on. "We don't know what they'll do to the other person. You're point on the rescue mission because you know more about KATO than any of us. If you get taken, we don't have enough information to get you both."

Travis drew a tight breath, visibly torn between wanting to fight her and seeing her point. "She can't go by herself."

"I'll go." I turned around. It was Cody, leaning against a pillar behind me. He laughed at me. "Don't look so surprised, Secret Spy. I'm on your side."

"I didn't mean—" I stumbled. "I just didn't expect—"

He smirked. "I know. I get you."

Travis still looked uneasy, but after a moment he nodded. "Okay. Let's start getting a plan together."

I separated myself for most of the hour, and this time, no one tried to bother me. Cody and I set out when the time came. The warehouse was only five blocks away, but it felt like so much farther. Cody didn't say anything, content to give me my quiet time, but I found now that I was so close to KATO, my nervous energy was too much to silently contain.

"Why did you agree to this?" I asked.

He looked down at me, curious. Probably more surprised that I had said anything than he was about the question itself. "Because I get it now," he said. "I get that you really didn't have a choice and what it meant for you to pick the IDA."

"That doesn't seem like it's enough for everyone." I grimaced thinking of Rachel. She'd barely spoken to me.

Cody shook his head. "Don't let Rachel get to you. It's just how she is."

I glanced at him out of the corner of my eye. "She has a right to be like that. I hurt her."

"Yeah," he said. "You did. But you were working for KATO."

I shook my head. "That shouldn't matter. I still chose to listen to them."

"Maybe it shouldn't," he said with a shrug. "But to some people it does. To *me* it does. You were keeping yourself alive." He shook his head, seeming annoyed with himself. "I should have trusted Travis. He had more encounters with you than any of us. If he could trust you, that should have been enough. I shouldn't have treated you the way I did. I owe you."

Now I had to laugh. "After everything I've done, you think you owe me?" I shook my head. "Why don't we call it even?"

He nodded. "Yeah, I think I can live with that."

We walked for a few more seconds in what seemed to be an oddly comfortable silence.

"They'll probably only knock you out," I said. "They've got too much going on at the headquarters. The last thing they're interested in is dealing with an extra body."

"Don't worry about me." Cody flashed his charming smile. "We've got a plan in place."

My nerves intensified as we got closer, but I was resigned. When we were a block away, we flipped the switch and just like that we were acting, playing the parts of two IDA agents scouting a building. We'd entered the warehouse, and after a meaningful look, Cody said, "We should split up. Cover more ground."

"Yeah," I said. "Good idea."

My heart was pounding with so much force I could feel it in my hands. Then out of nowhere something heavy hit my head, and my world went black.

Chapter Thirty-One

INSIDE

I woke up groggy and it took me a moment to remember what was going on. Once I did, I fought the urge to jump up. I had to *want* to be here. I pretended to sleep for an extra beat. This was it.

My eyes fluttered open. I was back in my old room, lying on the thin mat on the ground. The calm acceptance I had felt at the start of the mission had settled back in my stomach.

"Look who is finally awake," a voice to my right said in Korean. It was my handler, Chin Ho. I blinked a few times and focused on him.

"How long was I out for?" I asked. I glanced around the room. We were alone.

"Only about an hour," he said. His voice sharp and gruff, as usual. "When was your last injection?"

I swallowed hard. "Right before I left."

He considered me critically, then nodded. "Good." He pushed himself out of the chair. "Come with me."

I followed him without question. He led me out of my room and up to the main floor. We ended up on the other side of the building, standing outside the biggest room in the facility. My heart jumped. I had a good idea what I was going to see behind that door and I wanted no part of it. Chin Ho typed a code into the keypad and the door slid open. Behind it were rows and rows of big, round hover-crafts. Even though I was prepared, my breath caught.

They were finished, and from the looks of things, fully opera-tional. KATO had everything they needed to cross the DMZ.

"We're ready to invade?" I asked.

"We will be starting the missile prep momentarily," he said. "It needs a day and a half to prepare before it launches."

I kept myself calm and my breathing even. "What do you need from me?"

"We are pulling you out of the IDA for the time being. As far as they know, you have been kidnapped by your former agency. When we invade, we are stationing you in South Korea." I felt like I couldn't breathe. "Once the situation stabilizes, we will send you back to pre-pare for phase two."

It took me a minute to find my voice. I focused on the hovercrafts, doing my best to appear in awe of them so I didn't have to talk. It must have worked because a few moments later, Chin Ho said, "You should be very proud of your role in this."

"Thank you," I said, my stomach roiling. I stayed transfixed to hide how fast my mind was working. I had planned on the hover-crafts and the missile being in the same room, but they weren't. Everything was too spread out. I'd have to disarm the missile, take out the hovercrafts, and get the hovercraft technology out of their system. If they still had access to the tech, there was nothing to stop them from rebuilding and starting the process from the beginning. I didn't want to wait for the others, but I remembered what Travis had told me on the plane. They would be more at risk if they had to search the whole facility to find me, and there was no way I could get to all of those pieces without exposing myself. I needed to alter my goals. If I could spend my time here getting as much intel as I could, I would be able to pass it on to the rest of the team when they arrived.

"Let's go. I have some training to put you through," Chin Ho said. "Your job is going to be to blend into society and eliminate any Southern uprisings. This means you cannot be associated with us. We have to be creative about how we get you across the border."

I had plenty of questions, but I followed him silently. I was expecting him to lead me to the training room, but he threw me off when he opened a small closet door. Inside was a relatively compact trunk. Chin Ho opened the lid and pointed. "Get in."

I blinked a few times. He couldn't be serious. This wasn't the kind of training that was normal even for KATO. I wasn't even sure I would fit—and if I did, I would be crammed in tighter than a sushi roll. "What?"

I was out of practice and I never saw his fist coming. I stumbled and the right side of my jaw stung. When I straightened, Chin Ho gave me a deeply disapproving look. "It looks like you have had too much time on your own. Don't forget, you're not in charge of your own Gerex in here." I let a flash of fear cross my face; it just didn't mean what he thought it did. "You have to be packed into the hovercrafts, and you have barely more than a day to get used to it." Then I understood the plan. I couldn't be seen by a Southerner getting off a North Korean vessel. I would also bet most of the military members who would be on the hovercrafts wouldn't be cleared to know KATO was putting a spy on the ground. This way, I could be brought into the South covertly, as a supply chest, without any South Korean or unauthorized military official knowing about me.

I got in the trunk without another word. I had a plan, but I waited a few minutes to make sure I was alone before enacting it. Fortunately I could reach my boot. There were lock picks embedded in the soles. I'd been prepared in case I needed access to a room without an air duct, but now I was just glad I could pick the trunk's lock from inside. My joints were starting to ache when I finally lifted the lid and breathed in the quiet of the room.

My eyes adjusted quickly to the dark. The room was small, but the ventilation shaft was just as big as the rest in the facility. Since Chin Ho was letting me "practice" in small spaces, he had no reason to come looking for me for a while. I pulled myself up into the vent and got oriented. I knew the layout of these ducts better than the regular floor plan. I had only been caught once, and punished enough that no one ever thought I'd try it again. They didn't know that to me it only meant I had to be smarter.

I found my way to the director's office. It was empty, which wasn't too surprising. With something this big going on, he was probably a very busy person. I crawled to the vent a few rooms over—the conference room. It was packed with leaders and military officials discussing plans of attack. I'd never seen these two groups working together like this.

"We're sure the missile will work?" one of the military officials asked.

"It passed every simulation," the director said. "And we have the developer in the facility if anything goes wrong."

I bit my lip to keep myself from making a sound. Dr. Foster was in here. There was a good chance he was even on this floor. They wouldn't want to expose him to too much of headquarters.

I didn't have a lot of time. I knew KATO wouldn't let me starve and dinnertime would probably be within the next ninety minutes.

I moved through the vents expertly, checking each opening for anyone who might be Dr. Foster. I couldn't help him, but if I knew where he was, the others could when they got here.

I was ready to give up and head back to the closet when I found him. He was a few doors away from the hovercraft room. He was either asleep or unconscious, but I could see his chest rising and falling. He was alive.

I crawled back to my closet, then settled in the trunk again. I was there for about a half an hour before Chin Ho came back with a tray of some unidentifiable food. I hadn't thought about the food before I left, but now that I was back the idea of eating it made my stomach turn. But I didn't have a choice. He was watching me. I took my time, eating slowly. When I was done, he ordered me back in the trunk, saying he'd be back in the morning.

I picked the lock again. When I got out I stretched out on the floor. It was a huge shift from my comfortable bed, but I couldn't help feeling like I got off lucky. They left me alone. It was so much better than I could have hoped for.

I could never let my guard down at KATO. It wasn't until I got to the IDA that I realized how I'd adapted to being half asleep. I had fallen back into that routine easily. That night, I got enough sleep to be rested, while still being constantly on guard, ready to jump back into the trunk if I had to. I startled awake when I heard a key turning in a lock and curled up back inside the trunk.

Throughout the course of the next day, Chin Ho brought me out only to eat and use the bathroom. In between I crawled around the vents, checking on Dr. Foster and seeing if there was anything new I could find out. Aside from confirming Foster was still alive and learning that the missile prep had, in fact, been initiated, I hadn't come up with anything else.

After I finished lunch, Chin Ho pulled a vial and needle out of his pocket. I froze.

He misread my fear for excitement and smiled. "I figured you'd be ready. And you've been so good with your training, aside from that one incident."

I bit my lip, hard, trying to figure out how to get myself out of this. The only thing I knew was that there was no way I could let that back in my veins.

But I couldn't fight him. There was no logical reason for me to fight this. If I showed even the slightest resistance, Chin Ho would know and he'd interrogate me, then he'd kill me. He tied a tourniquet around my upper arm and I swallowed hard, thinking of the detox ahead of me, and how much harder it would be now that I knew what to expect. He filled the syringe with the Gerex. I breathed through my nose, trying to keep it together.

As he moved the needle closer, I was forced to admit that this was really happening. And now that it was so close and so real, I *wanted* it. Goose bumps came over me as the needle hovered above my skin. I braced myself for the wonderfully familiar searing burn, and the moments of bliss that would follow. I hadn't let myself think about the good part in so long and now that it was unbearably close, I felt overwhelmed.

A chill shot through me as the needle touched my elbow crease. I wasn't just ready for it, I was *desperate* for it.

Chapter Thirty-Two

FIGHT FOR CONTROL

Then the door banged open. "Get. Away from her," Nikki said, with her gun held out and a fierceness so different from her usual kind demeanor. I met her eyes, and I had never felt more transparent. She moved closer, pointing her gun at Chin Ho's skull. He froze with the needle on my skin, seconds away from puncturing. Even my tougher-than-steel handler didn't want to die.

Nikki leaned toward Chin Ho, her eyes widening when she saw what was in his hand. Then, in one easy motion, she knocked him out. "I got her," she said into her comm.

The syringe clattered on the ground and I dove for it. Nikki got there first. She snatched it away and sprayed the Gerex all over the floor. A fierce fury burned in my stomach—enough to make me want to attack her.

"Hey!" She grabbed my face, sandwiching it between her hands. "You don't need that. You *know* you don't need that. We have a job to do here and we need you with us."

I focused on her eyes and my breathing. I had a mission. A mission that had to be more important than anything. I felt the adrenaline start to flood my system. I nodded. "Yeah," I said; my voice sounded breathy and detached. "Yeah, I'm here."

She let me go and nodded. "Good." She handed me a comm and a gun. I took them from her, working the comm into my ear while she found Chin Ho's keys and locked him in the closet.

"We have a situation," I said, pressing the comm in so the rest of the team could hear me.

"Raven?" It was Travis. "Are you okay?"

"I'm fine," I said, burying my craving even deeper. "I have a lot to fill you in on." I told them everything I knew about the missile, the hovercrafts, and Dr. Foster.

"He's here?" Travis asked.

"I saw him this morning."

"Okay," Travis said, and I could practically hear him working out a plan, but I already had one.

"I'll get to the control room. I know where it is and I can get there faster," I said. That missile had to be stopped and I was the best person for the job. Even if it meant I'd leave here a KATO traitor. "Scorpion, get to Foster, and the rest of you take out the hovercrafts."

For a moment everyone was quiet, waiting to hear if they should listen to me or not. Then Travis spoke. "Do it."

"Command, did you get that?" I asked.

"Oh, I got it," Sam said. "I lost the hack into their feed but I'm working to get it back."

"Good," I said. "Because I'm going to need your help."

"Just keep your eyes open. They know I was in their system, so they're going to be looking for all of you."

"I'll see you later," Nikki said, before sprinting off to meet Cody and Rachel.

I held my gun low in front of me, then closed my eyes. I focused on the metal between my fingers. I'd done a lot of things in this facility, but running around with a weapon was something new. I took comfort in the feel of it in my hand and the power it gave me. Then I opened my eyes. I could do this.

I crept back to the main entry hall and ducked behind a pillar. I peered around it, down one of the hallways, then darted to the next pole. I didn't look back. "We're outside the room," Nikki said in my ear. I kept moving, quickly glancing around the pillar after each move, then hurrying to the next until I got to the hallway that was slightly off the atrium. I pushed my comm in. "Okay, Command. I'm staring at the door. I'll let you know when I'm outside it."

Then I heard a gun click a bullet into place near my ear. I stiffened.

"Well," Chin Ho said, his lips tight and his jaw locked. "This is quite the disappointment." I dropped my weapon without being asked. The closet didn't hold him. We were running out of time.

I stayed frozen, and my heart started to speed up. I was more terrified than I'd ever been. And for the first time in my life, I didn't see a way out.

In my ear Nikki, Cody, and Rachel were rushing Sam—they were still stuck outside the hovercraft room.

Chin Ho circled me, and when he came into my field of vision he had a vial of Gerex between the fingers of his other hand. "I saw it all over the floor. Which means you must be *desperate* by now." I was outside of their control and he knew it. He was so close to me I could feel his breath on my face. "Even if you have been off it for months, I know you still want it. As I'm sure you have figured out by now, it does not matter how long you have gone without it or how clean you think you are—you will *always* want it. It is how it was designed."

I swallowed hard, because he was right. I wanted it. My *mother* made me want it. But not as badly as he thought I did. I was on an assignment, and right then, that was all I felt.

I fixed him with a look of total disgust, breathing evenly through my nose and trying to think. I needed a plan. It didn't matter that I didn't have a weapon. I would *not* let him win. Not after everything I'd done to stay free.

"What?" He cocked his head to the side and stepped closer to me. "You are not even going to beg for forgiveness?"

I snapped. "You killed my *mother*. I don't have to ask you for *anything*." I quickly grabbed his wrists, then twisted, pointing the gun at the sky. Two shots fired off into the air. My cover may have been blown, but now I could use that to my advantage. It meant I didn't have to pretend anymore. I kneed Chin Ho in the groin, temporarily stunning him so I could knock the gun out of his hands.

Then Sam was in my ear. "Raven, what the hell are you doing?"

I kicked his legs out from under him and pressed my comm in. "I'm a little busy."

Chin Ho popped up and came at me, faking a punch to my head and landing one to my unprotected stomach. I forced myself to stand straight and fight. We battled until I got an advantage. I hit him in the head with enough force to make him stagger away from me. I saw his gun lying on the floor. I knew I couldn't get to it, but I had enough time to kick it far away from both of us.

He bounced back with an angry fire in his expression. He wasn't amused anymore. He started cursing at me, saying things designed to break me, and dangling the Gerex in front of me, hitting me with the biggest weakness I had, but it wasn't working.

He faked a punch, then tried to sweep my legs out from under me, but I saw through it and jumped up, kicking his stomach in the process. He sprawled across the floor, landing far too close to the gun. He glanced back at me with a mixture of delight and disappointment in his eyes, then army-crawled over to it. There was no way I could get to him before he got to the weapon, so I retreated, running back to the hallway I'd first come down—where my gun had been kicked aside.

I grabbed it and spun around to find Chin Ho on the floor with his gun on me. I liked my odds better in a hand-to-hand situation. He knew about a dozen moves to kill me in seconds, but I had always been quicker than he was. When it came to guns, however, he had the best shot in KATO.

For a moment we were both frozen in place. I edged closer to him, tightening my grip on the gun, trying to figure out a way I could *not* shoot him. I'd killed enough people because of him. I wasn't looking to add to that number, even if I *did* want him dead. "You need to come with me," he said.

I clenched my jaw, but kept walking. I didn't stop until I was practically standing on top of him. "Not a chance."

He sat up a little bit straighter. "You know I'll kill you if I have to."

I swallowed hard, knowing he wasn't bluffing. I fired two rounds fast. They sliced through his thigh, accurately hitting their target. I dodged to my left, knowing what was coming. He fired two shots of his own. The first cut into my right shoulder as I fell to the ground, and the second flew past me, so close to my ear that I could hear it. I swung my leg high as I fell, kicking the weapon out of his reach. I held mine tight in my left hand and pushed myself off the ground. I aimed for his head, wanting so badly to pull the trigger. But I couldn't. He'd raised me, and no matter how much I hated him, I couldn't kill him. I tipped the nose of the gun down to his stomach and fired.

I stood over him, panting and trying to ignore the pain shooting through my right arm. The bullet was still inside. I holstered my gun and reached for his, praying he would bleed out before he could get any kind of help. I gave him one last look and saw him squirming, before I moved toward the control room. I struggled to press my comm. "Command, did you get back online?"

"Give us a second," Sam said. "We're close."

"Get closer."

It was a few seconds before Sam answered. "Okay, I'm back in. You're right outside the control room and you've got KATO agents heading your way."

"How much time do I have?"

"I'd say about thirty seconds."

I exhaled. "Can you get me inside, then seal the door behind me?"

He was quiet for a moment. "Yeah," he said. "I can do that. But once you're in you're going to have ten or so agents to deal with."

I nodded. "That's okay; I can take them."

Then Travis's voice was grunting in my ear. "Don't get reckless."

"I'm not. Control is a secure, disarmed room." I could hear the KATO agents getting closer. "You worry about what you're doing and let me handle this."

"Just be careful." His voice was tense. I was afraid he was having problems, but I didn't ask. I trusted him to know what he was doing.

"Command, get me in that room."

The guards were getting closer. I could hear them storming the halls that led to the atrium. I would be surrounded in seconds.

"You're in!" Sam said.

I pulled the door open as dozens of agents poured out of the hallways. Bullets flew as I pushed the door shut. "Seal it now. And jam their system. I don't want anything getting in this room until I'm done."

I heard the room vacuum shut. I was using their own protection protocol against them. In case of emergency, this room, made solely of bulletproof glass, was supposed to seal itself. There was no way they'd be able to get in while Sam had a hold on their security system. I turned around and started taking out the tech operatives. They had all been through training, but they didn't practice regularly enough to be able to take me. Plus, the room bottlenecked in a way that made it impossible for more than two of them to get to me at the same time. I handled them quickly, even with my labored breathing and the pain shooting through my entire arm with every movement. I was down to one guy sitting at a computer in the center of the room.

"Raven, you got to hurry up," Sam said. "I've got one active computer trying to push me out."

"I see him."

I charged at his back, using the fact that he was distracted with Sam to my advantage. I knocked my gun hard on the top of his head and he flopped across the keyboard. I pushed him to the ground and took his seat. Then I tore a piece of his shirt off and used my teeth to tie it tight around my shoulder. I needed to control the bleeding to stay conscious. "Command, I've got the room," I said, once my wound was wrapped. "I need you to walk me through this."

"Okay," Sam said. "Priority one is shutting down the missile, but you have to do *exactly* what I tell you to."

I swallowed. "Where do I start?"

"You're sitting at the main computer, right?"

"If that was the last active computer, then yeah," I said.

Then Travis cut in. "He's dead."

I froze. "What?"

"Foster's dead." His voice was thick and heavy.

"He was alive a few hours ago."

Travis didn't say anything for a moment. "Stop the missile."

I knew what this meant to him. This was never *just* a mission. "Scorpion—"

"Focus," he said, with a sharp edge. "They can't win."

"Okay." I exhaled heavily. "Command, I'm at the computer."

"All right," Sam said. "I'm going to get in there and pull up the screen you need, then you need to take it from there. I can see your screen, but this can't be done remotely." He went quiet, then a few seconds later my monitor blinked and a dark background with complicated computer code filled the screen. My heart skipped.

In my head, Nikki asked for Travis to come help them. Cody and Rachel had chimed in and all four of them were talking back and forth.

I tried to focus on my task. I'd never felt so out of my league on a mission before. "What am I looking at?"

"It's the backdoor into the missile command," Sam said. "You need to find the line that starts with five zeros and a one."

I scanned the list of zeros and ones and dashes and carets. My stomach twisted. "I can't do this." My voice was barely above a whisper. "I'm not a hacker."

"Shut up," Sam said in a tone so bored I could practically hear the eye roll. "You're the most capable person I know. Relax, focus, and get to work."

I bounced my foot up and down, biting my lip hard as I took in the situation. He was right. I pushed aside the pain in my shoulder and pulled my chair close to the computer. "Okay, what do I need to do?"

"Find the five zeros and a one." His voice stayed calm, like he never doubted me. "You'll know you have the right line if there are two slashes after it. "I'm looking at it right now. It's halfway down your screen."

My eyes jumped. "Okay, I see it. Now what?"

"Go to the end of the line and type *exactly* what I'm about to tell you. And whatever you do, *do not* hit enter until I say so."

I waited for the rest of his directions, then followed them to the letter. I typed everything like he said, jumping from line to line as he told me. And after two minutes, he finally told me to hit enter.

"This is going to take a minute," Sam said. "Once the countdown was initiated, the control of the missile was shifted to the computer in the missile itself. This is rerouting the control back to the computer you're sitting at."

"So this is only half of it?" I asked, trying not to panic.

"Yes, but the second part isn't any harder," Sam said. "Just give me a minute."

I exhaled and glanced around the room while I waited. For the first time since I got in, I noticed the army of agents standing outside the door. I pushed my comm. "Hey, team? Are you almost finished what you're doing?"

"Yeah," Nikki said. "Why?"

"Because I've got about two dozen agents outside my door," I said. "There's no way I can get out of here on my own."

"Give me five minutes," Travis said. I heard metal scraping in the background. "Can the room you're in withstand an explosion?"

"Yeah," I said. "It was designed to. Why, what are you planning?"

"You worry about the missile. I'll worry about the agents."

"All right, Raven, you're up," Sam said. I looked back to the computer. The screen had turned green. "But here's the thing. I don't have a view or access to the computer anymore."

"What?" Panic shot through me. "Why?"

"Because the security this deep into the system is too advanced to hack. This is why you had to be on-site." His voice was calm, and it forced me to keep it together.

"But you can talk me though this?"

"Absolutely." I could practically hear the single nod of his head. "You're looking at a green screen now, right?"

"Yes." Relief flooded me. Just the fact that he knew that made me feel like I wasn't blind.

"Okay. I don't want you to freak out," Sam said, "but you can't make a mistake here. One wrong keystroke could ignite this thing early."

I grunted. "I don't know why you would think something like that would freak me out. I mean, it's not like any of this is over my head or anything." My sarcasm could not have been more apparent.

Travis cut back in. "The rest of the team is clearing out. The hovercrafts are destroyed and I'm en route to the control room."

"Copy that," Sam said. Then he turned his attention back to me. "You're going to be fine. Just take your time and type what I tell you."

I drew a shaky breath. "Okay. What's first?"

"First you need to find the computer's operational program." Sam told me what keys to hit. I tried to move as fast as I could, but I was so inexperienced in this area, and now millions of lives were sitting at the tips of my fingers. "You're doing good," Sam said after a few minutes.

"How could you possibly know that?" I asked.

"Because we can tell from the satellites that the missile hasn't launched," he said. "Just keep doing what you're doing."

I closed my eyes, taking a moment to refocus. "Okay. What's next?"

"Here's the big part," Sam said. "You need to override the countdown to make the computer think the device has already been launched."

I swallowed and nodded, even though he couldn't see me. "All right. Tell me what to do."

Sam walked me though the code and after a few nervous keystrokes, I was starting to feel more comfortable. I could tell by Sam's tone that we had to be getting close when Travis interrupted us.

"Stop what you're doing for a second," he said.

I froze. "Why?"

"Because I'm about to take care of the guards outside your door and I don't want you to make a mistake."

I sat up a little straighter. "Scorpion, what are you doing?"

But he didn't answer. The next second the hallway outside the control room lit up and an explosion shook the entire room so hard it knocked me off my chair. I stared at the windowed wall as the smoke cleared, at the agents sprawled across the floor. "You're going to want to hurry up," Travis said. "I'm sure backup is on its way."

I stumbled to my feet, thoughtlessly using my injured arm to try to help me off the ground. I gritted through the pain and got myself back in front of the computer screen. "Command, what's next?"

"Type eight, zero, one, five, six, three. Then hit enter twice." His voice was hurried and I knew we were running out of time.

I typed fast without stopping to second-guess myself. I hit enter. "Now what?"

There was a pause on Sam's end, like he was double-checking something. "Now you get the fuck out," he said finally.

"It's done?" I asked.

"Yes," he said. "And I erased the hovercraft data."

"Okay, give me a minute to wipe this." But that wasn't all I was doing. I started typing furiously. I knew KATO's computers enough to do a basic system search and there was one more thing I needed to do before we left. It took me seconds to find what I needed. Then I wiped the computer. "Now."

"Go!" Sam said. "I've got the door open."

"I'm right outside," Travis said.

I hurried down the small tunneled hall, jumping over the agents I had taken out when I'd come in. Travis was holding the door open for me when I got there.

"I can hear them gathering in the entry hallway," he said. Both of the exit shafts I knew about were in that direction. "Command, you got another way out for us?"

"Go to the back right corner of the atrium you're in. You'll find a hidden door that will take you down a tunnel. There's a way out from there."

Travis headed right over to the corner, but I stopped to take in the agents littered across the floor. I started to panic when I saw who *wasn't* there.

"Hey!" Travis barked when he noticed I wasn't with him. "Let's go!"

"He was here," I said.

"What are you talking about?" It was taking every ounce of patience he had not to completely snap at me.

"Chin Ho," I said. "I shot him, but he's not here anymore. He didn't die."

Some of the impatience left his face, and I could see a part of him wanted to find Chin Ho as much as I did. "We don't have time to look for him. We've got to get out of here while we have the chance." I didn't move. "Raven!" He spoke sharply enough to startle me back to life.

I hurried over to Travis, pushing Chin Ho out of my head.

"We're here," Travis said to Sam. Sam started rattling off a step-by-step process of exactly what we needed to do to get out of KATO. I focused on his voice and on Travis's movements, pushing myself to keep moving forward, fighting everything inside me that wanted to go back and finish what I had been too weak to do the first time.

Chapter Thirty-Three

HOLES

When we got to the end of the tunnel there was a tall ladder leading to a manhole. Travis went up first. I struggled, pain spiraling through my arm every time I had to grip the rung. When we got to the top, Travis reached to help me, but I pushed myself past him. The only reason I was keeping it together was because I kept moving forward and making myself focus. If I let him help me, I was done.

Travis had his tablet in his hand quickly and squinted at the GPS map. "We need to move this way, through the forest. The street we parked on is on the other side."

I nodded. "Let's get there fast." I led the way through the woods, with Travis right behind me.

"Let me see your shoulder," Travis said once we were safely covered by the trees.

I pulled away from him. "We don't have time. We need to keep moving."

"I need to see if you're okay." He was forcing himself to be patient.

"I'm *fine*." I grabbed his tablet and navigated through the forest, back toward the car. I heard him sigh in exasperation, hurrying to keep up. We moved quickly and quietly through the trees. I figured we had about a ten-minute head start before anyone started searching the surrounding area. They had no way of knowing how we got out of the building, which meant they would have to fan out and search the entire facility before they checked outside.

We zigged and zagged our way back to the car. I pulled open the passenger door. "We've got to move," I said. "They'll have people on the ground and road looking for us."

Travis jumped in the car and pressed hard on the gas pedal, putting enough distance between us and KATO before he slowed to a less noticeable speed. Once he had, I felt like I could finally catch my breath. And that was when I could really process everything that had happened. They killed Dr. Foster once they realized the IDA was inside. He knew too much for them to risk us getting a hold of him. He was alive this morning and I didn't even try to help him.

Then I blinked and I saw Chin Ho lying helplessly in front of me and I saw myself unable to do what was necessary. I slammed my good hand against the dash. "Damn it!" Angry tears slid down my face. I brushed them away roughly, furious they'd shown up at all.

"Hey!" Travis's voice was sharp. "Take it easy."

"I had him." I couldn't look at him. "They killed Foster." He stiffened, but I kept going. "And then I had him right in front of me and I couldn't—" I broke off, shook my head and leaned back into my seat.

"Who are we talking about?" He sounded cautious and I had a feeling he knew exactly who I was talking about, but I couldn't find my voice to answer. I didn't want to explain. I wasn't ready yet. Instead I stared out the window, and other than a few uncertain glances in my direction, Travis let me be. I replayed the entire encounter in my head. I had him lying in front of me.

I found myself shivering when Travis pulled the car to a stop a few blocks away from the safe house, which was right inside the city limits. He threw a jacket at me when we both got out of the car. "Put that on."

"I don't need—"

"You've got a bleeding hole in your shoulder that's going to draw more attention than we can afford. Put on the damn jacket."

I closed my eyes for a second and nodded. I got my good arm into the sleeve easily enough, but I struggled to get the right side over my shoulder. Travis came up behind me and dropped the jacket over it without a word. His arm moved to my back and pushed me forward. "Come on."

I followed half a step behind him, feeling slightly absentminded as I navigated the narrow streets and back roads until we got to the safe house. Travis locked the door behind us.

Nikki came out from a room in the back. "Thank God," she said.

"Where are the others?" Travis asked.

"Cody got caught on a broken pipe on the way out. Rachel's treating him in the back."

"He'll be okay?"

"He'll be fine. Rachel just needs some water." She answered Travis but her focus was on me. "Are you okay?"

I nodded. She didn't look like she was completely convinced, but the jacket hid any evidence that I was lying.

Travis steered me toward a room off to the left. "I need to talk to Joss for a second," he said to Nikki, "but I may need you in a little bit."

She nodded, a little confused. "Yeah, just let me know."

He opened the door and waited for me to step inside.

It was a medium-size bedroom with a small fireplace in the

corner and a double bed pushed up against the wall. Something about it made me feel antsy and claustrophobic. I started pacing, thinking about what Chin Ho had said to me and what I couldn't do to him. And what KATO had done to Dr. Foster.

"Let me see your shoulder," Travis said, bringing me back to the room. He stood in front of the door, watching me with his arms crossed. I was finally starting to let my guard down and I felt a little dizzy.

Travis put his hand on my good shoulder. I jumped when he touched me, but he didn't apologize. His face was etched with a confused and concerned expression that I'd seen before, but still stopped me in my tracks. He tilted my chin up, taking in my new bruise. "What *exactly* happened in there?"

I shook my head and dropped my gaze to the ground. "I wasn't being reckless."

He squeezed my shoulder a fraction tighter. "I didn't say you were, but I need to know what happened."

When I looked back up at him, I saw his jaw was set and determined. I sighed and nodded. Travis sat on the bed, guiding me down next to him. He watched me patiently, waiting for me to start talking.

"It wasn't as bad as it could have been," I said. I told him about waking up with Chin Ho watching me, and being forced into the trunk, but being able to pick my way out. "Nikki got there right before he stuck me. I got lucky."

"*Nothing* about KATO is lucky," he said. "How did you get shot?" Travis kept his voice even, but I noticed his eyes fixed on the spot that was bleeding beneath the jacket.

"Nikki knocked out Chin Ho and locked him in a closet. He got out somehow," I said. "He cornered me and shot at me, but missed. I fought him off and for a little while neither of us had guns. He went after his at one point so I went for mine." I swallowed and looked away. I couldn't look at him while I told the rest, and my voice dropped to a low whisper. "I had him on the ground right in front of me. I wanted to kill him *so* badly. But I couldn't." My voice broke. "I pulled the trigger, but I didn't hit anyplace that would put him down for good. I hoped he would bleed out."

"Hey." Travis had his hand on the back of my head, trying to get me to face him, but I wouldn't do it. "Jocelyn, look at me." I still didn't move. "*Please.*" There was a desperate edge to his voice that pulled at me. I turned my head up. His eyes were intense and firm, and his voice matched them when he spoke. "That wasn't weakness."

I stood up to get away from him, pacing ever so slightly in front of him. A small humorless laugh got away from me. "How is it not? I had, in front of me, the person who has caused me more pain in the past ten years than most people ever experience in a lifetime. He did it to me, and he's done it to others—maybe even Eliza." Anger ignited inside of me. "And I could have ended it all. But I didn't. Instead, I got shot and jeopardized a mission."

"You're trained to be a killer," he said, and paused until I stopped pacing and looked at him. "You're trained to believe that ending lives solves problems. It would have been *easy* to kill him. And if I had been the one that got to him, his blood would have been all over that facility for what he's done to you." I stepped away, feeling worse, but Travis was in my face, with a hand on me in seconds. "It takes more strength than I have *not* to put him down, especially given everything."

I shuddered and looked at the ground. "It doesn't feel that way."

He stepped back so he could drop his head and find my eyes. "Trust me."

I looked up at him and I wanted to. At least for now. I sighed. "I'm sorry we couldn't get to Dr. Foster in time."

"I don't want to think about that right now," he said. "But I do need to look at your shoulder. And this time I'm not asking." He arched his eyebrows pointedly at me and I nodded. He sat me back down on the edge of the bed, then he lifted the jacket off my shoulder, untied the makeshift tourniquet, and gently shifted my clothes so he could get a good look at the wound. He poked in exactly the wrong spot and I cried out. "Sorry," he said, glancing up. "The bullet's still in there. The good news is it looks like it's lodged in your tissue, which is the best-case scenario. Bad news is I'm going to have to get it out."

"Can't it wait until we get back?"

"It could if we knew for sure we'd be on a plane in less than forty-eight hours. But if something goes wrong and that doesn't happen you're going to have a problem."

I swallowed. I had never had a bullet removed from me in the field, and I'd never had anything like this done when I wasn't heavily drugged. "Have you done this before?"

He looked uneasy. "Yeah," he said. "But never with anyone as sober and aware as you're going to be."

I exhaled deeply. Strangely not feeling the aftermath trigger nearly at all. "I can handle it."

He tilted his head and I knew he wasn't convinced.

"You said this can't wait until we're extracted," I said.

"No," he said. "It can't."

"Then we really don't have a choice, do we?" I sounded more sure than I felt.

Travis shook his head slowly.

"Get what you need and let's get this started."

"Lie on the floor," he said, grabbing a pillow from the bed and dropping it at my feet. "It'll keep you more stable than anything else in this place."

I eased myself onto the ground as Travis moved around the room, picking up the first aid bag and a bottle of alcohol. He also built a fire in the fireplace. I knew why we needed the fire, but I wasn't ready to think about that yet. "Give me a minute to get Nikki," he said.

He came back with Nikki right behind him. I swallowed hard as he sat down next to me, and Nikki settled at my head.

"You know," she said, "when I ask you if you're okay, and you've got a gunshot wound, the right answer isn't yes."

I gave her a halfhearted smile that she didn't return.

Travis held a thick piece of rope in front of my mouth for me to bite on. "Try to keep your arm across your ribs," he said. I nodded.

"What do you need me to do?" Nikki asked.

"Keep her from moving." He started to cut the clothes around the wound. I winced when he poured alcohol over it.

Travis picked up a knife and cut my shoulder open a little bit wider. I cried out and tried not to squirm, but I couldn't help it. Travis's hand was on my face. "Hey." He spoke gently. "I know it's hard but I need you to stay as still as you can."

"I know," I grunted out, talking around the rope. "I'm sorry."

"It's okay." He looked deep into my eyes, trying to transfer some calm.

"Focus on me," Nikki said. "No matter what happens or what Travis does, keep your eyes on me. Okay?"

I breathed through my nose, fighting the pain. "Yeah. Okay. Just—go." I hated the desperation that crept into my voice.

Travis brushed a hand over my forehead. "Stay with me."

I nodded. His fingers lingered in my hair for another moment, then he grabbed the towels and pushed them into my hands so I'd have something to hold on to. He picked up the knife again and continued to widen the wound. I dug my fingers into the towels, gripping them so hard the cotton cut into me.

"You're doing good," Travis said, concentrating intently on my shoulder.

I panted through my nose and let out a cry of relief when the knife lifted off my skin.

"We're really getting into it now." He sterilized a pair of medical-grade tweezers. "I need to dig for the bullet and pull it out."

I fought to slow my heart down, but it was useless. "Do it," I grunted.

He gave me a hesitant look, like he didn't think I understood how much this would hurt. "Do everything you can to stay still," he said, looking more to Nikki than me. Nikki nodded.

"Okay." I tightened my fists around the towels. "Let's go."

He gave me one final look. "Keep your eyes on Nikki. Once I'm in there, I'm not coming out until I have the bullet. It'll be better that way."

I nodded. Travis turned back to my shoulder and I looked back to Nikki. She gave me an encouraging smile that only lasted for a moment. The tweezers brushed the edge of my wound. I focused on Nikki's eyes as she hovered over me as much as she could without getting in Travis's way. Then he hit something. The pain spiraled through my entire right side and I couldn't stay still. I was only vaguely aware of the tears streaming down the side of my face.

Nikki tried to hold me steady, but I was in too much pain.

"What did you do?" she asked him. But he wasn't paying attention to her.

"It's okay." Travis held my face in his hands. "You're okay. I just hit a nerve. Give it a minute to pass."

I breathed through my nose, trying not to throw up. The pain still echoed through me as I found my way back to Travis. He was leaning over me, searching my eyes, trying to anchor me. He came out without the bullet, despite what he promised. "Keep going."

He scanned my face like he was trying to read my mind. "You sure you're ready for more?"

"Please. Just do it." My voice was barely more than a whisper through the rope.

He nodded, never breaking my gaze. "I'm going to try a different angle."

He stepped around and settled above my head to try coming at the bullet from above. He directed Nikki to my left side, away from the injury. She was out of my field of vision, so this time I focused on Travis's forehead. His face was scrunched in concentration and his thought wrinkles were deep. I felt the tweezers back on the edge of my wound. They scraped through tissue and I squeezed my eyes tight.

"Come on, Raven. Stay with me."

I forced my eyes open again.

"Good." He sounded a little out of breath. "You're doing great."

I focused on his eyelashes. They were long and dark enough to make a girl jealous.

The tap of the tweezers around the bullet made me shudder. Travis froze. "Sorry," I said. Breathless pain tinged my voice.

"It's okay." He paused for a moment. "Listen, Jocelyn. I have the bullet. All I have to do is pull it out."

"Okay."

"It's going to hurt like hell, but I need you to not move. If you do, I may hit another nerve." His voice was calm, but I could hear the intensely serious undertone.

"I get it." I gritted my teeth and clutched the towels.

"Nikki, I need you to hold *both* of her shoulders."

"Both?" There was a fair amount of uncertainty in her voice.

"It'll hurt, but it will be worse if she moves."

"Okay." She still didn't sound sure, but she did what he asked. The pain in my shoulder intensified, but I told myself it would only be for another moment.

Travis took a deep breath. "One." He studied my face. I braced myself. "Two." He ripped the bullet out of my shoulder and this time I cried out, the rope falling out of my mouth. It was like he'd hit every nerve in my body. I rolled onto my shoulder, trying to protect it. Tears streamed down my face and I struggled to get enough air to breathe. Then I felt Travis and Nikki pulling me back over, onto my back. Travis propped my head up on his knees. "Don't do that. You're going to make it worse." He grabbed the alcohol and poured it into the hole in my shoulder. I tried to roll in the other direction, but Travis put the bottle down quickly and kept me still. "Just let it settle," he whispered.

He had one hand draped across my collarbone, and the other holding my good shoulder in place.

I panted and squirmed. My heart slammed against my ribs. "I can't breathe." My voice broke. "I can't—"

"I know." He moved his hand from my collarbone up to my hairline. "Give it a minute."

I swallowed and focused on taking each breath in. The agony eventually evaporated, but my shoulder was still killing me. I had never felt this much pain sober.

He squeezed me a little bit tighter. "We're almost done. I just—I just have to cauterize the wound."

I closed my eyes tight, and nodded. "I can handle it."

Travis looked disgusted at the prospect. "You've been burned enough." His fingers brushed my old scar. "I hate that I have to do it again."

I tried to smile. "It's okay. I know what to expect."

He exhaled heavily, not feeling any better. The fireplace was above my head. I could hear the wood shifting. Travis pressed his elbow into my good shoulder and his forearm across my collarbone, holding me in place. "Are you ready?"

I nodded and rolled my head into his stabilizing arm. Nikki grabbed my hand and squeezed. I closed my eyes and braced for the pain. I heard Travis lift the rod out of the fire. A few seconds later my shoulder exploded. I screamed into Travis's arm and he tightened his hold on me. I wasn't sure how long it lasted, but I was left gasping through tears.

He rubbed my hair, trying to soothe me. And the truth is, his being there kind of did.

"I need to do it one more time," he said. "It's not fully closed."

I was tired and sick to my stomach. I just wanted to be done, but I nodded into his arm. He dug his elbow into my good shoulder again, and I buried my face deeper into his bicep. This time he didn't hesitate before lowering the rod to my skin. We both wanted this over with.

Travis leaned over my wound when he pulled the rod away. "All right," he said. "It's closed."

I felt every muscle relax with relief. Then the door opened. It was Rachel.

"What the hell is going on in here?" she asked. I rolled back into Travis's arm. She was the last person I wanted to see me like this.

"She had a bullet in her shoulder," Nikki said.

"Well, give her something," Rachel snapped. "Before we have the neighbors reporting us."

I felt the muscles in Travis's arms tighten.

Nikki stood up to face her. "Get out."

"What?" Rachel sounded stunned.

"Go!" Travis practically growled at her. A few seconds later, the door slammed shut.

"Let's get you into a bed," Travis said, calmer, propping me up a little bit more.

"No." I tried to move away from him. "I want to stay here."

"You're not going to get the rest you need here." He sounded stressed and tired. "It's not that far. Nikki and I will help you."

I grimaced, but nodded and let them pull me to my feet. I staggered when we started walking, but they were quick to stabilize me.

"Easy," Travis said. He had my good arm draped around his neck, letting me lean against him for support. They got me over to the bed and eased me onto the edge. "Go check on Rachel and Cody," he said to Nikki. "I've got her." Nikki nodded, then gave me a final concerned look before leaving.

Once she was gone, Travis slipped in behind me, lying next to my good side. He slid his arm under my neck and along my collarbone again, only this time he was tilting my head onto his shoulder and away from the bullet hole.

"What are you doing?" I asked, barely able to get the words out through the exhaustion and pain.

"Making sure you don't move too much. If you pull the skin you could reopen the wound and we'll have to do it all over again." He squeezed me.

I rested my head on his shoulder and sighed. "Thank you."

"Get some rest."

I felt myself finally relax and drift off to sleep.

Chapter Thirty-Four

ESCAPE

I startled awake and sat up straight. Pain shot through my shoulder and I stifled my reaction.

"Take it easy," Travis said, annoyed, pressing me back down. "You lost a lot of blood, and it wasn't like we had any way of replacing it."

I swallowed the pain and took a few deep breaths. "How long did I sleep for?"

"A few hours." He leaned over me to take a look at the wound. "This looks good." He rubbed some antiseptic cream on it and I tried not to flinch. Then he covered the area with gauze and taped it into place.

I struggled to sit up straighter and this time he let me. "We've got to start moving," I said, wincing as I felt my injury with every slight movement.

"The others left a little while ago. We're trying to stagger our exits." He arched his eyebrows. "They're going to call us when we're ready to go, but I don't think I'm really liking the idea of moving you."

I shrugged my good shoulder. "It's not like we have a choice. The longer we stay here, the more likely it is that KATO is going to find us. If they figure out I haven't left, they'll scour the country looking for me."

Travis gave me a hard look. "If we go now and get ambushed, there's no way we're going to be able to hold off an attack," he said. "Not with the condition you're in."

I rolled my eyes. "It's going to be a little while before I can put up that kind of a fight. If we're going to make it out of this country we need to move *now*. Before they figure out we're still here. It's the only chance we're going to get."

His lips thinned and his eyebrow furrowed. He knew I was right, I could tell. Now he was just trying to come up with a way around it. After a few moments, he nodded. "Okay." He rooted through the backpack. "But first, lie back."

"What?" I asked. "Why?"

"Dr. March walked me through your acupuncture treatments. You have to be feeling it right now. If we're going to pull this off, I don't want to have to worry about that."

"The only thing I feel is the pain, which I'm guessing you can't do anything for," I said, and it was the truth. I would have taken anything for the pain if it wouldn't jeopardize what I'd worked for.

A sympathetic expression crossed his face. "Trust me, if I could do something for that, I would."

"I know," I said, smiling lightly. "The craving isn't that bad."

He considered me carefully. "I'd feel better if we did this to be sure."

I bit my lip and nodded, then lay back down. Travis sat down on the edge of the bed. He brushed my hair away from my ears and gently pushed the needles in.

He pulled them out after fifteen minutes. "You good?"

"Yeah." I sat up.

He held my eyes for another moment, then started moving around the room, packing things into the backpack. "Can you fire a gun with one hand?"

"Not as accurately," I said, "but I can hit my target."

He nodded and tossed me a gun. I caught it easily with my left hand. "I'll get in touch with Command and let them know we're ready. Then we'll move." He threw a balled-up piece of cloth at me. "Put that on. If you argue with me, we're not going."

I held it up and saw he'd made a sling for my arm. I took it without complaint and dragged myself into the bathroom with a change of clothes to try to get myself together. I flicked on the light. There were three bulbs, but only one of them was working. I struggled into a clean tank top and slipped the sling over my shoulder. Then I stared at myself in the mirror. My hair was flat, limp, and hung loosely around my face. My eyes were bloodshot with dark circles around them, and my face was startlingly pale, which I suspected was from the blood loss. I splashed some water on my face, leaned over the sink, and forced myself to breathe easy. We made it out of KATO, but we weren't safe yet. If they caught us now, Travis and the others would be dead, and I didn't even want to think about what they'd do to me.

Travis knocked on the door. "Joss?"

I tore my eyes away from the mirror. "Yeah." I opened the door quickly. "We ready?"

"They've got a team en route to China. We have to get across the border and meet them outside of Fushun," Travis said. "They'll swoop in and pick us up there."

"How are we getting out of the country?" I asked.

"Freight train." He leaned against the doorframe. "There's one leaving the station in half an hour. Sam said the others are already on one of the loaded cars. We have to get there before it leaves."

I shook my head. "They'll be searching the trains."

"I know," he said. "We're going to have to find a really good hiding spot. It's the best and most direct way out of the country. They'll never let you through an airport, and a bus or a car won't give us enough of a place to hide."

I bit my tongue and nodded. I hated it, but he was right.

"The train makes two stops on the way. One is before the border. My best guess is that they'll have a military presence on the train looking for us at any point from the time we leave until we get to China."

I swallowed. "So we pretty much need to find a car that has a place to keep us hidden the entire time."

"That's the idea."

"And we have half an hour to avoid the police, the military, and KATO; get on a train; and get hidden without anyone noticing we're there," I said. My voice was even.

He nodded. "That's it in a nutshell."

"Then we should probably get going." I tried to step out of the bathroom but he stopped me.

"We need to hide you better," he said, holding up a wig with bangs and straight shoulder-length black hair. "They don't know me well enough to know what to look for, but they know you. And if they see the two of us together they'll have no doubt who you are." He made sure to tuck my hair tightly under the wig before tugging it down as far as he could. His fingers brushed the burn on my neck as he lowered his hands. It fell just below the length of the wig. "We're going

330

to have to find something to cover that. If KATO's looking for distinguishing features, it's a dead giveaway. Here's your comm."

I grabbed it, not remembering anyone taking it out of my ear. He stepped away from me and went to the closet in the corner. The IDA seemed to stock their safe houses with essentials, including clothes and disguises. When Travis came back, he had a light scarf in his hand.

I took it from him and wrapped it twice around my neck with my good arm, making sure my scar was covered. "Do we have everything we need from here?"

Travis nodded. "We're good to go."

I stepped past him, then picked up my gun and put it in the waistband of my pants. I grabbed the jacket I had worn in, which was still sitting on the bed. "They'll be looking for someone with an injured arm," I said, struggling with the jacket. Again, I got my good arm in, but I couldn't get a good enough grip to pull it around me. I found myself more afraid now than I had been before this mission started. I flipped the jacket again, trying hopelessly to get it to land on my shoulder.

Travis went behind me and put the jacket over me. Even though I knew he was there, I jumped. He came around to stand in front of me and zipped it up so I wouldn't lose it if we had to run. He studied me intently. "Relax," he said, gripping my shoulder. "I've never seen you like this. I knew you were worried before, because there was no way you couldn't have been. But right now, it's written all over your face."

I swallowed. "They weren't looking for me before."

"They're not going to get you again," he said. His eyes met mine, and they weren't letting me go until I believed him.

"Okay." I was still terrified, but I nodded anyway. "Okay, let's go."

Travis grabbed the backpack and led me out the door.

Maneuvering through the city wasn't easy. The train station was about twenty minutes away by foot, so we had cut it pretty close. And we still had to find a way to get to the train undetected. I bit my tongue as we weaved through the crowd in the station. Every time someone bumped me, a searing pain shot through my right arm. We had one close encounter when we passed some of the People's Military. I ducked my head so the wig's hair hid my face. Travis grabbed my hand and pulled me closer. I caught on quickly. We were less suspicious if we looked like a couple.

Once we got outside onto the platform we worked our way to the edge of the crowd until we were standing next to a big yellow building. We had four minutes to get on the train. Travis pushed his comm. "Command, we're in position."

"Okay," Sam said. "The cameras are down for two minutes."

I pulled Travis behind the building and dropped his hand. We jumped down off the platform so we were level with the tracks and ran between the trains, putting a train in between us and the platform.

"Command, what train are we looking for?" I asked.

"You've got to get to the other side of the tracks. That's where they load the cargo-only trains. Once you're there, you're looking for train three-seven-four," Sam said.

Travis and I moved swiftly through the trains. We had a minute and a half before the cameras came back on. We ducked between the next row of cars and I stopped quickly, throwing my arm out to keep Travis from going any farther. There were voices coming from a few cars down. Travis shot me a grateful look and I peeked out around the edge of the train. The one we wanted was sitting on the tracks in front of us and three cars down.

I took in the situation and stepped back. "Everything is being loaded from the other side of the train. If we avoid the cars that are open and actively being loaded, we can make it."

Travis glanced at his watch. "We have thirty seconds before the cameras come back on."

I nodded, and the two of us darted across the gravel ground and pressed ourselves against the cars next us. I edged down the row with Travis close behind me, stopping when we got to the end of the train. I took in the brown cars of our train, listening to the workers loading.

I started to step across the small gap between the train we were hiding behind and the one we needed to get to, but Travis pulled me back. "Let me go first," he whispered. I didn't get it, but I nodded, trusting he had a reason.

He stepped in front of me, his back inches from my face. He darted quickly across the gap, then motioned me to follow. Once I was next to him, he edged down the side of the train, stopping short of the open car.

"Get this shit in the car," a worker said in Korean. "She's moving out."

Travis ducked down and slid under the opening.

"The cameras are live in fifteen seconds," Sam said.

I hunched down and followed Travis. He was an entire compartment ahead of me, and had the small door open at the head of the car. I hurried over to him.

"Ten seconds," Sam said.

Travis laced his fingers together and gestured for me to put my foot in his hands. Once I did, he lifted me up and I twisted so I landed on my good side.

"Five seconds."

Travis hoisted himself up and into the train, then jumped up quickly to pull the door shut.

"Cameras are live," Sam said. "Please tell me you made it."

"We're clear," I said, breathless. I heard one of the big cargo doors slamming shut outside, and then a second one. We had just barely dodged two catastrophes.

Travis grabbed my arm and pulled me away from the window. "Come on, we've got to find someplace to hide."

Chapter Thirty-Five

LAST TRAIN OUT

I'm going to patch you into the rest of the team," Sam said.

A few seconds later Cody's voice was in our heads. "You guys safe?" he asked.

"Yeah," Travis said. "Let us get a place to hide, then we'll check back in."

"Copy that."

Travis started shifting some cargo. The space was full of boxes, but they weren't stacked like I would have expected. They were spread and weaved across the car in a way that didn't make any sense. Some ran from the floor nearly up to the top of the ceiling, while the others came up to my waist. They were the perfect height for a seat even if I'd have to jump a little to get on one. Travis started in the back of the car, where the bigger boxes were, and I started at the front. I tried to shift the boxes around, but I couldn't move them.

"What's in these things?" I pushed harder, trying to make them budge, but they barely slid across the floor. Travis struggled with the bigger floor-to-ceiling boxes in the back.

"Come here for a second," he said, motioning to me. I maneuvered my way back. Travis pointed to the Korean writing on the box. "Korean isn't my strongest language, but I think that says it's steel."

"Yeah, that says steel." I sat down on top of one of the smaller boxes, and I yanked the scarf from around my neck, stuffing it in my jacket pocket. I was starting to feel like it was choking me. "How are we supposed to carve out a place to hide? We can barely make a path?"

"I can move the boxes," Travis said. The car jerked as the train started moving and I slid slightly on my steel block. The boxes themselves barely moved. The car we were in was completely cut off from the rest of the train, so no one could get to us while the train was in motion. We were given a reprieve until the next stop.

"You can't lift these." I didn't mean for my voice to hitch or for panic to creep in. "We wouldn't even be strong enough to lift them together."

Travis's eyebrows shot up. "Let's just get one thing straight. No matter what plan we come up with, there is absolutely no way you are moving or lifting anything."

I glared at him. "I'm not some weak-ass girl."

He smirked. "Trust me, I know that. You've kicked my ass on more than one occasion, but there's no point in finding a place to hide if you're going to pull your wound open and bleed all over the car. Once we're hidden, we need to stay that way, and I won't be able to close that up again. I need you in one piece for this, okay?"

I ripped off my wig and let out an irritated grunt, but nodded. "Then we need a different plan."

Travis turned around to lean next to me on the same block I was sitting on. I stared at the tall boxes waiting for an idea to pop out and announce itself to me. And then it did.

I jumped up to stand on the block so suddenly that it startled Travis, who glared up at me. "What are you doing?"

I stood on the tips of my toes and could just barely peek over the top of the tall boxes. But I saw exactly what I was hoping to see. There was a row of tall boxes along the back wall of the car, but right in front of that row, the boxes weren't lined up so neatly. There was one hole that would be perfect. Three tall boxes made a U against the left wall.

I looked back down at Travis, sizing him up.

"What are you thinking?" he asked.

"There's an opening in the middle of these boxes." I gestured toward the tower in front of us. "If we can swing the box at the back of the U out, we can slide this"—I tapped my toe on the shorter box I was standing on—"in the middle."

Travis's eyes widened. "That way we can drop into it."

"The only problem we're going to have is if someone stands on a short block like I just did to see if there are any holes," I said. "They'll find us in two seconds."

Now Travis was the one scanning the room, looking for some kind of answer. I sat back down on the box. He glanced down at the miniature square, then back up at me, wide-eyed. "I have a roll of medical tape. It's a steel block. We can cut the cardboard top off the box we're going to use and sit on the block itself, then tape the box top to the others so it'll at least look like there's another steel tower."

I tilted my head to the side, considering. "But if anyone touches it, they're going to know there isn't steel underneath the cardboard."

Travis shrugged. "I don't think we're going to get anything better."

I thought for a moment, weighing our options. Then Sam's voice was in our heads. "They're on to you. The Korean military combed through the security-camera footage at the station after they lost their feed. Raven, they found a shot of your face before the feed cut out. They've shut the train station down and ordered all trains to be searched at the nearest station."

I glanced at Travis. "Okay, let's do this."

He approached the tall steel tower against the wall and I followed him. "I thought we agreed you weren't going to make a bloody mess," he said.

I rolled my eyes. "I don't need to use my arm. I can use my good shoulder to push." His eyebrows knitted together and he gave me an expression that said this wasn't much better. I got defensive. "You can do most of the pushing, but this is a lot of steel. You're going to need help."

He shot me a stern look. "If you feel even the slightest bit worse, you better stop."

"I will." He knew it was the best he was going to get. I pulled a knife out of my pocket and handed it to Travis. He cut off the cardboard, exposing the steel, and put it on top of one of the other boxes.

It took a lot of work, and the pain in my shoulder did get a little worse, but not enough to matter. Eventually we had the towers open enough to fit the smaller block inside. Travis insisted on moving that one by himself and I let him. Once we had the small block enclosed, we moved another one of the other small blocks closer. Just close enough so we could use it to climb onto the taller ones. Travis helped me up onto the boxes. I waited for him to climb up and slide into the small rectangle of space before preparing to drop down myself.

"You're going to have to sit," I said. "You're too tall to hold the top up."

He rolled his eyes but didn't move. "And you're supposed to do this one-handed?"

I glared at him, annoyed, but I jumped down next to him. "Fine. You tape the first side so it'll stay and then I'll do the rest."

He debated for a moment, then ripped off pieces of medical tape and gave them to me to hold. He had cut the box so we had a little lip around the edges to work with. The box top popped up above the others slightly, but Travis was able to dip down and line the edges up perfectly.

"Go ahead," he said when he had finished. "It's all you."

He sat down on the smaller block and stretched his legs diagonally across. There was barely enough room for him to extend completely. The box top sagged slightly, but my head pushed it back into place when I straightened up. Travis snorted.

"What?" I asked, glancing down at him.

"It would figure that you're just stubborn enough to be the perfect height for your head to hold the box up." A ray of light from the small opening in the center of the box fell across his face. He shook his head. "Anything to keep you from asking for help."

I rolled my eyes. "Will you *please* just rip the tape?"

He laughed but did as I asked. A few minutes later I had us all taped in. I slid myself down onto the steel square, draping my legs over his so I could stretch out as much as possible. For a few moments, the only sound was me breathing harder than I intended. It wasn't until then that I had time to think—time to really comprehend the situation we were in.

It was only the two of us. We didn't have any tactical information and we had an entire intelligence agency and military looking for us. An agency that would kill Travis and do God knows what to me.

"All right, we're hidden," Travis said into the comms.

"Good," Cody said. "Raven, you holding up okay?"

I smiled lightly, despite the situation. "I think I should be asking you that."

"Please," he said. "I got a scratch. You got a bullet."

"I'm doing fine," I said.

"Glad to hear it."

"We're going dark until we get off the train," Travis said. "Command, do you copy?"

"Copy that," Sam said. "We'll be in touch when we're close to the inspection."

He leaned casually against the wall of the car, then rolled his head in my direction. "How's your shoulder?"

Throbbing, but manageable. "It's fine. I told Cody." I sounded breathless and unconvincing.

Travis shifted so he could get into the backpack next to my feet. He came back up with a flashlight, then leaned close to me and reached for the zipper of my jacket.

I pulled away. "What are you doing?"

He gave me a disgruntled look. "I'm trying to check your injury, since there's a good chance you're downplaying it." I glared at him. He raised his eyebrows. "Are you telling me I'm wrong?" My glare intensified and Travis nodded once. "That's what I thought." He unzipped it enough so he could slide the jacket off my shoulder. He pushed the sleeve of my tank top aside and carefully peeled the tape off my skin.

I studied his face as he examined my burned skin. He grimaced, but didn't look shocked. "Yep," he said. "The skin is pulled. Any harder and you'd have torn it open." He pulled the bandage all the way off, then went back to the bag for a clean one and some disinfectant. He threw me a disapproving look as he rebandaged me.

"What was I supposed to do?" I asked, a burst of anger shooting through me. "This isn't a situation where I have time to sit back and heal. Did you really think you would be able to move all this steel by yourself?"

"I would have gotten it eventually." There was an edge to his voice. He shook his head as he pressed the fresh bandage into place. "I spend so much time trying to keep you alive, the least you can do is work with me."

"I'm not a civilian," I said. "I've been keeping myself alive for longer than you've been training, and I'm not going to stop while KATO is after me." Something I had said, or the way I had said it, quieted him, but his eyes never lost their intensity.

"I never thought you would," Travis said. The frustration was gone from his voice and understanding settled in his face. "But I need you to stop fighting me. I'm on your side."

"I know." I dropped my eyes and rubbed my forehead. "I know. I'm sorry. I've—I have a lot of practice surviving KATO. But—" I took a deep breath. "I've never felt more helpless than I do right now."

My hands started shaking. Despite my treatment, and the fact that I hadn't felt a symptom until now. Saying this out loud brought it out of me. I studied my black pants, counting the holes, purposefully avoiding Travis. Which was why I was startled when his hand covered mine. He squeezed it tight like he was trying to take my symptoms away. "If they haven't gotten to us yet, they're not going to now." He said it with so much certainty I almost believed him.

But my head knew better. "They can catch us any second." I whispered like they were standing outside the boxes.

"If we don't give them a reason to look too closely at these boxes, they won't," he said.

I looked back up at him. "These guys can be very thorough." I pulled myself out of Travis's grip and leaned back against the steel, but Travis didn't take his hand back—it rested casually on my knee. And I couldn't help but find it comforting.

I kept my eyes shut for the next forty-five minutes. My stomach wouldn't stop twisting. I tried to picture a time after the next train stop, after the soldiers had searched the train, decided we weren't on board, and let us move on. But I didn't know how to believe that. I felt as if I was living on borrowed time. I should have been caught a long time ago. I was never loyal to KATO and my managing to keep it from them for so long was a miracle. I had to be running out of luck.

The train slowed to a stop, jarring me back to reality.

"Oh God," I said, doubling over. I wrapped my arm around myself and burrowed my face into my knees. This time I embraced the pain in my shoulder, grateful to feel something that wasn't dumbfounding fear or dread.

I felt Travis sit up a little bit straighter. His hands fell on my back and head, his fingers working their way through my hair, moving in small circles, trying to calm me down. But it wasn't working. If anything it reminded me that I wasn't the only one at risk. I heard the train car doors on both sides of us opening and closing. There were two teams, starting from either end of the train and working their way in. We were the third car from the end. I listened carefully, trying to determine how long we had until they were at our door.

It felt as if we were waiting an eternity. The only thing that kept me from throwing up was how much the smell would give us away. When the door finally opened I froze, completely petrified. Every muscle in my body was so tense and coiled that it probably took a foot off my height. Travis's hands stopped moving and pressed down on me, making me feel safer than it should. I heard their standard-issue shoes moving around the car. My heart was pounding so hard that I was sure Travis could feel it in my back.

A few grunted as they tried to move the boxes toward the front of the car, but that didn't stop a soldier from weaving his way to the back. I could hear his footsteps on the other side of the towers. My limbs were tingling themselves numb, and it was all I could do to keep myself from passing out.

"Steel," the soldier near us said. Then he knocked on the tower behind me. Travis pulled his knees into my legs and pressed down on me even harder. It was the only thing that stabilized me. "Should we see if they're behind it?"

There was some shuffling and some grunting and the tower started to move ever so slightly. I heard the tape begin to peel away from the box. I started breathing harder, trying to fight off hyperventilation. In all my years at KATO, I'd never had a panic attack, but the prospect of going back like this was enough to finally break me.

And then the movement stopped. I didn't have to look up to know the tape was barely hanging on. Then another voice said, "Don't waste the strength. It's just another box."

But the person next to us who had done the pushing didn't walk away. I heard the floorboards creak as he shifted his weight.

"Come on," a voice said from the front. "We've got other cars."

The guy next to us moved reluctantly to the front of the car, and the rest of the soldiers filed out, but I still didn't move. I knew the soldier who had been next to us wasn't ready to write off this car. He could still be out there. Travis must have had the same thoughts because he hadn't so much as flinched.

The train door closed and I was still afraid to do anything that might give myself away.

Sam's voice was in our ears. "The People's Military just radioed in. You guys are clear."

The train started moving and relief spread through me so quickly and intensely I was too overwhelmed to move. I felt Travis relax around me and start to rub my back again. He took his arm off my hair to answer Sam, and my head felt cold.

"Copy that," Travis said.

I couldn't process the reality. Travis nudged me gently, trying to get me to straighten up, but I couldn't. His mouth dropped to my ear. "Hey." His voice was soft enough to shatter me. "You're okay."

A sob I'd been holding in for years wrenched itself out. Travis shifted, keeping his right hand on my back, and sliding his left arm under me, pulling me closer and up into his chest. His one arm held me tight around the waist while the other ran the length of my back, surrounding me and grounding me. I gripped his forearm with so much force that it hurt to hold on, but it felt like I would die if I let go.

Travis didn't say anything. He anchored me while I let out years of built-up fear and tension, until I was incapable of making a sound.

Chapter Thirty-Six

HOME

Once we got near Fushun, we had to jump out of the train and sprint to a field to meet the extraction team. We had to get out of China fast, so the IDA sent a V22-Osprey, which has the ability to fly like a plane, but take off fast like a helicopter. We flew to Germany, where we were then transferred to a plane, and finally had access to a medical team. They tried to give me painkillers, but Travis stepped in and made sure they didn't. I lay down flat on my back. Now that I could finally relax, the pain in my shoulder was getting worse. Travis sat nearby, which I suspected was to make sure I didn't do any more damage to myself. Nikki was sitting with Cody on the other side of the plane. His "scratch" was more of a head gash. From what I could gather he also had a concussion.

I was surprised Rachel wasn't with him. Then I was even more surprised when she showed up next to me with a black bag in her hand. Travis leaned toward me, listening in.

"I—I heard your usual medical care involves acupuncture," she said. "Is that right?"

"Yeah," I said. "Why?"

She sat down on the edge of the bench. "Because I might be able to help with the pain." She opened the bag and started taking out some supplies.

"You know acupuncture?" Travis asked.

Rachel nodded. "One of my foster parents—one of the ones that I liked—taught me the basics. This is all the stuff they had on the plane. It may not do much, but I might be able to help."

I nodded, feeling desperate for relief.

She got to work, peeling back the bandages and putting some needles around my wound. "Why are you doing this?" I asked.

She stayed focused on her work so she wouldn't have to look me in the eye. "The comms stayed open after the train was cleared." She didn't have to say any more. My stomach dropped. They had all heard my breakdown. "I don't forgive you," she said. "But I have an idea what it's like to feel that way."

I couldn't completely explain it, but an understanding seemed to pass between us. I hadn't expected anyone to get that feeling, least of all her.

"Sit like that for a while," she said.

I let my guard down and let everything I was feeling fall away. It seemed like it was only a minute later when Rachel was back pulling the needles out of me. I sat up when she was done, and noticed the pain had shifted to a manageable level.

"We're not friends," she said. She packed up the supplies and started to walk away.

"Thank you," I said.

She turned back for half a moment and gave me a small nod.

Travis slid a little closer. "Did that help?"

"Yeah," I said, still a little shocked by Rachel. "I still feel it, but I can handle it better."

"That's good," he said.

"Listen—" I hesitated. I needed to tell him what I found out in KATO, but I didn't know how to broach the subject of Eliza without bringing up Dr. Foster's death. "I found something before we left KATO—"

Travis shook his head. "We can talk about it later."

"Travis, I think—"

"I mean it," he said. "It's been a long few days for all of us. Let your mind rest."

"But—"

He smirked. "Let *my* mind rest. *Please.*" Suddenly he looked more worn-out than I had realized. His eyes were surrounded by dark circles and he gave me a weary look.

I sighed and sunk into the seat. "Okay. Sure."

"Thank you," he said, leaning back and closing his eyes. But there was one more thing I needed him to know.

"I'm sorry I lost it like that," I said. His eyes snapped open. "I didn't mean to—especially on a mission. I didn't mean to let you down."

He shook his head. "Don't do that. You didn't let me down, you let me in. And I have *never* been more proud of a partner." I blinked a few times, completely stunned. He smiled and patted my knee. "Seriously. Cut yourself a break and get some rest."

I looked around the plane. The others had already fallen asleep, and I knew Travis wasn't far behind them. I tried to relax, letting what Travis said play over in my mind. It wasn't long before my eyes shut like everyone else's.

When I woke up I was in the medical wing at the IDA. I must have needed the rest more than I realized because I didn't even know I'd been moved. Cody slept in a bed next to me, and Travis sat on a chair by the wall at the foot of both our beds. He smiled when he saw I was awake. "You know, for someone who was so reluctant to rest, you slept more than anyone."

I sat up and rubbed my eyes. "What time is it?"

"After six," he said. "On Tuesday."

I slept for a whole day.

I looked back over at Cody. "How's he doing?"

Travis stood up and pulled the chair closer to me. "He woke up earlier today. Dr. March says he'll be fine. He's got a concussion like we thought, but only a mild one."

There was a knock on the door next to me and Sam poked his head around it.

"What are you doing here?" I asked.

He shrugged, as casual as ever. It was as if he hadn't just pulled off one of the biggest operations someone his age ever had—even if he hadn't been pulling all the strings. "I wanted to see how you made out." He came to stand next to Travis's chair.

"We made out fine thanks to you," I said.

He smirked. "Hey, I was just happy to get a chance. No one else would have trusted me like that."

I smiled. "Well, you've had my back from the beginning, which is more than a lot of people around here can say."

"Yeah," Sam said. "But I never thought it would get me something like this."

Travis laughed. "Karma's funny that way."

Sam leaned against my footboard. "Just so you know, I know about your secret."

My forehead tightened, confused. "What are you talking about?"

"The last search you did on KATO's computer," Sam said. "The one you didn't think I could see."

I rolled my eyes. "That wasn't a secret."

Travis shot me a confused look. "What are you talking about?"

"What I was trying to tell you on the plane," I said. "Before I got out of KATO's computer I looked up Eliza."

He straightened up, seeming suddenly more alert. "You what? So fast?"

"I may not be a full-fledged hacker, but I've had enough practice with KATO's system to know my way around." I paused, giving him a moment. "They'd had her in India since she was captured, but they recently moved her to Russia. Saint Petersburg to be exact. They have a safe house there. That's what the message on the flashdrive meant. She was the snake."

Travis's eyes sharpened and I could already tell he was planning. "We can handle a safe house. What else did you find? I need to get moving." I understood where he was coming from. We'd weakened KATO for the time being, but they'd be back. And there was every chance they'd be using Eliza to advance their next agenda.

"You're not going anywhere," I said.

"Jocelyn—"

"No." I was forceful enough to surprise them both. "After what happened to Dr. Foster, I know why you want to rush this. But you can't. If you do, you'll tip our hand and they'll move her, kill her, or use her against us. We have one chance to get this right. And besides, you're not going without me."

He was ready to fight me, but Sam intervened. "Man, come on.

She's got a hole in her shoulder. Cut her a break." Travis gave me a once-over and I could tell Sam was getting to him. I may have even seen a hint of guilt. Sam continued. "You've been looking for this Foster girl for a year. Now that you found her, rest up and plan it out."

"A year?" Travis asked. "You knew?"

Sam beamed. "I know everything. You're going to have to stop being surprised by that."

"You have such an innocent face," I said.

"Agent Lee tells me that all the time," Sam said.

Travis looked like he wanted to ask more questions, but he shook his head, thinking better of it. "When we *do* go in, you're on this with us."

Sam's eyebrows shot up. "You still want me to help?"

"Yeah." The corner of Travis's mouth turned up a fraction. "You know too much."

Sam laughed. "It's about time that paid off." He started backing toward the door. "I'll see you guys later. Feel better, KATO girl."

I waited until Sam was gone to turn back to Travis. "Seriously," I said. "I know what this means to you, but it means just as much to me. Don't do anything without me."

He rested his elbows on his knees, leaning forward. "I won't."

I studied him. Then something dawned on me. For the past month he'd repeatedly amazed me when he'd pick up things about me—small details that made me slightly uncomfortable with how well he seemed to know me. But in that moment I realized that I knew him as much as he knew me. "I know you're more upset about Foster than you're letting on."

I startled him enough to make him look up. "What do you mean?"

I arched an eyebrow at him. "Since when are you ready to jump on the first plane out with no plan?"

He just looked at me, completely transfixed. When he spoke his voice was hoarse. "He's dead because I couldn't do my job. I couldn't protect his kids, I couldn't fix my mistake, and I couldn't find his daughter in time to stop him from working for the enemy."

"But we can still do something about it," I said. "We stopped them from using his knowledge. And they were so afraid of us getting him that they killed him before he could reset the missile." I paused to give my words some weight. "We can still get Eliza. We can save her."

He pinched the bridge of his nose. "You're right." He only seemed slightly more convinced, but his resolved had increased. "Okay, you're right."

"It's going to be harder with my cover blown," I said. "They're gunning for me now."

He looked up at me, and he saw a fraction of the fear that I had been trying to hide. "We'll figure it out. We both have a stake in this. We'll find a way to make it work."

I sighed, feeling strangely content. Just then the door opened—this time without a knock. Agent Lee marched in with a spring in her step and a big smile on her face. "Jocelyn!" She was loud and excited and I knew it was more than just a successful mission. "Jocelyn, we found your father."

My heart stopped, and for a moment I couldn't feel anything but the sinking pit in my stomach. This was an entirely different kind of fear.

Acknowledgments

T he acknowledgments section of a first novel is about so much more than thanking the people who helped with this specific book. It's about thanking all of the people who have helped turn a dream into a reality. So, with that in mind, thanks to:

My agent, Michelle Wolfson, for the call that changed my life and for loving Jocelyn's story more than I could have ever hoped for. Your hard work and guidance through this whole process have been invaluable. Also, thank you for the thoughtful and encouraging email years before taking me on. You saw what I was trying to do long before I was actually doing it, which left me convinced that you would one day be the perfect agent for me and my work. I'm so grateful you felt the same way when the time came.

To Jill Santopolo, for seeing everything this book could be, and giving such inspiring notes from the very start. You have been so considerate and kind, which has made for a wonderful debut experience. I feel extremely lucky to call you my editor. Also thanks to Michael Green, Talia Benamy, Anne Heausler, Cindy Howle, Kristin Smith, Siobhan Gallagher, Semadar Megged, Lori Thorn, and everyone at Philomel and Penguin Young Readers who had a hand in turning this story into a real-thing-I-can-actually-hold. You are all truly awesome.

To my parents, Frank and Marianne Rogers, for supporting me in every way, and always knowing I'd end up here. Also, for giving me entirely too much power as a child. No, seriously—I'm pretty sure it's the reason I never doubted I had the power to make this happen.

To my sister, Katie Rogers, for being so imaginative with me as we were growing up. For always believing in me and sharing my love of stories. For accepting that I am both the bossy and annoying sister. And for tolerating the singing wake-up calls, messy toothpaste tubes, blaring music in my car, and *all of the things*. You really do put up with a lot—but I think we can both agree that it's so much more fun this way. Right? Yeah, I thought so.

To my cousins Shannon Rogers, Hunter Brutsche, Erin Rogers, Kellsey Rogers, and Seamus Rogers, who have always been more like siblings. Thanks for dreaming big with me, guys! You can officially start thinking about your rooms! (It just may be a while before you get them.)

Extra thanks to Hunter for answering every call, text, and question, and for teaching me what I needed to know to write this. There is not enough space here to completely describe how much you've helped me (but I'll add more in the next book, because I need your help with that, too).

Thanks to my grandparents Ellen Civatte, John Civatte, and Joan Rogers, for being the original biggest fans, and doing so much to inspire my imagination. To my aunts and uncles, Nancy Brutsche, Joan Latshaw, Dave Latshaw, Claire Mann, Dave Mann, Jimmy Rogers, and Colleen Rogers, along with my cousins Josh Latshaw and Jeremy Latshaw for being so supportive and sharing all of this with me. I'm so glad you are all my family. Additionally, thanks to Lisa Rice, Kevin

Rice, Lauren Rice, Lindsay Rice, Kevin Rice, Trish Carman, Chic Carman, Jerry Keil, and Paula Keil, for always taking an interest and redefining the term *extended family*. It means so much to me!

To Jessie Furia for fighting so hard against that awful idea. You changed the entire direction of the series for the better—Jocelyn has her strength because of you. And to Dana Celona for every detailed and thoughtful comment. And for understanding the importance and delight of torturing characters. You were the ally I needed.

To Maggie McGrath for being so enthusiastic, for questioning all the right things, and for being my friend for the past eleven years. Thank you for giving this and all of my books so much of your time and attention. You are unquestionably my person.

To my friends Susan Murphy and Mark Murphy (and their daughter Shannon Murphy) for the years of employment prior to this, and for believing in me as much as my own family. And to Jenn Lacko and Caitlin Naylor, for showing up at my house with champagne the night I got my agent, and for a lifetime of imagination and inspiration. It means everything to have you two on my side.

To Carla Spataro, Randall Brown, Richard Bank, and everyone at Rosemont College for developing such a solid MFA program. I learned so much in my time there. Also to my college writing instructors, Jim Kain and Joe Glass, for teaching awesome classes and proving that taking classes in writing wouldn't ruin the experience for me (it was something I was seriously concerned about at the time).

To all of the students I had the pleasure of working with during my time at Springfield High School, especially: Alex DeLuca, Alicia LeSage, Brianna Fox, Michael Strolli, Megan Yates, Dan Madonna, Bryan Biehl, Richie Brown, Steven Russo, James Leahan, Bradley

Lord, Kevin Swanick, Danny Swanick, Jimmy Swanick, Heather Sinkerton, Jack Schott, Steve Reger, Ryan Joyce, Mike Dougherty, Lou DiMichele, Nick Santana, Bill Flaherty, and Aysha Ray-Walker. I am better for knowing each of you.

Special thanks to: Dan Ketler, Vince Marra, and Pat McKnight for being a constant source of optimism and inspiration. To Amanda Brown for always being in my corner. And to Davis Caramanico for your superior naming skills and for taking an interest from the beginning.

Likewise, thanks to Zac Ondo for being the original noodle, letting me borrow your word, and making sure I got it right. Also for being so invested and always caring about what I was working on. Thanks to Courtney O'Connell (Courto!) for being one of the first people in my target audience to read my first novel. Your belief and enthusiasm helped me get here.

And, of course, thank you to Sam Mola for being yourself and inspiring so much of this story. When I started planning this, I had no intentions of giving any of the students in Jocelyn's class too big of a role. You inspired not only a character, but an entire direction for this story and I can't thank you enough for that.

Thanks to Vicky Rostovich, Adriana Lecuona, Mercedes Huff, Mary Pat Bowman, Mary Schwingen, Sharon Smith, Patricia Reynolds, Diane McGinty, Elise Woods, Mary Ann Clifford, Yvette Goslin, Jill Keithly, Gladys Ramirez-Wrease, and everyone at DCCC who I have been lucky enough to call colleagues. Your support has been overwhelming and is so appreciated. Nkenge Daniels, thank for reading and always talking writing with me (and for being so adorable!). And Emily Irwin, thank you for being such a self-aware human disaster.

(I haven't made proper use of this yet, but I will!) And also for caring, and continually thinking all of this is so cool.

To all of the Sixteen to Read and Sweet Sixteen members I have had the chance to get to know over this past year. Sharing this journey with you has been *everything*!

And last, to the two people who have impacted my creative life more than anyone or anything else:

Andrea Ridgley, thank you for being SO EXCITED when I decided publication was a goal back when we were in ninth grade, and for understanding, so completely, what it's like to create. For seeing the strengths in every first draft and seeming to know what the story is supposed to be long before I do. You are the absolute best first reader and an even better friend. My work and my life would be so much worse off without you.

And Denise Mroz, thank you for saying "yes" my junior year. For giving me a place in your room and in your life. For believing this would happen with such certainty, that it truly felt inevitable. For being the Lois to my Chloe. For showing me that pigs can fly, and Mrogers can make anything happen. I don't know who I'd be or what I'd be doing without you, but I know it wouldn't be this—which means I would be utterly miserable.